THE
MITHRAS
CONSPIRACY

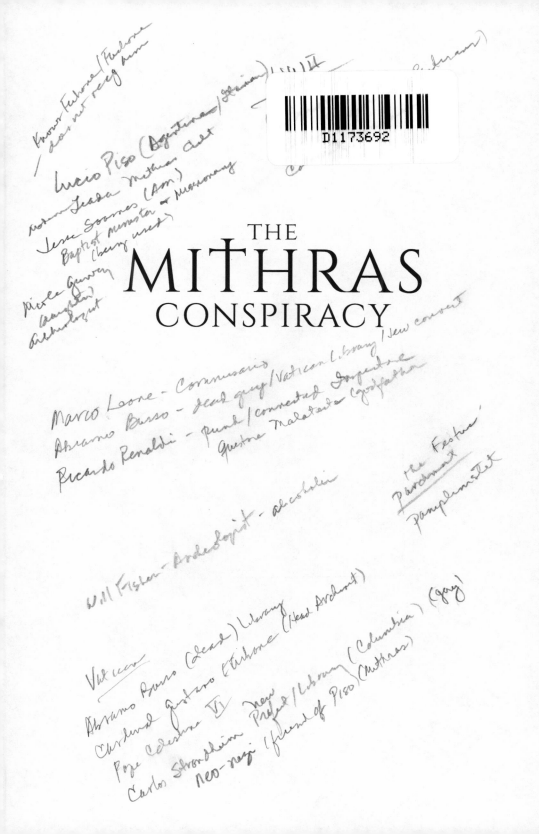

Known Fulvia / Fulvia
/ does not reappear

Lucio Piso (Agostino / Steiner)
now Testa Mithras Cult

Jesse Soames (Am.)
Baptist minister → Missionary
(being used)

Pierre Guvroy (daughter)
(archeologist)

Marco Leone - Commissario
Abramo Basso - dead guy / Vatican Library / New convert
Ricardo Renaldi - punk / connected Imperatore
Gustave Malatesta (godfather)

Will Fisher - Archeologist - alcoholic

the Festus
Parchment

Pamphlenatet

Vatican
Abramo Basso (dead) Library
Cardinal Gustavo Ettobre (Head Archivist)
Pope Celestine VI
Carlos Stronheim New Prefect / Library (Columbia) (gay)
Neo-nazi (friend of Piso) (Mithras)

THE MITHRAS CONSPIRACY

M. J. POLELLE

LIDO PRESS

Copyright © 2019 M. J. Polelle

Published by Lido Press, Sarasota, Florida
www.mjpolelle.com

Edited and designed by Girl Friday Productions
www.girlfridayproductions.com

Cover design: Paul Barrett
Project management: Sara Addicott

Cover image: eZeePics/Shutterstock

ISBN (paperback): 978-0-9600863-0-6
ISBN (ebook): 978-0-9600863-1-3

First edition

*To my wife, Donna, with me every step of the way,
and to my children, Mark, David, Beth, and Daniel.*

PROLOGUE

AD 392
DECEMBER 25
ROME, ITALY

In the century-old Baths of Caracalla, the potbellied Roman police officer known as the *vigilis* pounds his club on the door. "Open in the name of Emperor Theodosius." Flaming torches illuminate the mob's rage. "You are all under arrest." Silence from inside the room. The officer kicks the door open. Crumbling like the empire, red brick powders his face. Its chalky grit peppers his tongue and tickles his nostrils.

A ferret-faced informer slinks forward, jangling a ring of keys. He gives the ring to the officer and takes a gold coin in return. The officer rattles a key into the lock. The door moans open on rusted hinges. Like a serpent on fire, the mob undulates down the narrow, twisting rock-hewn stairs after the winded officer.

In the grotto, the mob brushes the officer aside and confronts the congregation. Fifteen men and seven youths cower wide eyed behind a mitered and scarlet-robed priest muttering prayers.

The attackers overturn a table set with bread loaves and jars of red wine in celebration of the day. From their cloaks, the mob pulls out axes and knives. They hack and stab. Blood and wine slick the white-tiled floor.

The mob leader struts behind the altar, where a sheet conceals the object of his suspicions. He rips off the sheet. In the shadowy glow of a brazier, he discerns a marble statue.

The statue depicts a bare-chested youth glaring with opal eyes. Yellow curls dangle under a stocking cap. Clothed in alien pants, the youth sits astride a bucking bull. He plunges a dagger into its flank with one hand and pulls up its snout with the other. A snake and a dog leap up in frozen motion to lap blood from the beast's wounds.

The mob clamors for the leader to mark the statue.

Claiming kinship to the illustrious Piso clan, a grizzled centurion—one of the worshippers attacked by the crowd—staggers up from the floor. He suffers another frenzy of fists and knife stabs before falling again.

A stonecutter chisels the sign of the cross into the forehead of the pagan god.

The cavern echoes with cries of "Hail to Jesus the Christ."

The centurion screams a curse of eternal vengeance on the attackers and their religion just before a knife slits his throat.

CHAPTER ONE

THE NEAR FUTURE
DECEMBER 27
ROME, ITALY

Commissario Marco Leone of the Polizia di Stato sighed over the water-soaked corpse in a black cassock lying facedown near the Four Heads Bridge. The Tiber buried its victims no better than Rome buried its past. The writhing whirlpools of the mud-yellow river concealed tree limbs, rocks, and who knew what other dangers. His grandmother used to wag a finger in warning. The overthrown gods of old reached from the past to drown little boys wandering too near.

Do they also take down priests?

"The case is yours," said the carabinieri police officer standing near Leone.

"Not what we agreed to. It's your turn."

When he'd joined the police, they told him the jurisdiction between the carabinieri and the Polizia di Stato was like spaghetti—snarled up and slippery.

"Just because a drunk or suicide drowns in the Tiber?" The officer puffed his chest, which was crisscrossed by a white bandolier. "That's not important enough for us."

Not important enough? Everyone knows these presumptuous carabinieri have red stripes running down the sides of their navy-blue pants so they can find their pockets.

"Come on, Marco. I'm busy with family this Christmas season." He made the sign of the cross with a grin. "You're Jewish. You have the time."

"Then convert." Leone shook his head. "I'm leaving for Chicago." The top brass of the Polizia di Stato had selected him for a professional enrichment program with the Chicago Police Department. He had to leave in two days if he wanted to escape the hidebound traditions of life in the eternal city. They didn't call it the New World for nothing.

A medical examiner slipped on latex gloves and eased the dead man faceup on the river walkway. Leone felt the fish eyes of the corpse boring through him. Sores dotted the face like salted cod too long in water. An eyelid missing. Bits of lip gone. The Tiber gods had collected their toll.

The examiner crouched down, slipping his hand under the cassock with a pickpocket's finesse. He fished out a plastic card from a wallet.

"Who is he?" Leone asked.

"Abramo Basso." The examiner scrutinized the card. "Connected to the Vatican Library."

"Abramo Basso?" Leone shook his head in disbelief. *Abramo Basso.* The name of his childhood chum hit him hard in the stomach like a sucker punch.

They had grown up together as dead-end toughs in the ghetto of Rome before gentrification. His best pal converted to Christianity and became a priest-scholar of classical studies. They fought. He felt guilty for refusing Abramo's olive branch. They lost touch. Each escaped the ghetto in his own way.

Leone knelt next to the corpse and examined it closely. Someone had burned the numerals 3, 6, and 5 into the skin. He had to find out who.

"I'll take this case after all." He looked up at the carabiniere. "This man was my friend."

Leone poked numbers on his cell and told his secretary, "Cancel my plane ticket to Chicago."

CHAPTER TWO

Back in his office, Commissario Marco Leone looked at the wall clock—4:25 p.m. Abramo Basso's sister would arrive at 4:30 p.m. sharp for her appointment. She had the punctuality of a Prussian. He adjusted his shirt collar and smoothed the hair on his head to camouflage a thin patch. She had once, so long ago, smoothed his hair that time in the rain when they strolled arm in arm over the cobblestones of Campo dei Fiori, and she had—

The office door swung open. His secretary announced, "Signora Miriam Sforno here to see you, Commissario."

Sforno? Wasn't her late husband's surname Adorno?

"Bring her in." He flicked lint from his trousers.

Clutching a yellow fiberglass case to her chest, she limped toward him. Her hobble had grown worse since they last met. And it was all his fault.

He arose from his desk and pecked her on the cheek. Touching her shoulder, he said, "You're as young as I remember."

"Fibbing was never your strong point, Marco." She grazed his cheek with a butterfly brush of her hand. "Don't change."

She dabbed at the misting in her eyes with a handkerchief. Just maybe the past could come alive. Did she feel the same way as he did?

"Abramo told me to give you this . . . if anything happened to him." She broke out sobbing and twisted the handkerchief.

He took the case from her and placed it on a credenza. He guided her to the chair next to his desk.

"Before I forget, thank you for the money," she said. "It was a hard time for you and me."

Her father had raged at Leone for crippling his daughter. Miriam's mother had died unexpectedly while Miriam recovered in a hospital. Miriam's father lost his job soon after. Marco and Miriam's plans of a life together were put on hold until they withered over time. She went her way; he went his. She married, had one child—a loser son—and lost her husband. Marco married, had one child—a disaffected daughter— and lost his wife to another man.

"What money?"

"Good thing you're not a card player." She smiled. "Shortly before his death, Abramo told me the money came from you."

"It was the least I could do." He fidgeted in his chair. "I was driving at the time of the accident. Not you."

"Still beating yourself up?" She leaned toward him. "You know perfectly well the police blamed the other driver."

"If I hadn't—"

"Enough." She waved her hand, brushing aside the topic. "They say you're divorced."

"Yes, but it's a long story. Maybe we could discuss it over dinner."

"Dinner?" She pulled back. "I'd like that . . . but I don't think it's possible."

Of course. How tactless. She still grieved for her brother. He had to keep things on a professional basis, for now. "Is the parchment in the case?"

She nodded, averting her eyes from the credenza. "My brother found the parchment while working in the Vatican Library. He took it because he feared the cardinal in charge, Gustavo Furbone, would suppress it. They quarreled about it when—"

"Furbone?" He leaned back in his chair. "Are you sure?"

"Yes. Do you know him?"

"I know him all right." Gustavo Furbone, then a careerist monsignor on the make, had once appeared at headquarters for an ecumenical blessing of police vehicles with a hippie rabbi. Another cockamamie idea cooked up by his boss, the *questore*, Pietro Malatesta. While the patchouli-scented rabbi murmured prayers, Furbone sprinkled holy water on police cars. Leone refused to let his undercover car be sprinkled. Furbone fumed, but the car remained a heathen. Leone lost track of the cleric except to note his steady ascension on the escalator of Vatican politics. "Please continue, Miriam."

"Abramo told me the cardinal threatened him if he didn't return the parchment."

"Idle ranting perhaps?"

"My brother didn't think so. He was scared." She leaned forward again, her voice tremulous. "Abramo came home one evening to find burglars ransacking his apartment. They pushed him down and fled."

The telephone rang. He let it go to voice mail.

"Abramo wanted Professor Will Fisher to examine the parchment. He's an American at the Gregorian university in town. My brother said that after himself, Fisher was the next best authority on early Christianity."

"Christianity?" Leone paused. "That's what this is all about?"

"I don't know." She put her handkerchief into her purse. "He said the less I knew, the better for me." She lowered her voice. "But he did say its contents . . . if true . . . could rattle the Church."

"Did my men make you identify your brother at the morgue?"

"They said they didn't need me. A fellow priest identified him."

Good. She was spared the sight.

"Did he ever mention the numbers three . . . six . . . five to you?"

"No . . . why?"

"Miriam." He ran a finger under his shirt collar. "Before we go any further, you must know I have a special interest in this case."

"Naturally. You and my brother, always getting on each other's nerves, yet mirror images of each other. That's why you couldn't get along."

She reached across the desk and took his hand.

"He wanted you involved if anything happened to him. Despite the quarrels, he trusted and respected you . . . though he'd never tell you to your face."

"That's not what I mean," he said, looking into her eyes.

"Please, Marco." She removed her hand. "I'm a married woman."

"But . . . But I heard your husband died."

"I remarried recently. His name is Rabbi Elia Sforno."

Leone's hopes tumbled back into the tomb of his memories.

CHAPTER THREE

"After you drop me off at headquarters, check out the vandalism at the Ardeatine Caves national memorial." Commissario Marco Leone turned to Inspector Riccardo Renaldi for a response. The inspector mumbled assent with eyes fixed straight ahead and hands squeezing the steering wheel.

"Why won't you let me do my job in the Basso case?" the inspector said, glancing across at his superior in the passenger seat. "My duty is to do the spadework."

"This case is a personal matter."

"You don't think I'm up to the job, right?"

"That's not it." But, truth be told, having the police chief as his application reference greased the wheels of Renaldi's admission to the Polizia di Stato. "Abramo Basso was my friend. I simply owe him and his sister."

"Exactly why you shouldn't get so involved. You can't be objective."

Leone didn't need unsolicited advice from *Il Piccolino* . . . the little guy . . . the moniker of one barely over a meter and a half in elevator shoes. With a nasty Napoleon complex to boot. Lucky for Renaldi the *polizia* no longer had a rigid height requirement.

"Is this about your estranged wife?" the inspector asked, turning a corner.

"She's got nothing to do—"

"Look." Renaldi pointed ahead to a crowd of demonstrators blocking the street. They were burning the prime minister in effigy. Flames shot up from a straw figure hanging from makeshift gallows. The inspector shifted into reverse.

"Don't retreat," Leone ordered. *"Avanti."*

"We need to wait for backup."

"Keep going forward . . . that's an order."

The squad car crept ahead. Flashers pulsated blue light. Renaldi switched on the singsong wail of the siren. A red paintball exploded on the hood and splattered the windshield. Leone reached across Renaldi and banged on the horn. The mob surrounded the car and rocked it back and forth. Seconds later a rock shattered the rear window.

Leone poked a Beretta 92FS pistol out the passenger window. Yelling curses, the mob backed away and opened a path. Almost running down a demonstrator, Renaldi lurched the car forward. Fellini-like flashes of clenched fists and grotesque faces wrapped in rage whizzed past Leone.

But for him this was no film. Italy was on the brink of collapse. The European Union was locked in negotiations with the playboy prime minister in a last-ditch attempt to arrange a bailout before the country defaulted on its bonds. Things were getting out of hand.

"Some of those guys were cops," Renaldi said. "What the hell are they up to?"

"The police unions have joined the protest against budget cuts."

"I don't care. Cops shouldn't agitate in the streets." The inspector turned off the siren and flashers. "Il Duce knew how to handle guys like that." He hit the steering wheel with his hand. "Communist scum."

Protestors held banners proclaiming the coming of proletarian power as the answer. Leone sighed in frustration. Did the protestors even remember what the question was? The empty slogans were dusted off once again. The national future was always the past in disguise. Nothing would ever change. Unless he got out of the country and out of his rut, neither would he.

The inspector pulled up in front of headquarters. He put his hand on Leone's arm. "It is about your wife, isn't it?"

"Will you get that out of your head?" He broke away from Renaldi's touch. "I knew Basso. How he thought. How he felt. I need to handle this case from the ground up."

"You two were separated at the time. You weren't involved with her."

"That's not the point." Leone got out and looked back through the open door. "The three-year wait for consensual divorce hadn't quite passed. We were still technically married."

"Only because this is Italy."

"Nonetheless. You put the horns of a cuckold on me."

"OK, OK. You're a technical cuckold." Renaldi took off his cap and ran his hand through his hair. "Why can't you let it go? It's ancient history."

Unlike his own hair, Renaldi had the thick, black wavy hair of a matinee idol that he'd never had and never would have. That must have attracted her.

Leone rubbed his balding crown. "How do you erase a memory, Riccardo?"

"By creating new ones."

He slammed the car door on the answer.

CHAPTER FOUR

Scanning the morning headline in the ivy-walled courtyard of Da Pappagallo restaurant, Marco Leone took a final drag on his half-finished cigarette.

SEISMIC TREMORS UNDER ROME

He ground the cigarette into a Cinzano ashtray. *Cracks in Foundation of Saint Peter's* read the subheading. His eyes moved on to the opening sentence. *Investigators are still determining the damage to—*

"December 31." Surprising him, the owner of Da Pappagallo plunked down a dish of tiramisu with a lighted candle. "It would have been your uncle's birthday today. He'd be proud of you for finding out his fate after the Nazis captured him." He patted Leone on the shoulder. "Bravo, Marco."

"You never forget."

"How could I? La Sirena deserved a bullet in the head. She betrayed him."

Did she? La Sirena had doubled as a Nazi informant in the ghetto. After the war, they said she ratted out Uncle Benjamin to the Nazis. Yet, even with a vigilante gun to her head, she admitted other betrayals but denied ever betraying her beloved Benjamin. The doubts haunted Leone. She had become the scapegoat. But if not her . . . *who?*

"You didn't forget him." The owner shrugged. "Why should I?"

Leone had no answer. Both his uncle and father had joined the Polizia di Stato in Rome. But it was the family story of Benjamin that made Leone idolize his uncle. Benjamin had created family turmoil by quitting the Polizia di Stato in opposition to Fascism. His uncle defied his only sibling, who remained with the polizia and even became a party member. The more Leone's father raved against his brother for resigning and becoming a partisan fighter, the more Leone considered Uncle Benjamin his wished-for father.

He looked up. The furled table umbrella flapped like a trapped bird. Snowflakes drifted down and danced around the tiramisu. A gust of wind rattled the newspaper and snuffed out the candle flame.

"Come out of the cold, Marco." The owner squeezed Leone's shoulder. "Watch the soccer game inside with the others. Lazio versus Sampdoria."

"I prefer to stay outside."

"What you prefer are these things." The owner picked up the cigarette butt from the ashtray. "Didn't you give these up?"

Leone rubbed his hands together for warmth. Earth tremors reaching 5.9 magnitude over the last several days. The upswing of an economic and political crisis filling the streets with beggars. Rare snow falling in Rome. The season seemed out of joint, except for the comforting aroma of roasted chestnuts sold by the street vendor.

"What are you doing for New Year's Eve?" the owner asked. "The tremors won't stop our party at the restaurant."

"What I've always done since the separation from my wife. Work overtime."

The owner stepped away to scold a busboy at the other end of the courtyard. Leone riffled newspaper pages to make sure he hadn't missed anything. His eyes drifted past the uncompleted crossword puzzle to a society column titled "The Return of Rome's Pride."

According to the newspaper, Lucio Piso, an international businessman and philanthropist, now living in Argentina, was returning to Rome—his birth city. Although abandoned by his mother and without a father, he turned his life of rags at home into one of riches abroad.

Why would one of the world's richest men return when those who could leave were abandoning the sinking ship of state Italy had become?

He found his answer in the last paragraph. An avid collector of Roman antiquities, the tycoon claimed DNA tests and ancient records in Constantinople proved he was descended from ancient Roman aristocracy. Lucio Piso believed destiny called him back to Rome. Leone shook his head at the delusion. Outside of his Midas touch, Mr. Moneybags was nothing but a vain and foolish plutocrat whose wealth fed charlatans and con men.

He flipped the newspaper onto the table and checked his cell messages before leaving for the office. A voice mail from Miriam. She must want to see him after all. As he punched in the retrieval code, he thought of the perfect place for dinner.

"Ciao, Marco. It's Miriam. Is there any way you can help my son, Shlomo, find a job with the police? I was too embarrassed to ask in your office. He's a good boy and just needs some work. It was good seeing you again. Take care."

The voice mail plummeted him back to earth, but he couldn't bear to delete it just yet. A job for Shlomo? As the saying went, it would be easier to find a white fly than a position for the shiftless Shlomo in the Polizia di Stato. But how could he deny her his help?

It was time to leave for work.

"How much do I owe . . . tiramisu included?"

"Nothing." The owner waved away the question with his hand. "Consider it a gift. You cops keep the bad guys away."

"No gifts for me or my men." He put on the table more than enough euros to cover everything. "Gifts come in pretty boxes . . . but with strings attached."

CHAPTER FIVE

"And so the religion swept across the Roman Empire. Archaeologists have unearthed hundreds of chapels from the Black Sea to Hadrian's Wall and from the German Rhineland to the Sahara Des—"

The hall door of the Pontifical Gregorian University squealed open at the top of the stairs leading down to the lecture platform. Professor Will Fisher looked up, startled. He let his reading glasses dangle from a lanyard. He clutched the lectern. Was the university rector coming to yank him out of class because of the heresy complaint? He couldn't stand the humiliation without his friend Jack.

Thank God. It was only the American student.

"Now, sir, that you've announced your presence, pray tell, what religion I was describing?"

"Christianity?"

The lecture hall resounded with the scorn of student hoots.

"A little late, historically speaking, just like your arrival."

Fisher swallowed more cutting words that were welling up. He had no business taking out his anxieties on this student. He himself had once arrived in Rome from Milwaukee, much like this young American, perplexed and lonely in a university with students from over one hundred countries.

"No, not Christianity." His tone lost its edge. "The religion was Mithraism and the god, Mithras. The belief emerged among the

Romans about a century before Christ. The Mithraists worshipped underground in cave-like spaces to honor their god born of rock."

His theatrical instincts compelled him to keep the audience engaged and awake at all costs. Could he stump the brightest student in the course? He looked up the rising rows of benches and called on the Spaniard in the third row.

"How many mithraeums . . . or mithraea, for you Latin sticklers . . . possibly existed in ancient Rome?"

"Between seven hundred and two thousand."

"Right again." He should have known the Spaniard would read ahead in the class handouts. "The religion overlapped the later rise of Christianity, declined sharply around the time of Emperor Constantine, and disappeared for good after Emperor Theodosius made Christianity the state religion at the end of the fourth century."

The wall clock showed it was time for the last act, last scene of his teaching performance. Like most professors, he chose to speak in Italian. The zest and operatic cadences of the language suited the liveliness of his teaching style. Not for nothing did students consider him the hottest teacher at the Gregorian.

Looking up the ascending rows of admiring faces, he gestured with his arms for greater effect. His theatrical skills as a former off-Broadway actor in short-lived plays served him well. Every outstanding professor like himself had to be a thespian of sorts. The center of attention, he now enjoyed the role of writer and director of his classroom productions in which he always played the leading role. If only he could live forever in the high of his teaching performances, he wouldn't need his false friend, Jack, who stabbed him in the back every time they reconciled.

"In conclusion," he said, bringing down the curtain, "Ernest Renan, the French scholar, remarked that if it had not been for Christianity, Mithraism would have prevailed in the lands of the Roman Empire." He packed up his notes. "Do you agree? Be prepared to justify your opinion next class."

Excusing himself from after-class questions by his student fans, he hurried, exhausted and exhilarated, to meet Jack. Closing the office door, he rummaged behind a thick volume on the lowest bookcase shelf. He needed Jack to help him in the encounter with the rector.

Fisher pulled out a skull-and-crossboned insecticide bottle plastered with poison warnings. A little Jack wouldn't hurt. Just a tad to steady the nerves. Jack deserved another chance.

Pouring Jack Daniels into a bottle emptied of insecticide as his peculiar brand of aversion therapy didn't fool the alcoholic demons. His hands moved as if on their own toward the bottle.

Deliver me from temptation . . . This time I can do it.

On his knees, he held the bottle in both hands outstretched, his head bent over. His hands inched the bottle closer to his face. He smacked his lips.

My God, my God, why hast thou forsake—

Someone knocked on the door and wouldn't stop. Had the rector come to give him the boot?

He returned Jack to his hiding place and opened the door with hands atremble.

CHAPTER SIX

"Commissario Leone." Professor Will Fisher winced. "I was expecting the rector. Weren't you coming tomorrow? I thought that's what we'd arranged."

"Sorry to disappoint. But it's important we talk now."

Why now? He can't suspect me of murdering Basso, can he?

"Come in, then."

"Is Inspector Renaldi watching your office, as I ordered?"

"I gave him a key." Fisher looked up and down the hallway before closing the door. "He's putting a guard on duty tomorrow."

The professor collected books from the sofa and dumped them onto his filing cabinet. Skis propped up against the cabinet clattered to the floor.

"You need to be careful." Leone replaced the skis against the cabinet. "You could hurt someone."

What does he mean? Could he think I hurt Basso?

"They belong to Wesley Bemis, my colleague on the Herculaneum dig."

"Ah, yes." Leone consulted his notebook. "The archaeologist from Brigham Young University in America." He put the notebook away. "Why are you two poking around in Herculaneum?"

The suspicious tone disturbed Fisher.

"We're simply resuming the unfinished excavation at the Villa of the Papyri." He dialed a combination lock on the top drawer of the filing cabinet and removed a yellow fiberglass case. He placed it on his desk and motioned for his visitor to take a seat on the sofa.

"Thank you for letting me examine this startling parchment," Fisher asked, snapping open the case. "How did you get it?"

"I ask the questions. You answer them." Leone folded his arms. "Before we get to the parchment . . . How did you and Abramo Basso get along?"

"Why do you ask?"

"Let's not beat the bush, as you Americans say," Leone said in English before lapsing back into Italian. "I've heard you and Father Basso were enemies."

Best not to correct his English. "You think I—"

"I think nothing yet. Please explain your relationship."

Dry-mouthed and wishing Italy had a Fifth Amendment, Fisher explained in a meandering monologue how Basso and he had lived parallel lives. They were classical scholars of renown. They both did groundbreaking research on ancient cults before Fisher's cantankerous friend had volunteered to help catalogue the entire collection of the Vatican Secret Archives. Each also had a scholarly interest in comparative religion. Basso became a Jesuit priest, but Fisher left the order before taking his vows.

"I compliment you, Professor Fisher. Your Italian is excellent."

"You really think so?" Fisher felt a warm glow inside, the kind his friend Jack could kindle. "That's good to know."

"Yes I do, which is why you'll understand my question . . . Did you kill Father Basso?"

"That's absurd."

"They say you two constantly fought when he was on the faculty here."

"If we were such bitter enemies, why on earth would he require you to bring me the parchment for examination?" Fisher had had enough. "Did you come to arrest me or discuss the parchment?"

"Arrest you?" Leone acted surprised. "Who said anything about arrest?" He pointed to the parchment. "What does it say?"

"I call it the Festus parchment. It's what experts call a palimpsest, a later writing superimposed on an earlier one. Fortunately, instead of scraping the older writing away, Pope Alexander the Second—"

"Please, Professor Fisher." Leone raised his clasped hands up and down. "No history lesson. I just need the translation."

"With a touch of ultraviolet light, I detected and translated a few more words than Basso could." Fisher put on reading glasses. "I'll now read my translation." The ex-actor cleared his throat for an audience of one.

> Porcius Festus to Paul of Tarsus, greeting . . . may you be recovered from . . . whenever you see glistening wet clay on a potter's wheel . . . falling sickness . . . you toil and preach too much . . . rest . . . Junius Annaeus Gallio, my colleague who protected your religious speech in Corinth has agreed to entreat his famous brother, Lucius Annaeus Seneca, to invite you to the learned discussions on religion in Herculaneum at the home of the illustrious . . . who . . . is . . . of Ga . . . Jul . . . Caesar . . . congratulations on your acquittal . . . beware court vipers in Rome . . . fortune is fickle . . . goodbye and be well.

"If true," Fisher said, snapping shut the case, "this is a religious bombshell."

"What do you mean?" Leone scratched his neck. "I only come across real bombs in my work."

Fisher took down a copy of the New Testament from his library shelf. "Some have speculated whether Saint Paul suffered from epilepsy. The Acts of the Apostles in chapter nine states—"

"I don't care about Paul's medical history. What about the learned discussions?"

"I wish I knew." Fisher closed the book. "We think the surviving letters between Paul and Seneca, the Roman statesman, author, and tutor to Nero, were all fabrications unmasked after the Middle Ages. Outcast Christians probably authored them to gain respectability by association with a leading figure of the day." The professor replaced the New Testament on the shelf. "This parchment suggests an even closer connection between Paul and Seneca."

"But like you said, just a fantasy of pious Christians."

"Like the New Testament, the parchment mentions the two judges who heard charges against Paul. No one, not even the writers of the New Testament, left behind the final verdict when Paul appealed to Nero." Fisher paused. "This says he was acquitted."

"One fantasy piled on another is still a fantasy." Leone rubbed his chin. "The parchment also mentions Herculaneum where you and Ves . . . Ves . . . Wesley Bemis are excavating," Leone said, overpowering the foreign W sound.

"I have a hunch about the missing letters." Fisher snapped his fingers. "If my feeling about the Festus parchment is right—"

The first few bars of the theme from *The Waltz of the Toreadors* sounded on Leone's cell. "Don't do anything until I get there," he said into the phone. "Understand?" He snapped the cell shut. "I must leave at once. Some brutal business at the Ardeatine Caves memorial."

"Do you still suspect me?"

"I recommend you not leave Rome."

CHAPTER SEVEN

Cardinal Gustavo Furbone strode across St. Peter's Square on a mission. He breezed past a Swiss guard checkpoint on the way to the secret archives of the Vatican. Rushing through corridors, he flashed identification in the face of a curator brash enough to offer challenge. The ends of his red sash swished around him like the tails of angry cats.

What was the new pope thinking? Celestine VI had ordered a complete cataloguing of the Vatican Secret Archives. Thousands upon thousands of documents lay on shelving stretching just over eighty-five kilometers. These dust-shrouded catacombs, where the written word sat putrefying, reeked of mildew and death. Furbone shrank from the archives as much as possible. But only he was the caretaker of the cemetery. He had to make that absolutely clear.

The pope's rash decision had enabled Abramo Basso to imperil the Church with the discovery of the Festus parchment. How many other unknown papers and books lay buried, waiting to damage Church interests if they ever resurfaced? As cardinal librarian and archivist of the documentary cemetery, he alone had the power to resurrect a document. Celestine VI compounded the danger by appointing as prefect of the secret archives a Vatican outsider, not even a cleric.

The cardinal tromped up the white marble staircase to the Meridian Hall on the first floor of the Tower of Winds. He stormed into a side room where Carlos Stroheim, the new prefect, sat slicing an apple on his desk. Grunting a greeting, the prefect carved the apple in half, then quarters, and finally eighths. He lined up the pieces with skin-cracked hands that were red and raw like crab claws. "Now, what can I do for you, Your Eminence?"

"You can hand over the Festus parchment."

They said this stooped half-breed with the hawk nose of a South American aborigine so loved the past he even slept nights in the secret archives despite staff objections.

"I would if I had it." The prefect squirted sanitizer liquid on his hands from a bottle and rubbed them together. Stroheim offered a glass jar to the cardinal, who seemed offended by the disappointing aesthetics of the prefect's pocked face. "Care for some?" The jar held what looked like small black marbles.

"What are they?"

"Roasted *hormigas culonas* . . . literally translated . . . big-assed ants."

"*Ugh.*" The cardinal gagged and waved away the bottle. "How disgusting."

"On the contrary." Stroheim tumbled out ants from the jar. "A rare delicacy from my region of Colombia." Eyes fixed on the cardinal, the prefect took his time crunching the ants before swallowing them with an audible gulp. Dabbing at the corners of his mouth with a napkin, he switched on a gold-toothed smile reeking of insolence.

The cardinal knew all too well the source of this insolence. Stroheim and the future Celestine VI had become fast friends in Nigeria, where the Colombian archival expert had modernized governmental records beyond all expectation in an astonishingly brief time. The pope did not forget his friend when the office of prefect fell vacant. Furbone had to manipulate the Colombian savage so as not to antagonize the pope.

The cardinal glanced at two assistant archivists cataloguing the documents in a wall-sized bookcase. The accursed bookcase. There, Abramo Basso, while working for Stroheim, had discovered an unsent parchment letter from Pope Alexander II inviting William the Conqueror to Rome. Under the Latin script, Basso had detected ancient writing that survived an unskillful attempt at erasure with milk and oat bran. The scandalous discovery purported to be a letter from Porcius Festus, the Roman governor of Judea, to Saint Paul in

Rome. After the prefect had dismissed the assistant archivists at the cardinal's request, Furbone tugged at his ear. "Where is it?"

"As you requested, I contacted persons gifted, shall we say, in the art of unofficial retrieval." The prefect paused. "They couldn't find the parchment in Basso's apartment."

"Saint Paul consorting with pagans." The cardinal wiped his brow with a lace handkerchief. He laid his hands on the front of Stroheim's desk. "No good can come of the Festus parchment."

"Come, come." Stroheim folded his hands. "The parchment belongs to the eleventh century, not the Roman period." The prefect circled his hand in the air. "At best, someone made a copy of a copy of a copy and so on. How accurate can it be? It's not the original."

"The problem is you think like a pedant." The cardinal frowned. "Many will believe it transmits the original with sufficient accuracy. Even the New Testament consists of copies of copies."

"Then why did Pope Alexander the Second try to erase it? He must have thought it a fake."

"Or a danger . . . as I think is the case." The cardinal tugged at his ear again. "How did Basso manage the theft?"

"He promised to store the parchment in an acid-free case inside one of the climate-controlled storerooms." The prefect gulped down a slice of apple. "Instead, he stole it."

"You're responsible for Basso's theft. What do you plan to do about it?"

"Commissario Leone wants to question me about the Basso homicide. I plan to answer his questions." The prefect took off his wire-rimmed glasses and wiped the lenses with his sleeve. "So glad I wasn't the one to threaten Basso."

"What will you tell the commissario?"

"See that?" The prefect rose and pulled out a packet of documents the size of a thick magazine. "That bookcase alone holds about nine thousand packets." He blew dust off the one in his hand. "Who knows what else we'll find?"

"Answer me. What will you say?"

"The truth. Basso stole the Festus parchment from the bookcase."

"That's not what I meant."

"What did you mean?"

Furbone tugged on his earlobe once more. "You didn't hear me threaten Basso . . . isn't that right?"

The image of his mother pulling on his earlobes in her rages flashed through the cardinal's mind. Embarrassed, he let go and awaited for the prefect's answer.

"It depends." The prefect sat down at his desk. "Will you allow Lucio Piso, my philanthropist friend back from Argentina, to purchase the Mithras statue?" He leaned toward the cardinal. "For his collection of Roman antiquities."

"With the cross cut into the forehead? Out of the question."

"But I negotiated its presence in our library with the director of Vatican Museums. Without me, it wouldn't even be here."

"And I'm the boss. And I say no."

"I could be mistaken." Stroheim scratched his head. "But I seem to recall you threatened Basso with physical harm if he didn't return the Festus parchment."

"You dare blackmail me? A cardinal of the church?"

"Ah, it's becoming clearer." The prefect took a fistful of ants from the jar and washed them down with mineral water. "I see and hear you threatening Basso in my presence."

The cardinal pulled out a cablegram from under his cassock. "I know," he said, inching closer to the prefect, "you were a leader in the Neo-Nazi Aryan Force in Colombia, all the while hiding behind your role as a respected national archivist." The cardinal tossed the cablegram onto the desk. "His Holiness should know his prefect from the Colombian slums even trafficked in narcotics."

Stroheim slumped back in his chair and ran his swollen hand through his hair. "You know." He shook his head. "My memory isn't what it used to be." He ran his hand over his chin. "I propose I only imagined you made a threat . . . just like you incorrectly imagined I was mixed up with the Aryan Force." He folded his hands across his stomach. "Am I right?"

"Of course." The cardinal smiled. "Memory plays tricks on us all."

CHAPTER EIGHT

Commissario Marco Leone descended, his eyes adjusting to the underground gloom of the World War II mausoleum in the Ardeatine Caves, now closed to the public for restoration. Inspector Renaldi and he stood alone in the fading glow of afternoon sun filtering through a slit around the sunken chamber's perimeter. A monolithic slab of concrete ceiling stark as skeleton bones rested on squat pillars close above hundreds of sarcophagi. Before investigating the outrage inside, Leone took a moment to admire the avant-garde architecture, unusual in a city anchored to the past.

"Are you okay?" Renaldi asked. "You're sweating."

"I'm fine."

"Have you thought of retiring? You're overdue."

"Sorry, Renaldi. You'll have to wait to take my job."

Rows of identical gray granite coffins contained the remains of over three hundred Nazi massacre victims, each victim personalized by name, age, profession, and photo. Had it not been for Leone, his Uncle Benjamin would have remained one of the unknown victims. By using cutting-edge DNA techniques and methodical spadework to determine his uncle's identity, he had made his reputation in the Polizia di Stato. They still called him the Bulldog for his personal and unrelenting crusade to find out what had happened to his uncle.

Bowing his head, he stuck a bouquet of white and pink chrysanthemums into the flower receptacle at the foot of his uncle's sarcophagus.

What barbarian had smeared a swastika and the number 365 on the sarcophagus? Like a virus, the number replicated itself across the rows of stone coffins. The swastika spoke for itself. But what to make of the number, the same one found on the forehead of the priest's corpse? The number of days in a year? A code of some kind? If only he could light up a cigarette in the sacred place and solve the puzzle.

"If the guilty partisans had surrendered, none of these unfortunates would have died."

He bristled at the intrusion of Renaldi's voice interrupting his private moment. The weight of grief stifled his instinct to strike back. Renaldi and those like him had to discredit the Resistance to preserve their image of a past bestowing meaning on their present. Like Uncle Benjamin used to say, better not argue with a fool lest bystanders be unable to tell the difference.

Renaldi's men paraded past Leone with five scraggly-haired punks in handcuffs on their way to police headquarters. Their garbage smell upset his stomach.

"I caught these perpetrators red-handed," the inspector said. "Case solved."

"Really?" Leone held his tongue. "Show me the mithraeum now."

After entering the adjacent mithraeum, Leone examined the barely visible frescoes of Mithras slaying the bull and also feasting with the sun god. "When did this cave come to light?"

"About two months ago, when they renovated the mausoleum." Renaldi pointed to a Latin inscription scrawled on the floor in bloodred letters: *In spelaeo velatis oculis NON illuduntur.* "What does it mean?"

"I'm not sure, but I know someone who might," Leone said, thinking of Professor Fisher. The inscription was too vivid to be ancient. Someone alive had scripted the graffiti. Sniffing incense, he looked around. "Let's examine that pot on the wall ledge."

Renaldi struggled, but even in his lift shoes, he could not quite wrap his fingers around the pot. Nudging the inspector aside, Leone put on gloves and took down the still-smoldering pot.

"I could have taken it down." The inspector's face flushed. "I'm not an invalid."

"It's not your size, for heaven's sake." Leone held up a gloved hand. "Just that you would have destroyed any fingerprints with your bare hands."

"The gang I arrested must have brought the incense."

"You're certain, are you?"

"Of course. You yourself always say that whenever times get bad, satanic cults pop up in Italy like poison mushrooms."

Leone walked toward the main room of the mithraeum. Through the opening, he saw an ancient altar and beyond that, an animal carcass lying in the charcoal embers of what looked like a campfire. "Is that it?"

"It's what I told you on the phone." They both entered the main room and beheld the scene. "The remains of a baby bull."

Animal flesh still filled dishes strewn on the floor. A drinking bowl and goblets, some overturned, rested around the circle of burned-out charcoal. An empty whiskey bottle lay off to the side. Whoever did this had left in a hurry, maybe surprised by some intrusion into their macabre feast.

"I have the lab results." The inspector held up the report. "It identifies bovine blood in the bowl, in the goblets, and all over the floor."

"So soon?"

"I have connections at the lab." Renaldi winked. "Let me work with you on the Basso case. I'd be an asset."

"You never worked a homicide case."

"I have to start sometime."

"No more, Renaldi. You have enough to do here." Fed up and feeling a surge of nausea, he fled the foul site of the mithraeum, a mixture of stale blood and sweet incense.

Reentering the mausoleum chamber, Leone tried to walk away his nausea through rows of coffins. Back pain glided up and down his spine like fingers playing on a keyboard. He'd have to consult a doctor before it affected his professional performance. Renaldi wanted his job. He suspected the predator inspector would eye him for any sign of weakness before swooping in for his position.

In the dim light, Leone stopped when he almost stepped on a knife resting next to a sarcophagus. It lay there with a pearl handle shaped like a snake's head. Dried blood splotched the emerald patina of the bronze blade. A spotted trail of blood wove to and fro alongside the sarcophagus.

Sensing Renaldi coming up behind him, he turned. "How could you miss this?" His finger pointed at the knife and spatters of blood.

"I hadn't finished my investigation." The inspector rubbed his palms up and down his thighs. "Before you barged in and took control, as though everything would fall apart if you weren't involved." Renaldi took a deep breath. "Anyway, I solved the case and arrested the culprits before you ever got here. I'll get their confessions at headquarters."

"You solved nothing."

"What do you mean?"

"The juvenile delinquents you arrested arrived after others had performed what looks like a cult rite of some kind. These young thugs you hauled off just took advantage of the earlier forced entry to see what they could steal for drug money."

"How could you know that?"

"One of the gang members you arrested is an undercover cop. He reports to me."

"And you didn't trust me, your own inspector, with this information?"

"I didn't need you."

"Then I'll find someone who does."

CHAPTER NINE

Hot morning wind splotched the silk of his ancient Roman tunic with sweat. The chauffeur gunned the Land Rover, twisting up the switchback roads into Argentine hill country toward the mansion retreat far from Piso Global Enterprises in Buenos Aires. Lucio Piso looked forward to the farewell theme party in his honor before he left for Rome. The trees stationed like sentinels along the road waved hosannas to him. Through shimmering air drunk with humidity, he saw his mansion poking in and out of sight at the top of the highest hill. Only an awaited telephone call from across the Atlantic clouded the celebration.

Servants creaked open the filigreed iron gates. On each side of the entrance stood a statue of Cupid pissing champagne into a pool. Guests filled fluted glasses with the champagne in salute to his arrival. The chauffeur drove over the stone bridge onto a driveway lined with BMWs and Mercedes Benzes. Piso ordered his driver to halt. In keeping with the classical motif, guests swarmed around in Roman togas and tunics. Piso needed to know about the call.

"Has he telephoned?"

"Not yet, sir."

The guests shouted greetings in Spanish and Italian, with a discordant one in German. The former Nazi military officer sat in a wheelchair with his portable oxygen tank. Didn't he know it was risky to speak German? Didn't he know he was supposed to dress up in a toga for the party? The once dashing military officer had gone senile.

For the sake of their money and connections, Piso checked his disgust for this dwindling collection of cranky Nazi geezers held together by weepy memories and fears of arrest. These has-beens dared press him for information about the underground movement that would overthrow the Italian government and shake Europe. A lack of discipline and genius had done in the Italian Masonic plotters of Propaganda Due in the 1980s. They had turned a coup attempt into a comic opera of ineptitude. He would not make the same mistake.

On foot, he led an entourage of guests and servants toward his four-story mansion. Statuary of Greek and Roman mythological figures lined the pathway to the open portal of his residence, where the majordomo handed Piso a towel monogrammed with his initials. Wiping beads of perspiration from his forehead, he took pride in these pagan masterpieces that he'd illegally recovered from Italian soil. They now belonged to a new government that could protect and cherish them. The rebirth of ancient glories nourished his spirit; the dull-as-dust commercial cover of a global business did not.

A woman screamed. As Piso drew near, she remained frozen and fixated on a log near her feet. On top of it, a pit viper rustled like fall leaves in the wind and prepared to spring at the woman. Piso flicked his towel toward the serpent with a skill honed from his years as an amateur bullfighter. The distraction caught its attention.

The viper lunged into the towel and fell writhing to the ground in a whirl of dust and cloth. With repeated stompings of his thick sandals, he smashed the serpent's head as it tried to escape. Piso raised the viper's body on high like a lifeless sausage in acknowledgment of the crowd's cheers before hurling it to the ground. In life's arena, he was the gladiator growing ever more powerful in the continual defeat of his adversaries.

Piso ordered a servant, who passed on the order in a chain of command down the hierarchy of servants, until four menials trotted out of the mansion hoisting a sedan chair on their shoulders. Elevated onto the vehicle by a swarm of hands and arms, he rode on a wave of victory to the front door of his mansion. At the entrance, his majordomo announced the caller from Rome would call back in twenty minutes.

"Let me out." Piso scrambled out of the sedan chair and stumbled. A menial steadied him before he hit the ground. "I must take the call in the privacy of my study."

***

After cleansing the telephone with sanitizer, the prefect of the Vatican Secret Archives clamped the receiver to his ear. The rhythmic tinkling of telephone rings in Argentina sounded to Stroheim like the crisp tones of ceremonial chimes in honor of Mithras at the break of Christmas morning in the Ardeatine Caves. The transoceanic voice of the Pater Patrum, the Father of Fathers, boomed into the prefect's ear.

"*Pronto.* Stroheim? Is that you?"

"It's me, the prefect of the Vat—"

"You bungler. Where is the parchment?"

"I don't know."

"Your life hangs in the balance."

"Forgive me, Pater Patrum." The prefect's voice cracked. "I swear I'll find it. I didn't know how much it meant to you."

"Do you take me for a fool? Basso told you the parchment referred to the Pisos of ancient Rome . . . my ancestors."

"On my mother's grave, I'll track down the Festus parchment."

"You have also stirred up the police with Basso's death."

"Forgive me, blessed representative of Mithras on earth." Hoping his flattery would help, the prefect bunched up the telephone cord in his hand. "We arranged for the reconsecration of the mithraeum and the initiation of the new Lion . . . as you requested . . . on December twenty-fifth, the birthday of Lord Mithras. Basso snooped and caught us performing the sacred ritual soon after midnight. He would have betrayed us."

"You idiot. Why did you not torture him to locate the parchment?"

"We didn't have time." Stroheim failed to rein in the panicked undertone of his voice. "He took us by surprise in the Ardeatine Caves. He ran for the exit. We cornered him. He struggled like a demon. I had to stab him with the ritual knife. We then disposed of the body by—"

"Disposed of the body? The police had no problem finding it in the Tiber."

"We won't get caught, I swear."

"How can you assure me?"

"When Commissario Leone interrogates me next week, I'll tell him about Cardinal Furbone's threat to harm Father Basso." Stroheim caught his breath. "The police will arrest the cardinal."

"Do not dare to implicate Cardinal Furbone."

"What? . . . I don't understand."

"You presume to demand an explanation . . . from me?"

"No, no Your Magnificence, that wasn't—"

"I have my own special plans for the cardinal." The voice of the Pater Patrum became clipped and fast. "I know about the calling card of swastikas and bull's blood the probationary Raven left on the coffins."

"The Raven drinks too much." *Somebody snitched. How can I save my darling?* "He knew the pope's blessing of the mausoleum angered you, so he tried to please you by desecrating the sarcophagi." The prefect ran his fingers back and forth over his forehead. "He won't cause more problems. I promise. I'll personally watch him. I'll—"

"He will assuredly cause no more problems. I have terminated your lover."

"No . . . It can't be. What will I do without him?"

"Do not fret. Unless you recover the parchment, you will join him."

***

From his ivory throne on the dais, Piso looked approvingly over the arrangements his household staff had made for the re-creation of an ancient Roman banquet in his honor. All he needed for a perfect evening was a favorable reply from Rome.

The movers and shakers of Argentina reclined uncomfortably on couches fashioned in the ancient Roman manner for one reason only. He wanted it so. Slave-costumed waiters served wild boar stuffed with dates from serving stations set up in the dining hall. Silver platters loaded with blood sausages rested next to heaping bowls of ostrich ragout, and small birds marinated in egg yolk with parrot tongues and jellyfish.

The thrumming of lute music in the background stopped.

"And now, my dear guests," Piso announced from the head table, "the highlight of Roman cuisine."

Shadows swam through blackish ooze in cauldrons heating up in front of the dais. The sulfurous stink of rotten eggs permeated the dining hall. Reclining guests nearby gasped. Some too degenerate to appreciate the strong sensations of life tried leaving their dining couches. To prevent their departure, security guards locked the exits. The sharp edge of Piso's rapier remarks shamed the fainthearted into returning to their places.

"I invite you to taste this specialty." His look spoke command and not request. "My chef has re-created a Roman *garum* sauce made from the gills, intestines, and blood of mackerel maturing in our hot Argentine sun for seven months, a sauce through which goatfish now swim, turning bright red as they die a well-seasoned death for your eating pleasure."

He took note not to trust those faces wrinkled in disgust as his staff served the goatfish. Piso knew the others feigned approval so as not to offend their host. *They eat just to please me.* His boyish glee at the sight of mayors and bishops eating the goatfish sated a hunger gnawing at him more than any hunger pangs he'd ever had. He wielded the power to control men, even what and how they ate.

Nothing was left to chance. The guests rose on prearranged cue to offer farewell toasts in honor of the host, each successive speaker trying to outdo the previous profusion of praise.

Out of script, a tipsy guest from the Ministry of Social Development cried from the back of the room, "You have all missed something. We cannot pass this day without public thanks to our generous host for his philanthropic support of orphanages, not only in Argentina, but throughout the world."

A round of applause erupted. Ambushed by surprise, Piso waved his hand for them to stop. He loathed publicity about the aid he gave to orphanages. It stirred up unwanted memories. "I, too, was once a throw-away child," he uttered in response. A sob broke through his clenched mouth before he could smother the display of weakness.

Fearful of his off-script outburst, he turned for deliverance to a messenger ascending the dais. Had the circumspect contribution to the campaign of the Italian prime minister borne fruit? The answer had arrived from Rome.

He read the message and shared the news with his guests. The Italian Ministry of Cultural Heritage and Activities had appointed him superintendent in charge of all excavations in the archaeological zone of ancient Herculaneum. The standing ovation from the audience of sycophants washed away the nightmare remembrance.

He could now control a project dear to his heart: the renewed excavation of the Villa of the Papyri in Herculaneum, the villa owned by the Pisos, his ancient relatives. He would finance the project from his own funds if he had to. Bad enough the Chinese financed the maintenance of nearby Pompeii with the obsequious gratitude of a bankrupt and feckless government.

The time had come to lay claim to his ancestral home and set in motion his plot of political revolution and social resurgence.

CHAPTER TEN

Back from his hilltop mansion, Lucio Piso sat in his penthouse atop an art deco building in Buenos Aires. His communications director hooked him up to a desktop Skype system, while an aide looked on. The wavy image of Cardinal Gustavo Furbone solidified on the monitor. A pectoral cross hung from his neck. After confirming all was in working order, the director left the room.

"A pleasure to make your acquaintance, Signor Piso."

Excellent. The pig does not remember me. "Likewise." *But I shall never forget.*

"Why did you insist I contact you from the Vatican on this device?"

The same jowls—pink and unlined like a baby's bottom.

"Your aide said the matter was too urgent to await my arrival in Rome. And I prefer to do business face to face . . . especially with persons I have never met."

"Will you do it?"

The same tic of pulling his ear under stress.

"Why not the police?"

"The recovery of the document requires confidentiality to avoid Church scandal."

"Why me?"

The cardinal ordered his offscreen aide out of the room.

"My brother, who owns a carnival store in Venice, recommends your discreet services . . . beyond the conventional ones offered by the police." The image of the cardinal moved closer. "More than legal means may be required in the retrieval."

"Ah yes, the proprietor of Sfaccia Sfumata. A fine man, your brother. He supplies my South American business interests with animal masks for the carnival celebration."

"I have a question . . . Yo-ur Emin-ence." Piso almost gagged pronouncing the title of office when he wanted to say *Your Hypocrisy.* "Do you know who now possesses the object in question?"

"Unfortunately, no." The cardinal sipped from a glass of water. "You're not recording this conversation, are you?" Even now the cardinal's lips puckered as he spoke, like those of a scavenger carp.

"To do so would benefit neither of us."

"In that case"—Furbone pulled his ear—"is the compensation sufficient?"

The fool pays me for finding what I seek while I pretend to seek on his behalf.

"Not quite." Piso drew closer to the monitor. "I also want the Mithras statue recovered by the Church. Stroheim sent me photographs of a mutilated statue of Mithras found by workmen digging around the church of Saints Nereus and Achilleus. I must have that statue with the cross on the forehead."

"But the government disputes our claim. They say it belongs to the Baths of Caracalla within sight of the church."

"I will take care of the government. Do I get it or not?"

"If you insist. The pagan idol means nothing to the Church."

"I do insist."

"One final thing." The cardinal tugged at his ear again. "When you recover the Festus parchment, contact me no matter the hour. Don't worry about disturbing me."

"Rest assured. I will never worry about disturbing you."

CHAPTER ELEVEN

In the study of his Buenos Aires penthouse, Lucio Piso took a break, rubbing his eyes. The flowchart of his financial empire was sprawled out on his custom-built desk of Carpathian elm. He put his arms behind his head and breathed a sigh of satisfaction. His interlocking businesses crisscrossed the globe in a potent tangle of disguised power. Just as all roads led to Rome, all his businesses led to his Argentine holding company, Piso Global Enterprises, where he doled out bribes and jobs in exchange for a base to operate under the law's radar. Only destiny could explain the rise from orphan beggar to one of the world's richest and most powerful men. The way Cardinal Furbone had fallen into his hands like ripe fruit confirmed this destiny.

About to commit suicide to escape grinding poverty and depression, he had inherited from a distant relative a farm on the verge of foreclosure in the Maremma backcountry. He turned a profit by selling olive oil and pasta across Italy. From there, he gobbled up one farm after another until he wound up the CEO of the largest European agribusiness. From agricultural dominance he branched out across the world with the manufacture of everything from beds to bullets. Tired of making things, he resolved to influence opinion by acquiring media outlets in Argentina and Italy. He would no longer remain hidden away as the financial angel and puppet master of playacting politicians. Soon he would emerge from the wings onto the world stage as a twenty-first century leader.

The real *he* was not the vulnerable shell called Lucio Piso. *No.* He was *in* Lucio but not *of* Lucio. His true self was the godhead within Lucio. By viewing Lucio as an object from above, he could guide Lucio the puppet on the path of power. Only the superman within had the wit to flee from the psychiatrists ready to kill him with pills and pala-ver. There was nothing wrong with him.

The intercom buzzed, interrupting his visions of glory. Piso pressed the blinking call button to hear his secretary say, "He called and apol-ogized for running late."

"Let me know when he arrives." Annoyed, Piso consulted his bejew-eled wristwatch. He had almost forgotten feeding time. He rushed to the aviary on the roof outside his apartment, where he rounded up a chirping chick. Behind wooden planks and wire mesh, a Harris's hawk fluttered its wings in a blur of chestnut-and-white color. He crushed the chick dead with a squeeze of his falconry glove and unlatched the aviary door. The hawk glided onto his gloved arm. Pausing only to gulp, the hawk tore off tidbits of feathers and flesh from the chick carcass held by Piso's protected fingers. Afterward, Piso returned to his desk to complete any paperwork needed before he would depart for Rome.

The intercom buzzed again. "He's arrived."

"Send him in at once."

Jesse Soames entered and shook hands with Piso. "It's so good to see you again, Lucio."

Piso winced at the use of his first name. If it had been any other employee, he would have reprimanded this presumptuous American informality. But Jesse Soames was an unwitting but important cog in the grand plan. Now head of Latin American operations for Piso Global Enterprises, he had served in Vietnam and won the Medal of Honor for heroism in Iraq.

Piso trusted Soames not because of his character but because of dirty little secrets he could use against him. With his nearly two-meter height, blue eyes, and blond buzz cut, Jesse Soames showcased the do-gooder face of Piso Global Enterprises that Piso wanted the world to see, while its other face went undetected. The Baptist mis-sionary work Soames did in his free time had enhanced the reputation of the worldwide conglomerate with humanitarian awards.

"My dear Soames, I am inexpressibly sorry about your wife." He forced his face to show a compassion he did not feel. "But I need you with me in Rome after you go back for the funeral. It would do you good. You could visit the grave of your grandfather, Colonel Soames."

"I'd like that. Because of his distinguished service, I chose a military career. The last time I visited his grave, I was doing liaison with the Italian military." Tears welled up in his eyes. "I should have been with her."

"You could not know she would die visiting friends and family in Georgia."

"My daughter . . . you remember? . . . Nicole, the archaeologist?"

"How could I forget? A talented woman full of promise."

"She's going to Amalfi for a wedding." Soames held his chin. "I suppose I could meet her in Rome."

"Meeting her there is a wonderful idea."

"We haven't seen each other for a while." Soames blew out a breath. "But what about Latin American operations? I'm supposed to launch our marketing drive here."

"I have made alternative arrangements."

"I should've known." Soames smiled. "You think of everything . . . but I'll bet you didn't think of the five new Baptist churches I planted in Argentina and their social service ministry. Who's going to tend them?"

"That is why I need you." Piso switched on the state-of-the-art 3-D wall television set for the afternoon news. "Look." Water cannons flushed away crowds surging toward the office of the Italian prime minister. The scene switched to the Testaccio district of Rome, where helmeted police in visors lobbed stun grenades into a charging crowd protesting the rape and dismemberment of a twenty-year-old girl by an illegal African immigrant. The flash bang of the grenades blinded and deafened the rioters. A line of soldiers fired rubber bullets toward those trying to regroup around a leader draped in the Italian flag.

"I heard about the Italian riots on the car radio." Soames looked away from the set toward Piso. "What's this got to do with me?"

"It is returning." Piso sat in his executive chair of ostrich hide. "Like the days before the Second World War. Economic misery. The tide of illegal immigrants from the cesspool of the Mideast. The rise of iron-willed men."

"I don't understand."

"I predict the Italian government will fall."

"So what's new?"

"This will be the last fall." Piso rose and leaned across his desk. "The impoverished and destitute multiply in Rome and brawl with illegal immigrants. Piso Global Enterprises must win goodwill . . . and, of course, help the hungry and sick. I want you to take your experience in working with the downtrodden to set up a relief agency in Rome with centers for food and shelter."

"Can I do Baptist missionary work over there?"

"Absolutely." Piso opened his arms. "Who am I to deny your Christianity?"

"Really?" Soames smiled. "But the Roman Catholic Church."

"The priests will not bother you. I have my contacts."

"Then I'm in."

"Bravo." Piso hugged Soames. "Will you shelter my friend from the States . . . a sad case . . . in one of the Rome soup kitchens you'll set up?"

"Of course."

"Do not forget . . . because I never forget."

CHAPTER TWELVE

Nicole Garvey knelt at the coffin of her stepmother in the Rock of Ages funeral home just outside Dublin, Georgia. With a face as dismal as a dried-apple carving in rouge, the deceased clutched a Bible with fingers withered down to talons. While mourners behind sang of the heavenly feast to come, Nicole only heard the late Mrs. Jesse Soames badgering a redheaded, pigtailed girl, whom she'd insisted on calling Nick, to learn the art of cooking. *You'll never catch a man, Nick*—a nickname the girl hated—*unless you learn to cook.* The Southern belle, lifeless in her Sunday best, had judged the pigtailed girl a hopeless tomboy misfit. Nicole no longer wore pigtails, but the memories remained.

Her father had never given up on her, though. How triumphant she had felt those times he rescued her from the kitchen, where she could do no right, to go camping with the Baptist Family Campout. The leaves had crunched under her feet, while masculine banter floated in the forest air scented with sputtering bacon and percolator coffee. She would press her ear against the inside of her sleeping tent to hear the fathers outside tell tales of Noah's Ark discovered in Turkey, and the Ark of the Covenant, sure to be found somewhere in Ethiopia. He nurtured her passion for archaeology all the way through a doctorate.

"Your stepmother was right proud of you." Her father's voice came from behind. He stood over her, his hand on her shoulder.

She stood up and hugged him. "I'm sure," she said. She finished the rest of her sentence to herself, *that she told me no man wants an overeducated tomboy digging up old bones.*

"She always wanted to help you, trying to teach you to cook and all."

"I know." Out of hurt pride and concern for her father, she never told him how his second wife would pinch her whenever she violated the code of the Southern belle. When he asked, she just made up lies to explain the black-and-blue marks on her arms.

"I was pretty lonely after your mother died."

"You had every right to remarry and be happy." She kissed his cheek. "I'm glad you did."

Glad for him, not for herself. She would never tell him how his second wife had insinuated Nicole was responsible for her mother's death due to complications while giving birth to her. He didn't deserve to have his peace of mind disturbed. The nastiness of her stepmother's guilt trips no longer existed unless she let it fester in her thoughts. The world beyond Georgia had cleansed from her mind the guilt that no tent revival meeting could.

"I want to thank you." He took both her hands into his. "You didn't have to come, but you did."

"I wanted to be here for you."

"Have you thought some more about meeting in Rome after your girlfriend's wedding?" He hugged her. "We both could use some R&R. Let's go visit the grave of your great-grandpa, Colonel Soames. I told you what a hero he was."

"My World War Two cloak-and-dagger great-granddad?" How she had loved to brag to other kids about his exploits. She withdrew from her father's embrace and looked at the floor. "I don't think I'm going to Cindy's wedding in Amalfi."

"Why not?"

"He'll drop the divorce proceedings." She grabbed her father's hands, wanting him to be happy for her. "He wants to work things out."

"After what he put you through . . . including that bimbo who—"

"Not here, please." She looked around to see if anyone had overheard. "Anyway," she whispered. "That was over a year ago."

"I don't want to tell you what to do," he said, escorting her to a side room. "But you shouldn't have let him back in."

"It's just temporary. He's had some water problems in his place."

"The man's nothing but a serial cheater." He rubbed the back of his neck. "Honey, it hurts me to say it, but you need to be more choosy in your men."

"And you should know . . ." She wasn't going to play tit for tat by hurting him with bad stepmother memories. "Just let us work it out."

CHAPTER THIRTEEN

Commissario Marco Leone fretted while Inspector Riccardo Renaldi wove the squad car through Rome's traffic jam to the Colosseum in morning air still gauzy with fog. "Hurry. I can't be late."

"I'm doing the best I can. Traffic jam. An accident up ahead."

A special alert came over the radio about a terrorist group called Egyptian Phoenix making unspecified threats unless Rome's obelisks were returned to Egypt.

"Our thanks for returning the Axum Obelisk to Ethiopia." Renaldi jolted to a stop centimeters from the rear end of the car ahead. "Now the Egyptians are making threats unless we return more."

"The special alert only referred to the Egyptian Phoenix. Not the Egyptian government."

"They're all the same."

"Why not return some of the ancient phallic symbols?" Leone rolled down the window to let some fresh air in. Riding with Renaldi made him more claustrophobic than usual. "Rome has twice the number remaining in Egypt."

"Never." The inspector cursed a driver cutting in front of him. "Next they'll want reparations for the conquest of Egypt two thousand years ago."

The Colosseum played peekaboo behind fog patches thickened with the yeast of pollution. During the intervals of its disappearance, Leone imagined a terrorist's bomb bringing down the Colosseum. If terrorists did not destroy it, time would likely do so. Because of the financial crisis, government funding for repair had ended, leaving only private donations. A neon-illuminated billboard in front of the Colosseum listed the major donors . . . World Heritage Fund, the Chinese Government Benevolent Fund, and Piso Global Enterprises. Lucio Piso . . . Mr. Moneybags was back home.

"What's the drug unit doing here in uniform?" Leone nudged Renaldi's elbow just as traffic picked up.

"My godfather reassigned the undercover narcs." Renaldi zoomed around two totaled vehicles by the side of the road, one smoking like a minivolcano. "To protect the Colosseum from Egyptian terrorists."

"You don't have to keep reminding me Malatesta's your godfather." Leone held up his hand with the tips of his thumb and forefinger nearly touching. "They were this close to catching those drug dealers until Malatesta pulled the plug."

If drug crimes increased, Questore Pietro Malatesta was sure to shift the blame to someone else for his decision to transfer the drug unit to guard work. Against Leone's advice, the questore had once ordered a drug courier's stomach pumped to recover a cocaine packet concealed in a condom. When the condom ruptured, causing death, the honorable Malatesta let Leone take the public-relations rap.

"I understand why you're so personally involved with drug crimes, Marco, but—"

"Commissario Leone . . . please."

"Forget it, then." The inspector gunned the engine and raced around a car, almost sideswiping it. "I have nothing to say . . . to you."

Forget it? How? Lorenza . . . his only child, working with drug addicts in a rehab program and becoming hooked herself, thanks to the crackhead patient turned boyfriend. She accused Leone of wanting a son instead of her. Days on end, after their fights, she would call herself Lorenzo instead of Lorenza just to spite him. She stopped talking to him after he arrested her in front of the Colosseum as a last-ditch effort to get her into a detox program.

If only Lorenza had taken his advice. If only she had not fallen for the druggie. If only his ex-wife would stop blaming him for their daughter's estrangement. *If only* . . . two useless words. One thing was certain. *Mondo cane* . . . dog world.

It's a dog's world.

He escaped his memories by reviewing the Abramo Basso investigative file. Owing Leone a favor, the lab director had prepared a supplemental report, using advanced DNA testing instead of traditional blood tests, that proved the blood on the snake-head knife was Abramo's. Experts traced the knife used for sacrificial purposes to one of ancient Rome's Mideastern provinces. "Guess what?" Leone looked up. "The blood on the knife is Basso's. Not that of a bull . . . as you predicted."

"I still think the gang I arrested had something to do with Basso's death. Remember the 365 cut into Basso's forehead and smeared on the sarcophagi?"

"Still blaming the gang, are you?" He had his own theory of the 365 puzzle. But he wanted to hear Renaldi out. "What about the 365?"

"The gang is part of a punk-rock group called Bong 365. See now?"

"Get over it, will you? Pure coincidence."

"Punk-rock bands also use Nazi symbols, like swastikas."

"I give up. Believe what you want." Last night it had come to him. That year spent at yeshiva might pay off after all. "The number could relate to the three hundred sixty-five *mitzvot* . . . the negative commandments of Judaism. And then those swastikas. Whoever killed Basso had to be an anti-Semite."

"Don't make this into one of those American hate crimes." The inspector made a sour face. "How many even knew this Catholic priest was a converted Jew? They killed Basso because he interrupted a satanic ceremony. Period."

"Just get moving." Goal for Renaldi. The inspector had a point. "I'm late."

As they drove past the Basilica of San Lorenzo, Leone's chest tightened. His ex-wife and he, full of laughter and spirits after a party, had once taken a taxi with a Somali driver unfamiliar with Rome. They let him roam lost through the streets with the mutual promise they would let fate name their child after the first church they passed. She had pointed to the Basilica of San Lorenzo and declared, "I hereby name her Lorenza."

He shook off the bittersweet remembrance by examining the autopsy report from the forensic pathologist. A sharp instrument had pierced Basso's chest. Even without the hand cuts indicating the victim had tried to protect himself, the stab wound showed Abramo was first murdered on land before winding up in the Tiber. The wound itself was fatal.

Most unusual was the fingerprint report. Partial prints on the knife found at the scene proved insufficient for identification. The worn-away ridges lacked detail. The abrasive material used by certain manual workers, such as bricklayers, could cause such prints. *Could it be—*

"We've arrived," Renaldi said. "Campo Verano Cemetery."

CHAPTER FOURTEEN

By the time Commissario Marco Leone arrived at the Verano cemetery, the priest had nearly finished the funeral service for Father Abramo Basso, immured behind a marble slab in the three-story Jesuit mausoleum. Students and faculty colleagues from the Pontifical Gregorian University swarmed the passageway lined on both sides with the marble slabs of the dead. Looking uneasy in the Christian crowd, old ghetto acquaintances greeted Leone with their disappointment that the Jew turned Jesuit was not buried in the Jewish section.

Why was Fisher so intent on meeting Leone after the service? Maybe the professor knew something that could solve the case. Maybe Fisher would even confess to Abramo's murder. Maybe Leone could make the plane to Chicago after all.

After the final prayer for the dead, Fisher led Leone outside to a stone bench near the entrance. "I never thought he'd become a Jesuit priest." Fisher sat down next to the commissario and kicked a pebble. "Instead, I was the one who couldn't make it."

"My time is limited." Leone tapped his foot. "Did you see me to make a confession?"

"I'm sorry for reminiscing." The professor crossed his arms and jutted his chin toward Leone. "But I have nothing to confess either to you or my spiritual confessor."

"Why, then, did you want to meet?"

"You should know Wesley Bemis has discovered a dedication inscription in the Villa of the Papyri. It confirms Lucius Calpurnius Piso Caesoninus as the builder of this ancient mansion in Herculaneum."

"Four Latin names for one old Roman are impressive, but to me they mean nothing." Leone checked his wristwatch. "Are we here to discuss ancient history?"

"I believe the Villa of the Papyri is the home mentioned in the Festus parchment." He handed Leone a sheet of paper. "I've underlined what I think are the missing words and letters of the Festus parchment referring to Seneca and Saint Paul. Kind of like a crossword puzzle."

"I like crossword puzzles." Leone scanned the sheet: . . . *in the home of the illustrious Lucius Calpurnius Piso Caesoninus who is the father-in-law of Gaius Julius Caesar . . .*

"We know from other sources," Fisher said, "old Lucius was the father-in-law of Julius Caesar."

"What's your point?"

"I believe," Fisher said, "the Festus parchment shows Apostle Paul, for some unknown reason, met Seneca, Nero's adviser, in the Villa of the Papyri where we're now excavating. We know a descendant of old Lucius, one Gaius Calpurnius Piso, who lived in the time of Paul, ran the place like an intellectual think tank. Earlier archaeologists have already recovered Greek poems and philosophical works and—"

"Stop for a minute." Leone held up a hand. "Even if the parchment's genuine, it doesn't say Seneca ever invited Paul." He handed the sheet back. "Save all this speculation for your next book. None of this helps solve the Basso murder."

Before the professor could respond, the ground rippled like a conveyor belt under the commissario's feet.

Afraid it was another of his dizzy spells, Leone braced for a fall.

A chunk of masonry fell from the Jesuit mausoleum and just missed Fisher's head.

"The tremors have returned." Fisher headed for the cemetery entrance. "Let's get out of here."

At the cemetery entrance, Leone and the professor waited in the open to make certain the shaking had ended. Nearby flower vendors taunted as cowards those competitors closing up their stalls in fear of further earth rumblings.

"They've stopped for now." Leone watched traffic thaw back into motion from its frozen state. He might as well hear the professor out. The quakes had delayed the arrival of Renaldi to take him back to headquarters. "What can you tell me about the Latin riddle in the Ardeatine Caves?"

"My research led me to something similar in an ancient Christian writing called *Questions of the Old and New Testament*." Fisher pulled out a leather-bound book from his briefcase. *"In spelaeo velatis oculis illuduntur."*

"What does it mean?"

"They are deceived in the cave with their eyes blindfolded."

"Who's deceived?"

"The early Christian writer that scholars call Ambrosiaster was ridiculing the initiation rites of the Roman cult devoted to the god Mithras." The professor returned the book to his briefcase. "The writer says the cult blindfolded initiates and had them flap their hands like wings and croak like ravens. Others roared like lions at a different stage of initiation. Some were even called soldiers, in a religious sense . . . like the song 'Onward Christian Soldiers.' They had their hands bound with chicken guts until someone named the Liberator severed the guts with a sword."

"You're overlooking something." Leone looked down the street but no sign of Renaldi. "The Latin words in the cave written in bull's blood included the word *non* in capital letters. *Non* means *not* in Italian as well as Latin." He put his hands on his hips. "Not deceived, Professor Fisher, is quite different from deceived."

"I didn't overlook it. I just don't know why it was added . . . yet." Fisher rubbed his right temple. "Whoever wrote it wanted to deny any deception."

"A ritual murder in a cave does not surprise me. This is, after all, a country fascinated with the deeds of sorcerers, occultists, and fortune tellers. But literate murderers engaged in theological disputations?" Leone threw up his hands in mock despair. "Spare me."

"The media have sensationalized the numbers found on Basso's forehead and in the caves." Fisher stooped over to drop coins into a street beggar's basket. He straightened up. "They've made the case into a black-magic homicide."

"Any ideas about those numbers, Professor?"

"What comes to mind is the number of days in a year."

"What would be the significance?"

"The Egyptians considered the god Thoth the creator of the three-hundred-sixty-five-day calendar." Fisher pointed to a newspaper kiosk nearby. "The papers are full of stories about the Egyptian Phoenix terrorist group. Do you believe there's a connection?"

"Some claim to see the image of Padre Pio, the Italian saint, on a church wall in the Philippines." Leone shrugged and sighed. "Believing is seeing, some say. I prefer to see before I believe. And I don't see any connection. The Egyptian Phoenix wants the return of obelisks, not a calendar."

As Fisher walked away to hail a taxi, Leone called out, "The ancient knife I told you about in the Vatican exhibition . . . Do you know who was in charge?"

"That would be Cardinal Gustavo Furbone." He entered the taxi and asked out the window, "Is his name helpful?"

"The most helpful information you've given me all day."

CHAPTER FIFTEEN

Shedding her shoes, Nicole Garvey dumped the day's mail onto the kitchen counter. She ripped open the envelope from the Harvard University Department of Anthropology. The dean regretted to inform her that due to budgetary constraints, her contract for the position of senior lecturer in classical archaeology would not be renewed.

She sat down to absorb a blow not unexpected. The dean had hinted as much before the semester ended. But it still smarted. She focused on the bright side. She had time now to reconnect with her husband by remaining in Georgia. She bore the greater fault for their estrangement. She had caused the long-distance nature of the marriage. It was her decision to traipse off to Harvard despite his law practice. He had given up his affair. It was now her turn to meet him halfway.

Forgoing her meditation time-out, Nicole turned to her emails. The rhythmic press of the Delete button offered its own satisfying mantra. Her finger poised over the intriguing squiggle of a news link. "Renewed Excavation at Villa of Papyri." She dipped into her private stash of Godiva chocolate, which was behind the monitor, and opened the link.

Dr. Will Fisher, professor of early Christianity at Pontifical Gregorian University in Rome, and Dr. Wesley Bemis of the Center for the Preservation of Ancient Religious Texts (CPART) at Brigham Young University are exploring the Villa of the Papyri in Herculaneum. The Piso clan of ancient Rome owned the villa in which previous excavators have found hundreds of carbonized scrolls now being opened and translated.

The eruption of Mount Vesuvius in AD 79 killed between 10,000 and 25,000 persons. Unlike her sister city of Pompeii, smothered under volcanic ash, Herculaneum perished in a river of volcanic mud. The result is that the interiors of buildings in Herculaneum are better preserved than in Pompeii but harder to excavate.

The project seeks a qualified archaeologist to fill a team vacancy.

The Wesley Bemis? She turned the name over in her mind during a much-needed bubble bath a little later on. It couldn't be, but it was. An airport reception committee of one, she had agreed to pick up the bubble gum–popping boy wonder with the cowboy hat. He came to lecture to the Harvard anthropology faculty on the use of multispectral imaging, or MSI for short, in deciphering ancient texts.

A former computer specialist at IBM, he possessed dual degrees in archaeology and papyrology. The creep had made a pass at her outside her car, placing his hands against the door on either side of her head and aiming an awkward kiss she deflected onto her cheek. She could still smell the faint odor of a decaying tooth on his breath. And what had she done? *Nothing.* Instead of kneeing him in the crotch, she cajoled him. They'd be late for his lecture if he persisted. He relented, but she still felt a flash of shame.

The opening for an archaeologist mentioned in the news link sparked her interest. The position could revive her career . . . if only she weren't wholeheartedly committed to repairing her broken marriage. If she tried as hard with her marriage as with her profession, she could put her marriage back together. Now was not the time to run off to Cindy's wedding on the Amalfi coast and especially not to an archaeological dig directed by the Mormon creep. She had to put her marriage first.

She emerged refreshed from her bath in anticipation of the reconciliation dinner with her husband. She had to hurry. He didn't like to be kept waiting. Before putting on her white terry-cloth robe, she rubbed the caffe latte birthmark shaped like a butterfly on her left arm. As a girl, she'd thought she could rub it off. The silly habit had stayed with her.

In the bedroom she found the bed unmade. Was stress playing tricks? She had made it up before leaving for her stepmother's funeral early that morning. She rubbed her eyes and looked again. Still there.

Long blonde hairs from another female like a serpent's spawn on his pillow.

She stumbled toward the dresser and pawed through the drawer she had set aside for him. A stack of overdue bills and jumbled clothes concealed a blue envelope with red striping. Through tears she struggled to read the letter.

> I love to feel the sweat from your body drip onto mine when we make love . . . I love to feel you deep inside . . . I love to taste . . . I love to . . .

Garvey threw the letter to the floor and collapsed into the granny rocking chair. She raced on the rocker as though it might transport her to a better place.

She had supported him in his desire to rise to the top of the law firm like pond scum. And this was her reward?

She slowed to a standstill, falling into fitful slumber. A banging on the door shattered her nightmare of choking on a ball of blonde hairs. She awoke from her long nap.

"Let me in, Nicole. It's me."

"I found your lover's letter."

"That's an old letter."

"One little problem, Mr. Einstein. It's dated a week ago."

"It's all a mistake."

"It sure was." Her marriage was a corpse. "We're finished. Get the divorce."

"Come on, Nicole. You can't mean that." He paused. "I'll see a counselor."

"You have the wrong Nicole." She bolted the safety latch on the door. "The one you want doesn't exist anymore. Now, go away."

CHAPTER SIXTEEN

First responders salvaged bodies from the rubble heaped up inside the Basilica of San Clemente. Commissario Marco Leone used his jacket to warm a survivor sitting dazed against a broken-limbed tree. Fragments of the church facade lay scattered on the ground. Paramedics either zipped up body bags or treated survivors while the wail of ambulances going and coming drowned out the moans of the wounded. Thick black smoke curling through gaps in the basilica roof stung the membranes of his nose. Leone asked, "Are you certain?"

The victim repeated his story. During the well-attended funeral Mass for a prominent politician, the closed casket in the center aisle had exploded in a blinding flash, like a resurrection. The victim paused to thank the saints for his late arrival, requiring him to take a position in the rear near a protective pillar. He fell unconscious after the blast until rescued.

Paramedics cut off the explanation and took him away on a stretcher. Before departing, a paramedic donated a cigarette to Leone. The commissario wanted to believe he could kick the habit by bumming cigarettes instead of buying them. Taking a drag, Leone took stock of the case. The victim's account fit the little he knew. In an abandoned flat not far from the basilica, his men had found the tuxedoed corpse. Whoever perpetrated this had used a remote-controlled explosive in place of the politician's corpse.

That day, many churchgoers didn't know the funeral would be their own. Early in his career, Leone had investigated a ransom case in the Campania where kidnappers had amputated the victim's ears. And in Rome, he had unraveled the cases of a drug-induced beheading of a baby and a student burned alive by her ex-boyfriend. He exhaled a blast of smoke.

Mondo cane. It's a dog's world.

As a schoolboy, he had visited the Basilica of San Clemente. A twelfth-century church built over a fourth-century church in turn built over a first-century apartment building. A street once separated the apartment building from a mansion owned by a Roman consul turned Christian convert and presumed martyr. The apartment building and mansion had buried even more ancient buildings destroyed by the Great Fire in the time of Nero. Rome struck him as a historical compost pile where the miasma of the past blemished the present.

"Commissario Leone . . . Come," Inspector Renaldi yelled from the police car.

Leone arrived to hear the dispatcher's voice from headquarters crackling over the radio. "A message to media outlets from an unidentified source claims this is the first installment of reparations owed by Christians. A terrorist group called the Egyptian Phoenix is suspected."

"I don't believe it." Leone threw his cigarette on the ground. "They've denied it. It's too sophisticated an operation for them."

"Questore Malatesta thinks they did it."

"Your godfather is gullible and delusional." With his foot, Leone ground the discarded cigarette into smithereens. "The Egyptian Phoenix wants the return of the obelisks, not reparations. Christians didn't take the obelisks. Ancient Romans did."

"But the questore says—"

"Nonsense."

It would not have surprised Leone if the perpetrators of the San Clemente bombing turned out to be homegrown visionaries drunk on desperation. Like contemporary youth, he had once felt the same anarchic urge to smash the existing social order to avoid suffocation. The Years of Lead—that time of youthful rage unleashed by the Red Brigades—changed his mind. They left only a terror trail of blood and bullets for him and his fellow officers to mop up.

The winds of change, whether the Reformation or the Enlightenment blowing across the lands of the north, had stopped at the Alps. Even the glories of the Renaissance, let alone the fiasco of Fascism, harkened back to the future. Change had no chance. Italy would remain smothered by the overflowing wealth of its history and culture even if it meant its inhabitants had to live the life of privileged custodians locked away in a marbled Disneyland museum.

His only wish was to seize the chance of escaping to Chicago for fresh air.

Near the basilica he interviewed a suspect his men had picked up in the vicinity. The detainee had nothing to do with the bombing. Yet, for their efforts, he thanked his inner circle of trusted officers nicknamed the Leone Squad for their devotion to him.

"How bad is the damage?" he asked a junior officer guarding the entrance.

"The inside's a mess. But the underground part, the ancient tunnels, including the pagan chapel dedicated to Mithras . . . some god or other . . . is intact."

"That will make the tourism bureau happy." Something clicked in Leone's brain. "You're supposed to be off duty after the bust yesterday." He held out his arms and flexed his muscles. "Who do you think you are? Hercules?"

"I want to help you here."

"Aren't you worried Malatesta might discipline you for violating policy?"

"Malatesta's—" The junior officer hesitated. "Malatesta's an asshole."

"A little respect, if you please," Leone said with a wink.

"The boys know he let you take the fall for the dead Somalian drug dealer."

"Get out of here, and get some sleep. That's an order." The commissario tapped the officer's shoulder. "Before I get you exiled to a Sicilian donkey town."

In a world other than mondo cane, this man could have been the son he never had.

CHAPTER SEVENTEEN

"He has to go." Jesse Soames watched the hungry poor of Rome shuffle up to the food table with empty bowls. "His son, Professor Fisher, lives here in Rome. Fisher can take him in."

"Out of the question. He's at the gates of death." Lucio Piso pushed his forefinger against the American's chest. "This operation belongs to Piso Global Enterprises. You run it at my pleasure."

"I don't mean to be ungrateful." Soames stepped back from Piso's touch. "But I can't stand him around here. Let his son take care of him."

"The son wants nothing to do with him. He even Anglicized his surname to Fisher from Fischer." Piso pointed to Otto Fischer, leaning on his walker and ladling out minestrone with a trembling hand. "And the poor man is too ashamed to look up his son in Rome, even though he yearns to."

"And he damned well should be." Soames jutted his chin. "I know why he fled the States. The Justice Department there is after him for his Nazi war crimes."

"He was just an underage youngster in the German military. They drafted him nonetheless because they needed more soldiers. He had to follow orders."

"My conscience won't let me do it."

Piso took Soames by the shoulders. "We must shelter this doddering old man, now a fugitive. If the Italian authorities learn he's in Rome, public hysteria will force his arrest for participation in the

Ardeatine Caves affair." Piso shook Soames. "We are his only hope, my dear friend."

"How can you defend him? He was part of the SS execution squad. They shot over three hundred of your countrymen in the Ardeatine Caves, their bodies piled up like stacks of cordwood."

"Blame the partisans. They attacked the German column. Today the partisans would be called terrorists. Only one thing counts." Piso held up one finger. "Fischer helped me, a defenseless youngster, during the German occupation. Nothing else counts."

"Look, Lucio, I appreciate the favors but—"

"Let us get one thing clear. I do no favors. I collect debts, and you owe me."

Otto Fischer stumbled, knocking over a basket of bread. An assistant rushed out of the kitchen to help him regain his balance.

"Owe you?"

"In Buenos Aires you promised to shelter a friend."

"I didn't know your friend was a war criminal."

"You must honor your promise."

"And if I don't?"

"Must it come to this?" Piso motioned for Fischer to approach them. "This poor man was present when his German comrades interrogated your grandfather about his terrorist activities with Italian partisans," Piso said to Soames.

The businessman helped the fugitive into a chair. "Now tell the colonel's grandson what you know."

Otto Fischer related how the Nazis captured Colonel Soames as a secret OSS agent sent by the Americans. Fischer stopped momentarily to catch his breath. Then he added that under interrogation, the colonel had revealed the names of his partisan accomplices, including one Benjamin Leone.

"You expect me to take the word of this Nazi?"

"You should. He shot Benjamin in the back of the head in the Ardeatine Caves."

"Who'd believe this fugitive's lies about a dead American hero?"

"Recognize this?" Piso took a black diary from his pearl-handled briefcase and handed it to Soames. It couldn't be. The handwriting was his grandfather's.

"Look," Piso said, "at the entry for April 28, 1944."

In the diary, Colonel Soames bemoaned the weakness of his flesh in revealing the names of Italian partisans to the Axis inquisitors.

"I can't believe it." Soames turned away from the diary. "They must have tortured him beyond endurance."

"He squealed so readily," Piso said, "that they spared his life."

"Another lie by this fugitive."

"Your grandfather had more than one weakness of the flesh." Piso leered. "He and La Sirena carried on an affair. She bore a child."

"La Sirena was my grandmother, and her daughter . . . my mother . . . was illegitimate." Soames blew out his lips. "So what? It's old news."

"There is more." Piso turned to Otto Fischer. "You had better tell him."

Jesse Soames put his hands over his ears, not wanting to hear that La Sirena had carried on a simultaneous affair with both Colonel Soames and Benjamin Leone. The father of La Sirena's child was Benjamin Leone and not Colonel Soames. Yet the mother told Otto Fischer she would claim the colonel as the father. She wanted her daughter to find a better life in the New World, even though Benjamin was the love of her life and the colonel just an enemy spy caught in her honey trap.

"No-o-o." Soames walked toward Otto Fischer with a raised fist. "I don't take the word of this Kraut. My daughter is the great-granddaughter of Colonel Soames and no one else."

Piso pushed him back. "Then look at this." He handed Soames a ragged sheet, browned by time. "It is an Italian birth certificate Fischer took from Benjamin Leone's pocket after the execution."

The sealed document listed Benjamin Leone as the father and the woman called La Sirena as the mother.

"You think this is enough to keep me quiet about this war criminal?"

"If not," Piso said, "how about that untoward incident in Vietnam? The My Lai Massacre. A participating officer escaped detection. Did you ever wonder who it could be? My sources know."

"How did . . . ?" Soames turned pale. "I did nothing wrong."

"The sources know how the officer falsified records to hide his involvement."

"I was just following . . ." He sat down and hung his head, his clenched fists banging against his cheeks.

"Exactly like Otto Fischer." Piso patted Jesse Soames on the head. "I can bury the past . . . as long as you follow my orders." He put his arm around Fischer. "This man stays here as long as I want."

CHAPTER EIGHTEEN

At his desk, Commissario Marco Leone thumbed through the investigative report of the San Clemente bombing while his secretary stonewalled journalists clamoring for an interview. But one thought drove out all others: someone had betrayed him. Just like Uncle Benjamin.

He fished out of the bottom desk drawer a black-and-white photograph. Uncle Benjamin wore a white shirt unbuttoned at the collar, his chest hair curled and sleek like the fur of a black sacrificial lamb. The picture was all he had left of a hero he never knew but admired from afar. Cut down in his late twenties by the Nazis, his uncle was everything his father wasn't . . . adventurous, independent, charming, and full of Torah righteousness even unto death.

Leone had little enough in common with a father who begat him late in life. A man of sullen silences, his father refused to tell him anything about the younger brother killed in the Ardeatine Caves. Leone turned to outsider hearsay about his uncle's feats and molded them into the role model of his imagination.

Inspector Riccardo Renaldi entered with an armful of files. "Here are the dossiers on the cold cases you wanted to review."

"You backstabbed me."

"I what?"

"Questore Malatesta told me I'm off the San Clemente case, and my trip to Chicago is on hold." He hooked his thumbs under his belt and looked up at Renaldi. "But I keep the Basso case. Stay out of it and away from me."

"I didn't squeal what you said about his views on the Egyptian Phoenix."

"How would you know the reason unless you snitched?"

"I might have complained a bit but . . ." Renaldi stopped speaking and dumped the files on Leone's desk. "What's the use? Nothing will change your mind." He backed away. "I tried, but you shut me out, just like everyone else who doesn't think you walk on water . . . including your ex." He pointed at Leone. "You doubled-crossed yourself."

"You can screw her, but don't screw with me." Leone brushed away the files. "You sold me out to Malatesta. Without him you wouldn't be here."

"Where would you be if not for your father's service in the Polizia di Stato?" Renaldi asked. "If your father were alive, he'd investigate the Egyptian Phoenix."

"The very same words used by Malatesta about my father . . . if he were alive, he'd investigate the Egyptian Phoenix." Leone leaned back in his chair. "Beyond coincidental, don't you think?"

"You never appreciated me." Renaldi walked to the door and turned. "You're not half the detective your father was."

His wonderful father who set a Fascist record for confessions by forcing castor oil down the throat of suspects until they shit in their pants.

"My father?" He stood up and leaned forward on his desk with both hands. "When you and your cronies drink to his memory, does anyone mention how he became so famous by sucking up to Fascists?"

"What kind of son are you? He was a patriot." The inspector's face reddened. "If you were fair—"

"If life were fair, I'd be able to transfer you to a remote beat where you'd spend the rest of your days directing tourists in bad English to the nearest ATM machine. But as the great JFK said: Life is not fair." Renaldi took several steps toward the door. "Come back. Where are you going with that file?"

"Quite interesting. It's about your father and the Ardeatine Caves. It was misfiled. But since you don't care about him . . ."

"Give it to me."

The inspector tossed the Ardeatine Caves dossier on the desk. "You're making a mistake." His voice sounded hoarse. "You will regret your mistake."

"Get out of my office."

***

Leone slipped out the side door of headquarters to evade reporters demanding answers to the San Clemente bombing.

He had worsened relations with Questore Malatesta by rejecting the Egyptian Phoenix theory and attacking Renaldi. Now that Chicago receded into the distance, only the antagonism toward Renaldi broke through his emotional numbness.

As early evening dimmed the city, he zigzagged down narrowing streets flanked by crumbling buildings to evade a reporter. He turned onto a crime-ridden backstreet reeking of uncollected garbage from a sanitation strike. On the upper floor of a tenement, a couple argued over money in the rising and falling melodies of an opera duet.

A shadow bobbed along behind a row of garbage bags. A tall bag tumbled over, spilling out stinking fish entrails. He fingered his concealed pistol. The shadow emerged from the protection of the last garbage bag . . . a dog with a missing hind leg. Tail wagging and tongue panting, the rib-prominent pointer hobbled toward Leone with burrs entangled in its hair.

Leone cursed relief and walked away down the center of the deserted backstreet. The three-footed clacking of claws on cobblestone trailed him. He clapped to scare off the pointer. The dog mistook the clapping as an invitation. Leone picked up his pace to shake off the unwelcome canine. Yelping came from behind. The pointer had tumbled over on the cobblestones made slippery by soapy water dumped into the street. It struggled to right itself but flopped over. He slipped a foot under the dog, probably infested with vermin, and gave it a leg up to standing position. White with orange blotches over each eye and an orange snout, the pointer looked up at Leone and whimpered.

Thinking it foolish to run from a miserable mutt, he slowed so he and the pointer could walk side by side. The mutt would leave him at some point anyway, like his ex-wife, like his daughter . . . maybe to forage in another backstreet for scraps, or . . . this is life after all . . . to be run over by a vehicle. No one would mourn this bundle of mange.

He came into a familiar neighborhood not far from his apartment. He would read the discovered dossier about his father and the Ardeatine Caves. And then, after downing leftovers for supper with so-so red wine, he would follow his routine of dozing off on the sofa with the TV left on.

At the door to his apartment complex, the pointer lay down shivering.

"God help me . . . You can stay." He scratched the pointer behind the ears. "I name you Mondocane after this dog world of ours."

CHAPTER NINETEEN

Looking at the time on her cell every quarter hour wouldn't make the Circumvesuviana train arrive any sooner in Sorrento for her bus connection to Amalfi. It wasn't just the wedding of her girlfriend she would miss if the train arrived late. Professor Fisher was interrupting his return trip to Rome from the Villa of the Papyri just to interview her in Amalfi.

Nicole Garvey had double-checked the train schedule and even arrived forty-five minutes early at the Naples central station. But how could she know a wildcat strike would delay train service just long enough to jeopardize her plans?

The train streaked past yellow buildings smeared with soot and hurtled into a tunnel, plunging her into darkness. Falling back into the plush seat, Garvey remembered her father's disturbed look when he had seen her off in Rome on the first leg of her trip to Naples. He seemed happy enough when he had opened up the social service center in Rome. What was bothering him now? His heart again? He didn't believe in talking about his own problems but only in trying to solve hers.

If she landed the position of assistant archaeologist for the Villa of the Papyri, her father wouldn't have to help her out to tide her over until the divorce settlement came through. He had done enough. She wanted back into the trenches of archaeology and away from the dust of research stacks and classroom chalkboard. Italy would recharge her life after waking from the evaporated dream of her marriage and the cloistered world of Harvard. She wasn't going to let her experience with Wesley Bemis scare her away from a chance to advance her career. If she got the job, she'd figure out how to deal with the Mormon lecher.

As soon as the train rocketed from the tunnel into the sunlight, she prepared for the interview by reviewing the modern technology Bemis planned to use in the renewed exploration of the Villa of the Papyri. Overlooking the Bay of Naples before the modern era, the Villa of the Papyri sank into the earth after the eruption of Mount Vesuvius. The volcanic explosion left nearly two thousand charcoal-like scrolls buried under the mud, waiting for archaeologists to discover them. The brittle sheets of carbonized papyrus, baked together like rolled filo dough in a Greek pastry shop, contained lost writings of the Greco-Roman world.

She'd had enough of the thumping bass leaking out from the head-phones of her teenage seatmate. She didn't have to take it anymore. She tapped his shoulder and asked him to stop. He glared. She glared back. He turned the music down and broke off eye contact.

She resumed preparation at her weakest point . . . the breakthrough technology promising to resurrect the carbon-based ink absorbed into the papyrus fabric blackened by the fire and heat of Mount Vesuvius. Multispectral imaging picked out the light wavelength reflected by the carbon in the ink. The ancient writing sprang, revived, from the papyrus background and became readable once again.

The problem remained of opening the bonded sheets of papyrus in order to apply imaging technology. Thanks to innovations of the space age, scientists had created a special gelatin that allowed the sheets of carbonized papyrus to loosen and unfold like flower petals. She learned from his Harvard lecture that Bemis, although a raunchy jerk in her eyes, had further advanced the potency of the gelatin beyond all expectations. His variation exponentially reduced the time needed to unravel the papyrus sheets. She had to face facts. The jerk was a genius. Dropping the name of Dr. Wesley Bemis, the professor's colleague in the excavation project, should score her some points in the interview.

"We have arrived in Sorrento," the conductor announced, just before the train doors jolted open.

She gathered her things and bolted down the aisle. The first to exit, she sprinted to the Amalfi-bound bus pulling out of the parking lot. She stood in front of it and waved her hands. The bus driver hit the brakes and honked the horn.

Behind the windshield, he waved her away.

She refused to move until he let her on.

CHAPTER TWENTY

Convertible top down in his red Maserati, Marco Leone snaked around hairpin turns, cliffs shearing down on his right into the foam-swept sea on the road to Amalfi. Hotels and villas hugged the mountainside below. Vehicles moved forward like windup toys on an asphalt ribbon past a medieval watchtower on the lookout for pirates long gone.

Cardinal Gustavo Furbone had given him the slip in Rome to avoid discussing Abramo's death. He'd outfox the prelate by ambushing him at the Amalfi wedding reception in honor of the cardinal's politician nephew and his American socialite bride.

Once he gave Carlos Stroheim a promise of confidentiality, the prefect of the Vatican Library revealed that the cardinal had threatened Abramo with harm for keeping the Festus parchment. The cardinal not only threatened Abramo but, according to Professor Fisher, had charge of the murder knife stolen from the Vatican collection. With luck, he'd wrap up the case and be off to Chicago.

He tried to stay focused on the case, but the dossier on his father found by Inspector Renaldi prevented that. Leone had pored over it the night before in disbelief. His father, an influential officer in the Polizia di Stato, could have saved Uncle Benjamin. An SS officer involved in the Ardeatine Caves executions had owed his father a favor. The Nazi offered the option of replacing Benjamin with a prison inmate to be selected by the Italian police. His father refused on the pretext it would violate proper police procedure. In cold blood, his father had let Benjamin die wrapped in the rhetoric of sanctimonious claptrap.

Except for a black Audi darting in and out of sight in his rearview mirror, no other vehicles traveled the road. Wind tousled his hair, just like those film clips of JFK at play with a full head of disheveled hair, so young and virile. He ran his hand through his own, feeling so free and alive, trying to channel his hero, until he touched the bald spot spreading like a stain at the crown of his head. Cold reality set in. He was no JFK.

He pressed the pedal harder to distance himself from the black Audi.

Commissario Leone, you have Addison's disease, his doctor had told him. *You're risking your health unless you take medication and change your lifestyle. You are no longer a young man, Commissario. Have you thought of a disability leave?*

The triumph of JFK over the same affliction gave him hope. But like his hero, he needed to keep his vulnerability hidden from those who wished him harm. Not a word to Inspector Renaldi, already circling around to grab his job title. To be ill was to be vulnerable in the world of mondo cane.

In his rearview mirror, the Audi speeding closer straddled the two lanes of travel.

Shifting to ease back pain, he daydreamed his youth alive again— the time Miriam and he, those many years ago, had spent a long weekend at the Luna Convento in Amalfi, both young and ignorant of how fate would tear them apart. He had serenaded Miriam amid the scents of lemon and orange trees with star sparklers pinned to a midnight-blue sky above a courtyard fit for Romeo and Juliet. He longed to claw back those times, to enchant her once again like a snake charmer, to rush with her, hand in hand, to their room, where he would . . . He caught the Audi zeroing in like a torpedo.

Does the idiot want to pass?

Losing sight of the Audi, he rounded a curve and slammed on the brakes to avoid crashing into road barricades. Two men in road-repair uniforms stood wearing masks shaped like ravens' heads.

"Stop. We have something to tell you," the shorter man said, as they sprinted toward the convertible.

"What the hell is this all about? Some kind of carnival stunt?"

The black Audi screeched to a stop behind him.

In his rearview mirror, the driver of the Audi wore a lion's mask.

A trap, his gut warned. He gunned the engine with a roar. The taller raven-headed man pulled out a pistol from his overalls. The convertible bucked forward, tossing aside the barrier, fishtailing for a few seconds, until Leone took control and raced down the highway with the Audi in pursuit.

Banging his horn before rounding an S curve with hands glued to the steering wheel, he swayed back and forth across the two lanes of travel without knowing if a vehicle was about to barrel around the mountain from the opposite direction.

The Audi dogged his tail. He steadied the Maserati on a straight patch of road before the next curve. A bullet from behind hit the dashboard.

The Audi closed in, its front tapping the Maserati's rear.

Horn blaring, Leone careened around a curve and hugged the mountainside lane to avoid a tumble over the cliff beyond the right lane. He prayed no car approached from the opposite direction. He'd won this round of Russian roulette.

The lion-masked driver of the Audi appeared on his right, neck and neck with the Maserati. The driver wasn't trying to pass. He wanted to smash the Maserati into the mountain. For a split second, the lion man turned toward him, his mask sparkling in the sunlight, impassive as death. In tandem, the Maserati and the Audi rounded a wide bend.

A flock of mountain goats materialized. Clipping goats on the right, he turned left and scraped the mountainside while braking. The lion driver veered right, catapulting the Audi off the road and down the mountainside.

A bloodied goat crashed through the Maserati's windshield.

The world went dead.

CHAPTER TWENTY-ONE

"The Festus parchment's gone. Someone broke into my filing cabinet." Soaked from the rain, Will Fisher leaned on his umbrella at the foot of the bed. "I stopped by to tell you on my way to Amalfi from the Villa of the Papyri to attend a wedding . . . and of course to cheer you up after your accident."

"You have a strange way of cheering me up," Marco Leone said. Hospitalized near Amalfi because of his brush with death on the way to his destination, Leone's headache grew worse with the news. He fished across his bed for a pack of Marlboros smuggled into the night-stand drawer. He needed to clear his brain. The hospital orderly had confiscated the contraband. He fell back, defeated, against the stack of pillows just as an officer from the Leone Squad brought in Mondocane for a visit. Leone asked the officer to wait outside.

"Where were the guards?" he asked Fisher. Mondocane's wet-dog smell from the rain cleared Leone's head. The pointer shook off rain-water from its back, almost slipping on one of his three legs.

"At the catacombs."

Mondocane nuzzled his nose into Leone's hand dangling over the bedside. "Inspector Renaldi was supposed to provide a guard."

"He had a tip the Egyptian Phoenix schemed an attack on the cat-acombs. He said he went there with the guard."

Patting the pointer on the head, Leone resolved to pursue disciplinary charges against Renaldi. Even if the Egyptian Phoenix threat were credible, he had an order to guard the parchment at all times.

Fisher snapped open his umbrella to dry and laid it at the foot of the bed.

"I hadn't planned on showering." Leone wiped the umbrella's scattered raindrops from his face. The gauche American perplexed him.

Renaldi's background check had been uncharacteristically superficial. The inspector blamed American privacy laws for the limited information. But with Renaldi, one never knew when his personal agenda took precedence.

Fisher's father had served in the German military, but Renaldi provided no details. Otto Fischer filed for bankruptcy and divorced. Arrested for shoplifting. Charges dropped. The son changed his surname from Fischer to Fisher and left Milwaukee for New York to become an actor of middling abilities. For reasons unknown, the son withdrew from the Jesuit order before taking vows but became a leading scholar on early Christianity and comparative religions.

"What do you know about the parchment's disappearance?"

"Absolutely nothing." Fisher's cheeks flushed red, and the color ran up his neck. "I'm an academic. Not a thief."

"I told you not to leave Rome." He struggled into a sitting position on the bed.

"Wesley Bemis needs an archaeological assistant immediately. I'm going to Amalfi, not just for the wedding, but to interview a candidate."

"Ah yes." He had almost forgotten. "Bemis. Your colleague with the skis in your office." The commissario sipped water. "You mentioned the parchment, didn't you?"

"He didn't steal it."

"Why so sure?"

"You told me to keep the parchment a secret."

"Just like I told you not to leave Rome?"

CHAPTER TWENTY-TWO

At an outdoor table in the Piazza del Duomo of Amalfi, Nicole Garvey sipped limoncello and looked up the sixty-two cathedral steps. Cindy posed on high for photographs with her aristocrat husband, a rising political star in the Italian parliament. The sun reflected honey gold off the twelfth-century bell tower of green and yellow glazed tiles. Her friend looked picture-perfect in her strapless, thigh-high wedding dress with a ruffled train of tulle. Cindy had not lost her sassy sense of fashion.

To their own internal tune, a gray-haired couple danced a fox-trot before a platform decorated with red, white, and green bunting. An official orated from the platform with the same Italian tricolors on the sash crisscrossing his chest. Above the music, she heard the words *tutti* . . . all . . . and *frutti* . . . fruits, something about protecting Amalfi fruits.

Her stepmother had ordered her not to chew Tutti Frutti gum. It was unladylike. Being unladylike had not prevented Cindy from snatching the gold ring of happiness as life rushed past them both, leaving the archaeologist to dig in the dirt for broken things left by the dead. Everything always seemed to work out for Cindy.

"Hello, Dr. Garvey?" said a voice from behind.

She turned. "Yes?"

"I'm Professor Will Fisher."

His introduction sounded on the perimeter of her attention, which was fixed on his starlight-blue eyes. "Oh, I thought we were meeting later." She offered her hand. His grip felt warm and firm.

"I finished my work at the Villa of the Papyri earlier than expected. So, I took up Cardinal Furbone's invitation to attend the wedding."

"You know the cardinal?"

"He attended the Pontifical Gregorian University of Rome where I teach." A dimple accentuated the smile on his left cheek. "Everyone at the school knows him. He's a go-to alumnus, a mover and shaker."

Behind him, Cindy floated down the stairway to a gaggle of relatives at the bottom, a butterfly bride in her lemon-chiffon dress under a barrage of colored confetti thrown by guests lining the path of descent.

"This won't take long." He held her résumé.

Had he made up his mind already? Her study of the Villa of the Papyri and the state-of-the-art technology had paid off. She aced the professor's questions.

Fisher said he knew an Italian archaeologist she had worked with as a graduate student at the Etruscan excavation of Populonia in Tuscany. The professor let slip his interviewer poker face for a moment by remarking that the colleague from that archaeological dig had recommended her. The wind was at her back.

The presence of Wesley Bemis on the project still troubled her. On her résumé, she mentioned meeting Bemis when he had lectured at Harvard about his breakthrough technology. The lecherous advance of the Brigham Young whiz kid on that occasion left him as a wild card in her new job. Fisher didn't say anything about his colleague, so she said nothing. She refused to let the presence of Bemis in the project influence her decision.

"That'll do." Fisher put away the résumé. "No need for more questions. I'd like you to join us in excavating the Villa of the Papyri."

"With pleasure, Professor Fisher."

"Call me Will. Glad to have you on our team." He looked at his watch. "I should go back to the villa. Wes . . . Dr. Bemis . . . thinks we're close to finding the Latin library in the villa."

"Latin library?"

"Aside from snippets of Latin comedy and history, the works recovered so far were written in Greek. The most famous recovery to date concerns writings by Philodemus, the Greek poet, probably a house-guest. We suspect a treasure trove of lost works still exists somewhere in the villa."

"Like what?"

"Horace, the Roman poet, dedicated his *Ars Poetica* to the owner's sons. He must have given them an original copy. Virgil was friends with Philodemus and Horace. I'll bet early editions of his epic *Aeneid* are still in the villa. Somewhere in that mansion my gut tells me rests the heart of Piso's library. Undiscovered works not just of the Greeks, but also a wealth of Latin writings, including Livy, Cicero, and Julius Caesar, Piso's son-in-law."

His passion for discovering the mother lode of classical literature, so obvious in the rising tone of his voice and the sparkle in his eyes, captivated her. Neither her father nor her ex had shown this in their work. She disliked dampening his flame, but she had to speak up. "Isn't it possible the occupants removed the library before the eruption obliterated the villa?"

"It's possible, not probable." His tone switched to cool logic. "The inhabitants had grown accustomed to tremors in the region. Evidence indicates they ignored the early warnings for some four days. Some sixteen thousand people perished." He sipped Cinzano vermouth on the rocks. "They were caught flat-footed before—"

Behind him, Cindy approached arm in arm with her Prince Charming husband.

"—and past excavations recovered not just scrolls left behind but valuable statuary and personal—"

Cindy waved. She waved back.

"—and that's why I think the scrolls are still buried."

Some people had all the luck. What to say to her after all this time? Excusing herself, Garvey rose to embrace the bride. "I'm really happy for you," she said, hugging Cindy and trying to mean every word. They pulled away, the ever-gorgeous Cindy, a little tipsy, looking tan and radiant.

Cindy eyed Fisher and steadied herself. "Who's the hunk?"

The face of Cindy's tuxedoed husband betrayed a ripple of displeasure before clouding over with the practiced cordiality of a politician on the make. Mortified, Garvey dug her fingernails into her palms.

Fisher joked away the tension by pretending to look for a hunk. She released her fingernails. They would hit it off just fine working together.

His presence helped her feel less inadequate with Cindy. Cindy introduced her husband as the head of a parliamentary committee investigating subversive organizations and dangerous cults. After exchanging pleasantries, the husband excused himself to greet guests a few yards in front of his wife.

Just then, a motorcycle putt-putted into the piazza, like a snorting mechanical bull, forcing its way through the scattering crowd. It jerked to a halt in front of the husband. A motorcycle passenger dressed like a tuxedoed bridegroom pulled something shiny from his pocket. He wore a flat hat with facial netting. Similar anti-insect headgear had been used on archaeological digs in Mexico.

Cindy's husband bent over to retrieve a purse dropped by a woman seconds before the motorcycle passenger fired a pistol.

Fisher pushed Garvey to the ground and covered her with his body. She raised her head.

Cindy lay prone, returning a fish-eyed gaze. Her blood snaked over the pavement.

Cursing his veiled accomplice, the motorcycle driver roared out of the piazza.

CHAPTER TWENTY-THREE

Near midnight, Inspector Riccardo Renaldi waited on the subway platform of Line B at the Colosseo metro stop in Rome. He looked up and down the platform. A drunk wobbled out toward the exit on the bumpy yellow warning stripes along the tracks.

Where are they? Renaldi thought, slamming a rolled newspaper into his palm. They better not have stood him up.

They all took him for granted. They might forget teasing him about his short height, but his memory was long. He had no regrets about stealing the Festus parchment. They deserved it. And after all he did for Leone, even digging up dirt on Otto Fischer, that Jewish atheist-communist still treated him like trash. At least he omitted Fischer's membership in a Nazi SS unit stationed in Rome. He would show them all how much they underestimated him.

All in black, Carlos Stroheim entered the platform with a body-builder type wearing tinted glasses and looking ripped enough to be on steroids. As the prefect approached, the bodybuilder remained at attention with arms folded like intertwined baby hams. The prefect and the inspector pretended to be strangers waiting for a train side by side on the platform, each obscuring his face with an opened newspaper. "You kept me waiting."

"Bit of a stickler, aren't you?" Stroheim looked at his watch. "I'm only ten minutes late."

"Don't let it happen again."

"Easy there." The prefect glanced sideways at the inspector. "Rest assured we value your services. Our leader is grateful for delivery of the Festus parchment."

"I want to meet the Pater Patrum personally."

"How did you know his title?"

"Don't underestimate a sleuth like me." Renaldi tapped the prefect's arm. "I put two and two together about you and this cabal called Roma Rinata."

"His identity remains secret for now." The prefect lowered his newspaper and looked around. "If you disobey orders . . ." He pointed to the bodybuilder. "You'll wind up a dead man."

"Don't try to intimidate me." Renaldi raised a fist. Stroheim's companion ran up and put the inspector in an arm lock. A train rattled toward the platform. He threatened to throw the inspector onto the tracks.

They were going to kill him.

"Let him go."

The bodybuilder followed orders.

"I just need to be appreciated." Renaldi rubbed an arm. "At one time or another I joined the Republican Fascist Party, the Tricolor Flame party, the National Front, the New Force, the Social Action group, the Italian Social Movement, not to mention the National Vanguard . . . The bumblers all ignored me."

Before continuing, he pretended to read his newspaper as two passengers left a train and headed for the exit.

"The buzz on the street is something big is about to happen, a return to the glory days. In this national crisis, I want to throw myself into a cause worthy of me." Renaldi stood as tall as he could in his elevator shoes. "Am I accepted into Roma Rinata or not?"

"We need people like you." The prefect revealed a gold-toothed smile. "The Pater Patrum agrees to probationary status. But you must understand, everything is on a needs-to-know basis."

"Sure, sure." Renaldi shrugged. "Just tell him I need to see him personally."

"If you insist."

"I do." Renaldi puffed his chest out. He had stood up for himself. "Let's shake on the deal."

"No offense." Stroheim withdrew his hand from Renaldi's attempted grasp. "Too many germs."

While waiting the agreed twenty minutes before leaving, Inspector Renaldi felt triumphant. He had found a cause that gave him meaning. Its strength would be his. He would no longer be small.

CHAPTER TWENTY-FOUR

In his darkened apartment, Marco Leone lay on a sofa, his head resting on a pillow under the glow of a lone floor lamp. The nightmare replay of his brush with death on the way to Amalfi had startled him awake. Tail wagging, Mondocane shambled from a corner of the living room to lie down on the floor beside him. Perhaps some late-night reading would lull him back to sleep. When they removed his leg cast next week, he'd have a better chance at untroubled sleep. He rubbed Mondocane's back before taking the police report off the end table. Too comfortable to hop on his crutches for his reading glasses, he squinted at the text.

The Amalfi police suspected the bridegroom's ex-lover had hired professional assassins to kill the Cindy woman at her wedding for revenge. The hypothesis would work for a Verdi opera plot, but it didn't quite persuade him.

More likely someone wanted the bridegroom dead. Cardinal Furbone's nephew, after all, chaired a committee of the Italian parliament investigating the rise of political extremism and antisocial cults posing a threat to public morals. The nephew's aggressiveness in carrying out his mission had earned him death threats from both the far left and the far right of the political spectrum.

Witnesses reported the victim's new husband had bent down to pick up something right before the shooting. The shooter could have been aiming at the husband and mistakenly hit the bride standing directly behind him. Strangest of all, the witnesses unanimously agreed the shooter dressed like the bridegroom except for the added apparel of a hat with facial netting.

Unable to jump onto the sofa, Mondocane curled up next to it.

Leone crooked his forearm over his forehead and yawned before returning to the puzzle.

If the netting had concealment as its purpose, why not a ski cap or something less exotic? The driver of the motorcycle wore a ski cap.

The licking of his hand by Mondocane kept him from drowsing off.

And then there was the business of the flare-up between the driver and the passenger on the motorcycle. He turned back to page ten to make sure. He was right. Again, all the witnesses reported some kind of argument between the assailants right after the shooting, but before they escaped.

The Amalfi investigator thought the driver could have been upset because the getaway was taking too long. But the driver had control of the motorcycle. Something went wrong with the plan. The murder of the wrong person would explain the argument between the killers. An innocent women instead of a parliamentarian too zealous for his own good.

His mind whirled around with medication and supposition.

His cell vibrated on the coffee table. Leone grabbed for it under the unpaid bills and old newspapers.

"Sorry for the late call, Commissario. I just received the results."

"Go on."

"They found the lion mask in roadside underbrush near the incinerated vehicle. Made of crystal manufactured on Murano island. Sold to an artisan who crafted glass carnival masks depicting animals, including lions. Limited number sold to only two retailers, one now out of business and the other, Sfaccia Sfumata, in Venice."

"Excellent work." He rubbed sleep from his eyes. "Make cooperative arrangements with the Venice police. As soon as my cast is off, I'm going to Venice." The Amalfi nightmare flashed into his mind. "What about my would-be assassins?"

"The two impersonating road workers escaped without a trace. The guy in the Audi plummeted off the mountain road into the valley. The Audi exploded. He looked like fried calamari when they found him."

"Finally we have something." The goddess Fortuna had smiled . . . even if it was an upside-down frown.

"One other thing, Commissario." A throat cleared on the other end of the line. "We've just received an anonymous warning. The Egyptian Phoenix threatens to destroy another church."

CHAPTER TWENTY-FIVE

Disguised as the Pater Patrum, Lucio Piso stood on the ruined foundation of a Roman bathhouse in the Maremma countryside of Tuscany clad in the alabaster mask of the god Mithras, ghostly white in the noonday sun. In his right hand, he held a gold-plated crosier studded with precious stones. To cool his head, he removed a miter matching the scarlet color of his velvet slippers. The breeze billowed his pantaloons of ancient Persian design. Cicadas strumming in the swelter fell silent at the sound of a vehicle chugging closer over the clayish soil.

He replaced his miter and drew up to full height, planting the crosier in front to lay claim to destiny. The way to national salvation ran through his genius. Had not that fortune-telling crone in the hills foretold his future greatness? Kneeling in the dust, she had kissed his hands and raised her cataract-clouded eyes to his, hailing him as rescuer of the nation, as she pocketed the wad of cash an aide had slipped into her hand. Mussolini had only drained the malaria-infested swamps of the Maremma. How much more Piso would do in power. He would restore the native faith driven out by the apostles of fanaticism from the Mideast. The Maremma bull, and not the cross, was the symbol of this land.

As a diversionary tactic, he would frame the Egyptian Phoenix for attacks on Catholic churches. His genius demanded he wait until Roma Rinata was strong enough to come out of the shadows and seize power. Then he could take credit for the attacks and the social revolution accompanying his political one.

A battered van rounded the boulder and stuttered to a stop. Two men in lion masks led Riccardo Renaldi out. They removed his blindfold and earplugs. He blinked and placed the edge of his hand over his eyebrows. "Who are you? A bishop?" He rubbed his eyes. "Where am I?"

"My dear Renaldi, I am the Pater Patrum you demanded to meet." He raised his crosier. "I am the representative of Mithras on earth."

"Why don't you reveal yourself?"

"My time has not yet come."

"When will you initiate me into Roma Rinata?" His voice grew confident. "I kept my promise to Carlos Stroheim. Without me you wouldn't have the Festus parchment."

"You have been paid."

"I didn't do it for the money. I want to belong."

"The Pater Patrum thanks you, but we must be certain of your loyalty. Too much is at stake." He pounded the crosier to assert his authority. "You were a police officer after all."

"I was an outstanding one until Leone engineered my suspension." Renaldi cursed and raised his fist. "I'll make him taste my vengeance."

"Not unless and until I say so . . . if you want to join us. Is that clear?"

"I understand." He doffed his cap and wrung it in his hands. "Thank you for the job as chief security officer at the Villa of the Papyri. I need the work."

"You will be my eyes and ears at the villa."

"Do you have an in with Lucio Piso, the superintendent?" Renaldi inquired.

"I know him all right. He's my inferior and does my bidding."

The deception was delicious. Renaldi did not know the Pater Patrum inhabited the body of Lucio Piso. Secrecy gave him control, and control made him the master of puppets like Renaldi. Soon he could pull enough puppet strings to take over.

"My own godfather, Questore Pietro Malatesta, didn't even lift a finger to save me."

"To be betrayed by one's godfather is a terrible thing indeed. But if you pass your probation, you will have Roma Rinata to protect you."

"There's another reason I wanted to see you today." Renaldi wiped the sweat off his brow with his sleeve. "There's a problem at the Villa of the Papyri."

"What?"

The Pater Patrum listened with towering rage as Renaldi related the problem with the don of the most vicious camorra clan in Naples. The clan boss threatened to hold up any further excavations until something was done to "wet his beak." Some in the government already looked for any excuse to stop the excavation. The camorra complication would kill the excavation project by calling work stoppages if it did not receive kickback and bribe money. The country was on the verge of complete paralysis.

Unthinkable.

An anachronistic group of criminal maggots feasting on the decay of ancient Rome would not stand in the way of destiny.

His genius had the answer. It never failed.

"Have no fear. The problem is solved." The Pater Patrum cackled behind the alabaster mask. "The don will wet many beaks."

CHAPTER TWENTY-SIX

Wearing a matador's cape, Lucio Piso waved on the Italian cowboys called *butteri*. On horseback they circled the white bull twisting its horns toward one tormentor and then the other, each jamming a lance into its back. Sheets of blood matted the bull's flanks. He admired this native bull stock, solid as marble, the descendent of prehistoric bulls fossilized all over the Maremma territory. The bull charged the cape with decorated darts quivering in its back like bloodsuckers.

Sun rays slithered through the cracks of the ruined Roman amphitheater onto Piso's cape as it swirled away like a magician's trick revealing a twisted and screaming body lashed to a post. The naked torso bore the full brunt of the charge and fell silent forever, a companion piece to another broken and bloodied corpse tethered to a post six meters away. A *buttero* shot the bull in the head.

The animal knelt on its forelegs.

It moaned and keeled over in the sand.

"Clean up this mess . . . now." Piso's command echoed around the amphitheater ruins. "I'm expecting a visitor." Henchmen seated for the performance in stone box seats reserved for dignitaries millennia ago jumped to obedience.

He spat in the faces of the two corpses lashed to posts. The buffoons had killed the wrong victim. Their failure allowed the chairperson of a powerful parliamentary committee to live and continue his crusade against subversive organizations and criminal cults.

***

After cleaning himself up, Lucio Piso passed time waiting for his visitor under a grape arbor at the hilltop entrance of his farmhouse made of flaking and fissured travertine stone near the ancient Roman town of Rusellae. His high-priced team of lawyers had concealed the purchase of the hideaway headquarters in tangled layers of newfangled imported American trust law.

A spider pounced on a mosquito entwined in a web among the grape leaves.

Down in the lowland, two menials led Cardinal Gustavo Furbone up the winding path to the farmhouse. Lugging a satchel, the cardinal stopped to rest against a boulder, a blob of human suet under a black cassock and scarlet sash.

Inside his peasant abode, Piso scrutinized Furbone's puff-pastry face across a table of log-hewn wood. His puppet body yearned to reach across the table and squeeze the pig's fleshy throat with both hands.

Detached and above the fray, the real Lucio hidden inside the puppet body knew better. His inner genius recognized the gift of time in which to prepare a dish best served cold . . . vengeance. The predator pedophile still did not recognize the victim after all the passing years, but the victim never forgot. His real self could objectively view the puppet's life, as though played out on a screen.

A boy named Lucio had once lived on the streets of Rome after World War II with hunger and death his playmates. The boy's father died on the Russian front, fighting for the Axis. The mother abandoned him in a church and died soon after of tuberculosis. The boy's American savior soldier named Colonel Soames, flush with chewing gum, Hershey bars, and cigarettes, fed and clothed him. He placed the boy in an orphanage run by a young priest. The priest, oh so kind and solicitous, had taken a special interest in the boy, even tutoring the waif.

The priest's hand on the boy's knee led to visits by the priest to the boy's bedroom under cover of night.

"Call me Gustavo," the young priest had said, sliding into bed and probing and kissing where the boy should not have been probed and kissed.

Should he tell anyone, the young priest had said, he would be thrown out into the streets again and suffer the pains of eternal hell for disobeying a priest of God.

But all this had happened to Lucio the puppet and not the real Lucio inside the puppet, who'd escaped through the puppet's eyes and hid inside a crack in the ceiling. As long as the puppet boy kept his stare fixed on the crack, the real Lucio felt nothing, suffered nothing, feared nothing, loved nothing.

Confusion and depression had become the boy's twin playmates in a whirlwind of sexual abuse that ripped his boyhood up by the roots. He grew up, fighting shame and self-loathing, only one step ahead of suicide, until he completely walled off the misery, coming to the full revelation he was like a god, two persons in one, an outer puppet and an inner superhuman hovering above vulnerability.

The superhuman genius had taught the puppet Lucio either to dominate or be dominated. Better one day as a lion than a thousand as a sheep. Clawing and punching his way to the top of the business world, he gained supreme confidence in his ability to dominate. Neither lesser mortals nor lavish expense deterred him from proving to himself that through the Piso name of his father, he had inherited the DNA of greatness, reaching back to the elite clan of the ancient Pisos. Nothing else could explain his meteoric ascent in society to the brink of total supremacy.

"Is something wrong?" the cardinal asked.

"Not anymore."

"Here." The cardinal hoisted the satchel onto the table. "The retainer for your efforts is inside." He unlocked the satchel and pushed it toward Piso. "You won't offend me by verifying the amount. The balance will be paid upon completion of the retrieval."

"My search for the Festus parchment is not about the money, Your Eminence." The bile in his belly churned at the title of respect.

"I do this for my faith" . . . *Faith that you and those like you will be swept away.*

"Your piety becomes you." The cardinal pulled at his ear. "I don't mean to be impatient, but it's been a while . . . Have you made any progress in your search?"

"We toil day and night."

Furbone's ignorance that Renaldi had already given the Festus parchment to the Pater Patrum made Piso want to giggle at the secret double-cross of the predator cardinal.

"And, my dear Cardinal Furbone, do you not forget something?"

"The statue of Mithras with the cross in the forehead?"

"That was part of the deal. Was it not?"

"The pagan idol should've been left in the earth . . . or destroyed."

"I want it for my collection of antiquities."

"Agreed. I'll make sure it is delivered." The cardinal stood up to go. "Notify me as soon as you recover the parchment. It belongs to the Church."

It belongs to me, the descendent of the Pisos.

"It's important." Furbone touched his ear. "Don't forget."

"How could I ever forget?"

CHAPTER TWENTY-SEVEN

From the second story of an abandoned Venetian palazzo, Marco Leone stared across a backwater canal into a store window highlighting carnival masks. Spinal pain made him question his judgment in coming to Venice against medical advice and having to endure the stakeout of Sfaccia Sfumata. The Venetian inspector leading the operation seemed more intent on cracking a prostitution ring inside the store than helping to solve the attempt on his Roman colleague's life.

Unable to see into the interior of the store, Leone walked over to the humming electronic surveillance equipment operated by technicians in headphones. The monitor screen burst into a flash of light and wavy lines. The interior of the first floor across the stagnant canal came into focus. The monitor fed by hidden cameras inside the store showed only display cases and wall racks filled with animal masks of every variety and color. The technicians switched monitor surveillance to an upper floor of Sfaccia Sfumata.

The camera caught old men and girls cavorting virtually naked except for their Venetian Carnival masks. When they tired of the orgiastic foreplay, couples drifted off hand in hand from the bacchanalian revelry to back storerooms. The technicians and Venetian police overseeing the surveillance hooted and whistled.

"Why are you wasting my time on this porno show?" Leone lit up a mooched Marlboro. "Your prostitution case won't stand up."

"I think it will. Minor girls are involved." The Venetian inspector put his fingertips together and smirked. "Look, Commissario, be patient. You are in Venice now. Do as the Venetian police do."

"What about the attempt on my life in Amalfi?" Leone blew out a smoke stream. "Cardinal Furbone's brother sells lion masks like the one worn by the guy who tried to force me off the road. That's why I'm here. Have you forgotten?"

"We know. You've told us often enough." The Venetian waved the cigarette haze away. "No smoking here. This is work space."

"Get serious. This chilly dump is closed and the company bankrupt."

"Fire hazard. Combustible liquids on this floor."

This wasn't his turf. He had to back off.

"Will you at least get the customer list you promised?" Leone ground out his cigarette on the concrete floor.

After the Venetian inspector left to get the list, Leone took another look at the monitor screen. Fully dressed, only one figure remained in the room. He still sat immobile on a throne chair. Under a flat black hat, the figure wore a black satin robe embroidered with stars and a white ruff at the neck. He hid his face behind the classic carnival mask of the plague doctor with the exaggerated white beak thought to protect against infection.

Who was this voyeur?

The Venetian inspector returned with the names of the store's customers. Leone scanned the list of over a hundred people. The shop had sold many kinds of masks of popular animals, including those of ravens and lions. Forty-six customers had at one time or another purchased either raven or lion masks. The list did not distinguish between lion masks made of crystal, like the one his would-be assassin had worn, and the more usual ones of papier-mâché. Ten customers had purchased both lion and raven masks. An international corporation called Piso Global Enterprises caught his eye because of Lucio Piso, its billionaire founder.

The Venetian looked away from the monitor. "We make our move now," he said to Leone.

Undercover cops disguised as construction workers crossed the bridge over the canal toward Sfaccia Sfumata on the other side. Waiting for them, a cop dressed as a tourist guide teamed up with two colleagues playing the role of utility workers. The faux nuns passing by the store shed their habits and morphed into female police officers. They all converged at the front door of Sfaccia Sfumata and forced their way in. Shaking his head in admiration, Leone smiled. The coordinated and intricate images of undercover police on the move were worth a spot in the Venice film festival.

An undercover cop in hard hat and safety vest burst into the room. "This guy says you want to see him." The cop looked at Leone. "Do you know him?"

"Shlomo Adorno." What did the shiftless offspring of Miriam's first husband want? The son had changed from bad to worse. He had grown into a ferret-faced thief and petty con man sporting long hair and an unkempt beard the color and texture of chicks' down. "What are you doing here?" Leone said. "Can't you see I'm busy?"

"That's it, you two." The exasperated inspector lapsed into Venetian dialect. "We have work to do." He pointed up. "Settle your business in the office upstairs."

Before the two left the room, the monitor screen showed the disheveled revelers stumbling down the stairs into the arms of the police. Two officers escorted the masked plague doctor fully dressed in his midnight attire out of monitor range.

"Bring the plague doctor over here," the Venetian inspector ordered over his cell phone. "I want to peek under the mask he refuses to remove."

***

"I need to get back downstairs." Leone fidgeted on the other side of a battered conference table in the office of the bankrupt construction company. "I told your mother I'd try to find you something after I return to Rome."

Shlomo sat in shadows. Such light as existed slid through a begrimed window shielded by shutters with broken slats. The former owners had the foresight to spirit away the Murano chandelier, but not the cut-rate office furniture adorned with watermarks and scratches.

"It's not about you and me pleasing my mother anymore." Shlomo slumped in a chair missing an armrest. "I'm broke and desperate for work. I came to Venice to collect a debt, but the deadbeat pulled a fast one and skipped town."

Pulling a fast one on Shlomo? Not likely. He was a master con.

"The rumor is you and Rocco are thick as this and doing well for yourselves." He tapped the sides of his two index fingers together. "If I can prove you two are pickpocketing on buses again, I'll bust you personally, your mother notwithstanding."

"Rocco's gone underground." Shlomo folded his hands on the table and rubbed his thumbs together. "He acted strange. Talked vaguely about joining some secret organization, more powerful than the Mafia."

Full of interest, Leone leaned forward over the table. Before he came to Venice, the gradual disappearance of the common thugs and underworld muscle making up his day had disturbed him. Every so often, one or the other surfaced before ducking below the radar again. The calm on the streets felt ominous, even though crime had taken a dive. No one knew anything, which meant someone knew something. Maybe Shlomo was that someone. "Tell me everything you know."

A bar of sunlight streamed through the shutters across Shlomo's face like an interrogation lamp. He shielded his eyes.

"That's just it." Shlomo moved the chair out of the sun. "I don't know much. But maybe I can help you."

"You? Help me?" Leone raised his eyebrows. "How?"

"Rocco said I should consider joining. Everything is organized into cells, the left hand not knowing what the right hand does. There's some kind of initiation period, and you know how good I am at—"

"Conning people? I sure do." Leone rubbed his chin. Something big was in the air, and it had to involve the terrorist acts in Rome. Shlomo might be able to pull it off. "You want to work undercover for me, is that it?"

Shlomo nodded. "If we can work something out."

"We can. See me when I get back to Rome."

"Good." Shlomo cleared his throat. "One other thing. My stepfather, Rabbi Elia Sforno, has an urgent favor to ask of you."

Miriam's husband was a man of superior airs who boasted of an alleged kinship to Ovadia Sforno, the illustrious sixteenth-century rabbi. Elia Sforno had a history of beseeching the Polizia di Stato for dubious favors whenever he needed to affect the course of justice. It was not his style to do so directly but only through fixers and flunkies. Yet, for Miriam's former lover to reveal this about her well-reputed husband would smack of sour grapes. "What does he want?"

"The Mormons are at it again. Using the genealogies of—"

The office door slammed open. The undercover Venetian cop in the disguise of a construction worker entered. "Come downstairs, Commissario." He beckoned with his hand. "We've removed the mask of the plague doctor. Our inspector says you're in for a surprise."

Leone bolted out the door to learn the identity of the voyeur in black.

***

Back downstairs on the second floor, the inspector and the unmasked plague doctor remained silent as Leone entered the room.

"Mamma mia." Leone folded his hands in front of his chest. "If it isn't Cardinal Gustavo Furbone . . . the ringmaster of orgies."

"It's not what you think." The cardinal crushed the mask of the plague doctor in his hands.

"I'm sure it's much worse."

"I had nothing to do with my brother's debauchery." Furbone shifted on his feet, tugging at his ear. "You're trying to ruin my career."

"Don't tell me what I'm trying to do." Leone faced the cardinal eye to eye. "You've been evading me. What do you know about crystal lion masks sold in Sfaccia Sfumata?"

"A little respect, if you please. He is a cardinal after all." The Venetian inspector raised his hand. "I'm allowing you to ask questions as a courtesy. Watch yourself."

"Am I my brother's keeper?" The cardinal's face grew smug. "Ask my brother about the lion masks he sells."

Leone bristled but held his tongue. The cardinal apparently drew strength from the inspector's obsequiousness.

"We just did, Your Eminence." The inspector shrugged. "He won't talk."

"And I know nothing about my brother's business." The cardinal moved to put on his coat. "I must be about my own business for His Holiness, Celestine the Sixth."

"Not so fast." Leone stepped before the cardinal. "If you please," he added after detecting a disapproving glint in the inspector's eyes. "A witness says you threatened Abramo Basso shortly before his death."

"It was Stroheim who tattled on me, wasn't it?" The cardinal shrugged. "Sure, I was angry about Basso's theft, but I didn't kill him."

"Thanks for confirming Stroheim's accusation." Leone smiled, thinking of Miriam's account in his office. "By the way, I also have someone else who confirms the threat."

"Will you take long?" The inspector sighed. "I have to get back to the station."

"Probably not." He expected the cardinal to confess any minute. "Weren't you in charge of the Roman artifacts exhibition sponsored by the Vatican?" Leone asked. "The one displaying the knife used to murder Basso?"

"In name only." The cardinal folded the coat over his arm. "As cardinal librarian and archivist, I was the most important person in the Vatican Library. But staff took care of details not worthy of my attention."

"But you had access to the knife."

"Not unless you can prove I smashed the case and stole it shortly before the murder." The cardinal put on his coat. "Your expression says you know nothing of the theft report filed with the Vatican Gendarmerie Corps. Anyone could have stolen it. Our police never found the culprit." The cardinal put on his hat. "You really should work more closely with Vatican law enforcement."

"Time's up." The inspector tapped his watch. "I'm letting His Eminence go."

"You're what?" Leone glared at the inspector. "You can hold him on the prostitution charge. You yourself said minors were involved."

"His Eminence informed me he came to Venice on papal business and just happened to be visiting his brother. The obscene activities took him by surprise."

"Surprise?" Leone slapped his forehead with his palm. "Naked girls a surprise?"

"Exactly so." The cardinal buttoned his coat. "My black-sheep brother trapped me. He had the doors locked. His conduct has shocked me profoundly."

"My men verified the locked doors. Even the upstairs one."

"No mystery there," Leone said. "They wanted to keep intruders out and their activities secret." He blocked the door to prevent the cardinal from leaving. "What's the brother say?"

"He backs up the cardinal's version of events."

"The brother is covering up for the cardinal, can't you see?" Leone pointed to the surveillance equipment. "The camera doesn't lie. We all saw him in the costume of the plague doctor. No one forced him into the costume. He sat there and watched."

"As I told the inspector," Furbone said, rubbing his ear, "at my brother's suggestion, I tried on the costume as a joke in the dressing room with the door closed. I heard people come up the stairs. When I exited, I was shocked to see people undressing. *Dumbfounded* would be a better word. I just had to sit down, paralyzed at how depraved my brother had become. He tricked me."

"Do you expect us to believe that fairy tale?" Leone folded his arms and turned to the inspector. "Do your duty and arrest him."

"That does it." The inspector ordered Leone away from the door. "As you said, the camera doesn't lie. We have no proof whatsoever he touched anyone, let alone engaged in . . . well, you know. Watching is not prostitution. Let the cardinal go."

"Just let me ask one more question . . . a professional courtesy."

"No, no." The inspector wagged his forefinger sideways. "You don't know when to stop. No more telling me what to do. No more questions."

"That's all right." The cardinal made no attempt to hide his smirk. "Let him ask."

"Where were you, a little after midnight on Christmas day, when Basso was murdered?"

"You've got me there, Commissario Leone." The cardinal held his hands up as though he were surrendering. "I was helping Pope Celestine the Sixth celebrate Midnight Mass in St. Peter's."

"Do . . . do you have"—Leone recovered his composure—"any witnesses to support that claim?"

"You don't have to answer, Your Eminence."

"I have just a few witnesses of questionable character." The cardinal put on his hat and smiled from ear to ear. "About a hundred priests and bishops who celebrated the Mass alongside us."

Avoiding eye contact, Leone let the cardinal pass.

CHAPTER TWENTY-EIGHT

The Hotel Elysian staff squeaked open the ceiling-to-floor French doors to the terrace overlooking the Bay of Naples. A breeze from over the water refreshed Marco Leone as he admired the purple velvet sky at twilight. The hydrocortisone tablets for Addison's disease made him a new man. His energy and weight returned. And so did his appetite. The decision to attend the banquet was the right one. Aside from the sumptuous cuisine he looked forward to, he would do both himself and his good friend on the Naples police force a favor.

During his recuperative vacation at the friend's home in Naples, Leone had received a call from Professor Will Fisher. Unable at the last minute to attend, Fisher wanted Leone to replace him at a fundraiser banquet for the Villa of the Papyri sponsored by Lucio Piso, the new superintendent of Herculaneum excavations. Piso had arranged for Dr. Wesley Bemis and Don Perugino to attend as guests of honor and receive awards.

Leone's friend urged him to attend. The Naples police needed an unknown face to keep tabs on Don Perugino as part of their undercover program for the continuous shadowing of the most powerful gangster in Calabria. They hoped Leone's attendance would provide some answers to their questions about the affair.

Why would the superintendent named international CEO of the year by the *Worldwide Business Review* suck up to the camorra clans by inviting Don Perugino as an honored guest? Even more surprisingly, he wondered why Don Perugino, the head of the most powerful camorra crime family, had accepted. The mobster's hunger for respect and recognition must have overcome his legendary caution.

The hundred or so camorra clans led by Perugino had moved beyond prostitution, robbery, bribery, kidnapping, and the corrupt waste disposal business, threatening to make Naples a cesspool of toxins. With speedboats, they now facilitated the bootlegging of drugs, illegal aliens, and tax-free cigarettes beyond the Bay of Naples. A Nigerian criminal mafia called the Black Axe had entered Sicily concealed within the swarms of illegal and desperate immigrants fleeing Africa in rickety boats. They had recently entered Calabria. After a bloody showdown caused by their invasion of camorra turf, the two criminal organizations made their peace. The Black Axe paid a tax on their illegal activities to the camorra and handled prostitution, still considered shameful by some old-timer camorristi.

For opium and cash, the camorristi even smuggled Islamic jihadists from offshore ships to the slums of Naples, where their terrorist cells incubated. From there, the mobsters guided them north beyond Italy through a network of safe houses before injecting them into the arteries of Europe in preparation for terror attacks.

Aside from helping out a fellow officer in Naples, he had his own reasons to attend, one professional and the other personal, both involving Wesley Bemis, the Mormon American archaeologist from Brigham Young University. The presence of the archaeologist's skis in Fisher's office when he visited the Pontifical Gregorian University showed that Bemis had access to the office and, therefore, could have stolen the Festus parchment.

He would have to keep his personal issue with the American separate from the professional interests as best he could. The Mormon had converted dead Jews in Switzerland. According to Shlomo, Rabbi Elia Sforno wanted him to do something about it. In other circumstances, he might have done exactly nothing for his least-favorite rabbi. He had enough problems in this world without hypothetical ones in the next. But Uncle Benjamin was one of the dead Jews. And that indignity made all the difference.

***

Interrupting his thoughts, guests breaking for dinner entered the ballroom at the conclusion of the cocktail hour in the reception hall. The hotel manager approached with two men and rubbed his hands together. "Would you be so good, Commissario Leone, as to take a seat at another table?"

"Why?"

"May I present Don Perugino?" The manager bowed toward the don. "He has brought an unexpected companion to dine with him."

"How does that concern me?"

A pencil-mustached man with a beach-ball stomach, the don scowled at the commissario. His beefy companion, no doubt the bodyguard, assessed the room and nearby tables with deep-set eyes.

"I'm afraid there's a misunderstanding. We need places at this reserved table for our honorees and their companions and . . ." The hotel manager cleared his throat. "And Professor Fisher is absent. So, I would appreciate your most gracious understanding in letting Don Perugino's companion take your place."

"Professor Fisher asked me to take his place at this table, so I'm now the companion of Dr. Wesley Bemis, an honoree." Leone pointed at the bodyguard. "I'll bet this man's name wasn't even on the guest list."

The bodyguard stepped toward Leone. The don touched the man's wrist. The bodyguard stepped back.

"Please be so kind as to sit at another table." The manger held out his hands in supplication. "You would do me a great service."

"This place card has my name on it." The commissario held it up. "I'm staying."

Damned if I'll move for the likes of this hoodlum and his goon.

Frozen in a deadlock of eyeball intimidation with the don, Leone waited while the hotel manager stepped up to the dais and interrupted Piso's conversation with the mayor. The superintendent of Herculaneum excavations left the dais and came to the table. With a smile and arm around the don, Piso invited the leading racketeer of Naples and his bodyguard to join him and the mayor on the more prestigious dais looking down on the tables.

Piso reminded the don to first have his picture taken on the terrace. If he would but hurry over to the balcony, Piso assured the don the city dignitaries would soon join him for a group picture. The don's stone expression looked like it might crumble in gratitude. His face quickly recovered its death-mask appearance. Before leaving for the terrace with his companion, the don whispered into the commissario's ear, "Up yours, flatfoot."

"Why," Leone asked Piso, "does a man like you stoop to honor that slimeball?"

"Are you always so brash, Commissario?"

"You didn't answer my question."

"Not every question deserves an answer." Piso sighed. "What a pity. So much energy misdirected." Piso waved to a guest across the room. "I must leave . . . but I feel we shall meet again."

**

While Leone went round and round with theories of why Lucio Piso acted so warmly toward Don Perugino, a slender man with bright eyes sat next to him and introduced himself as Dr. Wesley Bemis.

"I am Commissario Marco Leone from Rome," he said in English. "Professor Fisher asked me to take his place." He hoped his English, boned up at night school, would put the archaeologist at ease. "For long, Dr. Fisher, I desired to discuss an affair with you."

"Vall me Ves." Bemis shook hands with Leone. "Vill ed yewd vantid to awk vid me."

"More clearly, please." Leone touched his ear. Was this some unfathomable American dialect?

To his astonishment, the American pulled out a wad of bubble gum from his mouth and folded it discreetly into a napkin.

"Sorry, but the gum helps me avoid stimulants, like coffee and alcohol."

"I do not understand, Dr. Fisher."

"Call me Wes." He shook hands again as though the prior handshake wasn't valid. "I'm a Latter-day Saint . . . Mormon for short . . . and it's against my religion to imbibe."

"Not to beat the bush." Americans liked getting right to the point. "Someone stole an ancient parchment from Professor Fisher's office. What do you know about it?"

"Oh, you mean *beat around the bush*."

"Only answer my question, please."

Leone fumed over the garbled idiom his night school instructor had given him.

"I know nothing about the theft." The Mormon looked perplexed. "I never knew about the parchment until it was stolen. Will promised to tell no one what he was working on. And he kept that promise."

"I have no reason now to believe he didn't."

"May we speak Italian? I used to be a Mormon missionary in Italy."

"As you wish."

Bemis pushed away the shrimp appetizer. "Cooked in wine."

"No coffee? No wine?" The Mormon's religious rigor reminded Leone of the Talmudic dietary injunctions dulling whatever religious appetite he once had. "I fear you have come to a most unsuitable country. Now, back to the parchment," Leone said. "Between the time Professor Fisher last saw it and the time he discovered it missing, you were in Rome. Weren't you?"

"No, I was not."

"But I know you were not excavating at Herculaneum."

By suddenly switching topics, he hoped to put Bemis on the defensive and crack open the truth about the parchment when he doubled back.

"By the way, you must stop converting dead Jews to Mormonism in Switzerland. Even the Church of Latter-day Saints has agreed not to—"

"The interfaith settlement only prohibits conversions in Italy. Not in Switzerland."

"Look here. You baptized and converted my dead uncle, someone born a Jew and died a Jew, a hero in the Resistance, one who knew nothing of Mormonism. You violated his memory and stand to create legal trouble for yourself. If you don't stop these baptisms, I intend to call a fellow detective in Switzerland . . ." Leone sounded absurd to himself. Theological mind games would not bring back Uncle Benjamin.

"I plan no more baptisms and conversions in Switzerland." Bemis held up a hand of appeasement. "Golly . . . I'm sorry for any offense."

"I accept your apology, but what about the Festus parchment?" Leone leaned closer to Bemis. "You had a key to Professor Fisher's office. You even kept your skis in his office."

"Correct."

"Now we are getting somewhere." Leone waved away a waiter. "If you tell me everything, it will go better for you."

"I've nothing to hide." Bemis cleared his throat. "At the time of the theft I was in Switzerland baptizing dead converts. Troublemakers told all sorts of lies to the police about our activities. To calm things down, I agreed to let Detective Mattias Boller check up on me. He said you two were good friends. I'm certain he'll support my alibi. Any more questions, Commissario?"

"Nothing more." He had come up empty-handed. All he could do was leave a hook dangling in the water without any bait. "But if you think of anything, let me know."

A staccato burst of gunfire rang out. Screaming guests stumbled into the grand ballroom from the terrace. Leone raced toward the terrace along the wall to avoid any bullets in case the firing resumed. Two attackers carried AK-47s and wore beaked masks of black in the shape of ravens' heads. They had hooded the don and were dragging him off the balcony onto the platform of a hydraulic lift the commissario had seen earlier at a nearby construction site. As the platform descended, Leone sprinted to the balustrades, almost stepping on the don's bodyguard sprawled out on the terrace in a pool of blood. He looked over the balustrades and ducked when a gunshot sprayed wall plaster around him. The sound of a racing motor came from below. A black van roared out from underneath the terrace to the shoreline down the road. The kidnappers hustled the don out of the van and into a docked speedboat.

The boat churned up a trail of milky spume on its way into the Bay of Naples.

CHAPTER TWENTY-NINE

In the foothills of Mount Vesuvius, Marco Leone shrank from the supine body of a naked and dead Don Perugino sprawled beside an abandoned well from which the police had extracted him. Angry puffs of ruptured red flesh pockmarked the remains of the most feared gangster in the Campania region. In place of the eyes, only bloodied sockets remained. Raven scouts circled in a cloudless sky bleached faded blue by the noonday sun. The main flock, larger than any he had ever seen, retreated to the roof of an elongated farmhouse and the branches of nearby oak trees. They waited to return to their feast once the meddling humans left.

Mondocane barked and tugged at his leash, straining to get at the birds until Leone hushed him. He ordered the dog to sit. Mondocane cocked his head as if to say he didn't understand.

"*Animali* . . . those bastards who did this," the local police inspector repeated to himself, kneeling over the corpse. He raised and kissed a lifeless hand.

The obsequiousness of the gesture repelled Leone. The inspector either had a questionable relationship with the deceased or at least wanted the bystanders behind police lines to believe he did. The ambiguousness of southerners in their relationship with the underworld eluded his comprehension.

After rising unsteadily to his feet, the Neapolitan inspector issued his pronouncement to the commissario: "Camorristi committed this atrocity."

A barely tolerated interloper from Rome, Leone had scant chance of challenging that rush to judgment. But his doubts remained. No camorra thug would dare make a move against Don Perugino. It was joked that if an underling even farted, Perugino knew about it. Everyone assumed the deceased's cutthroat brothers would have made short work of any would-be assassin. True, the clans clashed in periods of underworld anarchy. But they now enjoyed unprecedented peace with a remarkable increase of illegal profits. They had no reason to risk police intervention in their affairs through the commission of this theatrical abomination.

Kidnapping the chieftain of the most powerful clan and penning him up nude without food or water, to be pecked dead in a dried-up well swarming with starving ravens was a sure invitation to public outrage and clan revenge. Even the lowest Neanderthal in the camorra understood the distinction between a murder of criminal necessity and what he now saw before him—an act of sociopathic savagery amounting to a death warrant for the perpetrators.

No, he would not press his doubts on the Neapolitan inspector working the case. The understaffed police force of the region would not take kindly to a stranger depriving them of another opportunity to blame yet another unsolved murder on the camorra. It might even cause trouble for his friend on the Naples force to know such an unbeliever. Better not to cast doubt on their faith in the all-pervasive influence of the camorra. Such faith absolved the police of the duty to look beyond the obvious, confirmed the public cynicism that organized crime got away with murder, and pleased the dons by making them appear omnipotent and omnipresent when they were neither.

The banshee wail of a woman shoving her way through the crowd to the corpse unnerved the commissario. Leone pulled Mondocane back on the leash so the woman could pass. She struggled with a police officer and broke free, accidentally ripping her black dress across the waist. She flung herself on the dead body and kissed it between her sobs and petitions to heaven. No matter how vile Don Perugino, Leone realized love was bestowed, not earned. If he were to die that day, no one would mourn him like this woman mourned the dead mobster. Perugino had died a lucky man. At least one person truly mourned the don. Mondocane whined and worked his moist muzzle into the commissario's hand.

Ravens circled in the sky.

What did they signify?

CHAPTER THIRTY

"How much farther?" Nicole Garvey asked.

"Not much." Will Fisher stopped to adjust his LED-lit helmet. "Watch out. The ceiling's lower here."

She followed through the twists and turns of a shaft leading down to unexplored levels of the Villa of the Papyri. A chill ran through her. Was it due to the temperature drop? Or her vision of the Mount Vesuvius eruption in AD 79?

The avalanche of molten rock, mud, and ash—what professionals called the pyroclastic flow—skinned alive the inhabitants of Herculaneum with gases over four hundred degrees Celsuis, almost a thousand degrees Fahrenheit, and buried the remains over thirty meters underground.

They entered a small rectangular room, possibly an ancient bedroom. Their flashlights skittered across the walls, revealing fruits, fish, and geometric designs. The workmen had left a wheelbarrow filled with hardened mud and rocks. The flooring consisted of an interlocking pattern of apple-green and white floor tiles in the shapes of pentagrams, many broken or crumbled into powder.

"This is the first room we uncovered."

"Find anything?"

"Nothing."

He thought a treasure trove of the ancient world waited down here. She couldn't share his optimism. The occupants had probably removed all valuables before disaster struck.

"Wes'll meet us here any minute." He looked at the floor. "It's time I come clean."

With rapt attention, she listened as he told her the story of the Festus parchment entrusted to him by Commissario Marco Leone and his involvement as a consultant in the homicide of Father Abramo Basso. He explained how Porcius Festus had agreed to arrange a meeting between Saint Paul and Seneca, the famous Roman, in the Villa of the Papyri.

Why hadn't he told her earlier about the Festus parchment? She didn't like secrets. Her stepmother had so many nasty ones. But he confided in her now, and that was the important thing.

"Commissario Leone blames me for the parchment theft." He rubbed his hands over his face. "It was my responsibility."

"Not so." She wanted to reassure him with a touch. "The police were in charge."

The low warble of a whistle floated up the shaft.

"It's Wes." Fisher blew his own whistle in reply. "He's coming."

***

From the shaft, Wesley Bemis popped into the room and brushed off his clothes.

"Great news, pardner," he said, eyes fixed on Fisher. "I discovered a library today. I think we struck gold . . . the Latin library of lost Roman literature."

"Congratulations." Fisher pumped his colleague's hand. "Excuse me. This is Nicole Garvey. I hired her to help you with the archaeology."

"I know we've discussed hiring someone." Bemis crossed his arms, ignoring Garvey. "Still, you should have run this by me first."

"Any problem?"

"I don't have a problem." Bemis kept his eyes off Garvey. "Does she?"

"I answered all her questions, Wes. She's satisfied with the hiring terms."

"Remember me?" Garvey refused to play the demure mute while the Mormon played dumb. "We met at Logan Airport for your Harvard lecture. I picked you up instead of letting you pick me—"

"I don't remember." The Mormon's voice cracked. "I . . . I give so many lectures, you know." He rubbed his neck and turned to Fisher. "Silly me, I almost forgot to tell you. Commissario Leone called me."

"About the shooting of Don Perugino in Naples?"

"Nope. He's coming here to question Renaldi about the Festus parchment." He slapped Fisher on the back. "Looks like you're off the hot seat, pardner."

"That's a relief," Fisher replied. "I wish he liked me more."

"Let's get to work." Bemis headed for the shaft. "Time's a-wasting."

They edged single file down the shaft to the new discovery. If Bemis wanted to stonewall his sexual harassment, she'd have to put up with it. The professor wasn't likely to take her word over that of his colleague.

She paused on the forty-five-degree decline to brush away fine powder sprinkling down on her helmet and clothes. She spit away the mildew taste on her lips.

The Mormon had charge of the project and the final say. She hated the idea of him getting away with his actions, though she needed the work. But if he ever tried to lay hands on her again—

"Oh . . . my God." She bent over and covered her hair with her hands. A bat bounced off her arm on its way up the shaft. A few more whirred past.

"They're gone." Fisher put his arm around her shoulder. "It's okay."

From a hole in the ceiling where the shaft ended, the three dropped into the rectangular shape of the presumed Latin library. With flashlight beams crisscrossing through the gloom, they probed the wall facing them. Images of grain stalks and flower garlands blotched with mold bordered a plain wall painted a tomato-red color.

Bemis turned on a halogen lantern. Unlike the plain wall, the two sidewalls abutting it at right angles bore frescoes. One sidewall depicted a woman reading a scroll and the other, a man writing on papyrus.

"This is a library all right." Fisher laughed, translating the Latin words at the top of the plain wall. "Kind reader, be so courteous as to reroll the papyrus scrolls when done so that the gods and the master of this house will bless you."

The pyroclastic flow released by Mount Vesuvius had barreled through Herculaneum and crashed its way into buildings. Charred wooden shelves and cabinets along the library walls testified to the tragedy. "Look at those," she said. A few cylinders hung out of collapsing cabinets and even fewer clung to splintered shelves. She looked down. Far more cylinders lay helter-skelter on the floor. "They look like giant charcoal sticks."

"They're carbonized papyrus scrolls," Fisher said. "Like ones found in the villa years ago." He hovered over a pile of scrolls. "We have to examine them right away."

"Hold your horses, pardner." Bemis held up his hand. "I still have to set up my equipment at the National Archaeological Museum in Naples, besides inventorying everything for Riccardo Renaldi, the superintendent's right-hand man."

He aimed the halogen lantern at the wall behind Fisher and Garvey. "Now, for the main event . . . turn around and behold Mithras with a twist."

Their flashlights working the wall behind them, Garvey made out a red plaster surface decorated with a border of miniature bulls and fish. Because of the shine, she surmised the ancient craftsmen had mixed lime and marble dust with the plaster. In the center of the well-preserved wall stood two fresco figures shaking hands. One had to be the iconic Mithras, a haloed young man in a conical cap folded forward, wearing a star-studded cape. Curly hair spilled out under the cap. Saint Augustine had called this Roman god "that fellow with the cap."

But Mithras was not alone. He shook hands with another haloed male bearing the face of Apollo. The Apollo fresco sported a trident over his shoulder. A lamb and a peacock rested at his feet. Two smaller figures sat cross-legged on either side of the larger ones. One of the seated figures held a torch facing down and the other a torch facing up.

Below the tableau, a row of five Roman numerals stuck to the wall. Incised on separate bronze plates, the numbers read from left to right: . . . III . . . , VIII . . . , VI . . . , VIII . . . , V. A sixth plate had fallen on the floor. The wall bore the imprint of the fallen VIII as the last number in the series.

"Amazing," Fisher said. "Here's Cautes." He pointed to the diminutive figure holding a flaming torch upright. "And Cautopates." He turned his finger to the form holding the torch down. "And they're both in Phrygian caps, just like their master—the god Mithras."

"Question," Garvey said, tapping Fisher on the shoulder. "Who's shaking hands with Mithras?"

"Could be an early depiction of Jesus Christ." He held up his hands to forestall objections. "Early Christians used the lamb and peacock as religious symbols. The figure's also holding a trident, another Christian symbol."

"Not so darn fast." Bemis put his hand on Fisher's shoulder. "Lambs, peacocks, tridents . . . pre-Christian art also used these critters. And Neptune was the most famous trident holder of all."

"But don't you see?" Fisher asked. "The interlocking motif of bulls—identified with Mithras the bull slayer, and the fish—an acronym for Jesus, showed some friendly relation between Mithras and Jesus Christ."

"Hold on. You're spinning." Bemis shook his head. "With no yarn."

"I don't think the figure is Jesus Christ." It made her uncomfortable to speak in support of Bemis. "That's the head of Apollo, not Christ."

"Since no one knew how Jesus looked," Fisher replied, "they used the head of Apollo sometimes to represent Jesus. Other times they used that of Hermes or Orpheus."

"A Christian connection won't work." She looked around the room. "Julius Caesar's father-in-law built this place, long before the birth of Jesus Christ."

"You're overlooking something." He couldn't take his eyes off the mural. "Even if you think the Festus parchment linking Saint Paul and Roman elite at the villa is a fake, the New Testament records Paul landed at nearby Puteoli on his way to Rome. He then preached in Rome under house arrest for about twenty years before the eruption of Mount Vesuvius in 79 AD." Fisher opened his hands as if the conclusion were obvious. "Plenty of time for the Christian message to reach this pagan resort town."

"Look, Will." She put a hand on her hip. "No conclusive archaeological evidence shows Christianity reached Pompeii or Herculaneum before the eruption."

"Face it, pardner." Bemis lowered the halogen lantern. "No way of knowing who's right. This wall may have ears, but it doesn't have a tongue."

"Maybe it's trying to say something with those Roman numerals." Fisher picked up the fallen number VIII with cotton gloves and held it close to its original location on the wall. After returning the number to the floor, he removed his gloves and scribbled in a notebook.

"They're just numbers." Bemis shrugged. "They don't say anything."

"Translated into the Arabic numerals we use," Garvey said, "the sequence reads . . . three . . . eight . . . six . . . eight again . . . five . . . and the last eight fallen to the ground. What does it mean?"

Bemis scratched his head. "I'll be a monkey's uncle if I know."

"I was talking to Will."

"I have a hunch." Fisher looked toward the ceiling. "But I want to make sure."

CHAPTER THIRTY-ONE

Outside the concrete wall and steel gate sealing off the Villa of the Papyri, Nicole Garvey cupped her hands over her eyes. "Where are Bemis and Renaldi? They're late."

"Let's wait a few more minutes," Will Fisher replied.

Laundry fluttered from the balconies of tenements quarantining the decaying buildings of ancient Herculaneum from modern Ercolano. The afternoon sun ate into the ghost town of roofless buildings crumbling with neglect in fields of weeds and wildflowers. Rain and air pollution joined the assault on the past. Pigeons pecked away at the rotted-out rafters supporting their nests. Will Fisher tossed a stone at a pigeon flock befouling the Villa of the Papyri. "Damn birds."

"Ditto," she said, watching the whirl of wings flap into the sky. Fate mocked Herculaneum's struggle to stay above ground with daily bombardments of pigeon droppings. In their wisdom, the authorities deemed it illegal to shoot pigeons but legal for falconers to kill them. The site decayed while the politicians picked nits.

The midnight call from her father still rattled her. He had sounded more depressed this time, but he wouldn't talk about it. John Wayne heroes kept their troubles to themselves. He refused her offer to return to Rome and help out. He didn't want to jeopardize her new job.

Colonel Soames, her great-grandfather, had committed suicide and lay buried in Rome. Her father's visit to the grave yesterday had left him more morose than ever. He wasn't supposed to visit until they could go together. Why did he? Was he, God forbid, thinking of imitating his grandfather? If something happened—

Fisher checked the time on his cell. "We've waited enough for Wes and Renaldi."

"Why does Renaldi insist on chaperoning us in the villa?"

"A new security measure. He suspects trespassers."

"I'm not buying it." She hitched up her backpack. "We're not trespassers, and we'd report any."

"What can I do?" He pursed his lips. "Wes is the boss. And he wants it."

His resignation irritated her.

After their descent to the newly discovered Latin library, Fisher photographed the mural of Mithras and his mystery friend. He sat cross-legged on the floor to photograph the Roman numerals at the bottom of the mural and one on the ground.

She sat next to him. "Enough suspense, Will. What does the mural mean?"

Fisher put the camera down. "Ever hear of gematria?"

"A code of numbers representing letters or words. Like a cryptogram." She smiled at the memory. "I won a prize in Bible school for knowing the Book of Revelation refers in code to a beast whose number is three sixes . . . Nero's name, the Antichrist."

"You have the idea." He had the tone of a professor validating a star pupil. "Ancient writers, including Saint Jerome, calculated the name of the god Mithras in Greek letters as equaling three hundred and sixty-five." Fisher shrugged, looking puzzled. "So what, you ask?" He prompted her with a circular motion of his right hand.

"OK, Professor. I ask." She laughed. "But no more showboating. Tell me."

"We have the Greek letters in the word Mithras equaling three hundred and sixty-five. Next we must puzzle out the name of the person shaking hands with Mithras." He opened his notebook to show her. "Eight hundred and eighty-eight is the numerical name of Jesus in Greek letters." He tapped the page with his finger several times.

"What does this have to do with the mural?"

"Both sets of numbers," he said pointing, "are on that wall."

"All I see is one number . . . three, eight, six, eight, five, and a final eight."

"Look again." He held out his notebook for her to see the six letters he had copied down. Red highlighter marked the three, the six, and the five, and a blue highlighter marked the three eights. "The names of Mithras and Jesus are numerically woven together."

"No way." She shook her head. "You're seeing what you want to see. You know how would-be prophets always find hidden meanings in the Bible."

"The symmetry of the three eights counterbalances the three sixes."

"That's exactly what I mean." She stood up. "You're reading things into the text, just like the ancients. It's like the coincidental similarities between the lives of Abraham Lincoln and JFK. No mystical connection there, just the human need to find meaning in patterns where none exists."

"But that's the point." He stood up in front of her and banged his notebook against his hip. "We can't look at this fresco through the contemporary glasses of scientific rationalism. We have to look through their eyes. Those letters had religious meaning."

She was about to dismiss his interpretation with the fact the Greek alphabet had nothing to do with the fresco. The numerals on the wall were Latin. And the Romans spoke . . . She caught herself. Of course they spoke Latin, but the educated class, like those in this mansion, often preferred Greek. Greek was the language of the literary works so far discovered in the villa. Even Saint Paul wrote to the Romans in Greek.

"Do you have a better idea why those numerals are up there?" Fisher drummed the notebook with his fingers. "They must relate to the fresco. Otherwise their positions make no sense."

"Assuming you're right," she said, "then some kind of relationship exists between the first Christians in Rome and their Mithraic contemporaries."

"That is precisely what—" Fisher stopped in midsentence and stared at the plain wall on the opposite side of the room. "Didn't the archaeology interns clean off that wall yesterday?" he said, his back turned to her and eyes fixated on the wall.

"Yes. Why?"

"That explains why we didn't notice it before."

"Notice what?"

"Look at that wall." He went over to the far wall. "What do you see?"

Unlike the other walls, the tomato-red plaster had a slapdash quality. The ancient artisans had applied the plaster unevenly. They hadn't even decorated it with frescoes.

"Except for the coarse workmanship, I don't see anything special."

"Come closer."

She followed his flashlight beam around the edge of a different color tone in the center of the wall. Against the background of the tomato-red color appeared the apparition of an arch in the form of an inverted U shape. The arch had the tone of darker red, something like raspberry.

An optical illusion? Garvey ran her fingers through her hair. The Romans mastered the three-dimensional illusion known as trompe-l'oeil. But nothing about the two-dimensional arch suggested trompe-l'oeil.

Just a coincidence of different paints?

"Look here." He stretched to examine the wall above the arch. "Where the lighter red plaster has chipped away, I can see brickwork underneath."

He lowered his gaze to the wall center. Close up, the tomato-red background of the wall clearly enclosed the outline of an arch in faded raspberry paint. He peered into a crack in the archway. He shoved a pen through the crack as far as it could go and turned it into a hole.

"Be careful. Keep the site intact."

Fisher peeked through the hole.

"Looks like rotted lattice. Why no brick?"

His walkie-talkie beeped. He pressed the Push to Talk button.

"I copy you, Wes. Where are you?"

"I had a last-minute problem. Some visiting Mormon missionaries."

"Too bad you're not here. I think I solved the Roman numbers mystery."

"Good for you, pardner . . . but Renaldi wants to see me. Have to go. Over."

The Mormon's voice boomed over the walkie-talkie like the voice of God. The creep would like the comparison.

"Tell him we waited, but he never showed up. Later, Wes. Out."

Fisher ran his fingers across the archway.

"Don't touch it, Will. You could damage the wall."

He pressed his fingers against the archway—it broke apart.

Plaster chunks and wood splinters fell to the ground. The LED light on Garvey's helmet illuminated the swirling dust from the collapsing archway. She covered her mouth and nose with a handkerchief. Coughing, she squinted at him through the haze. His coughing joined hers. With his hands over his face, he sat slumped down on the floor, his back to the broken wall. Tying her sweater over her nose and mouth, she squatted in front of him. Plaster dust covered him. After the haze settled, she removed her sweater from her face and shook his shoulder.

"Look behind you," she said, rising. He staggered up and turned around.

The image of an archway had given way to a real archway leading into the darkness of an adjoining room.

"Somebody." He coughed. "Somebody wanted the entrance sealed." He brushed himself off. "Let's check it out."

The walkie-talkie beeped. He pressed the Push to Talk button.

"Bemis here. Renaldi is having a fit. You went in without him. Come back right now . . . Do you copy me?"

"Ten four." The walkie-talkie crackled. "Can't we work something out?" Fisher adjusted a knob. The crackling stopped. "We're on to something big, a new room next to the library. Over."

"Oh my heck . . . He's ordering you out. Get out now."

"He can't stop us," Garvey said, taking the walkie-talkie from Fisher.

"Is that Nicole?"

"The professional name is Dr. Garvey . . . if you please . . . Dr. Bemis."

"This is serious . . . Dr. Garvey. I want to be nice. Please leave."

"What can Renaldi do? File a complaint going nowhere?"

"Flippin' crud," proclaimed the voice of God, "Renaldi has authority to shut us down on the spot. Talk some sense into that . . . that female. Over and out."

CHAPTER THIRTY-TWO

Outside the ruins of the Mithraeum of the Seven Gates in Ostia Antica, Lucio Piso paced back and forth at half past midnight. Around this subterranean chapel of Mithras in ancient Rome's port, nothing stirred but whispers in the wind. Unless he hung up on Renaldi's litany of excuses, he would be late for his star role and risk electronic detection.

"One fact remains. Against orders, you let the American archaeologists into the Villa of the Papyri without you." Piso remembered what he had told Renaldi when, disguised as the Pater Patrum, he first met him in the Maremma. "You told me the Pater Patrum wanted you at the villa as his eyes and ears."

"I beg the Pater Patrum to forgive me."

The power of his alter ego comforted Lucio Piso.

"Tell the Pater Patrum I promise to do better."

"Of course." How he loved deceiving the world with his alter ego.

"I must go." Piso cut over to the mithraeum entrance. "If you want to join Roma Rinata, do not fail the Pater Patrum again." To avoid police tracking, Piso smashed the burner cell phone.

He had to keep stringing the runt along.

Piso put on the alabaster mask of Mithras. He took a deep breath and closed his eyes until he could feel himself transfigured into the Pater Patrum, the supreme Father of Fathers. The exalted representative of Mithras on earth, he opened his eyes and entered the underground sanctuary.

Platforms on both sides of the room paralleled a central aisle running up to an altar at the far end. A floor mosaic of black-and-white squares depicted seven gates representing the seven hierarchical stages of initiation and spiritual purification. In the regalia of their spiritual hierarchy, Roma Rinata members sat on the platform to the left of the entering Pater Patrum. The candidates for promotion waited on the platform to the right.

Behind the square altar, a semicircular niche opened into a wall stained with the faded colors of sun and fire. In preparation for the initiation ceremony, the Ravens had placed in the niche an icon of Mithras slaying the bull on behalf of mankind.

How could the slain divinity of Christianity replace the slayer divinity of Mithraism? A slave religion over a warrior religion? It must not stand. After twenty centuries of error, Mithras returned to his place of honor in the niche.

A masked Raven assisted him in donning the crimson robe brocaded with gold filigree over his white tunic. From the Raven, he took the golden crosier encrusted with rare gems and his shepherd's crook of office. Another masked Raven set on his head the miter headpiece of office. The eyes of all upon him, the Pater Patrum strode to the altar behind two dwarfs, Cautopates and Cautes, dressed as the mythological torchbearers.

"I am death," Cautopates chanted, holding a burning torch upside down. "I am the resurrection," Cautes responded, holding a like torch right side up. Before the altar, the Pater Patrum turned to his flock, Cautopates on one side and Cautes on the other.

Reenacting an ancient ritual, the sole candidate for the elevated rank of Miles—a Soldier of Mithras—walked blindfolded down the aisle, hands bound by chicken guts. He knelt at the feet of the Pater Patrum. Carlos Stroheim, the disguised Pater for the Vatican district of Rome, stood by the candidate's side as his sponsor.

He, the Pater Patrum, the Father of all Fathers, reigned supreme at the apex of a resurrected and updated Mithras cult. More than fifty lesser Fathers, like Stroheim, operating in and around Rome, stood ready to rise up with their cells of conspirators in a coup d'état inspired by the Mithras cult. All the ranks of Mithras formed the leaven of the coming revolution.

He was the new Pater Patrum, sprung to life, after a long line of Pater Patrums had died out with a whimper in the fourth century AD. They had waned just as the Christian popes of Rome waxed, appropriating the name *papa* from the departed pagan popes. The lower ranks were his elite corps in the coming revolution. The Fathers, who enforced his commands, were the elite of the elite.

He trusted Carlos Stroheim the least, though the man was deferential as a slave. The prefect of the Vatican Secret Archives had bungled the search of Abramo Basso's apartment, blundered by murdering Basso in the Ardeatine Caves, and botched the ambush of Marco Leone in the mountains of Amalfi. Yet, Stroheim remained the sole Trojan horse inside the Vatican—for now. When his usefulness ended, the Maremma bulls would gore him to death.

After placing a laurel wreath on the bowed head of the Soldier candidate, Carlos Stroheim removed the candidate's blindfold and handed the Pater Patrum a sword. Chanting *Nama . . . Nama . . . Sebesio*, the Mithraic invocation whose meaning had become lost in time, the Pater Patrum sliced away the chicken entrails binding the candidate's hands. "Now liberated from the bondage of your former beliefs," the Pater Patrum intoned, "you are free to wear a victor's crown."

The candidate removed the wreath and placed it on his shoulder while reciting the proscribed words, "Mithras is my only crown, Roma Rinata my salvation, and the Pater Patrum my leader on earth."

As Pater Patrum, he had added the phrase about Roma Rinata and himself . . . but so what? Just as he had instituted the masks and garb for the seven stages of organizational progression, his was the genius to stitch together with new cloth the surviving shreds of ancient rituals.

What little the world knew of Mithraism came mostly from the biased pens of Christian contemporaries who mocked it and feared its curious resemblance to aspects of Christianity. He had to build upon such scant knowledge and mold it to his purposes. A reshaped Mithraism would reinforce his grab for political and social control. Just as the Emperor Constantine needed Christianity to create one religion in one empire, he would do the same with this more ancient religion.

"I hereby declare you a Soldier of Mithras." The Pater Patrum tapped the candidate's scalp with the crosier.

Two masked Lions readied the ten candidates for their initiation into the lowest rank of Raven. On the Pater Patrum's signal, the ten flapped their arms and croaked like birds, shuffling around a vat of water three times one way and three times the other. One by one, they dunked their heads into the vat until they could no longer hold their breath. Each head bobbed up in turn, gasping in symbolic rebirth.

These true believers held him in awe. He could do no wrong. To so skillfully shepherd these acolytes clad only in loin cloths confirmed the superiority of his real self. Before him bowed the refuse of the streets, the skinheads, the petty criminals, the social misfits. They considered their lives worthless, with nothing to lose and everything to gain if they followed their leader and his cause. He would give them what everyone needed, something to live for, and more importantly for his purposes, something to die for. He was the artisan. They were the clay to be molded as he saw fit.

At his command, they recited singsong the Roma Rinata creed he had composed: "I believe in the genius of the Pater Patrum, our Holy Father of Fathers, in the communion of all brothers of Mithras, in the social and political regeneration of Italy, in the conversion of Europe, and in the resurrection of the empire."

When they finished, two masked Lions passed around trays filled with circular loaves of bread. The Lions poured wine into goblets held in outstretched arms. That miserable commissario Marco Leone had caused the death of his bravest Lion catapulted over an Amalfi mountain—the only one honored with a lion mask of glass instead of papier-mâché.

"Candidates for the Raven rank," he said, "I hold in my left hand the bread of Mithras warmed in the sun to absorb its divine rays, as prescribed by our spiritual ancestors, to become as hard as you in the coming battle. And in my right, I hold a cup of wine to fortify us in the days ahead.

"By eating this bread and drinking this wine, on this new day named after the sun, a day sacred to Lord Mithras, you become one with the sun god. By doing so, you imitate Lord Mithras himself, who ascended to the heavens after sharing a banquet with the sun god, and then became one with him. So—"

"I must ask something before I agree to become a Raven."

Who dares interrupt?

Rocco—the broad-shouldered candidate from Sicily, no more than thirty, broken nosed, scarred across the right cheek, uncouth and vigorous—the spitting image of Caravaggio.

Two Lions ran at Rocco. He raised his fists in self-defense.

"Leave him be." The Pater Patrum crooked his forefinger. "Come forward."

Flanked by the two Lions, Rocco swaggered up to the Pater Patrum. The Lions tried pushing him onto his knees. He resisted. The Pater Patrum commanded the Lions to leave him alone. The Raven candidate wore only a loin cloth and a gold cross around the neck.

"What, my son, do you wish to ask?"

"To get sworn in as a Raven . . ." Rocco looked around and then lowered his voice. "To become a Raven, do I have to believe this . . . pardon the expression . . . bullcrap?"

Shock dumbfounded the Pater Patrum.

"I see you wear a Christian cross. This is not allowed."

"It's just a piece of jewelry."

"If so, remove it."

"I promised my mother to never remove it. That's the only reason I wear it." His hands clenched and reopened and clenched again. "I believe in her, not the cross. She gave me life. I owe her mine. I only believe in what I can sense and understand."

"Because you love your mother, you wear it." The Pater Patrum distilled the Sicilian's meaning, as if his words would help him understand. They did not. He had never experienced father or mother or love. He was an abandoned orphan.

"Now then." The Pater Patrum collected himself and raised his crosier. "It is not a matter of belief. It is a matter of outward compliance. You need only respect our symbols in the same way you honor your mother with the cross. Can you do that for the sake of Roma Rinata, which, like your mother, offers you a new life?"

"I can."

"Good, my son. Now return to your post."

The Pater Patrum rapped his crosier on the floor. One by one, the new Ravens knelt before him. Each in turn extended his hand straight out and interlocked his fingers with the fingers of the Pater Patrum.

They pumped hands three times to complete their secret handshake of recognition.

"I, the Pater Patrum," he said, marking each candidate's forehead with ashes, "hereby admit you to the rank of Raven on your ascension up the celestial ladder through the seven stages of rebirth."

As each new Raven received his assignment from Carlos Stroheim, a senior Lion approached the Pater Patrum. "How prudent, most holy Pater Patrum, not to make a scene. A scene is what the Sicilian scoffer would have wanted." He embraced the Pater Patrum and whispered in his ear. "Give the order, and I'll take care of Rocco."

"Take care of him?" The Pater Patrum shook the Lion's shoulders. "Yes, yes. By all means, take care you not harm a hair of his head if you wish to preserve your own head."

The other Ravens followed Rocco out of the mithraeum.

"For that Raven, more lionhearted than my Lions, I have conceived a special mission."

CHAPTER THIRTY-THREE

Sunglasses protected Nicole Garvey's eyes, puffy from worry and lack of sleep after a late return from Rome. Workers fretting about the absence of birds and the presence of green-tinted clouds whirling in the sky carted volcanic rock from the Villa of the Papyri.

Outside the historic villa, the chained guard dog howled at Mount Vesuvius, about six kilometers away. The wind, foretelling rain, kicked up, brushing through Garvey's hair. The yowling and the desperation of the dog straining against the chain and biting its leg put her nerves on edge even more than the report of wells gone dry overnight. The volcano spewed up a billowing cloud of ash and smoke more ominous than the daily witches' brew of wispy vapors slithering through its vents.

A pack of unseen dogs in the stretch of modern tenements between Mount Vesuvius and Herculaneum accompanied the howling with their yapping. An underground sea of red-hot molten rock sloshed a little under 248 kilometers under the only active volcano in Europe, a ticking time bomb waiting to explode once again.

The Mormon boy wonder let her cool her heels outside the administrative field tent on purpose. She suspected payback for disputing his order to evacuate the room behind the collapsed wall down below.

Or was it about her trip to Rome?

It didn't matter. She did the right thing in visiting her father, even if it shook her to the core. A man who once adored his grandfather refused to show her the grave of Colonel Soames. What scared her even more was the way he cursed her great-grandfather and refused to talk about him. She wanted to shake him and make him talk, but it wouldn't have done any good. Nothing could make him talk once he clammed up. She spent her time in Rome just trying to keep him from sinking deeper into depression. He promised to see a doctor, but she despaired he would. What if he should . . .

"Come in." Renaldi jerked this thumb toward the tent next to the Villa of the Papyri. "He wants to see you."

Her father's state of mind and the hubbub about the recent tremors jangled her nerves enough without having to deal with the Mormon.

Like a penitent schoolgirl, she stood before a folding table full of cluttered papers. Bemis sat behind the table on a folding chair. He played his game of pretending not to notice her. She would not lose her cool. Her job was on the line.

"You did not have my permission to leave." He took the unusual step of looking her directly in the eyes. "I can't allow that."

Renaldi stood beside the table like an attack dog at the ready.

"I had to see my father in Rome." She struggled to confide in Bemis. "He served in Iraq. He's having a hard time."

"You had a job to do here, Nicole."

"Dr. Garvey."

"Whatever." Bemis stacked papers on his table. "Fact remains you went AWOL."

"I'm here now. We're supposed to help Will examine the room he uncovered."

"His name, Dr. Garvey," Bemis said, looking pleased with himself, "is Dr. Fisher."

"She wasn't supposed to leave the villa without notification." Renaldi glanced at Bemis. "Get it over with. I have to check on Fisher below."

Bemis nodded to Renaldi and puffed his cheeks. "I'm afraid your conduct won't do." Bemis removed his cowboy hat and fanned himself before plopping it back on his head. "I don't like doing this," he said, smiling, "but—"

"Great news." Will Fisher pushed aside the tent flaps and rushed in. "I found a stunning wall inscription down there. Come see."

"Wonderful, pardner." Bemis shook Fisher's hand. "I'd love to see it."

"Are you ready to descend with me?"

"Her." Bemis nodded at Nicole. "She went AWOL on us."

"No, she didn't." Fisher laughed. "I forgot to tell you. Dr. Garvey told me she had to see her father on a medical emergency. I gave her permission because you and Renaldi weren't available."

"You forgot to tell us?" Renaldi rolled his eyes. "I don't believe you."

"My pardner here does have a bad memory." Bemis reached for his rucksack. "He's notorious for forgetting his class schedule."

"Yep . . ." Fisher clowned, holding out the lapels on his shirt. "I'm the original absentminded professor."

He lied to save her job. She'd be happy to repay the debt . . . with interest.

"Follow me." Fisher stood at the tent entrance. "I'm eager to get back."

"Next time, see me." Bemis paused until Fisher had left the tent. "I'm sure we can work something out . . . Nicole." His smile verged on a leer. "Let's get going. We've work to do."

He chilled her even in the day's heat.

**

Inside the Latin library, the workmen had removed the remaining debris. Renaldi stayed behind to supervise the workers packing boxes with the carbonized scrolls discovered earlier in the library. He delayed shipment of the scrolls to the National Archaeological Museum in Naples until he verified that the number of scrolls Fisher had counted and prepared matched the inventory tally in his hand. Because he personally answered to Lucio Piso, Renaldi warned Fisher that everything had better be in order.

Garvey and Bemis trailed Fisher into the murkiness of the adjacent room the professor had stumbled into.

"My turn for surprises, lady and gentleman." Fisher made an exaggerated bow. "Welcome to the scriptorium."

"Scriptorium?" Garvey asked. "I didn't expect it."

"Before the medieval monks," Fisher said, "superrich Romans sometimes had a scriptorium for writing and copying letters and documents . . . not just a library."

"Here's proof." Fisher stood beside stacks of blank papyrus sheets resting on what appeared to be a decayed pallet. "This papyrus looks like top-notch stock for the scribes."

"You had better—"

"I know, I know, Wes. I've already inventoried these scrolls to keep Renaldi happy."

Fisher cleared his throat. "Ta-da . . . Now, my friends, switch on your lamps and look at that wall. It's going to make us famous."

He walked to the other side of the scriptorium and held up his lamp. Underneath mosaics showing male figures copying papyrus scrolls, Fisher traced with a flashlight in his other hand the Latin letters *C, H, R, I, S, T, U, S* running horizontally across the wall.

"I was wrong." Garvey held her breath. "Christianity came to Herculaneum before the eruption."

Fisher ran his flashlight vertically down the wall, revealing *M, I, T, R, A.* The two words formed a cross sharing the common letter *I.*

"*Mitra* . . . the Latin root word for the English word *miter* worn during religious services." He lowered the flashlight beam to the floor. "I wonder." He rubbed his chin. "Ancient sources refer to the Magi, the Persian priest-astrologers, as wearing a kind of turban . . . and maybe the inscription means Christ is a high priest."

"By golly, you're jumping to a conclusion." Bemis aimed his flashlight at the cruciform words. "It could also refer to the Roman god Mithras, sometimes called Mitra. The miters worn by Mithraic priests only later evolved into the English word for headpieces worn by important ecclesiastics."

"Your interpretation imagines a connection between Mithras and Christ. That's jumping to an even bigger conclusion than what Professor Fisher suggested." Garvey put a hand on her hip. "I don't buy it."

"Don't get so angry, little lady." Bemis made a happy face. "Professor Fisher and I were just making suggestions."

She wanted to deny she was angry. But she knew the game he played. When he felt offended, he'd try to bait her into getting testy so she could be labeled the naughty archaeologist. She wouldn't take the bait.

"Time out. It's been a long day," Fisher said. "We all agree on one thing. The inscription is the first clear proof that Christianity reached Herculaneum before the eruption in 79 AD. I think we should—"

Renaldi shouted over from the Latin library into the scriptorium. He needed Fisher to help him pack the scrolls for shipment.

***

As soon as Fisher left for the Latin library, Garvey moved away from Bemis to avoid his stare. His gazes disturbed her. She preferred it when he avoided eye contact.

"Let's get to work." She turned her back on him.

At the other end of the room, she bent down on hands and knees. Behind her flashed the Mormon's camera, snapping a picture of the wall inscription. She brushed away the dust and debris in search of whatever archaeological evidence she could find. Maybe something would shed light on their discoveries in the Latin library and scriptorium.

Garvey came across what looked like blanched animal skin, maybe intended for parchment. She punched a hole in a ziplock bag to avoid condensation inside and labeled it. She spooned the skin into the bag and crawled farther along, brushing the floor detritus into a dustpan and sifting its contents. Scraps of reed pens, inkwells, feathers, and papyrus lay along the wall. Even without the identifying wall mosaics, these scraps indicated a scriptorium. She inserted the specimens into separate ziplock bags.

An object that looked like a cylinder poked out of a pile of debris in a shadowy corner of the room.

As she crawled toward the object, something crept down her back like giant spider legs. She twisted around in a panic to confront the spiders.

The Mormon had his hand on her butt.

Garvey flung the hand off and scrambled to her feet.

He had a leer pasted on his face.

She kneed him in the balls.

He backed away, bent over and yelping.

Her indignation melted into satisfaction.

"Stay away." Garvey took a breath. "You touch me again, and I'll report you to the superintendent . . . and the police."

Bemis spread his hand over his face. "I'm so sorry," he said through his fingers. He put his hands down. "Don't tell anyone . . . please, please. I won't do it again. I promise." He crossed his heart. Before she could respond, he ran out of the scriptorium.

***

When Fisher returned to the scriptorium, Garvey was about to examine a strange container surrounded by what looked like a collapsed table.

"What's up with Wes?" Fisher said. "He just ran by on his way out of the villa . . . like he'd seen a ghost."

"Bemis?" She stalled, her mind in overdrive about what to say.

Say nothing.

Bemis had looked more afraid of her than she of him. The boy wonder would probably let the incident drop because of his embarrassment. Anyway, it was her word against his if she complained. Renaldi would believe him, and she didn't want to find out whom Will would believe. This groundbreaking dig would make her career if she kept her head. He wouldn't mess with her again. She felt in charge of her life for the first time in a long time.

"Oh, that . . . He left complaining of pains in his tummy." She groped for a plausible explanation. "Maybe something he had for breakfast."

"He ate what he always eats." Will stroked his chin. "Oatmeal and prunes."

"Forget about Bemis." She tugged at his sleeve. "C'mon, I found something on the floor."

Setting down her lantern nearby, she bent over to examine a wooden cylinder the size of a hatbox. It had to be a Roman scroll box. A scroll peeked through the cracked lid. The location of the scriptorium and its sealed archway had lessened the impact of the volcanic flow. The scroll inside had to be in better shape than the shriveled papyrus lumps found unprotected in the Latin library.

"I see a writing on this side of the box." Fisher was on his knees. "A word . . . *CALLINICUS* . . . in capital letters."

"Over here." Garvey blew away dust. "I see words . . . *SACERDOS MITHRAE*—priest of Mithras."

"I can see through the crack on top." Will leaned closer over the lid. "The scroll looks in excellent condition."

"Do we have to tell Renaldi about this?"

"Of course." He looked surprised. "Wes wants Renaldi kept in the loop."

"I don't trust Renaldi."

Why doesn't Will ever stand up to the Mormon?

"Wes knows what he's doing."

"Does he now?" Garvey got to her feet, hands on hips. "When you were gone, Bemis . . ." She couldn't let the boy wonder's juvenile behavior get in the way of this archaeological bonanza. "Praised your archaeological instincts." She crossed her fingers behind her back. "Time to get back to work while you pack this for shipment to the Naples museum."

Creeping her way toward an unexamined corner of the room, she swept up dust and debris clouding the surface of the floor and sifted them through her sieve. Kicking up a fine powder with the methodical strokes of her brush, she uncovered a ring attached to the center of a metal disk, resembling an engraved manhole cover, about a meter in diameter.

"Will, come here. I found something. It's a trapdoor."

"Shall we?" Eager to pull, she fingered the ring.

Fisher's walkie-talkie beeped. He held up his hand for her to wait while he answered the call.

"Bemis to Fisher, Bemis to Fisher . . . Do you copy?"

"I copy. What's up? . . . We need to open a trapdoor."

"The Vesuvius Observatory just issued an advisory. Increased seismic activity around the volcano . . . Get out now."

CHAPTER THIRTY-FOUR

Dr. Wesley Bemis, adherent of the Church of Jesus Christ of Latter-day Saints, stewed over his predicament of overseeing twenty-first-century technology in the midst of erotic statuary from ancient Greece and Rome. "This is no place for me," he said, throwing a blanket over the statue of Pan making love to a goat.

"We can work here undisturbed," Fisher said. "The director has barred the public with the renovation pretext." He winked. "In Italy, a closed museum wing is normal. No one will suspect what we're up to."

Bemis reconsidered the situation. Unless Fisher had persuaded Cardinal Furbone to use his influence on the museum director, they wouldn't have a workplace so close to the Villa of the Papyri. The clincher was the free use of the Gabinetto Segreto. The cardinal had more influence than Bemis thought possible. Even if they could find another location, the excavation budget didn't allow for additional rental fees.

"OK. I'll put up with this." Bemis crossed his arms. "But this is no place for Missy Garvey."

"No problem." Fisher looked up from the Callinicus scroll, which he'd named after the scribe who wrote it. "Nicole's taking a break visiting in Sorrento. After the tremors quiet down, we'll resume work in the villa."

"So, it's Nicole now, not Dr. Garvey."

"She and I are colleagues, aren't we?"

"Superintendent Piso and Renaldi set the excavation rules." Bemis looked up from his technology manual. "Will she accept their authority?"

"Nicole understands perfectly."

"I'm not so sure. She delayed your evacuation from the scriptorium."

"She was right. We had to save the Callinicus papyrus from any earthquake."

"But at the price of context." Bemis closed his technological manual. "You snatched the Callinicus scroll from its setting."

"C'mon, Wes. Nicole and I are professionals. We photographed the papyrus container where we found it."

"Renaldi's furious you didn't leave when ordered."

"No surprise there. He's getting more paranoid by the day."

"Watch it with her. She's trouble."

"Maybe for you, not for me." Fisher turned back to his translation of the Callinicus letter. "I've work to do, and you need to do your technological magic on the carbonized scrolls from the Latin library."

"Later. I'm dying to read your translation." Unlike the carbonized scrolls, he didn't need to use the magic of multispectral imaging and CT scan equipment on the Callinicus scroll.

"First things first." Fisher removed a special camera from its crate. "I must photograph the Callinicus letter, just in case—"

"Anything happens to the original. Got it."

Thanks to its entombment in the scriptorium, the Callinicus scroll had escaped the pyroclastic flow from Mount Vesuvius better than expected. The ability of the Piso clan to afford the best papyrus and ink in the ancient world hadn't hurt either. His colleague wouldn't need his technological skills to translate this scroll.

"My photos aren't just an insurance policy against loss." Fisher adjusted the camera. "Major universities will clamor for copies of the text."

"Will the photos harm the papyrus?"

"Nope. The special lighting has a low thermal temperature."

Fisher blew away dust from the papyrus as brittle as dried leaves. He mounted the sheets between glass panes before photographing the text. According to Fisher, this Callinicus wrote in a chicken-scratching style of cursive Latin difficult to read. Except for the occasional dot, the ancient writer further complicated things by following the custom of running all the letters together with no spacing between words, sentences, or paragraphs.

Bemis's face clouded over with worry. "Shouldn't we carbon-date the letter?"

"What's the point?" Fisher asked in return. "Someone bricked up the scriptorium in the first century AD, and the eruption sealed it until we discovered it. The chain of custody is unbroken. It has to be authentic."

"Let's do it anyway, just to dot our i's and cross our t's."

"But the writing style and papyrus are typical of the first century." Fisher polished his magnifying glass with a cloth. He tightened his lips and relaxed them. "You're right. This letter is too important. I'll take minimal samples from the papyrus for carbon-dating."

***

Returning from what he called a pornography break, Bemis opened the door to the Gabinetto Segreto to find his colleague rubbing a fist into one eye and yawning. He had removed swatches of blank papyrus from the Callinicus letter and prepared them for delivery to the Center for Data and Diagnostics, better known as CEDAD, for carbon-dating.

"I'm making steady progress." Fisher looked ecstatic. "My advice is to sit down before reading what I've translated so far." He handed off the partial translation to Bemis before hurrying back to his workstation.

TO PAUL OF TARSUS FROM MARCUS LOLLIANUS CALLINICUS

Greetings to Paul, a preacher of Christ, from Marcus, a priest of Mithras.

I pray this letter transmitted to you by your servant, Timothy, finds you safe from Nero's wrath. I, now recovering from a broken left leg, write this in the villa of Gaius Calpurnius Piso on the second day before the calends of October in the year after the Great Fire of Rome from whose destruction only a third of the

municipal districts escaped. The object of an imperial manhunt, I quiver like a cornered boar secreted
away here with my trusted slave. Only fond memories
of our friendship console me. Vivid is the day of your
arrival in Rome four years ago, the talk of the town,
an exotic and charismatic visionary from Judea, the
land of fanatics, prophets, and rebels. You wrote and
preached as a Roman citizen awaiting the outcome of
your appeal to Nero's court from the accusations of
your Jerusalem enemies. So unlike my occasionally
long-winded Asiatic rhetoric, the simple elegance of
your message touched not only the heart of Burrus
in charge of your house arrest, but even Seneca, the
chairperson of the secret imperial commission on religious unity for which I am the scribe. How could this
Nero once have been so dispassionate as to acquit you
after two years of loosely supervised house arrest, he
himself saying that Rome, the home of a hundred gods,
had room for one more, and then possessed by the
Furies disband the imperial commission and turn on
the Christians and their friends after the Great Fire?
I hesitate—

Who was pounding on the door of the Gabinetto Segreto?

Bemis pulled back the deadbolt from the steel door installed to
keep out determined looters. Kicking and shoving, a stream of Italian
schoolchildren flooded into the forbidden room. *"Non entrare,"* Bemis
yelled in his most authoritarian Italian with no effect.

Their ringleader ran around, knocking off the towels Bemis had
draped over offending penises and breasts and drawing the tittering
attention of his classmates to the "wee-wee" dangling from the goat
man. Their teacher shooed them out of the room with a litany of colorful threats; Bemis slammed the door shut and reset the crossbar.

He returned to the translation.

Credible men of the fire brigades claim that a fringe
group of Judean fanatics committed the arson to

hasten the return of the Christ you preach. According to an Egyptian oracle, the ascent of Sirius, the Dog Star, on that humid night in July portended the fall of Rome. They say the arsonists desired to force the fulfillment of this Egyptian prophecy to make way for the kingdom of the Christ. Some Christ followers, or at least those claiming to be, asserted that the divine Christ had miraculously ignited the fire, which would not be difficult even for a lesser god in a city built of so much wood, and that they merely assisted the hand of Christ with their own torches. In any case, numerous witnesses attested that mysterious figures either prevented attempts to fight the fire or actually abetted it. In support of this version of events, I have heard that Gaius Calpurnius Piso, the star-crossed owner of this villa where I hide, agitated behind the scenes to incite the mob in aid of his attempt to overthrow Nero, our unhinged mother slayer. Another version of the Great Fire exists. Those senators who bemoan the loss of power, and some out-of-touch intellectuals seeking to bring back the republic, assert that Nero made the Christ followers into scapegoats for a fire he secretly started for his own twisted purposes of either building a new Rome or more likely, obtaining the projected property for his outlandish Domus Aurea palace at fire-bargain prices. I find this unlikely because the fire started quite distant from the proposed construction site and even destroyed his existing palace on the Palatine Hill. Even though now out of his mind in other respects, Nero has always remained avariciously sane in protecting his own possessions. Which version of events is true, only the gods know for certain. But, alas, either version has triggered our death warrants if we are captured, you as the preacher of the Christ and me as your friend. Jewish elders—

The "Hallelujah" chorus ringtone sounded. Bemis answered his cell.

"Renaldi here. Is it translated?"

"Yes. I'm reading it now." He kept his voice low.

"I want it for Piso."

"But we need to—"

"I'm coming over now. Have it ready . . . or else."

The line went dead.

***

Better to say nothing for the moment. Bemis didn't want a run-in with Fisher over Renaldi until he finished reading the Callinicus letter.

> Jewish elders in Rome, fearing Nero's vengeance would fall on them as well, have publicly denounced your Christ followers as blasphemous heretics deluded by a false messiah and have prohibited further dialogue with Christ followers, especially since Nero turned devil no longer presses for a common basis of religious beliefs. Be wise and stay away from those you now have no hope of persuading to your views of the Jewish prophecies and who risk their lives by associating with you. After the Great Fire, Nero ordered the arrest of all Jews belonging to the Christ sect, now called Christians by some, and anyone associated with them, including me and many others in my congregation of Mithras. Some Jews repulsed by his behavior even refer in code to Nero as the ruler of Babylon. Nero has torched so many Christ followers fastened onto crosses that their burning flesh lights up the night sky. Whom the gods would destroy, they first make mad, and our emperor is now as mad as they come.

"When do I get the remaining translation?" Bemis asked. "I can't wait."

Fisher rubbed his eyes. "Just about done."

While his colleague completed the translation, Bemis passed the time reflecting on the personal importance of the Callinicus letter. He took the Book of Mormon from his duffel bag and, leafing through it, pondered the Great Apostasy in which the early Church lost its way by diluting the message of the Lord with paganism. And didn't the Callinicus letter show the early seeds of the apostasy? And wouldn't that corrupting friendship between pagan and Christian of course lead to—

***

"Here's the rest of the translation." Fisher rubbed his hand across his brow. "Shouldn't you be decoding the carbonized scrolls with your gadgets?"

"Later." Bemis waved Fisher off. "I have to see how this story ends."

> And now the worst news of all. Gaius Calpurnius Piso, our mutual friend, committed suicide on the emperor's order. Nero crushed Piso's conspiracy in the nest as it was about to hatch. Even our beloved Seneca had to commit suicide because Nero suspected he, too, was involved. Gone with this amiable Stoic are his plans for a universal brotherhood in a unified empire grounded on the natural law of Supreme Reason, what the Greeks call Logos, the Word. Yet, being Roman, he found, as you know, Greek theorizing impractical for the underpinning of virtue so necessary for the welfare of the empire. From your accounts of the Christ, he detected a common ethical basis for the mass of humanity, which does not consist of Greek philosophers. His divine soul and all his dreams have now ascended to the highest level of the stars where he makes his new home.

Divine soul? Ascended to the highest level of the stars? New home? Fisher shouldn't jump to conclusions. To make certain, Bemis checked the mounted photograph of the Callinicus text. Although his Latin was not at Fisher's level, he seconded the professor's translation.

Even Callinicus apparently anticipated Mormon belief. Men can become gods. And this pagan's belief was even compatible with the Mormon notion that the best of the best might rule over their own planets in the afterlife. Seneca and Callinicus were on the right track. And he was the one to help them go further down the track of knowledge to the Mormon destination. If he could no longer baptize dead Jews, he still had dead pagans to convert.

> Think me not an ungrateful guest, but our host, Gaius Calpurnius Piso, is the cause of our calamity. His followers urged him to claim and seize the throne as soon as Nero uncovered the plot. Instead, he dithered in the temple of Ceres like an aimless child. That pretty boy of straw, so unlike his illustrious ancestors, has through lack of courage, despite all his charms, ruined the Piso clan and all his friends by his ineptitude. Know, dear friend, I shall not betray you just as you would not betray me. My notes on the symposium remain where . . . What? I hear noise on the floor above . . . I must hide in the meeting place of the imperial commission under the trapdoor until I know who . . . I will finish this letter later . . . You will remain close to me in death as in life.

"Holy macaroni, Will. This Callinicus letter is dyn-a-mite," Bemis shouted to his colleague across the Gabinetto Segreto.

"Who called you earlier?" Looking pleased, Fisher stretched his arms and neck. "Anything important?"

"Not really. Just Renaldi."

"I have had it up to here." Fisher lifted his index finger to his throat. "He accused me of faking the papyrus inventory until I set him straight . . . What's he want?"

"The Callinicus letter."

"We've gone over this before." Fisher wrung his hands. "He can't have it."

"I have no choice, Will." Bemis licked his lower lip. "I don't want to pull rank, but you must turn it over. He'll arrive any minute."

"You should've postponed telling him about the letter."

"Very Jesuitical." He regretted his pique unworthy of a Latter-day Saint. "Piso will fire us all and hire a new archaeological team."

"No way." Fisher rolled his eyes. "You can't do it. If you—"

A banging on the door drowned out Fisher's voice.

"This is Renaldi . . . Hand over the Callinicus letter now."

CHAPTER THIRTY-FIVE

Fluted glasses with leftover prosecco and plates of uneaten sweets littered the buffet table of Lucio Piso's office in the town of Ercolano, built over Herculaneum. Piso waved farewell to the last of the village's elite as they departed the reception given for the new superintendent of excavations in Herculaneum. He ushered Will Fisher into his chambers, which looked more like a luxury suite than a governmental office.

Riccardo Renaldi's presence meant unpleasantness.

"Congratulations on your discovery of the Callinicus letter." Piso toasted with the prosecco remaining in his glass. "Join me?"

"No . . . no, thank you." Fisher swallowed hard. "I don't drink."

"What can I do for you?" Piso asked.

"The Callinicus letter is just the beginning." Fisher sat on the sofa indicated by Piso. "Renaldi ordered Dr. Garvey and me out of the scriptorium because of volcanic activity . . . just as we prepared to open the trapdoor in the floor. We need to go back."

"Unfortunately, an official alert exists." Piso shrugged. "As the superintendent of excavations, I must appear prudent for a bit." He winked. "But trust me."

"That's why we should go in tomorrow." Fisher rubbed his hands together. "We barely escaped with the Callinicus letter. An earthquake could destroy priceless scrolls under the trapdoor. Callinicus was, after all, the scribe to the imperial commission."

"My hands are temporarily tied because of an annoying function-ary." Piso smiled, crossing his hands at the wrists. "But soon my name alone will cut through even Italian bureaucracy." His hands burst free from the imaginary restraints. "For personal reasons, I am as eager as you to explore what lies beneath the trapdoor."

Fisher leaned toward Piso at the other end of the sofa. "Then at least return the Callinicus scroll to us." The professor looked up at Renaldi standing behind his boss and flashing a sneer. "The one he seized from us."

"You and I work for the Honorable Lucio Piso," Renaldi said. "The Callinicus scroll belongs to—"

"Silence." Piso's command directed at Renaldi startled Fisher.

Renaldi reeled back like a dog kicked by its master.

"My dear professor." Piso's voice dropped back to the silky smooth-ness of a charmer mixed with a tad of the con man. "For forty years a handful of scholars monopolized the study of the Dead Sea Scrolls until the Israel Antiquities Authority forced publication to the whole world." His stare chilled Fisher. "I will not permit the Callinicus letter to suffer the frivolity of academics. Do you understand?"

"But I gave you a copy of my translation."

"With all due respect, I would like another expert to review the original."

"Who would that be?"

"I am not at liberty to say." Piso smirked. "My expert is shy."

"The original must not be put at risk."

"I don't need to be lectured. I'm not one of your students." Piso shifted back to amiability. "I promise to return it to you for storage in the Gabinetto Segreto in the Naples museum."

"I'd like to transfer the blank papyrus sheets I found to the Vatican Library for safekeeping and mold removal." Fisher turned to Renaldi. He needed the security chief on board. "I have properly accounted for and inventoried the unused papyrus, haven't I?"

Renaldi scowled and acquiesced with a curt nod of his head.

"Granted, then," Piso said with the tone of a potentate.

Fisher dreaded relaying Nicole's ultimatum. He disliked conflict. But Nicole had insisted.

At the door, Fisher cleared this throat. "One final request. When you permit us to explore under the trapdoor, we would like to go without a guard . . . I mean escort."

"And if I do not grant such permission?"

"Dr. Garvey will resign from the project."

"Impossible." Renaldi was in his face. "You and the American woman already violated my security order by entering the Latin library without me."

"Permission granted," Piso said.

"What?" Renaldi's lips parted and eyes widened. "My authority is being undermined, Honorable Special Superintendent of Excavations."

"Never forget your place, Renaldi. You do what I say."

CHAPTER THIRTY-SIX

Giving the slip to paparazzi, Will Fisher and Nicole Garvey dashed up the stairs into the basilica of Santa Prisca hand in hand. By overruling his reluctance to go public with the Callinicus translation before authentication, Lucio Piso had done the unexpected favor of making Fisher a media star overnight.

The publicity circus Garvey shunned, he embraced. The last week had been a whirlwind of press interviews and television shows backgrounded with comely eye candy. Newshounds begged interviews from the photogenic professor. The sight of his face on TV thrilled him more than the adulation of students ever could.

The Callinicus hoopla had gone viral. Fisher's Twitter followers already exceeded one hundred thousand. The attack on the Callinicus letter by a Vatican faction led by Cardinal Furbone amplified the media frenzy. Scholarly journals begged him to write for immediate publication anything he chose about the relationship between Mithraism and Christianity.

He had to figure out a way of walking the tightrope of public acclaim without further jeopardizing his career at the university. The scandal-hungry reporters staked out near the church doors were bound to learn of the heresy rumors against him. With time, he could solve the problem. For now, he just needed his friend to steady him.

"Where are you off to?" Garvey asked.

"I have to check out the mithraeum below the church." It had to sound urgent. "*The Bulletin of Mithras Research* wants the final edit of my article ASAP."

"Why can't we both go?"

"I made special arrangements. Only one allowed." They never asked him to come alone, but the restriction sounded plausible. "Gotta go." He almost stumbled over the kneeler on the way out of the pew.

***

Below the church, Fisher stood before a rectangular room with a barrel-vaulted ceiling painted a faded blue. An underground chill rolled over his skin. In the alcove near the mithraeum entrance once existed a shrine to the birth of Mithras.

His snuffling nap disturbed by the professor's arrival, the custodian snorted himself awake and smoothed his hedgehog hair. Scowling, he verified the visitor's identification. The custodian grabbed Fisher's satchel. "I need to see what's inside."

"Do you know who I am?"

"A man." The custodian opened the straps. He extracted a book, a notepad, a pocket recorder, colored pencils, and a pint-sized bottle of cut glass decorated with a cross surrounded by wines. "What's this?"

"A container with holy water . . . blessed by Pope Celestine the Sixth."

After returning the satchel and its contents, the custodian yawned and waved him inside.

Fisher strolled down the aisle of the mithraeum with its raised platforms on either side toward the altar in the front. The north wall showed Mithras and the sun god sharing a meal as a procession of Lion initiates approached. The south wall depicted a procession with figures from each of the seven grades of initiation. While Garvey waited above, he wept below, tossing back Jack Daniels from a holy water container in the chapel of the god Mithras.

Unknown to Garvey, the board of trustees of the Pontifical Gregorian University of Rome, known affectionately to students as the Greg, had suspended him from his teaching duties. The Congregation for the Doctrine of the Faith had triggered his suspension for suspicion of heresy in his latest book. They said he undermined the faith by condoning syncretism of the world's major religious systems under the banner of "one God with many names."

All roads led to Rome. Why couldn't all roads lead to God? Had not the Church absorbed the symbols and traditions and beliefs of other religions? Could any religion be a world religion if it did not? Saint Paul understood this. Why didn't the congregation? He hoped Cardinal Furbone, the temporary prefect of the congregation after the death of its director, might reverse its prior opinion.

He euthanized his questions with another slug of consolation from his good friend in the holy water container, Mr. Jack Daniels.

New questions sprang up. Why should he sabotage his career prospects with in-your-face opinions? Others, like Abramo Basso, believed as he did, but they kept their heads down and mouths shut. He might still save himself if he recanted like Galileo. He should throw himself at the feet of the new prefect of the congregation and beg for mercy. Wasn't humbling oneself a virtue? Like obedience?

Wiping away tears with his sleeve, he reproved himself for his maudlin weakness. Fisher groped along the walls of the mithraeum in search of one particular inscription. He had to make sure he got it right in his article. His eyes scanned the rough walls. SWEET ARE THE LIVERS OF THE BIRDS BUT WORRY REIGNS. What worries? That puzzling piece of graffiti wasn't what he sought. He found another. YOU MUST CONDUCT THE RITE THROUGH CLOUDED TIMES. What was the rite? No one really knew for sure. It wasn't called a mystery religion for nothing. What clouded times? The barbarians at the gates? The followers of Mithras under attack? Only the dead writer knew. What he was looking for must be farther on. He moved forward along the walls.

RECEIVE THE INCENSE-BURNING LIONS, O HOLY FATHER, THROUGH WHOM WE OFFER INCENSE, THROUGH WHOM WE ARE CONSUMED. When he first encountered these words in graduate school, he thought of Christian saints, like Saint John of the Cross, who claimed to be consumed by the fire of divine love. No one knew whether the writer of the verse had the same feeling. All the living knew was that the Lion grade had something to do with fire. Was it a purification ritual before moving up to the rank of Perses . . . the Persian? No certain answer existed but all the more reason why scholars like him could write tomes without fear of contradiction.

He hurried farther from the custodian's stare. He had to stay away before his breath or glassy eyes betrayed him. He had to keep his pal Jack a secret. Out of the custodian's sight, he spotted what he came for. AND YOU SAVED US AFTER HAVING SHED THE ETERNAL BLOOD. Some said this inscription proved Mithras was a savior god like Christ. Others even saw this as another indication of a Christianity infused by Mithraic belief. His forthcoming article would claim a different meaning. It meant the bull's blood, not the blood of Mithras, saved mankind. Mithras never shed blood in atonement for the sins of mankind. The typical mithraeum depicted wheat and grapes flowing from either the blood of the bull or the bull's tail, gifts to mankind from its death. Maybe his more orthodox interpretation would help get the Congregation for the Doctrine of the Faith off his back.

Fisher scuttled away as he heard the custodian's steps come closer. Trying to settle himself, he focused on the mural of Mithras slaying the bull, what scholars called the *tauroctony*, the mystical and mysterious icon of Mithraic ritual. An artistic sunbeam shone from the top left onto Mithras in his starry cloak as he stabbed the bull to death. A dog and a snake leaped up to lick the bull's blood while a scorpion clawed the bull's testicles. A miniature pictograph showed Helios the sun god kneeling to Mithras while in another pictograph Helios and Mithras shook hands.

"Can I have some?" Fisher startled to hear the words behind him. He turned. The custodian stared at him. His mind went blank with panic.

"I said . . . Can I have some?"

"Some what?"

"The holy water, of course. I want some for my wife."

"It's for . . . my friend . . . He's sick . . . very sick. He needs it . . . for his cure."

The custodian grunted acquiescence and walked back to his station.

Fisher hung his head. What have I become?

***

Returning to the upper world, Fisher encountered people sitting in pain on the steps of the church or lying dead on the pavement. Others stumbled and pushed through the doors of Santa Prisca like disoriented bumblebees in their frenzy to get out. Moving unsteadily toward the entrance to help out, he felt the sting of a bleach-like smell bite its way through his nose and mouth. Wisps of a greenish haze drifted out the doors, flung wide open. With tearing eyes and congested lungs, he retreated from the church to the street.

Fits of coughing broke out all around. Hugging herself with blistered arms, a woman sat on the pavement and retched into the street. The high-pitched hysteria of approaching sirens grew louder. Two ambulances and a police cruiser were already parked near a garden at the side of the church. Inside the garden, he found blue-suited paramedics attending persons suffering from breathing problems. He spotted Nicole sitting on a garden bench. A paramedic administered oxygen to her. The paramedic removed the oxygen mask. "Thank God, Nicole," Fisher said. "You're alive."

She rubbed her eyes. "It was terrible."

"What happened?" Fisher held her hand.

"Two men came onto the altar before Mass . . . deacons? Altar boys? I don't know."

She gasped. The paramedic shot her more oxygen and suggested she not speak.

"A yellowish-orange mask, helmets with spokes—like rays from the sun, sticking out . . . a tube running into the neck of the surplice. They put something into the incense burners. They swung the burners back and forth . . . strange chanting. Dirty, green mist came out . . . people sick and . . ."

Her head rocked in spasms of coughing. She stopped. Paramedics took her away to a nearby hospital for observation.

As the professor watched the ambulance leave and prepared to reach into the satchel for advice from Jack Daniels, he felt a tap on his shoulder. Commissario Marco Leone.

"What happened to Nicole?" Fisher asked.

"Another terrorist attack. We think chlorine gas."

"It burned my nose." Fisher jammed on sunglasses to thwart Leone from detecting Jack in his eyes. "She said something strange." He watched a victim being carried away on a stretcher. "About two men on the altar. They wore helmets, with tubing, resembling the sun."

"The poor woman is in shock." Leone brushed away a fly. "Her emotions distorted her perception."

"Wait a minute." Fisher ran his hand over his face. "I saw a mural of Helios or Sol, as the Romans called him, in the mithraeum below the church. The sun god in the mural had a yellow-orange complexion, eyes uplifted to the sky, and rays shooting out from the head."

"Just coincidence."

"I wish I had the certainty you did."

Leone took two Perugina hard-mint candies from his pocket.

"Why? You academics thrive on uncertainty."

He offered one to Fisher.

Fisher wondered if Leone had detected alcohol on his breath. He plopped the mint into his mouth.

"By the way," Fisher said, desperate to turn the conversation away from himself, "have you turned up anything on the San Clemente bombing?"

"Yesterday my men found an untraceable burner cell phone in a warehouse, not far from San Clemente, where the perpetrators dumped the corpse. In place of the corpse, they substituted explosives in the closed casket before the service began." The commissario's face looked puzzled. "On the cell, someone calling himself the Pater Patrum, Father of Fathers in Latin, left a message: 'Take care the explosion does not damage the mithraeum under the church.'"

"That phrase referred to the highest post in the Mithraic mystery cult."

"Still trying to sell me a Mithras connection?"

"Look, Commissario, I'm not trying to sell anything." He pointed to the church behind him. "Two churches, this and San Clemente, both attacked and both built over mithraeums. An anonymous Pater Patrum doesn't want the mithraeum harmed." Fisher placed an arm on his hip. "And you're telling me there's no connection?"

"If one swallow doesn't make a spring, then neither do two."

"How about a third swallow?" His friend Jack told him it was time to stand up for himself. The professor ripped off his sunglasses and fixed eyes on the commissario. "The numbers three, six, five on Abramo

Basso's forehead and also in the Ardeatine Caves where they discovered a new mithraeum . . . I figured out the meaning of the numbers."

"Don't stop now."

"Those numbers are an ancient code for the name of Mithras. I found the same numbers in the Villa of the Papyri under a mural containing Mithras."

"You're also going to suggest the bull's blood in the Ardeatine Caves is another connection to the ancient cult of Rome."

"What do you think?" The professor smiled. "The facts speak for themselves."

"You're invited to my office." Leone threw up his hands. "Who knows? Maybe you can convert me . . . but bring more facts."

CHAPTER THIRTY-SEVEN

"I wasn't hallucinating." Nicole Garvey clutched the art book to her chest in the battleship-gray office of Commissario Leone. "I saw them enter the sanctuary with masks just like this." She opened the book and tapped a photograph. The picture depicted Sol the sun god in the mithraeum under Santa Prisca.

"Professor Fisher influenced you. He showed you this after the gas attack."

"I do my own thinking."

Her red hair flared like his mother's had when she was young.

"What about the power of suggestion in traumatic situations? A crime victim often assumes the perpetrator must be one of the suspects in police mug shots."

"I know what I saw."

Like Saint Prisca, who would not renounce Christianity, even though reportedly imprisoned, whipped, starved, set afire, doused with boiling fat, set before uninterested lions, and finally beheaded out of exasperation, this woman was stubborn.

Isn't that what they said about him behind his back?

The flashing blinker on his desk phone indicated an incoming call. He picked up the receiver. "Commissario Leone, we found a mask in a dump site . . . just like the one she described, the sun god . . . and two pressurized cylinders disguised as incense burners." He hung up the phone.

"If you consider me a hysterical female, let me know." She rose partway as if to leave her chair. "I'd be happy to go."

"Please, Dr. Garvey." He waved the palms of his hands toward the floor. "Calm yourself. Patience."

"I only came because Professor Fisher requested I meet him here." She sat down. "For the Mithras briefing he set up with you."

"You were right, Dr. Garvey. My men found the gas cylinders and one of the masks . . . like you described to Professor Fisher." Though he disliked being wrong, he liked her spunk even more. "Facts are facts."

"Where's Professor Fisher?"

"Late."

Heedless of past admonitions to knock before entering, Leone's secretary burst in to report the professor had just arrived. The way Garvey looked at Fisher when the secretary showed him into the office did not escape the commissario's eyes. Was something going on between them?

The professor set up the laptop for his PowerPoint presentation on Mithraism. Leone felt an impulse to protect Garvey from Fisher. From what, he did not know. As though she were his daughter. Women with broken wings touched him.

"The followers of Mithras," Fisher started, "were organized into small congregations. Equality prevailed inside the mithraeum, whether a slave or senator. Only religious ranking made a difference."

"Except for women," Garvey said. "They shut out women."

"Excluding half the population," Fisher said, "helps explain why Christianity survived and Mithraism did not."

He fiddled with his defiant laptop.

"The similarities to Christianity have intrigued scholars, including Dr. Martin Luther King, who did a theological paper on the similarities. The Mithraists had ritual meals, a form of baptism, seven stages of spiritual growth, ethical principles, and a savior who mediated between divinity and humanity before ascending into the heavens. The belief in the struggle between good and evil no doubt appealed to the many soldiers who joined."

"That's why the good Cardinal Furbone fears the Callinicus letter." Leone pushed the papers on his desk to one side so the professor would have more room for his laptop. "He's afraid Mithraism undermines Christian belief."

"So did some early Church fathers, like Tertullian and Justin Martyr." Fisher's laptop started percolating signs of life. "They felt threatened enough to claim the devil invented similarities so that when Christianity arrived, the faithful would be deceived."

"In fairness," Garvey said, "no one really knows for certain who, if anyone, copied from whom. Every religious movement, whether Buddhism or Christianity, has to speak in the symbolic language of the culture it's trying to convert."

His technological tussles rewarded, Fisher opened the PowerPoint slideshow illustrating the Mithras cult in an order of dramatic perfection he had honed over years of teaching. He skipped over the less relevant slides of how initiates might have marked their foreheads.

"Behold the seven grades of spiritual development in the cult of Mithras."

At his introduction, the laptop blinked and sputtered as though it were about to expire, but then the monitor revived with a healthy glow.

Corax = Raven
Nymphus = Bridegroom
Miles = Soldier
Leo = Lion
Perseus = Persian
Heliodromus = Courier of the Sun
Pater = Father
Pater Patrum = "The chief of the fathers, a sort of pope, who always lived in Rome"—Catholic Encyclopedia

"Seven?" Garvey asked. "Like the seven sacraments you Catholics have?"

"Some see a connection." Fisher adjusted the monitor image. "Others say the seven stages correspond to seven heavenly gates souls passed through to reach the highest heaven."

"The men who gassed me at Santa Prisca. They could have represented Heliodromus, the courier of the sun god."

"And don't forget the shooter on the motorcycle who attacked us at Cindy's wedding," Fisher said. "He wore a veil over his face like this." He clicked his way to slides showing an image of the Nymphus.

"Some think the Nymphus rank symbolized the love of Mithras, the way a bride loves her husband, or the way Catholic nuns were said to be brides of Christ. Or maybe the veil just means that until the veil of the flesh is lifted, no one can see the truth."

"The veil of a bride? Doesn't make sense to me." Garvey shook her head. "The Nymphus had to be a male, a bridegroom, not a female. Mithraism was a fraternity, no women allowed."

"Good point." Fisher rubbed his chin with thumb and finger. "That's why it's a mystery religion," he joked. "We have few answers."

"And my lion-masked attacker on the road to Amalfi, are you saying—"

Leone's secretary interrupted his statement as she doddered into his office again without knocking. Stared at, she justified her intrusion with welcome news. The vet had called. Mondocane only suffered from an ear infection, nothing more serious.

She atoned for her disruption by volunteering to pick up Mondocane from the vet and reminding the commissario to take his medication before she closed the door on her way out. Leone forgave his office mother, whose good heart compensated for her more than occasional lack of discretion.

"Are you saying"—Leone downed a hydrocortisone pill with water for his Addison's—"that the lion mask of my attacker represented the Leo rank on your chart?"

"Possibly," Fisher replied. "A twisted version of Mithraic symbolism."

"And you'd have me further believe the raven-masked abductors of Don Perugino also flaunted the disguise of Corax, the Raven rank."

"Worth considering . . . unless you have a better theory." Fisher played other slides showing archaeological images of the Raven rank. "This rank probably symbolized the death of an initiate's prior life. Going back to ancient Persia where some say the cult originated, the custom was to place dead bodies on funeral towers so ravens could eat them and—"

"Please, Professor Fisher." The commissario's face grew pained. "I just had lunch . . . I get the idea." He checked the time on his cell phone. "Fourteen minutes after two. I must leave in a few minutes." He slid the current issue of *Corriere della Sera* across the desk to Garvey and Fisher. "It says here the Egyptian Phoenix plans to protest around the obelisk at the Palazzo Chigi. The prime minister fears they will storm his residence in the palazzo." He tapped his middle finger on the desk. "Anything else?"

"One other thing." Fisher turned off the presentation. "On what day, Commissario, was Father Basso murdered in the Ardeatine Caves mausoleum?"

"December twenty-fifth, Christmas Day . . . but what does that have to do with anything?"

"Whose birthday do we celebrate?"

"Please, Professor Fisher." Leone folded his hands as though in prayer and moved them up and down. "Just get on with it."

"Pardon me, Commissario." Fisher looked hurt. "I'll keep it short. The Romans celebrated the birthday of Sol Invictus—the Unconquered Sun—on December twenty-fifth, the same day we celebrate the birth of Jesus Christ. Sunday was also a holy day for both belief systems."

"What does this have to do with Mithraism?"

"Sculptures," Fisher said, "show Mithras and Sol Invictus dining together on a table draped with bull hide. Over time, Mithras and Sol merged into one deity. The birthday of Sol became that of Mithras as well."

"And the first Christians," Garvey said, "picked December twenty-fifth for the day of Christ's birth to coincide with the pagan festival."

"True." Fisher put away his laptop. "The pagan intelligentsia of the time had moved toward a belief in one god."

"Class is about to end, Professor." Leone looked at the sky out his window and put on his black leather trench coat. It was time to meet with Shlomo, his unruly informant, working undercover. "I have to leave. What's your point?"

"Once Christianity became the state religion, archaeological evidence indicates mithraeums were ransacked and destroyed. The era of live and let live had ended. Christians built churches over mithraeums. The worm turned, and the Church was now on top."

"In retaliation," Garvey said, "the pagan Egyptians of Alexandria hanged the city's bishop for building a Christian church on top of a mithraeum."

"You're telling me this is historical payback?" The commissario put on a gray fedora. "Give me a break."

"Face it. Somebody doesn't like churches built over mithraeums." Fisher followed Leone and Garvey out the door. "According to the media, Questore Malatesta thinks the Egyptian Phoenix bombed San Clemente and Santa Prisca."

"I disagree," Leone said. "The Egyptian Phoenix wants the return of the obelisks, not revenge. We interrogated several leaders of the group yesterday. They claimed an imposter tipster framed them."

"I think we all agree the Egyptians aren't involved." After speaking, Garvey looked at Fisher. He nodded his assent.

"Good. We agree on something at least." Leone closed his office door. "But I don't believe I'll need to chase more disguised loonies."

"I'm not so sure," Fisher said. "I'd also keep an eye on other churches erected over mithraeums."

CHAPTER THIRTY-EIGHT

Riccardo Renaldi knuckled his eyes and blinked until they adjusted to the glare of the noonday sun. They didn't have to blindfold him so hard. The Roman Rinata underling in the car acted not as a comrade but as a guard. He didn't deserve this treatment.

At the guard's directive, Renaldi sat at a picnic table outside a farmhouse made of travertine. A tomato patch flourished on one side, and on the other, wild sunflowers had gone to seed.

Across the table sat Carlos Stroheim, mumbling German through a sanitary mask to an old man picking at his thumb. The old man wheezed, resting one liver-spotted hand on the table and the other on a walker.

Without revealing the stranger's name, Stroheim introduced him as originally from the South Tyrol region and a dear friend of the Pater Patrum. The dear friend recuperated as a houseguest after a bout of pneumonia.

"Use the Italian name," Renaldi said. "The Alto Adige belongs to Italy now."

The mystery man's accented Italian confirmed he came not only from the region bordering Switzerland and Austria, but was an ethnic German with one foot in the grave.

After the nameless introduction, the prefect resumed his conversation with the old man. They purposely cut Renaldi out of the conversation by speaking a language sounding to his ears like barking dogs.

Returning the disrespect instead of acquiescing to it, he poured himself a tumbler of red wine from the carafe on the table and helped himself to the last piece of cheese without their permission. They took him for granted despite all he had done. He poured more wine and yet more. Locked up in their babble, they paid him no attention. The old man laughed so hard at what Stroheim said that he fell into a coughing fit. They had to be talking about him, probably even mocking his height.

He had made an appointment to speak with the Pater Patrum personally. Who was this potato eater cutting into his appointed time? The Chinese had wiped out his father's shoemaking business with their cutthroat competition. He'd had it up to here with these foreigners.

"Tell me this guy's name." Renaldi banged the empty tumbler on the table. "And speak Italian."

"Otto. And he prefers German." Stroheim scrubbed his cracked, sore, red hands with antiseptic.

"Screw him. He's supposed to be Italian." He reached for the carafe, but it was empty. "What's his family name? You gave him my full name."

"It's not important."

"It is to me." Renaldi stood up. "I'm important." He collapsed back down.

"Of course you are," Stroheim said, moving the wine carafe back to his side of the table. "Yesterday the Pater Patrum said your initiation was just around the corner."

"Really?" A tight smile flickered on Renaldi's face.

Maybe he would be somebody after all.

"Really. He has great things in store for you."

"Then I deserve to report directly to the Pater Patrum . . . without going through you or Lucio Piso."

"I promise to look into it."

"Let's shake on it." Renaldi held out his hand.

"Sorry." Stroheim shrank away. "Germs. I have enough concerns with Otto."

"Give me the exact date of my initiation."

"Not now. I have to take care of Otto. I promise I'll—"

"I demand to see the Pater Patrum now."

"Something's come up. You have to wait."

"I want to know his identity."

"What you're asking compromises operations."

"You know his identity."

"I'm in the inner circle." Stroheim stood up. "Let's talk later when the wine's not talking."

"Don't patronize me." Renaldi grabbed for the prefect's throat across the table. His arms wouldn't reach.

They're laughing at me.

"I'll see the Pater Patrum on my own. I'll show you." Renaldi tore across the yard toward the front door of the farmhouse into the open arms of two guards.

When he awoke, bouncing along blindfolded with a headache and a bump on his head, he had no idea where the car was taking him. After some time, the driver stopped the vehicle. His Roma Rinata handlers removed his blindfold and dumped him in front of his apartment building in Rome before driving off. Lying abandoned in the gutter, he vowed revenge.

CHAPTER THIRTY-NINE

At 3:30 a.m. on Good Friday morning, not far from the Corso Italia in the town of Sorrento, Cardinal Gustavo Furbone, the local boy made good, sat alone on a purple-cushioned cathedral chair. Fighting sleep, he waited by the curb in the reserved area cordoned off with velvet ropes and stanchions from the press of common people. Chopin's Funeral March op. 35, rose dirgelike in the distance as the White Procession began its journey on its way past the area reserved for dignitaries. Nodding off and then snorting himself awake, the cardinal heard the slow and steady beat of the lugubrious rhythm come closer. They would meet soon.

Brandishing torches, the devotees in white-hooded robes with eye slits turned the corner at the far end of the street and stepped like zombies toward him in slow-motion cadence.

"What's this?" asked a pink-haired punk teen in a USA tank top up against the velvet ropes of the reserved area. "The Ku Klux Klan?"

The ring in her navel was too much for the cardinal. "Be quiet," he ordered. "Have you no shame?"

The procession leader carried a wooden cross over his shoulder past the reserved area. He stopped to welcome the town's guest of honor in a voice muffled by his hooded face. It had taken far longer than he deserved, but at last the town recognized the cardinal's importance, even if only the trivial title of honorary chairperson for Holy Week activities.

The procession leader was not the one he had come to meet. They had been young men when they left Sorrento to make their fortunes. What did he look like now? He was somewhere in the long procession.

Down the street came a marcher with the hammer and nails commemorating the Crucifixion. He walked past the cardinal. Then came another with the water bowl and towel recalling the washing of hands by Pontius Pilate. Neither was the awaited one.

Had he taken fright and not come as agreed?

The next bearer of a Passion symbol had the appearance of a diminutive ghost swathed in a white-hooded robe with eye slits. Could it be? This bantam ghost jangled a sack representing the thirty pieces of silver paid to Judas for his betrayal. The Jesus betrayer incognito walked over to the reserved area. Beating his chest with his fist in simulated atonement, the Judas figure fell to his knees before the cardinal's chair for a blessing.

That action signaled he had arrived.

"Why, Riccardo, did you insist on meeting at this ungodly hour?" The cardinal lowered his head and voice. "Still playing games of cloak-and-dagger, just like when we were boys in Sorrento."

"I fear for my life." Riccardo Renaldi looked up and down the street. "If Piso finds out."

"Come, come. He's simply a wealthy bureaucrat now. Not an executioner."

"That's what you think. He represents forces."

The cardinal sighed. "Let's get to the point." He leaned forward in his cathedral chair over Renaldi's bowed head as though hearing a confession. "I agree to retain you on your terms. Can you do your part of reporting what they find under the trapdoor?"

"Don't underestimate me like the others." The hooded face looked into the cardinal's. "I have my sources. If you want, I can steal or destroy scrolls they find."

"Steal? Destroy?" The cardinal made the sign of the cross over Renaldi's head. "I'm simply protecting Holy Mother Church from further scandal. The dangerous text of the Callinicus letter already circulates among the public."

"What lives by history dies by history."

"Spare me your epigrams." The cardinal placed his hand on Renaldi's head in the guise of a blessing. "Now go."

"What about the original of the Callinicus letter?"

"Let's wait until Piso gives it back to Fisher for storage in the Naples museum."

"Why? You think I can't outwit Piso?"

"The charred scrolls are already at the Naples museum. Once the Callinicus scroll arrives, we can take care of them all together." The cardinal lowered his voice. "Certain arrangements have been made."

"Don't question my abilities again." Renaldi rose to his feet. "That person you hired to retrieve the Festus document botched the job. I wouldn't have failed you. Who was it?"

"Lucio Piso."

"Piso?" The Judas figure laughed, causing spectators to eye him with disapproval. "That cunning bastard." He brought his laughter under control. "My eyes are open now."

"Watch your tongue," the cardinal ordered. "This is Good Friday morning." He flipped his hand toward the procession. "Now get back at once before suspicion arises."

Renaldi rejoined the procession winding down the street just as a statue of the sorrowful Madonna standing on a flower-bedecked litter hoisted on the shoulders of four hooded acolytes lurched around the corner up the street in search of her son. Transfixed by her gaze, the cardinal covered his eyes with his hands and pulled his earlobe.

Through the mist of incense, his own mother's coal-black eyes pierced him. Those eyes. She was coming for him.

In another bout of deranged fury, his mother staggered toward him with her fists. The yet-to-be cardinal pleaded and put up a child's arms in defense, but her face remained impenetrably depressed with lifeless black eyes. She pulled his ears and bashed him unconscious for being the seed of the monster male who had deserted her while pregnant.

The Madonna passed him by.

He needed more than sleep. He need to get a grip before things fell apart.

CHAPTER FORTY

Above Cardinal Gustavo Furbone's desk hung a painting of Jesus directing his disciples to let the little children come unto him. As though rendered speechless by a stroke, the cardinal looked pained.

Before the cardinal's stare, Lucio Piso squirmed in his seat. Did the summons to appear mean Furbone now recognized the man whose boyhood he had stolen? Uneasy with the silence, Piso pointed to the painting. "Yours?"

"Just an inferior piece of art I inherited with the office."

"If memory serves . . . it's better for a person to drown with a mill-stone around the neck than to corrupt a child."

"Matthew eighteen, verse six. My sentiments exactly."

"I am so glad we both agree, Your Eminence."

Leaning forward in his chair, the cardinal squeezed lemon juice into his tea.

Piso still felt the squeeze of the hand on his buttocks as though it were happening now. Over fifty years ago he had watched this degenerate take to his afternoon habit of tea drinking right after sexually abusing little boy Lucio. His hands yearned to squeeze the cardinal's neck. *It is a mortal sin to disobey me,* the degenerate had said, puffed up with the overpowering authority of his priestly office.

"Wouldn't you like some tea?" The cardinal reached for the teapot.

"Forgive me, Your Eminence. What did you say?"

"Tea?"

"No, thank you." His mouth ran dry, and his voice grew hoarse. "It upsets my stomach."

"I know you . . ."

He recognizes me. He is on guard. My plan is undone.

". . . think my assignment to the Congregation for the Doctrine of the Faith is permanent. Not so." The cardinal sipped his tea. "I have higher aspirations."

"Of course." Fortune had not deserted him after all. "I should think pope someday."

"You recognize my ability already, do you?"

"I can think of no one more suited."

"God bless you, my son." The cardinal put down his cup. "I called you here to discuss . . . a private matter."

The Fates had lifted him up only to dash him down into despair.

"Please do not take offense, Signor Piso." The cardinal dabbed his lips with a linen napkin. "I appreciate what you have done . . . but I no longer wish to retain you to recover the Festus letter."

The superintendent of excavations shivered in the exaltation of his deliverance. The ancestral genius within him had saved the day. Like a great general way up on a hill where no enemy could touch him, he foresaw victory in the fog-receding future.

"I fully understand. My best efforts have been unavailing."

"You're not offended?" The cardinal dabbed his forehead with the napkin. "I worried you would be. I prefer to remain friends."

"Offended? Not at all. You have relieved me of a great burden."

"As a token of friendship, you may keep the retainer."

"And the Mithras statue with the cross in the forehead? I must have it."

"With pleasure. Good riddance to the devil's delusion."

While the cardinal called to postpone a tailor's visit to measure his own girth for vestments, Piso checked a text message from Commissario Marco Leone of the Polizia di Stato in Rome. When he arrived at the Villa of the Papyri, the commissario wanted the superintendent of Herculaneum excavations to make Riccardo Renaldi available for questioning about the missing Festus letter.

What to be done with Renaldi now a thorn in his side?

The cardinal hung up the phone.

"I am concerned about your involvement in something else."

"Oh?" Was he but a plaything of the gods?

"My source says your archaeologists have discovered a trapdoor in the Villa of the Papyri."

"Your source?"

"And they think more scrolls lie beneath."

"Who?"

"You must revoke permission for their entry into the villa."

"I must?" The insolence. "They already entered this morning."

"Then have someone watch them. Take what they find and alert me."

"Who might that be, pray tell? Riccardo Renaldi perhaps."

"Please." The cardinal tugged at his ear. "I ask a favor, as one friend to another."

"I must know the source's identity."

"I shouldn't tell you."

"No, you should not." Piso put his hands on the cardinal's desk. "If you want it to get out about your orgy in—"

"How did—" Furbone staggered to his feet. "Did you know?"

"I make it my business to know."

"It is Renaldi."

"Rest easy now, my good cardinal. I see no need to spread gossip about you."

"You won't hold it against him, will you?"

"Of course not. He is my security chief. How could I be secure without him?" Piso made an exaggerated sign of the cross. "We are on the same side. That of Mother Church."

"God loves a forgiving heart, my son." The cardinal splayed his hands across the bulge of his belly and sighed. "One minor point. I understand you will store the original of the Callinicus scroll in the Naples Archaeological Museum."

"Renaldi again?"

The cardinal nodded.

"My devoted Renaldi is correct. I deliver it this week to be kept with the charred scrolls found in the Latin library." The cardinal wanted something. "What would you have me do?"

"Nothing at all." The cardinal's face turned serious. He placed his hands on the desk and leaned in toward Piso. "I approve of keeping them all in one place . . . including any new finds."

"What a good memory my security chief has." Piso stroked his chin. "Are you sure you don't want me to do something for you . . . as one friend to another?"

"Just curious." The cardinal tugged his ear. "But . . . as one friend to another . . . I was disappointed your office released the Callinicus translation before consulting me." He stood up from his desk. "It will disturb the faithful."

"Have faith, Your Eminence. It's only an unofficial translation of an unauthenticated scroll." Piso followed the cardinal's lead in standing up as the meeting drew to an end. "Would you like a Vatican expert to verify the translation?"

"That would be premature."

"Why?" What was the whited sepulcher up to?

"Things happen." The cardinal smiled. "Your audience is over."

The cardinal held out his ringed finger to end further discussion.

The inner Pater Patrum watched Lucio, the puppet boy, kiss the ring.

After leaving the office, Piso vomited in the nearest toilet.

CHAPTER FORTY-ONE

A gray-ponytailed classics expert in a rumpled suit pored over the text of the Callinicus letter for the last time in a seedy suburb outside Naples with the shades down. A victim of incipient dementia aggravated by accumulated grievances, the ex-professor had committed the indiscretion of assaulting his university dean during a faculty meeting.

Forced into retirement, he shook his head free of the academic nightmare. His work this evening required complete attention to detail. Writing lewd Latin phrases for greeting cards would not keep his stomach satisfied if he failed to please his anonymous client operating through a straw man.

If he got this right, he would have enough money to sue the university and then some left over for a vacation in Greece. How those arrogant assholes at the university would envy his access to an original scroll . . . if they only knew. When he thought it safe, he might even break the secrecy pledge to his anonymous client. The world should know of the Callinicus letter and his linguistic prowess.

He closed his eyes and took three yoga breaths to steady his head and hand. The ex-professor absorbed every squiggle of the Callinicus lettering as though it were a familiar musical score running through his head. He could even see the writing style of Callinicus in his sleep. He prepared to forge the handwriting of the long-dead Roman.

He first examined the Latin translation of the Italian text he had been given and then the clean sheet of papyrus. Who were these guys? What they said was counterfeit papyrus looked like the real thing.

A maestro of dead languages, he picked up the reed pen like a conductor's baton before transcribing his Latin translation onto the papyrus. Under bright light, he hunched over and scratched the first of many Latin letters in impeccable homage to Roman calligraphy of the first century AD.

Near midnight, he yawned and stretched. He put on a torn over-coat and headed into the night with his Latin masterpiece. At the meeting place, he handed it over and received in payment strangulation by garrote.

The hit man answered his cell. "Do you have it?" he heard.

"I do, Pater Patrum."

"Enter unseen at night into the villa."

"Should I tell Renaldi?"

"Not a word to him. Only you and I must know."

After the police found the hit man dead, only the Pater Patrum knew.

CHAPTER FORTY-TWO

Nicole Garvey's day looked promising. Lucio Piso had kept his promise to return the original of the Callinicus letter to the National
Archaeological Museum in Naples for safe-keeping and further work
along with the carbonized scrolls. The Vesuvius Observatory had
downgraded the earthquake alarm to a cautionary level. As if in con-
firmation, the sun emerged behind white clouds against a pale blue
sky. The wind shrank to a warm breeze on her face. The guard dogs
drowsed unperturbed near the entrance. And, best of all, Lucio Piso
had given Will and her permission to explore under the trapdoor of the
scriptorium without the presence of Riccardo Renaldi. All that nagged
in the back of her mind was the public statement of a Neapolitan volcanologist who claimed his controversial radon-gas detector indicated
elevated danger remained.

"Do you think they'll sue him?" she asked Will.

"The local prosecutor says he'll investigate the volcanologist for
unnecessarily arousing public alarm." Will checked over his gear. "The
National Institute of Geophysics says the radon-detector gizmo is
unreliable."

"Maybe the whole country's about to blow." She showed Will a
newspaper. "Even Rome has temblor problems again."

"Just coincidence." Will held her arm. "Look, Nicole . . . We don't
have to descend today."

"And not explore what's under the trapdoor? Not on your life." She retied a bootlace. "We'll finish up in no time and get out even if Vesuvius blows."

She tried forgetting that the Romans in AD 79 thought the same way.

"My thoughts exactly." Fisher picked up the front end of the collapsible extension ladder. "We should go before Piso changes his mind."

She held up the rear of the ladder while Fisher held the front and led the way to the shaft in the villa. Before starting their descent into the underworld, she stuck out her tongue at the security camera Renaldi had installed at the entrance to the shaft. To her delight, Wesley Bemis was out of the way at the museum in Naples, where he worked with his fancy technology on the treasure trove of burnt scrolls they had found in the Latin library. "What happens when the security camera tips off Renaldi we weren't with Bemis in Naples?"

"Not to fear." Fisher motioned for her to crouch as they angled the ladder through the tunnel. "Piso stood up for us against Renaldi. The security chief is on thin ice with his boss."

Something about Piso didn't inspire the same trust in her. Smitten with the wacky notion he was related to the ancient Piso clan, the superintendent wanted the villa explored as badly as they did. Yet, his way of referring to the villa as "my villa" in the literal sense creeped her out. She had met his type before. He manipulated people like arm's-length pawns in some private game to which he alone knew the rules.

They passed through the Latin library with the mural of Mithras and his controversial companion into the scriptorium where Fisher had discovered the intertwined names of Mithras and Christ.

They walked over to the trapdoor of the scriptorium and pulled it open. She poked her flashlight into the abyss. The rotted-out form of what once was a ladder lay on the dark floor below. They lowered the extension ladder through the opening until it steadied itself on the floor.

About to descend, Garvey said, "Did you hear something?"

"I wouldn't worry. Just a few rocks falling or some plaster collapsing." He grinned, poking his forefinger at the floor above. "Fixer-uppers like this need a lot of rehab."

His reassurance made her laugh. Where were guys like this when she was growing up? Not hearing anything more, Garvey stepped down the ladder.

"I'm leaving my lamp up here," Fisher said, following her down. "Too much other stuff to carry."

She thudded onto the floor with her feet and looked up. Her helmet light caught him straining under the backpack, taking one tentative step down at a time. Only the sound of water dripping somewhere broke the tomb-like silence. He started to fall but braced himself on the ladder. The clamminess of the chamber tightened its grip around her throat and chest.

Their underground world turned to light as her portable lamp powered on and absorbed the feebleness of their LED headlamps.

A mithraeum came into view.

Raised platforms on either side of a central aisle ended under the trapdoor. Their lamplight skittered along the faded red wall on their left, revealing algae blossoms sprouting from cracks.

The ground murmured under her feet like a truck passing through and stopped as soon as she became aware of it. "Let's finish up as quickly as we can . . . and get out of here."

"Nothing unusual." The crack in his voice betrayed a diminishing confidence. "But I agree. Better to be safe than you know what."

Under the semicircular apse at the front of the mithraeum stood a magnificent altar of rose marble nearly two meters across and incised with the iconography of bulls and fish. Flush against the curved wall of the apse, a bench of white marble veined in red glittered in the glare of their lamplight. Unlike the plain stone platforms, this bench must have been reserved for dignitaries.

On the wall above the bench, a fresco of Phrygian-capped Mithras wielding a sword on top of a bucking bull stared at them. The washed-out blue of buckled plaster represented the heavens. The golden color of the sun, dulled with age, shot out rays in all directions. One ray longer than the others descended onto the sword-wielding arm of Mithras.

A scroll wrapped in linen poked out of a terra-cotta jar placed along the altar.

Will scrutinized the title in Latin on a red tag attached to the scroll. He translated it as something called the Unity Report. While he snapped a photo of the apse wall, she painstakingly deposited the Unity Report inside a polyester insulated carrier.

Garvey felt a tap on her shoulder.

"Didn't mean to scare you . . . Do you know what this discovery means?" he asked, grinning with his back to the Mithras mural on the wall over the marble bench.

Before she could reply, Fisher's eyes opened wide. He looked gape-jawed over her right shoulder.

Was something wrong?

She turned to face the trapdoor entrance to the mithraeum.

Renaldi pointed a pistol at them. "Sorry to interrupt you two love-birds." He snatched the carrier with the Unity Report off the altar. "Hands up."

"Piso said we didn't need your permission to enter." She refused to raise her hands. She changed her mind when he pointed the pistol in her direction.

"To hell with Piso." Renaldi looked at the gun and then at her. "Ignore my commands again, and I'll shoot you."

"You've gone too far this time," Will said, his hand raised. "Stealing a cultural asset."

"Not as far as I'm going to go, thanks to this." He held up the Unity Report in the carrier.

A rumble rolled through the mithraeum like the stirring of a giant trapped in the earth. Plaster fell. The floor shook as if on rollers. She and Will clung together.

They were all doomed.

Renaldi fell. The carrier dropped to one side and the pistol to the other. Fisher and Renaldi scrambled for the gun. Seizing it first, Renaldi fired a shot, just missing Fisher's head. He ordered the pair down on their stomachs with hands on their heads.

Renaldi scrambled up the ladder without the scroll carrier.

Almost at the top, he swayed on the ladder as another tremor struck.

He grabbed the edge of the trapdoor opening with both hands.

The extension ladder fell onto the mithraeum floor.

Dangling, he hoisted himself through the opening and slammed the trapdoor shut.

CHAPTER FORTY-THREE

Seeing a lamp left nearby, Marco Leone shot a flashlight beam down the open trapdoor. Through the opening, a modern extension ladder lay on top of ancient wood. "Are you down there, Renaldi?"

No answer.

"Professor Fisher, Dr. Garvey, anybody . . . are you—"

"Thank God it's you, Commissario." Fisher stumbled into the illuminating arc of the flashlight. He looked up, blinking, before shielding his eyes from the light with his hands.

"Where's Renaldi?" Leone diverted the flashlight from Fisher's eyes. "I had an appointment to question him. But he's hiding from me."

"When you find him," Garvey said, coming out of the shadows, "ask about the gun he pulled on us."

"Gun?"

"Hold your questions, please, until we get out of here." She raised the extension ladder and scrambled up first.

Leone helped her through the opening. "Where did he go?"

She brushed off her jeans. "Wish we knew. He forgot to tell us."

Sassy as ever, Leone thought.

After Fisher emerged, Leone followed them toward the perimeter gate as they explained Renaldi's attempt to steal the priceless Unity Report. Fisher and Garvey, holding the scroll case, passed through the villa gate. Leone froze just before going through. Renaldi had mounted closed-circuit monitors on either side to spy on anyone entering or leaving.

"What's the matter?" Garvey asked.

Sweeping back and forth in a tight arc, the monitors had already captured images of Garvey and Fisher passing through the gate with the polyester carrier holding the Unity Report. The commissario was too far behind for the limited sweep of the cameras to detect his presence.

Leone fell to the ground and crawled under the electronic eyes until he was beyond their range on the other side.

"What are you doing?" Garvey said, hands on hips. "We have to get away before Renaldi returns."

"We don't know where Renaldi's gone, right?" Leone stopped talking to brush off his pants. With dismay, he looked at the scuffs on his polished Bruno Magli wing-tip shoes. "And we're outnumbered by his men, right?" Their silence confirmed his view. "When they see you two on the monitor with the Unity Report, they'll go after you, not me."

"Reminds me of fishing." The professor looked at the ground. "And we're the bait."

"Give me the scroll." Leone held out his hands. "The security cameras did not see me exit. They only saw Dr. Garvey exit with the scroll. Instead of taking the scroll in my car, I can catch the next Circumvesuviana train to Naples on foot. I'll meet up with Dr. Bemis at the Gabinetto Segreto. You two join me and analyze the scroll in safety while I arrange for police protection."

"Problem." Garvey looked worried. "What if Renaldi spots you boarding at the Ercolano station?"

"Renaldi knows I hate taking trains." He nodded in the direction of the station. "The train station isn't far. If I hurry, I can catch the next one."

"What," Garvey asked, "if Renaldi or his men stop us?"

"Doesn't matter. By then the scroll and I will be gone."

"I'll keep that in mind," Garvey said, "while he's waterboarding us."

On his race to meet the train, Leone dodged tourists and street vendors to arrive winded at the Ercolano station. Huffing and puffing, he flashed his identification in the eyes of the conductor about to blow his departure whistle. The conductor waited until the commissario plunged into the last car of the graffiti-tagged train just before the doors hissed shut.

As the train chugged away, the conductor telephoned the guard on duty at the Villa of the Papyri. "The man Riccardo Renaldi warned about just boarded the train to Naples . . . with some kind of plastic container."

**

The sunlight streaming through a window in the Gabinetto Segreto of the National Archaeological Museum in Naples fell in a band along the white lining of Wesley Bemis's open sleeping bag. The clanging of the malfunctioning air conditioner had disturbed his sleep and that of his grad-student assistant. Refusing to bunk down in the room another night, the assistant had left for accommodations at a nearby hotel. It took a dedicated Latter-day Saint like him to protect the carbonized scrolls around the clock while he coaxed out their secrets.

Fisher and Miss Uppity Woman hadn't called. What hanky-panky were they up to?

He rolled on his daily smile like lipstick. He would need it when he got into it again with the museum director about the temperamental air conditioner. The director was already on his case because of the project's delay in vacating the Gabinetto Segreto. The director had ordered workmen to pile up paint supplies outside the door of the room so that they could begin renovations as soon as the Americans moved out. With a lacquered smile rivaling his own, the director explained the supplies would provide a cover story for the *"Chiuso per Restauro"* sign—Closed for Restoration—on the outside of the door.

Bemis suspected the physical inconvenience and odors of the paint supplies stored outside the door were a not-so-subtle attempt to pressure the Americans out of the Gabinetto Segreto. He would love to leave the rent-free den of debauchery as soon as possible, but aside from a budget now in the red, he was at a critical point in his work. He had to figure out how to free the past locked up in carbonized papyrus sheets bunched like onion layers and as brittle as potato chips.

The burnt scroll on his worktable was no Callinicus letter protected from the molten fury of Mount Vesuvius. No matter how he manipulated his CT scanning equipment, he could not tease the text of the charred scroll onto his computer monitor. The resolution wasn't good enough. Letters written in black ink remained imprisoned in the deeper blackness of the volcano-scorched papyrus. The carbon-based nature of the ink, probably a mixture of soot or charcoal bound with a gluing agent, most likely explained the failure. His equipment only deciphered the iron-based ink more commonly used in the Middle Ages.

He prided himself on Plan B: his multispectral imaging equipment. The upside of the equipment was that the ink type would not pose a problem. Once he found the right waveband on the light spectrum with his revolving disk of filters, the text would appear as if by magic. The downside was that he would need to first unravel the fragile scrolls with chemical peel. Even with the advanced form of chemical peel available, the museum director had to give him additional time to finish.

Someday soon, archaeologists would not have to fuss with opening the delicate scrolls. Synchrotrons the size of football fields, like the one at Argonne National Laboratory outside Chicago, would accelerate particles around a gigantic ring at almost the speed of light to generate X-rays one hundred billion times stronger than his equipment. He could almost see the trapped scroll script read like the morning's newspaper.

The "Hallelujah" chorus ringtone ended his professional analysis. Sleep-deprived, he fumbled for his cell.

Where had his assistant put it?

He followed the sounds of the Mormon Tabernacle Choir behind the statue of Pan copulating with a goat. He put a hand over his eyes and retrieved the cell with the other.

"This is Commissario Leone. I'm coming to see you."

"Speak up. I can barely hear you . . . Why?"

"I'm on a train. Your colleagues gave me a scroll found under the trapdoor."

He awaited the return of Leone's voice from a dead zone.

"Renaldi tried to steal the scroll called the Unity Report with a gun."

"Oh my heck." He put a hand to his forehead. "Where are my colleagues?"

"We're all meeting you at the museum. Did Renaldi contact you?"

"He called. Furious I didn't tell him the whereabouts of Fisher and Garvey."

"Did he ask about me?"

"Said he knew where to find you, Commissario."

"Stay put till I get there. Do not let Renaldi in. He's armed and dangerous."

**

Speeding along the A3 highway, Riccardo Renaldi was not a happy man.

After Leone left the Villa of the Papyri and the tremors stopped, he had hoped to return from his hideout in Sorrento to retake the scroll from the Americans penned under the trapdoor.

Instead, the security guards monitoring the villa gate had called earlier to report. The guard stationed at the surveillance camera recorded Leone entering the villa but not leaving. The security force detained the Americans, who no longer possessed the container. They refused to talk. After noticing the commissario's automobile still parked on the grounds but unable to find him, the guard received a call from the conductor, who identified Leone boarding the train for Naples with a container in his arms.

The container had to hold the scroll.

After the telephone conversation with the guard, Renaldi received on his visor-mounted Bluetooth another call from Cardinal Gustavo Furbone.

"Your voice mail disturbed me. What do you mean the Americans found a new scroll under the trapdoor? You're supposed to prevent that."

"There's been a problem."

"I'm not paying for problems."

"It's under control. Leone is most likely taking it to Naples by train."

"Let me contact Lucio Piso to help you."

"No, no, no . . . I don't need that man's help. I don't need anyone's help."

He couldn't take a chance of losing Leone in the crowded Naples station. He had to do something right now before he failed again. Narrowly avoiding a collision, Renaldi screeched the car to a halt at the train station right before Naples.

"Don't worry, Gustavo. I'm boarding the train at Barra and taking the scroll from Leone."

***

After ending his call to Bemis, Leone imagined himself a soccer player about to break clear and score. He was only a few stops away from the Stazione Centrale in the Piazza Garibaldi of Naples. From there he could cab it to the museum and arrive in no time. He would set the Naples police straight on Renaldi's attempted armed robbery of the cultural treasure he now clutched. Placing the polyester container on the empty seat next to him, he let go his death grip.

A drunk, the only other passenger in the car, opened bloodshot eyes and stared at the container. Leone got up with the scroll box and made his way down the aisle to an empty seat at the very front of the car. The drunk resumed snoring. He wouldn't be a problem. The train whistle blew, its wheels grinding and screeching. The train slowed, approaching the Barra station not far from the main one in Naples. With one hand on the scroll box, the commissario took a deep breath and closed his eyes to relax.

The train jolted to a stop. The rear door of the car whooshed open. Passengers shuffled in behind him. The door whooshed closed. Footsteps padded down the aisle. Someone sat down in the seat behind him. Footsteps continued to the front of the car. On guard, the commissario opened his eyes.

A bearded man faced him at the front of the car, less than a meter away. A purple felt cap in the shape of a cone was perched on his head. He wore an ocher tunic with long sleeves and loose-fitting salmon trousers. A little over a foot long, a sheathed sword dangled from a cincture over his right thigh. Yellow satin footwear curved up at the toes. A black mask concealed his face.

The man offered brochures for a play in Naples based on the *Arabian Nights* tale of Princess Scheherazade, the story of a woman who prevented Shahryar, a Persian king, from killing her by enchanting him with stories lasting a thousand and one nights. He announced he played the role of the Persian king, and anyone attending the play with a brochure would receive a ten percent discount. He bowed, passed out a few brochures, and seated himself in the rear of the car. One never knew what sort of weirdo, con man, or would-be musician one would find on the Circumvesuviana.

"Give me the scroll," Renaldi whispered into Leone's ears from the seat behind. A second later, a pistol barrel pressed against his neck. "And don't make a scene."

"You won't get away with it."

"I'm arresting you for stealing a cultural artifact."

The pistol barrel burrowed into his flesh.

"You're arresting me?"

"Hand it over."

"You can't arrest me. You're suspended."

"Fork it over now, or I shoot."

***

The pounding on the door stopped. Wesley Bemis couldn't make out the voice on the other side. The crackling and popping outside prevented a clear identification. The voice stopped. He wasn't going to reveal his presence, no matter what.

It had to be Renaldi or one of his assistants. Leone had warned that the security chief of the villa was on his way, armed and dangerous. Not that it would have made any difference. Bemis wasn't about to open the door for anyone until the commissario arrived.

What is Renaldi up to?

Sweat leaked out, dampening the two-piece Mormon underwear he refused to shed. The air conditioner must have broken down completely. He gulped down the last bottle of *acqua minerale*, warm as dishwater. The fuzziness in his sleep-deprived head grew worse. He had to get fresh air. Even the door was warm. He felt his head. Warm. He must have a fever. Whoever hid behind the door would have left.

He slid back the dead bolt. The doorknob burned his hand. He wrapped his shirt around the knob.

What's going on?

He opened the door to an inferno rushing in.

***

"Tickets, please." Doing a random check, the conductor barged through the front door of the car. The commissario felt the pistol withdraw from the back of his neck. The train slowed, rocking side to side like an oversized cradle, as they approached the Naples Stazione Centrale. The conductor gave the tickets a distant once-over and hightailed to the front of the train as quickly as he came.

Now or never.

Leone lunged through the glass sliding door left swinging open by the conductor and slammed it shut in Renaldi's face. Nestling the scroll box under his left arm, he barricaded the door with his body and held the door handle closed with his right hand. His hand blanched, aching with the pressure. He yelled for help. Without looking back, the conductor passed through the forward cars toward the front. The only other passenger in the car was a beggar boy standing with an accordion behind Leone.

The train eased into the Naples central station. While his ex-colleague struggled to fling it open, Leone battled to keep the glass door closed. Staring into Renaldi's hate-filled eyes, Leone felt the deft fingers of the boy trying to filch his billfold.

The little bastard.

Renaldi caught the commissario off guard and ripped open the door. Almost falling, Leone grabbed the neck of the beggar boy with one hand and spun him into Renaldi. The accordion crashed to the floor in an explosion of cacophonous chords. Thrown back against the door, Renaldi recovered and stepped forward. He drew a Baikal pistol fitted with a silencer and pointed it at Leone.

Gliding through the open door like an apparition, King Shahryar halted behind Renaldi.

"Give me the box." Renaldi gestured with his fingers. "Or you're dead."

The king drew his sword from his sheath.

"Drop the gun," Leone said, staring at the apparition, "or you'll be the dead one."

"You fool. What do you—"

The king plunged the sword into Renaldi's back. The train came to a full stop. Renaldi slumped to the floor. The exit doors whooshed open onto the passenger platform of the Stazione Centrale.

"Who are you?" Leone asked.

"Take the scroll box and go," the Persian king said, jumping out the open door and boarding a baggage trailer lying in wait. The driver threw a blanket over the king and beeped the trailer out of sight through a horde of passengers scampering away.

Leone hurried out of the station and caught a taxi to the Gabinetto Segreto.

***

His head full of questions and no answers, Leone saw black smoke billowing from the National Archaeological Museum as the taxi pulled up. A fire truck pumped an arc of water into the building. He elbowed through the crowd of gawkers to the entrance, where paramedics wheeled Wesley Bemis out on a stretcher bed. Burns scorched his face almost beyond recognition.

Leone's friend, the inspector on the Naples police force, stood in conversation with the museum director. The inspector broke off his conversation to greet Leone. "So, you're back in Naples. A bachelor like you can't stay away from my wife's cooking, can you?" He hugged Leone.

From him, Leone learned the museum had stored a collection of painting supplies near the Gabinetto Segreto. The Naples police found the suspected arsonist burned to death, apparently trapped by the inferno. A sniffer dog picked up traces of kerosene, the probable accelerant, leading from the suspect's vehicle up through the museum to the Gabinetto Segreto. The police believed they recovered the kerosene can used in the arson. The dead body still clutched the container. Examination revealed a pinhole puncture in the bottom of the can.

That defect had led the sniffer dog from the vehicle to the arson site inside the museum.

"Who did it?" Leone asked.

"We're still checking out the dental work." The inspector raised the visor of his hat with a forefinger. "We found a phone number in his charred wallet. It's for Cardinal Furbone's office. Know him?"

"All too well."

"Now, about your . . . incident . . . on the train. We have some talking to do."

"You heard already?"

"My investigators are at the station." The friend shook his head. "Doesn't look good for you."

"I can explain."

"Really?" The inspector rolled his eyes. "'Oh, a Persian king just came by and saved me.' Sure. Before you explain," the inspector's face turned serious. "Renaldi arrived at the hospital . . . dead."

"And you suspect me of killing him? I know leaving the scene doesn't look good." Leone reached for a nonexistent smoke in his shirt pocket. "Could you give me a cigarette?"

"Gave it up on doctor's orders." The inspector smirked. "Relax, the beggar boy and several other witnesses cleared you. We also found Renaldi's pistol. The crazy pants leaping out of the train and running away is our suspected killer." He nudged Leone's shoulder. "I was just playing you."

"You rotten prankster." Leone nudged back with a grin.

He was free. Now that the Gabinetto Segreto had gone up in flames, he had to find another place to hide the Americans until they could decipher the Unity Report, away from danger.

"What's inside?" The inspector pointed to the container. "Something valuable enough for Renaldi to kill?"

Aside from probable theft of the Festus parchment, Leone explained how his ex-colleague had tried to take control of the discoveries in the Villa of the Papyri and almost killed him for the Unity Report. Renaldi had to be working on behalf of someone willing to pay big money for ancient documents.

"Too bad," the inspector said, "about the original of the Callinicus papyrus."

"What do you mean?"

"It was inside the Gabinetto Segreto with the carbonized scrolls." The officer looked at the museum director. "He says they all went up in smoke."

"Too bad Lucio Piso kept his promise to return the Callinicus papyrus to the museum." Leone grimaced with the determination nothing would happen to the Unity Report. "That's why I need to get this new scroll to the Americans, so they can translate it in safety. Before someone tries to take it." Leone scanned the crowd for likely thieves. "Don't take it from me. You don't need—"

"Don't worry." His officer friend held up a hand. "I'm only an agent on the Naples force, and you're a big-shot commissario from Rome. Besides, I don't need the red tape involved with a cultural artifact. Just take care of it."

"No problem." He patted the scroll box under his arm. "Like my own baby."

"All I need to do is one thing." The inspector sighed. "Find the loony masquerading as a Persian king, take his statement, and give him a medal for saving your life."

"That should be easy." The commissario pulled a playbill from his pocket. "He gave me this. He's the star in the play."

"Unfortunately, my Roman Sherlock Holmes, there's no such theater in Naples."

CHAPTER FORTY-FOUR

Back in Rome, Marco Leone entered the questura with a spring in his step. "Not bad," he answered a colleague concerned about his health.

"Not bad?" The colleague raised an eyebrow. "For you that's like being on top of the world."

"Hush." Leone put a finger to his lips. "The Fates will hear you."

"Lucky for you the actor happened on the scene."

Leone kept his thoughts to himself. The person costumed as a Persian king didn't just happen to be at the right place at the right time. That person ordered him to take the scroll from the train and go. He'd known about the scroll box. The Persian king saved him from being killed, but the lion-masked assassin in Amalfi and the raven assistants tried to kill him. Did two rival bands of costumed terrorists exist? Would he ever get to the bottom of things?

Only in a nightmare did he get to the bottom of something. He was trying to find the depth of a chasm splitting the earth open. As he reached the edge of the abyss, he tumbled in backward with winged demons in raven masks swirling down after him. When he twisted forward in midair to learn what lay at the bottom, he stared into the eyeless sockets of Don Perugino's corpse welcoming him to the underworld with outstretched arms.

Why hasn't Shlomo reported in? Without more information from him, the investigation would stall. He hadn't made contact in weeks. If he had a new money source, probably petty thievery, that might explain the lack of contact. Rumor had it he now scammed tourists outside the Colosseum. The slacker informant needed screws applied to spur motivation.

"The Waltz of the Toreadors" interrupted his thoughts.

Moving past ringing telephones and document-stuffed cabinets, Leone ducked into an alcove to answer his cell.

"The Americans have arrived," said the manager of the Castello of Julius II in Ostia. "I've now paid back the favor, Commissario. Right?"

"Of course."

"I've got my job to think about. If the boss finds out . . ."

"Don't worry. The castle is closed to the public for repairs."

"Who are these Smiths, Jack and Jill, anyway?"

"I told you. They're honeymooners."

"Give me a break. They're like two cold pieces of codfish."

"They're not Latin lovers. So what?"

"I don't like this."

"Who cares what you . . . All right. I'll tell you . . . but keep it a secret."

"On my mother's grave."

Considering it indiscreet to point out his mother was still alive, Leone played upon the manager's love of spy novels. "They're CIA agents using the honeymoon as a cover." His imagination spun into overdrive. "They need a safe house for a few days to analyze documents from Russian governmental archives. Very hush-hush." Now for the finishing touch. "An official commendation awaits you if you do your patriotic duty."

"Thanks for including me in the operation." The voice swelled with pride. "You can count on me to keep mum."

***

Marco Leone snagged a copy of *Il Messaggero* from his secretary's out-stretched hand, in keeping with their morning ritual, on the way to his office. "It's a Brioschi day," she spoke to his back. The code phrase meant the day's news would upset him.

Slamming the office door shut, he collapsed into his chair and saw it smack on the first page—the lurid tale of a suspended police inspector, Riccardo Renaldi, killed in Naples while trying to murder Marco Leone, a police commissario.

The intercom buzzed.

"Commissario—"

"What now?"

"Questore Malatesta on line one. And turn on the RAI News channel."

"Hello?" He pretended he didn't know who was calling. "Who is this?"

"It's me, Questore Malatesta. I want to make it like it never happened."

As the TV screen showed the bloodstains in the Circumvesuviana car where Renaldi died, the unctuous voice-over lamented the "fratricidal frenzy" that had seized the "trouble-plagued" Polizia di Stato in Rome.

Distracted by the TV, Leone asked, "Like what never happened?"

"What Renaldi tried to do to you."

"Never happened? Your godson almost murdered me."

The TV faded to a reporter at the scene in the middle of an interview with the beggar boy who saw a "circus clown" save Commissario Leone.

"You misunderstand. I mean my taking you off the terrorist attacks on the churches." A pause on the line. "You're back on the case. No hard feelings?"

The TV faded to the RAI News anchorman. With ominous music in the background, the TV celebrity thundered about the need to investigate Questore Pietro Malatesta for hiring his godson. Even Italian nepotism had limits.

"What about the Chicago sabbatical I was promised?"

"Restored. No problem."

"Another thing." He had him where he wanted him. "I want additional time in Chicago."

"OK, OK. Just get to the bottom of the terrorism and the Basso murder. Don't forget to look into the Egyptian Phoenix . . . And Marco . . . another thing."

"What?"

"If I go down, your trip to Chicago goes down with me. Ciao."

***

It was going to be one of those days. The commissario's stomach churned. He gulped a Brioschi with water before concentrating on *Il Messaggero's* lead story. The carabinieri had swooped down on a controversial Baptist soup kitchen operated by an American named Jesse Soames to arrest a war criminal named Otto Fischer hiding out "under the noses of the Polizia di Stato."

Another black eye for the department.

He popped a second Brioschi. To make matters worse, the carabinieri had failed to even notify the Polizia di Stato of the raid. It was too much to expect they would invite their comrades in law enforcement to share the honors of arrest. A photo of a decrepit Otto Fischer contrasted with another showing a younger and smugger version in full Nazi regalia. At least the lead story had pushed the department's public relations fiasco in Naples off the front page of *Il Messaggero.*

"Commissario—"

The intercom again.

"Who is it this time? The pope?"

"Close. Your carabinieri friend from the Tiber beat is here."

"Let him cool his heels for twenty minutes."

After twenty minutes, his secretary brought in the police officer from the carabinieri without knocking. *Will she ever remember to knock?*

"You've got a nerve coming here after failing to notify us about the Nazi bust."

"This is my thanks for giving you the Basso murder case?" His visitor made a tsk sound with tongue and teeth. "Our interagency agreement only requires joint interrogation of persons who may be of mutual interest. Not prior notification."

"Then why are you here? Just to rub it in?"

"We're interrogating a witness—Jesse Soames. I came with a personal invitation."

"Why should his interrogation interest me?"

"Believe me. It will."

"When?"

"In forty-five minutes."

"So soon? You should have told me earlier."

"The interagency agreement—"

"Doesn't specify a time. I know." He ran his fingers through his hair. "Where?"

"Our interrogation room."

"Why not ours?"

"Take it or leave it."

CHAPTER FORTY-FIVE

Arriving late, Leone sat behind a table next to the special deputy interrogator of the carabinieri. Before them, Jesse Soames sat in a stainless steel chair bolted to the floor at the edge of a circle of illumination cast from a table lamp.

Outside the circle sat a row of carabinieri cadets along the wall framed in shadow, like the black border of a condolence card. Although Leone found the newer generation of carabinieri well educated and skilled, the special deputy represented an older generation too often undereducated and underskilled.

What other carabinieri interrogator would have the audacity to take a statement in dress parade regalia? He wore it all, the two-cornered *lucerna* hat with red plume, the silver epaulet on his right shoulder, the white strap across his chest, and even the operatic cape of midnight blue. The special deputy's boast that this exercise in vanity intimidated subjects into confessing dumbfounded even his carabinieri colleagues.

"Who is this man?" Soames scrutinized Leone.

"I am Commissioner Marco Leone of the Rome police."

"What is your relationship to Lucio Piso?" the special deputy asked Soames.

"My employer." Soames swallowed hard. "He's not a friend."

"Are you the father of Nicole Garvey?" Leone asked.

"Yes."

"Enough." The special deputy fumbled through papers on the table. "Need I remind you, Commissario Leone," he said, waving a sheet from the pile, "that our interagency agreement here stipulates you do not ask questions?"

"No need." Leone shrugged. "You just did."

"Your grandfather—" Sentence unfinished, the special deputy reached down to pull out a folder from the briefcase at his feet. "Your grandfather, Colonel Soames, was an American OSS agent operating behind German lines in Rome, correct?"

"Yes he was, but what does that—"

"At war's end he took a special interest in the young Lucio Piso." The interrogator waved a paper at the witness. "He used his OSS influence to place Lucio in an orphanage operated by Monsignor Gustavo Furbone, now a cardinal, did he not?"

"Yes, but—"

"Isn't it true you attended a birthday party for Superintendent Piso in Buenos Aires at his expense?"

How would they know? Leone wondered.

Soames's eyebrows tightened. "He was my employer after all."

Unlike the Polizia di Stato, the carabinieri had deep intelligence sources Leone could only dream of because the carabinieri were part of the military. That competitive advantage grated on him.

"You say he is not a friend. Yet the record shows a history of family friendship." The special deputy started to rise but sat down again. "Why do you accuse Superintendent Piso of hiding a war criminal called Otto Fischer?"

"Because it's true. He hid Otto Fischer at my mission in Rome without my consent." Soames's shout resumed its whisper-like quality. "I thought we were friends. Not anymore."

"Lucio Piso denies knowing anything about Fischer's past."

"He lies. He tried to stop me from turning Fischer in."

"Didn't you conceal the truth about your service in Vietnam?"

"Lucio Piso told you, didn't he? He doesn't have his facts right."

Leone had had enough. "What does his service in Vietnam have to do with Otto Fischer?"

"If you persist, Commissario Leone, you'll have to leave . . . and miss the part of the interrogation you wouldn't want to miss." The special deputy turned back to Soames. "Otto Fischer, now in our custody, also denies Piso knew about his Nazi past."

"They both lie."

"Beware." The special deputy became agitated. "Superintendent Piso is a respected citizen, a recipient of a knight's title, and a confidant of the prime minister himself."

"Maybe I should get a lawyer."

"You're only a witness, not a suspect. You're not entitled to one." The special deputy seemed hesitant. "Anyway, things will go better for you without one."

"When is this over? I must meet my church members at the Colosseum."

"Very soon." The special deputy gave Leone an oddly sympathetic look. "The Nazis captured your grandfather in Rome," he told Soames. "A woman called La Sirena betrayed him, and he in turn betrayed the underground Resistance."

"How dare you smear his name." Soames rose. "The Nazis tortured him." Cadets moved forward out of the shadows. He quieted down without need for restraint.

Taking the special deputy aside, Leone warned he could not let him harass the witness with irrelevancies. Unless the harassment stopped, he would leave.

The special deputy advised Leone that if he left, he would regret missing important information.

The special deputy resumed questioning.

"In fact, didn't your grandfather reveal the identity of Benjamin Leone, a partisan fighter, later killed in the Ardeatine Caves?"

"That was my uncle." Leone stood up.

"Easy, Commissario." The special deputy put his hand on Leone's shoulder and coaxed him back into his seat. "Just one more question. Who shot Benjamin Leone in the Ardeatine Caves?"

"Fischer admitted he did. That's why I reported him to the carabinieri." Soames rubbed his hands as though washing them. "I knew Piso wouldn't." He turned to Leone. "Please forgive my grandfather."

"Will forgiveness bring back my uncle? Forgiveness changes nothing."

***

The day after the interrogation, what seemed to be a workaday homicide report crossing Leone's desk riveted his attention.

A bystander summoned a police patrol to the Colosseum, where
they found the dead body of one Jesse Soames. At the Colosseum, he
had met tourists from his Baptist congregation to show them around
Rome. The suspect, who wore a "What Would Jesus Do" T-shirt and
claimed to be a Baptist convert, asked Soames to pose for a picture
with a co-suspect costumed as a street performer playing the role of
Roman soldier. Witnesses described the so-called Roman soldier as
wearing the usual gear of breastplate, red tunic, plumed helmet, and
what appeared to be a cardboard sword. The sword was in fact one of
sharp steel. While the suspect with the T-shirt photographed the pose,
the other suspect fatally stabbed Soames. A black getaway vehicle with
false license plates appeared on the scene. A police officer on his day
off mortally wounded the man with the T-shirt as the suspect tried to
escape into the vehicle. The suspect with the T-shirt was later identified as a low-level pimp known to hire himself out for sundry forms
of criminal activity. The co-suspect street performer escaped in the
vehicle.

Putting down the report, Leone realized Professor Fisher's
Mithraism interpretation could no longer be dismissed as improb-
able. The links in the chain of events were too many. Raven, Lion,
Bridegroom, Persian, and now . . . the Soldier. It fit the few cloak-and-
dagger tidbits Shlomo had fed him before falling off the radar screen.

Which rank of Mithraic killer would strike next, and who would die?

Where was Shlomo?

CHAPTER FORTY-SIX

Leone found his informant outside the Domus Aurea—Nero's Golden House.

On a folding step stool near the imperial mansion, Shlomo, in Giorgio Armani sunglasses with a tall-stemmed plastic sunflower in hand, lectured a tourist crowd. Over the entrance, he said, once loomed a hundred-foot statue of Nero. After Nero's death, the Romans refashioned this Colossus Neronis into the image of the unconquered sun god—Sol Invictus. Twenty-four elephants moved the statue to Rome's amphitheater, named the Colosseum after the giant bronze sculpture.

"Where's the statue?" asked a matron in pixie-gelled hair.

She clenched the hand of a boy in black horn-rims.

"Vanished." Shlomo sipped from his thermos. "No one knows how or when."

She clapped a hand over the boy's mouth as he struggled to speak.

Leone aspired to Shlomo's command of English. Amazing what a subsidized year in London could do if one had an indulgent mother. Enough history. Time for answers.

He elbowed up to Shlomo. "Let's talk."

They moved to a private spot under a shade tree.

"What kind of new scam is this, Shlomo?"

"No scam." Eyes darting to the sides, Shlomo licked his lips. "I needed a plausible cover job, and they needed tour guides for the reopened Domus."

"You're supposed to work for us. What do you have?"

"Not here." Shlomo licked his lips twice. "They might see us together."

"When do we talk?"

"Inside. Safer there."

"Why did you cut off contact?"

"Things are moving fast. I have to be careful."

"Take it easy."

Shlomo's edginess meant he knew something.

Behind Shlomo's sunflower held on high, the tour group shuffled down the decline of an underground corridor to a honeycomb of interior walls fanning out before them. Outside the octagonal room, Shlomo mounted the folding step stool.

"Two major events occurred in sixty-four AD." Shlomo waved his sunflower for attention. "First, Nero's Great Fire. I'm sure you heard about it. But I doubt many of you know about the second. A failed conspiracy to assassinate Nero."

The hand over mouth came a second too late. "What about the orgies?"

"Adult tour only," Shlomo said, winking.

He pumped his plastic sunflower to quiet the crowd.

"As I was saying . . . the conspirators wanted to replace Nero with Gaius Calpurnius Piso, whose family owned the Villa of the Papyri. Nero discovered the plot afoot. He suspected Seneca, his former tutor and adviser, a philosopher, a statesman, and a dramatist, all rolled up into one. To no avail, Seneca retired from public life to avoid the emperor's wrath. Nero executed Seneca, Piso, and many others on his march into madness."

Working his way through the crowd, Leone kept his voice low but insistent.

"Step down so we can talk."

"We're taking a short break, ladies and gentlemen." Shlomo waved the plastic sunflower. "Go inside the octagonal room with its wonderful cupola open to the sky. What did Nero use it for? A dining room? An art gallery? After the break, I'll continue my commentary."

Making sure no one tailed them into the off-limits hallway, Shlomo waved Leone into the room of the Gilded Vault. "We can talk in here."

"What have you found out?" Leone asked.

"They call themselves Roma Rinata. Something big is cooking."

"What? I need to know."

"I don't know. I suspect an assassination."

"Of course." Leone clapped his hands. "The prime minister. They can pin the blame on the Egyptian Phoenix." He needed specifics. "When and where?"

"I don't know. Until my initiation, I'm in the dark."

"They're initiating you?"

"Rocco hinted it would be soon."

"Good." Leone studied the stuccoed rectangles of the barrel-vaulted ceiling. "Where's Rocco?"

"I don't know." Shlomo touched the commissario's arm. "Leave him alone. If you contact him, they'll know I'm a snitch."

"I want more information."

"Did you know," Shlomo said, pointing to the ceiling, "Raphael and Michelangelo shimmied down the shafts into the half-buried rooms of the Domus Aurea to study Roman frescoes?"

"Quit stalling."

"I gotta get back. Break's over."

"When do I get details?" He shook Shlomo's arms. "Terrorism isn't good for the tourist business."

Shlomo slumped, dropping the plastic sunflower.

"For God's sake, stand up straight like a man. Are you on drugs?"

Shlomo broke away and bumped against a wall. "I want out."

"Out?" Leone cursed. "Remember our deal?"

"I'm the one dealing with madmen." He picked up the sunflower. "They think they can resurrect the Roman Empire."

"You owe me."

"I sure don't owe you my life. I know what they do to traitors."

"You can't stop. Lives are at stake."

"You can't bully people to do whatever you want." Shlomo stepped up to the commissario. "No one owes anybody anything." He threw the plastic sunflower. Leone ducked. The sunflower skidded across the floor. "I'll quit if I want."

"If you drop out, they'll know you're a snitch. You'll be a goner for sure."

"No, no, I don't believe it." Shlomo wrapped his arms around himself. "They won't if I get out now. But once I get initiated . . ." Shlomo drew his index finger across his throat. "I gotta get out now."

"I do have an ace to play." Leone tapped Shlomo's chest. "If you don't stay in, at least a little longer, it could just be . . . you know how bureaucracies are . . . leaking like a spaghetti sieve and all . . . and word may get out you were an informer and then . . ." Leone paused. "Fill in the blanks."

"You bastard. You're bluffing."

"Try me and find out."

CHAPTER FORTY-SEVEN

In his private study adorned with African masks, Pope Celestine VI hung up the phone on the dire news. The ripple of earthquake tremors plaguing Rome had taken their toll. A consulting architect specializing in structural engineering warned that unless His Holiness shored up its foundation, St. Peter's Basilica verged on catastrophic collapse.

The basilica resembled a set of top-heavy building blocks, the present sixteenth-century structure built over Emperor Constantine's fourth-century basilica, which rested on a Roman cemetery. The repair cost would be enormous. But if he did nothing, the cupola of the basilica threatened to give way. He shuddered, imagining the dome, forty-five stories high, raining chunks of death on worshippers below. He rocked his aching head from side to side with both hands.

What to do?

Every problem awakened his urge to resign like his namesake predecessor. The similarities disturbed him. In the thirteenth century, Celestine V had chastised his fellow cardinals for their procrastination in electing a pope, just as he had. As a result, the Sacred College of Cardinals elected him to the position, just as they had his namesake predecessor. God's little joke on him for his sanctimoniousness. Like Celestine V in the Middle Ages, he yearned to shed the weight of the papacy for a life of simplicity.

He could follow the more recent example of Benedict XVI by retiring and perhaps establishing a tradition for a papal age limit. But what about the expectations of his African brothers and sisters for the first undisputed African black on the throne of Saint Peter? How could he let them down? But the true letdown would be collapsing under the strain.

What to do?

His eighty-third birthday a week ago made him long for a return to the life of a priest ministering to the poor and sick in the Nigerian bush of his birth. The ten rooms of the papal apartments enclosed in the Apostolic Palace with far more rooms overwhelmed him. He had lived his early years in a single-room hut where his mother and an occasional medicine man tended his polio. He survived with a permanent limp in his left leg. Had the priest-doctor not appeared at the hut and called him forth like Lazarus into the world of Western medicine and Christianity, who knows what he would have become?

He knew what he had not become. He was no skilled administrator, no learned theologian, no charismatic leader. As his Jesuit confessor intuited from the beginning, he had a need to be needed . . . and the truth was the Vatican Roman Curia neither needed nor wanted him. He could no longer tool around in the sidecar of a motorcycle driven by his private secretary, as he had done in the hinterland of Africa. Such behavior offended powerful acolytes devoted to Vatican conformity.

The ring of the telephone shook him out of his despondency.

His Nigerian private secretary.

"Yes?" the pope answered, pleased to speak English.

"Are you ready to meet the architect?"

"I forgot." The pope clamped his palm to his forehead. "I need to finish overdue paperwork. Please postpone the meeting for an hour with my apologies."

"Cardinal Furbone . . . you know, the pope in waiting . . . is fuming, as usual. As administrator of St. Peter's Basilica, he insists on attending."

"Sounds like trouble."

"I told you not to appoint him administrator. You're in soup all right."

He chuckled at his secretary's Nigerian idiom.

"Very well. Invite Cardinal Furbone . . . and please . . . be nice to him."

"Why did you appoint him?"

"Whatever his flaws, he is my best administrator."

"Be careful. I'd shine my eyes on that cardinal if I were you."

He found his spectacles behind the graduation photograph taken at a Nigerian seminary. What a merry troupe of priestly pranksters they were, full of high jinks and hopes. Hiding his spectacles as a joke was something they would have done.

Turning serious, he realized he had to stop his memory lapses. He must not go dotty like his papal namesake who doled out Church sinecures in the Middle Ages to whoever asked, sometimes awarding the same position to different persons. The anonymous gossips in the Vatican, the "crows" as insiders called them, had already spread the rumor that childhood polio had jumbled the Holy Father's mind.

He studied the petition signed by prominent members of a traditionalist society representing North American Catholics. It warned of his misguided outreach to the Muslims of Africa. That outreach would only accelerate the mixture of Christianity and Islam some scholars called a new religion of Chrislam. The petition condemned the contamination of the true faith with the heresy of syncretism. They said he had to draw a theological line in the sand. But they overlooked a problem. Lines didn't last long in the African sand. He had just finished a draft of his response when his personal secretary telephoned.

"Cardinal Furbone and the architect await you in the library."

"My leg's acting up. Please bring them to my study."

"Remember the proverb, Your Holiness. Leopards lurk in dark corners."

His sly secretary meant the leopards rampant on the Furbone coat of arms.

***

"I would prefer Cardinal Furbone stay." At the pope's words, displeasure spread across the architect's face. The anticleric took it amiss that the cardinal had appeared without his prior knowledge.

Despite the bad blood between them, the pope wanted to please both men. He needed the expertise of the architect renowned for his innovative work with reinforced concrete and floating foundations.

But he also needed the cardinal to run St. Peter's Basilica and interpret this alien country called the Vatican.

The cardinal had become his right-hand man and would like to take over the left hand as well. The ferocity of the cardinal's career ambitions could be turned to his advantage. Given the prelate's hunger for the triple-crowned papal tiara, Furbone would be delighted to facilitate his resignation from the throne of Saint Peter, should he so choose.

"My staff had the good fortune of finding this in the Vatican archives." The architect held up a photograph of an architectural draft of St. Peter's Basilica in red chalk.

"The peculiarity of the handwriting looks familiar." The pope rose from his desk chair for a closer look. He ignored the cardinal's warning about walking alone without help. The pope wiped from his mind the uncharitable image of a vulture impatient for its victim's demise. "Who drafted this?"

"Michelangelo." The architect held up the photograph. "The master perfected earlier drafts. My proposal for repair keeps intact Michelangelo's vision."

The architect explained that Emperor Constantine wanted to construct the original basilica on the side of Vatican Hill, slanting down toward a Roman cemetery. The emperor needed more than twenty-eight thousand cubic meters of soil to level off the foundation. To do so, he decapitated the top of the hill for landfill. Heedless of reverence for the dead, Constantine knocked off mausoleum roofs below and filled them with dirt.

"Who are you to judge the first Christian emperor?" The cardinal glared at the architect. "The Orthodox Church declares him a saint."

"That's a miracle in itself for a man who not only executed his wife and son but also declared himself a companion of the pagan god Sol Invictus."

"Please." Celestine VI raised his hands in supplication for the bickering to cease. "Architect Moretti, be so good as to finish your report."

"The name is Manetti, Your Holiness."

"My apologies." His memory had failed him again. The cardinal said nothing, but before the day was over, the shadow whisperers in Vatican corners would say His Holiness was losing it. And maybe they were right in a way. He was losing patience by pretending to be something he wasn't. In defiance of what Furbone thought proper protocol, he removed his white skullcap. The cardinal winced. The thing never fit right, floating on his thick thatch of salt-and-pepper corkscrew hair. "Please continue . . . Architect Manetti."

Manetti unrolled a blueprint of the proposed repair across the conference table to help explain the crux of the problem. When the Renaissance master builders raised the present St. Peter's Basilica with a facade of over 140 tons on top of Constantine's earlier basilica, the foundation of the Renaissance basilica did not settle evenly. Cracks snaked down that facade. Other cracks erupted in the vaults below the main altar. Underwater springs added to the problem of an unstable foundation ever since the excavations of Pius VII. The unprecedented wave of earth tremors further destabilized the foundation. More quakes, and the structure could come crashing down.

"Geniuses built this edifice. It has stood for centuries," the cardinal said. "God watches over his church."

"It took one hundred twenty years to complete St. Peter's," the architect replied. "It could destruct in minutes if we delay." He tapped the blueprint with his rubber-tipped pointer. "We need a decision, Your Holiness . . . as soon as possible."

"Your own report says you'll disturb the holy ground under the main altar." The cardinal tapped a crumpled document with his forefinger. "Out of the question."

"We have no choice." The architect shrugged, avoiding the cardinal's eyes. "We can minimize any damage."

Celestine VI had hoped for a more robust rebuttal of the cardinal's objection. Only weeks before, he had toured the necropolis under St. Peter's. He saw the ancient drawing of Christ in the form of the sun god driving two white steeds into the heavens and the cartoonish drawing of what some said was a bald-headed Saint Peter. The sacred Vatican Grottoes contained the tombs of nearly 150 popes, plus a king or two, and a queen. A priceless heritage lay under St. Peter's Basilica.

What to do?

"We are on the precipice of disaster, Your Holiness. We cannot postpone this any longer. The quakes could return anytime." The architect rolled up his blueprint. "You must decide now."

***

After meeting with Architect Manetti and Cardinal Furbone, the pope canceled all appointments. He retired to the study after picking at his favorite meal of fish stew and pounded yams prepared indifferently by a German Benedictine nun. His eyes glazed over, and his mind shut down as he pored over blueprints and documents related to the proposed buttressing of St. Peter's Basilica.

On the rooftop of the Apostolic Palace, he strolled under trees and along the flower beds in his garden of Gethsemane. Trouble stalked his papacy. The Vatican power brokers no longer bothered to camouflage their faultfinding out of his presence with flattery in his presence. They no longer feared him. Even the anticlerical architect—What's his name?—had called him Your Holiness whereas Cardinal Furbone had not.

What to do?

Shortly before midnight, Celestine VI looked up from his desk. The study lit up like a lone candle against the outside darkness blanketing St. Peter's Square. He removed his spectacles and rubbed the bridge of his nose. He rang up the papal secretary to proclaim his decision before he changed his mind again.

CHAPTER FORTY-EIGHT

In a conference room of CEDAD, Commissario Leone paced like an expectant father. If he wasn't on a mission for the American archaeologists and the advancement of his investigation, he wouldn't have worn himself out by traveling to the distant center located in the heel of Italy. Exasperated by continuous excuses for the delay in carbon-dating the previously sent samples from the Callinicus letter, Will Fisher had implored him to personally deliver samples from the Unity Report to CEDAD to move things along. With the original Callinicus letter destroyed in the museum arson, it was critical to carbon-date the Callinicus samples if the photographic copies were to be authenticated. While the Americans translated the Unity Report in the Castello of Julius II in secrecy, Leone stewed until the scientists pronounced the birth date of the samples from both documents.

Fat, black thunderhead clouds swept off the Adriatic toward the city like UFOs. Why hadn't the Americans faxed the translation yet? Had something gone wrong?

To make matters worse, the CEDAD staff killed time with mind-numbing explanations of injection magnets, gas ionization detectors, beryllium lines, and whatnot, until the physicist-director made up his mind whether to close the center before student-led demonstrators trashed it.

Ranks of riot police wielding shields and batons formed up between the building and the protestors. The demonstrators taunted the front rank with placards and banners. STOP NUCLEAR MADNESS read an oversized sign held up by a pair of protestors in skeleton-imaged jumpsuits. The pair darted back and forth, coming ever closer to the front rank, baiting the police to charge. From the window, his trained eye detected masked figures gathering rocks and bottles at the rear of the demonstration. Negotiators from both sides stepped into the no-man's-land between battle lines while a wind kicked up, blowing debris across the clearing.

Leone slumped, exhausted, onto a sofa. The tension had resurrected the craving. He took a cinnamon stick from his shirt pocket. He rolled one end around in his mouth, and following his doctor's advice, he tried to imagine the taste of bittersweet wood was the taste of a cigarette. It wasn't working. Maybe he should try bubble gum like Wesley Bemis. Hoping he could still pull it off, he closed his eyes and breathed in and out as though he were inhaling and exhaling nonexistent cigarette smoke.

"Am I interrupting?"

He opened his eyes to see the physicist-director standing over him in a white lab coat.

"What's in your mouth?"

Jumping to his feet, he jammed the cinnamon stick back into his shirt pocket. "Never mind that. What about the test results?"

"Is that all you're worried about?" The physicist-director looked toward the window. "They're threatening to destroy the center, and you want us to continue." He jutted out his chin. "For the safety of the staff, I plan to send everyone home until this riot ends."

Lightning flashed through the window followed by the roar of a thunderclap. Rain pelted the glass. Leone called the physicist-director to the window. The protest melted away into clumps of drenched demonstrators scampering helter-skelter for cover with shirts and signs over their heads.

"The heavens have spoken. If the protestors return, the local police have promised me to provide round-the-clock protection." Leone made a shooing movement with the back of his hand. "With the greatest respect I urge you to get me those results."

***

At dawn on the top story of the Castello of Julius II in Ostia, Will Fisher startled awake in a castle built for the Warrior Pope, Julius II. Outside the walls, the putt putt of a motorcycle revving up broke the morning calm.

Across the stone floor, Nicole, exhausted from her late-night return to the castle after her father's funeral, had fallen asleep on her sleeping bag in her clothes. Her T-shirt revealed a coffee-colored birthmark on her upper arm. The butterfly mark fluttered in sync with her breathing as if preparing to fly. She mumbled, rolling over on her side, and faced the wall. The joke on the back of her T-shirt—"An Archaeologist Is Someone Whose Career Is in Ruins"—was on him. His career was in ruins, not hers.

Not enough that his father had deserted him and his mother in Milwaukee, the war criminal had left lies behind. The old wreck of a man fabricated the story about being drafted into the German army and sitting out the war at a desk job in Bavaria. He had instead volunteered for the SS unit involved in the Ardeatine Caves massacre. Now under arrest in Rome, his father had crossed the ocean and messed up his life once again.

Circumstances forced him to tell Nicole about his university dismissal. She would find out anyway. But he didn't have to tell her about his father. The paparazzi scavengers were too busy gorging on the details of his father's war crimes to examine the family tree—at least for now. He had done what he could to sever his identity as the son of Otto Fischer. Changing the spelling of his last name was not enough. He had to figure out how to better fudge his filial connection to the war criminal. He might just deny Otto Fischer's paternity. Who would believe a broken-down Nazi?

His friend Jack Daniels offered solace from the thermos emblazoned with the words: "My Blood Type Is Caffeine." The professor struggled to avoid the thermos. He could not let alcohol screw up his career. With the aid of a lighted magnifying glass and Latin reference works, they had translated enough to know the Unity Report was a bombshell.

The humidification chamber and the cutting-edge gelatin had uncurled the papyrus in record time. The barely legible Latin letters, bunched horizontally across the papyrus, looked like black musical notes erupting across an almond-colored score sheet from a symphony lost in time. He picked up the partial translation from a worktable. He could already hear the applause of acclaim resounding down the corridors of academia for his stupendous discovery.

Nicole mumbled herself awake. She lifted herself on the sleeping bag, her eyes puffy and filled with tears. They exchanged good mornings.

"He was a good man." She rubbed a tear away. "If only I knew what tormented him before he died."

"You couldn't know. He wouldn't say what troubled him."

"Just a tight-lipped hero, my dad." She forced a crooked smile. "Where are you going?"

"The Neanderthals on the faculty call me a bomb thrower."

"Why do you care what they think?"

He waved the translation above his head.

"Wait till they read the bomb I'm faxing to Commissario Leone."

***

Holding an incoming fax, the CEDAD secretary bustled into the conference room just in time to avoid bumping into Leone. "Excuse me. This is for you, Commissario."

"You were to inform me when the fax arrived. I was to pick it up."

"I didn't read a word . . . if that's what you're insinuating." She placed a hand on her hip. "Please don't tie up our fax machine. At CEDAD we have work to do."

So much for Fisher's paranoia that a fax was more secure because a computer could be hacked. Upon the secretary's departure, Leone read the cover-page notation from Professor Fisher. The placement of a scroll rod near the opening sentences in the Unity Report smudged them so they could not be read. His eyes darted to what could be deciphered.

Seneca: Callinicus will record your words as my notary.
Paul: Why can I not report directly to Emperor Nero?
Seneca: Because the emperor desires your connection with
      him kept secret. He wishes the plausibility of denial
      should this project be exposed.

Paul: Why must my words be written? You are his counselor. You can report to him confidentially without
arousing curiosity, just like before.

Seneca: I am now retired. In any case, the emperor does
not trust my words any longer but only your report in
your own words. Oral words fly away, written ones stay.

Paul: I beg the emperor's forgiveness for the delay in my
report.

Seneca: The emperor did not summon you to Rome from
a backwater province in the guise of a successful legal
appeal by a Roman citizen only to be snubbed.

Paul: I beg forgiveness. My affliction forced me to bed.

Seneca: The emperor's instructions were clear. With our
support you agreed to organize one religion in one
empire for Jew and non-Jew alike based on the most
useful elements of Jewish and non-Jewish religious
traditions.

Paul: So I have tried to the best of my ability. I have used the
Mithras cult in my native city of Tarsus as my model. I
have turned Jesus into Mithras and Mithras into Jesus.
The Jewish sect of Jesus and the cult of Mithras seek a
brotherhood of men under God beyond the artificial-
ity of social and ethnic distinctions, just as you Stoics
profess.

Seneca: That is all well and good. But you have committed
a serious blunder by promoting the Jewish messiah as
the divine son of God. The emperor did not grant you
license to turn this Jewish preacher into a divinity. By
so doing you have not only offended the emperor who
claims divinity but also your Jewish brethren. They
believe you commit blasphemy and are no longer a Jew.

Paul: I am all things to all people.

Seneca: But you have become the wrong thing to us.

Paul: I needed to connect the abstract monotheism of the
Jews to the culture of Greece and Rome. The Jews pro-
hibit images of God and fear to utter his true name.
Are there not here in Rome statues of Apollo, Venus,

and the other gods that are the wonders of the world? Do you not glory in their names far and wide? How then shall we worship God through Jesus unless he has a divine status? I have combined the best of the Jewish and non-Jewish religions.

Seneca: But combined to such a dangerous extreme, my dear fellow. The God of the Jews overshadows our gods in perfection. The Jews say we are made in his image whereas Jupiter seems to me more made in ours.

MORE DYNAMITE TO FOLLOW . . . WILL

***

After Fisher returned from the fax machine, Garvey asked, "Before we get to work, have you reconsidered my concerns about the Unity Report?"

"You know, that butterfly mark on your arm." He readied the magnifying glass for a new assault on the report. "Around here it means your pregnant mother had an unfulfilled wish. The possibility of fulfillment is reborn in the child."

"Stop stalling, Professor." She became serious. "My only wish is to warn you. Your bombshell could explode in our faces."

"We've been through this. You told me about your doubts." He folded his arms across his chest. "The Unity Report says: 'I am all things to all people.' Saint Paul uses the same phrase in his first letter to the Corinthians."

"What does that prove?" She shook her head. "Ancient forgers inserted what a reader might expect to find. It made the forgery more plausible."

"It's just as possible Paul repeated a pet phrase. People do it all the time."

"We're not going to settle this now. Let's get to work."

Despite their divergent views, she liked the way he relied on her paleographic expertise when it came to deciphering the identity of particular letters. With him, she was part of a team instead of an appendage. Whenever they differed on the meaning of a word or phrase, he listened and treated her as an equal, even though classical languages were his specialty. She hadn't often found this in other men, certainly not her ex-husband nor her father. They were cocksure about everything. In the days before GPS, Will would've been the guy who stopped to ask for directions when lost.

In the Unity Report, the As were not difficult to identify, though they lacked crossbars. But the similarity of the Es and Fs took time. The writer—if a forger—had used the same cursive style as in the Callinicus letter. The Roman playwright Plautus had compared the style to the scratching of a hen's foot. Wouldn't a document like this have been penned in the more formal and legible rustic-capital style? The writing showed starts and stops, as if the author had hesitated numerous times before completing letters and words.

Garvey shared her thoughts. "Whoever wrote this paused a lot. The penmanship doesn't flow evenly as in the Callinicus letter. I think this is a different person."

"Maybe a scribe wrote the letter. Callinicus says in his unfinished letter he had a slave with him." He rubbed his finger along his chin. "Anyway, you have to admit the formation of the letters is the same in both documents, even the individual peculiarities."

"Too much the same, if you ask me." She shook her head. "If I were you, I wouldn't bet the ranch on the report's authenticity."

"Truce," he said, shaking her hand, "until we get word from Leone on the results of the carbon-dating test."

***

"Get away from the fax machine." Commissario Leone tapped the shoulder of the CEDAD physicist from behind. "I'm expecting an important fax."

"Go away." Without turning, the physicist continued tinkering with the machine as it whirred and flashed a blinking yellow light. "I'm trying to fix this damn relic. I need to send something. Our computer's down."

He reached around the physicist's head and flashed police ID in the man's eyes.

"OK. I'm going." The physicist gathered his papers. "But you fix it."

The commissario struggled with the glitch until the blinking yellow light stopped. The machine purred and disgorged the additional translation from its jaws.

Paul: Warn the emperor. The more rabid followers of this Jesus mutter about burning down the new Babylon. This is their code word for Rome. But I believe this nothing but idle talk.

Seneca: That is not for you to decide. Understood?

Paul: Of course.

Seneca: This unrest is the result of your apocalyptic preaching. Instead of pacifying the Jews here and in Judaea, you have stirred up the rabble. Even certain followers of this messiah no longer trust you. The technicalities of Jewish law must not be abolished all at once. You do things too impetuously.

Paul: What would the emperor have me do? Peter and the others in Jerusalem consider Jewish law eternal.

Seneca: One thing at a time. The Jews will not sacrifice to the emperor as a god, but we compromised. They sacrifice to their God on behalf of the emperor. That suffices for them and for us.

Paul: I have done so with the Sabbath. My letter to the Romans leaves Sabbath observance to the conscience of each person, neither condemning nor demanding observance.

Seneca: That was well done. The forced idleness of the Jewish Sabbath has always bothered me. It only spawns thoughts of rebellion.

Paul: I have nothing more to report at this time.

Seneca: Next time, tell me the names and plans of those who threaten to burn Rome. The emperor needs to know everything. Or you might never again be able to tell us anything.

Paul: By Mithras and Jesus, I will. I swear loyalty to the emperor.

Seneca: As we all do. But be careful. Your life and mine
    depend on it.

THIS IS THE END. NOW FOR THE FALLOUT . . . WILL

***

To celebrate their complete translation of the Unity Report, Fisher and
Garvey picnicked on panini and Chianti outside the Baths of Mithras
in Ostia Antica. Wildflowers poked up through the cracked marble
ruin they made their picnic table. Basking in the sun, she leaned back
and ran her fingers over her collarbone up her neck and through her
hair.

"Do you think," he said, "we fooled the manager of the Castello of
Julius II?"

"Yep." She twirled a lock of hair. "Would've fooled me."

They had embellished their honeymoon cover story to the point of
holding hands while asking the manager for directions to the Baths of
Mithras. Fisher planted a kiss on her cheek on their way out of the castle. The kiss wasn't in her version of the honeymoon script. It melted
her cheek like fire on wax.

"My former acting skills are a little rusty."

She felt the spot where he had kissed her. "Not so rusty, Will." She
ran her hand down the red sundress over her thigh.

"To us, partner . . . or pardner . . . as Wes would say." He clinked his
wineglass with hers.

She winced at the mention of Wesley Bemis. "To us."

After their picnic, he offered a hand to help her down the brick
steps to the mithraeum beneath the ancient baths. She didn't need help
but used it as an excuse to meld her hand into his.

They walked through the mithraeum entrance. She pointed out
two holes in the ceiling opening up to the sky without any obstruction
from the baths. Under the opening stood an iconic sculpture of Mithras
slaying the bull. An altar and two small brick columns stood before the
sculpture. On a sunny day, the ancient congregation must have con-
templated sunlight streaming through the holes onto the sculpture in
the way sunlight streams through church windows onto an altar cross.

Her eyes caught something odd. "What's on that bench?" She picked up a mask. "Look, Will . . . a raven mask."

"The Raven rank of Mithras." He turned it over in his hand. "They've been using this mithraeum. We have to tell Commissario Leone."

While searching for other objects left behind, she stumbled on a rock. He grabbed her before she fell. His arms around her shoulders, she looked into his face. She sucked in the scent of musk from his neck. He pressed his lips to hers. He drew his head back. With her right hand, she lowered his head back down and kissed him with an urgency he repaid. She steadied herself and pulled away. "We're alone now. No need to playact."

"Who's playacting?"

His smartphone buzzed.

"Commissario Leone. Good timing. What do you have?"

"The scientists told me one thousand nine hundred fifty-six years for both the Unity Report and the Callinicus letter, give or take fifty years."

"Nineteen centuries for both? Wonderful news." He shot her an I-told-you-so look. "Science has settled things."

"I'm sure it hasn't," Leone said. "Ciao."

CHAPTER FORTY-NINE

"You'll miss the turn," Leone warned Renaldi's replacement from Turin. "Turn left now."

He looked askance at this Inspector Rossi, unfamiliar with the streets of Rome. The short sleeves of his summer blue shirt exposed the tattooed phrase *"La Famiglia Sempre"* on his forearm. *The Family Forever?* Would he turn into another homesick transfer unable to make the grade? "God help us," Leone said under his breath.

"Faster, faster." Leone resolved not to fail. "We've got to stop it this time." Shlomo's overdue contact that morning about a threat to the church of Santo Stefano Rotondo fit the Mithraic hypothesis. The church rested on a second-century mithraeum near the barracks of Roman legionnaires transferred from imperial provinces. When he pressed Shlomo for details, the line had gone dead. He rocked in the passenger seat of the squad car as if his energy could speed it up.

The vehicle screeched to a stop.

Leone ran into the round building known as the Hungarian national church in Rome with Rossi right behind. The commissario shoved his way through a circle of mourners past the ring of colonnades encircling the altar. Near the altar lay a closed casket on purple cushions. Yellow roses adorned the casket. Around it, wreaths of white and yellow chrysanthemums huddled on latticework. At the altar, a priest in a purple-and-gold chasuble stood ready to begin the funeral service.

The slurred sibilants and hard consonants of a strange language, sounding like the buzz of agitated bees, surrounded Leone. "Hungarian," Rossi whispered into his ear.

"What is the meaning of this intrusion?" the priest asked in accented Italian.

"A police investigation." Leone removed his hat. "Why a closed casket?"

"A Hungarian diplomat died in an automobile accident. The accident mutilated his features." The buzzing of the mourners grew louder. "What do you want? I must begin this service."

It's San Clemente all over again. The revelation shook Leone.

"The casket contains a bomb. Clear the church at once."

The priest gasped. He ordered everyone out before a bomb exploded.

Answering the commissario's call, two bomb-disposal specialists in protective gear arrived, looking like astronauts. From the church rear, Leone watched the bomb squad work. He rejected their advice to wait outside.

The specialists lowered their helmet visors. The heavyset one set to work opening the casket lid with a long, flat strip of metal. While prying the lid open, he slipped on yellow roses fallen from the casket. The metal strip clanged on the floor.

The lid banged shut.

Leone hit the floor.

No explosion. He still lived.

"The point," Leone said, getting on his feet, "is to defuse the bomb without blowing us up."

Full of apologies, the specialist reopened the casket lid far enough to peek inside. He motioned his colleague to take a peek. Taking off their helmets, they closed the lid and looked bullets at Leone.

"Speak up. What did you see?"

"Disfigured corpse," the heavyset one replied. "No bomb. The point, Commissario, is to call us only for bomb threats."

They packed up their tools. "We're leaving," the other one added. "You do the apologies."

Leone's apologies did nothing to soothe the deceased's brother, who tongue-lashed him in both Hungarian and Italian with some colorful English phrases for emphasis. Other mourners backed Leone against a wall depicting Christian martyrs in baths of boiling pitch or with hands set afire or spears thrust through their throats. Subjected to his own self-inflicted tribulation, Leone bought off their wrath with the promise of a church donation to atone for his blunder.

Leone waved off Rossi's offer of a ride home. He wandered through the park of the Villa Celimontana, where protestors gathered around the smallest obelisk in Rome and demanded its return to Egypt. When he arrived home alone, Mondocane licked away the wound of Shlomo's false information.

CHAPTER FIFTY

Inside the climate-controlled consultation room of the Vatican Library, Fisher pondered the blank papyrus sheets shipped from the Villa of the Papyri. The staff had done a superb job of removing mold spots with a spatula plus a mixture of ethanol and water. He consulted his notes on the quantity and dimensions of the papyrus sheets before shipment. He examined the sheets.

Something was off.

He cross-checked the sheets and notes again.

No mistake.

When he deposited the sheets with the library, the numbers matched. Now they didn't. He turned to the library assistant accompanying him. "Sheets are missing."

"How could that be?"

"That's what I want to know. What about the staff?"

"If you're insinuating—"

"I'm insinuating nothing." His heart raced. "Did anyone else examine the papyrus?"

"Just another professor."

"Another professor?"

"I thought you knew. Someone cleared by Superintendent Piso's office."

The professor's name clicked. A gifted classics scholar whose mind went off the rails. After assaulting a dean, he had disappeared under the radar of academic gossip.

***

By the time Fisher exited the cab in front of the Marriot Park Hotel, the public hearing on the authenticity of the Callinicus letter and the Unity Report had already begun in the Michelangelo Ballroom. In conjunction with Brigham Young University and the Vatican, the Ministry of Cultural Heritage and Activities sponsored the hearing. The scrolls riveted public attention and pushed aside all other news. Even the anticlerical and secular parts of the city feared the papyrus revelations. If Christianity were undermined, would tourists still visit and help fill the coffers of a Rome teetering on bankruptcy?

Ushers shepherded him to his seat on the dais just in time to hear Cardinal Furbone's spokesperson blast the Callinicus letter and Unity Report as forgeries inspired by a Mormon agenda. The agenda was intent on proving the pagan corruption of early Christianity through what Mormons called the Great Apostasy in order to justify what they considered the reestablishment of true Christianity by the revelations of Joseph Smith, their founder. When the spokesperson's attack degenerated into repetitive bombast, Fisher checked his voice mails on the sly.

Still in the hospital for third-degree burns, Wes Bemis, poor man, had called yet again. The arson at the National Archaeological Museum scarred not only his body but his mind. He had a paranoid's conviction of an anti-Mormon mob lurking around the hospital to burn it down and get at him. The caustic tone of the cardinal's spokesperson reminded Fisher that even paranoids have enemies, and one prominent enemy was Cardinal Gustavo Furbone.

When Nicole rose to speak, Fisher knew her integrity forced her to make common cause with the Vatican spokesperson on the Unity Report. Although she thought the Callinicus letter genuine, her suspicion of the Unity Report, she said, began with its provenance. For such a confidential report to be left in the open for others to find struck her as peculiar. The writing style and the apparent hesitancy in the application of ink further raised her suspicions.

Bringing science to bear, she disclosed what the Unity Report revealed under a multispectral scanner. The ink did not show the type of aging or quality consistent with the ancient time period of the document. It also contained a suspicious degree of iron content not typically found in ink until the early Middle Ages. She concluded a forger had written modern text on ancient papyrus authenticated by carbon-14 testing.

When his turn came, Fisher walked to the lectern on leaden feet. Why had he appeared on a vulgar TV variety show a week earlier to hype carbon-14 testing as proof the Callinicus letter and the Unity Report were both authentic? He had broadcasted his professional misjudgment about the Unity Report to the entire country and beyond.

After a moment of stammering, he confessed to the audience that the blank papyrus sheets inventoried at the Villa of the Papyri and stored at the Vatican library had gone missing. The inventoried sheets also bore the same characteristics of scraping and washing Dr. Garvey observed on the Unity Report. Because the papyrologists at the library had completed those restorative tasks on all the sheets, he concluded the Unity Report was written on blank papyrus taken from the Villa of the Papyri, and most likely purloined by a visitor to the storage bunker of the Vatican Library.

He should have listened to her. He hesitated but he had no choice. He needed his friend Jack to console him.

He gripped the lectern to steady himself. A modern forger had concocted the Unity Report on ancient papyrus. He gulped. Therefore, he apologized to Dr. Garvey and others for his earlier view and retracted any public comments to the contrary.

"What about the Callinicus letter?" A reporter stood up. "Is that a forgery too?"

"I was too hasty with my assessment of the Unity Report," Fisher said. "But I will say carbon-14 testing and paleography . . . the study of ancient writings . . . validate the age of the Callinicus letter. Like Dr. Garvey said, the Unity Report problems do not apply to the Callinicus letter."

"I have no such hesitation." The Vatican spokesperson interrupted. "The Callinicus letter is also a Mormon forgery. If the Unity Report is a modern forgery on ancient papyrus, why shouldn't the same conclusion apply to the alleged copies of the Callinicus letter? Where is the original of the Callinicus letter? Gone up in smoke because of arson at the National Archaeological Museum. Rather convenient, don't you think, if you want to prevent conclusive authentication. How do we know the photographed . . . alleged . . . copies of the Callinicus letter weren't concocted out of thin air? At the center of all this is a Mormon, Dr. Wesley Bemis, aided and abetted by these two Americans with a bias against the Roman Catholic Church."

"Any last word, Professor Fisher?"

"My last word is defamation . . . like in defamation lawsuit, if the Vatican representative doesn't stop making false accusations."

Nicole winked and gave him the look.

The look meant he didn't need Jack for consolation later that night.

CHAPTER FIFTY-ONE

"Hey Rocco," a coworker said. "Did you know that a Sicilian is just a black African who's good at swimming?"

Rocco struck the bicep of his upraised left arm with his right hand in a classic gesture of defiance. "Up yours, you Roman cretin." He walked toward the coworker with clenched fists but stopped short. His mission was too important to be jeopardized.

Over twenty-one meters in the air, the two workmen glared at each other on the aluminum-tube scaffolding surrounding the pink granite obelisk in the center of St. Peter's Square. Others returned to festooning the obelisk for a special Mass of Deliverance from the earth tremors afflicting Rome.

Rocco squeezed the yellow-and-white bunting in his hands as though it were his heckler's throat. When begging for work up north, a train conductor outside Rome had pointed to a train map of the Italian mainland and Sicily. He stomped his foot. The boot of Italy stomps Sicily, the conductor said. The Roman bastards would pay soon enough.

"Knock it off, you two." On the other side of the scaffolding, the burly boss, his hands full of nylon bunting, followed up his command with a string of curses. "The Mass of Deliverance is tomorrow. No one leaves until we finish beautifying this twenty-five meter prick with the papal colors."

Rocco diverted his rage by contemplating the crowd milling below like mindless insects over cobblestones sectioned off by lines of white travertine. Laborers positioned potted olive trees around the obelisk base. The insects prepared to celebrate the special Mass of Deliverance outdoors the following morning. Because the tremors had cracked the steps of St. Peter's Basilica, on Sunday morning the pope would instead celebrate the Mass of Deliverance next to the obelisk flanked by two fountains.

"He's just an ignoramus trying to provoke you." The boss put his arm around Rocco. "Forgive him. He's even too dumb to find his ass."

"Never." Rocco broke free. "I don't forgive . . . and I don't forget."

"How did it go?" The boss looked down and then into Rocco's eyes. "With your mother's medical exam, I mean."

"That's my business." He turned his back and returned to fixing the flapping bunting on the obelisk. "I must finish up."

How did it go? Rocco wondered. He distrusted these smooth-talking sawbones in Rome, but he had no choice. Even though moving his aunt and mother to Rome had taken his last euro, only superior medical treatment offered his mother the hope of salvation. After the consummation of his masterpiece tomorrow, he would dine with her and brave whatever prognosis fate had dealt her. She insisted on getting out of bed to make his favorite dish of pasta with sardines and pine nuts. Only she mattered to him. After the Pater Patrum saw the spectacular results of his craftsmanship, he would have more than enough money for his mama.

The metal cross at the top of the obelisk glinted in the sun. Some said the cross contained a piece of the wooden cross from Christ's crucifixion. The Pater Patrum ranted that the papacy had substituted the cross of the obelisk for an ancient metal globe containing the ashes of Julius Caesar. They were all out of their minds. How could they get so worked up over past events distorted by memory and devoured by the black hole of history? But the Pater Patrum paid handsomely, and in the credo of the mighty euro Rocco believed. He could feel it and buy things with it. And save his mother with it.

When quitting time came, cleanup remained. To the delight of the crew, he volunteered to stay behind and take care of it himself. The boss thanked him. Even the worker who had taunted him shook hands, adding he had nothing against Sicilians—in fact, his barber was one.

After their departure, Rocco reached into his duffel bag and pulled out sticks of military-grade C-4 explosives.

CHAPTER FIFTY-TWO

The next day, clouds like cotton candy swirling in soot loomed over St. Peter's Square on the somber Sunday morning set for the Mass of Deliverance. From the viewing gallery on the dome of St. Peter's Basilica, Rocco trained his binoculars on the fifty thousand persons packed around the obelisk. A cantor intoned Psalm 22—*My God, why have you forsaken me?*—joined by organ music and thousands of swelling voices.

Professional pride demanded he be present to observe his handiwork during the hours-long ritual. The insects below could then no longer claim that because the obelisk had witnessed the upside-down crucifixion of Saint Peter, it was divinely destined to never collapse. Out there, another Roma Rinata craftsman, unknown to him, would bring this religious service to an explosive finale at any moment. Cells of operatives, unknown to one another, worked independently toward a master plan known only to the Pater Patrum. If one cell of the organism were eradicated, the Pater Patrum could replicate it without compromising the others.

His cell phone vibrated with an incoming call.

It had to wait until the final act of his masterwork.

The players in the ritual below appeared to him like a beehive in concentric circles of hierarchy. At the base of the obelisk sat the mitered Celestine VI, the queen bee, swathed in a vestment of scarlet brocaded in gold. Surrounding the base sat the drones in three sections:

the cardinals in scarlet, the bishops in purple, and the priests in white. Waving handkerchiefs and banners, the worker-bee laity, buzzing with excitement, stood behind the roped-off seating area. The only exception to the iron law of hierarchy was the pope's insistence the front row be reserved for the gravely ill. The chants of *"Viva il Papa"* puzzled Rocco, who was unable to comprehend such devotion to a stranger.

The Mass would end soon. When would the grand finale arrive? Had something gone wrong? He checked voice mails. Several from his aunt. Was it about his mother? Next to him an old woman in a black dress and white hair in a bun fingered a rosary. She reminded him that cell phone calls were not allowed. Anyone else he would have told to go to hell, but she looked too much like his mother. He pocketed his cell.

A police helicopter drifted from the southeast in a flight path over St. Peter's Square toward the northwest. Rocco raised his binoculars to the obelisk. A strip of bunting had come loose near the top, flapping in the wind. He scraped the side of his face with his fingernails. What if the pilot saw a C-4 stick behind the bunting?

The helicopter veered to the east and away like a dragonfly uninterested in the terrain. When he was a boy, his mother would fondle his hair and say he was born under a lucky star. He longed to hear her voice. The old woman in black had moved away. He took out his cell and punched in his aunt's telephone number.

"Yes?"

"It's me. Rocco."

"Where are you, Rocco? I kept calling, but you didn't answer."

"How's Mama?"

"The medical report is bad . . . very bad."

"Let me talk to her."

"I can't. She went to St. Peter's Square."

"What? Where did you say?"

"The Mass of Deliverance. Her nun friend gave her a ticket for the front row reserved for the sick. The pope will bless them. Your mother prays for a medical miracle."

"Jesus Christ." He hung up, stunned. He punched in some numbers and stopped. They'll trace the call. He ran as fast as he could from the viewing gallery and took the elevator down. He punched the ground-floor button again and again to make the elevator go faster.

He ran from the square to the nearest bar, which had just opened for business. The retro fifties pub displayed an antique pay phone in one corner and in the other a jukebox playing "Angel Mother" in the background: *Angel Mother, I am overjoyed we are together at last . . .* He deposited a coin in the pay phone and dialed.

"Police?"

"This is the police emergency number."

Angel Mother, you are in my heart always.

"A bomb is about to go off in St. Peter's by remote control."

"What's your name?"

Angel Mother, caressing your face, I am at peace.

"That's not important."

"Where are you?"

Your fingers, so frail and slender, I hold them never to let go.

"Hurry, for the love of God. The obelisk is riddled with C-4 about to explode."

"How would you know?"

"I put it there."

CHAPTER FIFTY-THREE

Leone awoke from a Sunday doze on his sofa to feel Mondocane licking his face. The kitchen telephone rang on and on, overpowering the TV chatter. The caller would be his ex-wife demanding to know why the great detective had no information about their missing daughter. Grateful his voice mail didn't work, he had no obligation of a return call when she hung up without a message.

Waiting for the ringing to stop, Leone snapped off two pieces of cold sausage from the fridge. Mondocane snapped up one on the fly. Leone ate the other one before downing five milligrams of hydrocortisone to fight off fatigue and aches. The continued ringing of the telephone jangled his nerves. *Will she never give up?* Avoid stress, the doctor had said without explaining how a detective did that. He grabbed the telephone receiver. "I told you I don't have any information."

"What?"

Enzo Rossi. His new inspector.

Eyes on the television, Leone said, "Sorry. I thought you were somebody else."

The TV showed the pope sitting on stage in front of the obelisk.

"Why the call?"

"An anonymous tipster reported a bomb about to go off in St. Peter's Square."

"Might be another prankster."

"He knew about C-4. Said it would detonate on the Vatican obelisk."

Celestine VI talked to an assistant holding a palm frond.

"Did you trace the call?"

"Couldn't. He used a pay phone."

"Pay phone? Only a few of those antiques left."

"I have a hunch about the location. Should I check it out?"

Professor Fisher had warned about the possibility of St. Peter's resting on ground used for Mithraic ceremonies. Some interpreted the incomplete Latin word *Petr* on an ancient fragment under the basilica as referring not to Saint Peter but to *rock-born* Mithras. *Petrus* in Latin meant *rock*, and upon this rock the Church was to be built.

"Do you hear me, Commissario? Should I check out my hunch?"

"We don't have time. Get a bomb squad over to the square right away."

On three legs, Mondocane hobbled over to Leone and brushed against him.

"And then pick me up." Leone massaged the dog's throat. "I'll wait downstairs. We're going to St. Peter's Square."

The TV showed a drizzle floating down into the square. The yellow-and-white bunting on the obelisk snapped in the wind. The pope looked upward, and within seconds two umbrellas vied for the honor of shielding his head. Like mushrooms, umbrellas popped open throughout the throng. The TV camera operator panned the transparent pope mobile crawling to a stop just behind the seated clergy. The driver exited and stood at attention.

"Get the pope the hell out of there," Leone ordered the TV set, just before grabbing his blue Gore-Tex police jacket on his way out of the apartment.

CHAPTER FIFTY-FOUR

"Out of the way," Leone yelled at a trucker blocking Inspector Rossi's attempt to pass. The inspector swerved the squad car around the truck and revved the engine on the way to St. Peter's Square. The wipers clicked back and forth across the wet windshield with the regularity of a time bomb.

Even if Roma Rinata wasn't involved, Celestine VI had wild-eyed enemies who would stop at nothing to harm him. Leone kept an eye on Christian extremists who claimed the closet-Muslim pontiff was the Antichrist, as well as on Muslim extremists who never forgave his teenage conversion to Christianity. He feared another Santo Stefano Rotondo fiasco, but even more, a dead pope. He'd lose face if the call was a hoax, and a pope if it was not . . . unless he arrived in time.

The squad car jolted onto the sidewalk, stopping less than a foot away from boxes of blood oranges arranged before a grocery window. The inspector got out and surveyed the vehicle.

"What's going on, Rossi?"

"We blew a tire."

Leone scrambled out the door and into the grocery. He ordered the owner to switch the overhead TV to the Mass in St. Peter's Square. The unctuous voice of the announcer opined the ceremony might be terminated if the drizzle worsened. A contingent of Swiss guards waited for Celestine VI to descend the makeshift platform decorated with flowers.

Rossi's voice came from behind. "The rain'll prevent an explosion."

"Not if it's C-4."

Murmuring among themselves, several customers stared at Inspector Rossi's arm. "Put this on, Rossi." Leone tossed his jacket to the inspector. "Most citizens don't like tattoos on their police."

"You can call me Enzo."

"Let's keep it professional, Inspector Rossi," Leone said, keeping his eyes on the TV. "Find out what's taking the bomb squad so long."

Just then the crowd in the square parted as the bomb squad sprinted through the opening to the obelisk. Swiss guards closed ranks before the platform stairway, where the pope stood blessing the seriously ill in the first row before he descended. Their captain and the bomb squad leader huddled alone in discussion.

"What's taking so long?" Leone asked the TV set.

The announcer proclaimed the cessation of rain a sign from God. A rainbow formed over St. Peter's Square. Umbrellas snapped shut. The services would continue.

Leone jammed numbers on his cell. The bomb squad leader answered.

"Stop the chitchat." He pressed the cell against his ear. "Get the pope out and disperse the crowd at once. Do you understand?"

"We can't. The captain demands identification. He says we could be terrorists masquerading as the bomb squad. He says he can handle things without us."

"Are his brains up his ass?"

"It's a power play. He won't budge."

"To hell with him. Use force to get through if you have to."

"Bravo. A shootout between us and them on national TV. Good thinking."

"Put the cretin on your cell. I'll talk to him."

The clock above the TV set ticked on.

The TV camera zoomed in for a close-up. As the pope prepared to leave the platform, an honor guard of Swiss soldiers in red-plumed helmets waited behind their captain with upraised pikes. The captain motioned the driver of the pope mobile forward.

"Put the captain on your cell, I said."

"He refuses to talk to you, Commissario."

The camera zoomed closer on the captain. That horse face with the beady eyes struck a chord in Leone's brain. Where had he seen it before?

"If he doesn't talk to me, I'll order his arrest."

"For what?"

"I'll think of something."

"Shouldn't we call the head of the Vatican Gendarmerie? He once worked for us."

"This is a major crime. It's beyond the Vatican security cops."

"You don't have jurisdiction in this instance." It was the captain of the Swiss guard speaking in guttural Italian on the cell. "The Swiss guard is responsible for the personal security of the Holy Father. We don't need you."

That voice. Where had he heard it before?

"C-4 is set to explode on the obelisk any moment. What are you going to do? Spear the C-4 sticks with your pikes? Let the squad through."

In this instance. That pretentious phrase sounded familiar. The speaker's identity was on the tip of his tongue. He knew better than to force it.

"I will consult my Vatican colleague, the inspector general of the gendarmerie."

"We don't have time."

"I can't let you interrupt a religious service on mere suspicion."

"The service is over and you know it."

"I forbid your men to scare the faithful."

"I got it." The commissario felt a rush of remembrance. "In this instance," he said, "you're going to let them pass if you know what's good for you."

"Who are you to order me around?"

"I am Commissario Marco Leone . . . remember? I let you go after I caught you with the underage boy in the metro, late one night, with your pantaloons down." He pressed his advantage. "I'll arrest you for public indecency if you so much as set one toe outside the Vatican."

Over the speakerphone Leone heard the captain say to his men, "In this instance, let them pass."

***

A basket crane rumbling behind them, the bomb squad hustled past the Swiss guards toward the obelisk. Assistants escorted the limping pope down the platform stairs. The basket lowered to let the bomb experts board. Forming ranks along his path, the Swiss guards waited for Celestine VI to limp over to the pope mobile.

The basket ascended alongside the obelisk.

"Hurry," Leone muttered to himself—or was it a prayer?

Celestine VI stopped to bless a bawling youngster offered up by a pair of hands from the human mass straining at the barriers separating them from the Holy Father.

Leone and Rossi looked at each other in resignation. Nightmare memories flitted through Leone's mind like ghosts. Dealey Plaza, 1963. His hero, JFK, tempting fate. JFK shot dead like a deer in the crosshairs of an assassin's rifle. The mental scars of the Secret Service officers who failed to prevent it.

Not again.

A chain of explosions ripped across the TV screen in bursts of white-hot flashes. An orange fireball burst into plumes of gray smoke roiling around the obelisk. The three-hundred-ton column of granite tottered and tumbled, raining stone chunks like meteorites on nearby chairs. Obelisk fragments shot into the more distant crowd with shrapnel force. The giant TV screens set up in St. Peter's Square keeled over and shattered on the ground.

As the floating debris settled, a battlefield of bodies lay near the explosion, some writhing, some deadly still. Those toward the rear of the assembly trampled over one another in a frenzy of flight. The cries in the square mingled with those of the customers inside the grocery. The stump of the obelisk remained upright, jagged and pitted. Breaking into sobs, the TV announcer exclaimed, "Holy Mary, Mother of God!" He pulled himself together and stated the obvious: terrorists had struck down the Holy Father.

CHAPTER FIFTY-FIVE

Outside the Gemelli Polyclinic, Marco Leone waited in the squad car for news. He noticed that armed police checked visitor identification at the entrance. Questore Malatesta had fanned suspicion by reminding news outlets that a Muslim had tried to assassinate Pope John Paul II. And, as Leone predicted, the questore blamed the Egyptian Phoenix for the act of terrorism because it involved an obelisk, and obelisks were their obsession.

A woman in black, reminding Leone of his grandmother, led a circle of other black-clothed women in a public recitation of the rosary under the tenth-floor room reserved for the pope. Young and old, the concerned and the curious clustered around the polyclinic in anticipation of a statement from the hospital on the pope's condition. Just like the death of JFK, his idol, Leone suspected that Celestine VI hadn't made it either. It was a dog's world. The hospital staff must be figuring out how to break the bad news.

Inspector Rossi exited the hospital with a downcast expression.

Not waiting for the inspector to speak, Leone said, "He's dead, isn't he?"

"Not unless being in a coma is dead."

"They don't want to admit he's dead."

"Why wouldn't they? More problems if they hide things." He looked down into the passenger window. "They asked us to say nothing about the coma until they announce it." Rossi took the driver's seat. "Any news about the attack?"

"Semtex maybe, probably military-grade C-4. A sophisticated operation using autonomous acoustic detonation." Reading Rossi's blank expression, Leone added, "The first blast generates sound waves setting off a chain reaction of explosions."

"Questore Malatesta." Rossi hunched over the steering wheel. "Would you believe he's telling people my tattoo . . . *La Famiglia Sempre* . . . is unacceptable because it suggests a crime family. Since when is devotion to one's family suspect in Italy?"

"Forget it. The man's an idiot."

"I can't. He found a police directive banning tattoos on the force if they are indicative of a quote . . . abnormal personality . . . unquote. I have to see a psychiatrist for an evaluation."

"Really?" Leone laughed until he felt it in his belly, unable to remember the last time he had laughed so hard. He patted Rossi on the shoulder. "Don't worry. I know the department psychiatrist. He thinks Malatesta is the crazy one for referring these tattoo cases."

Rossi brightened. "I saved the good news for last."

"Good news? Must be a mistake."

"Were you always such an optimist, Commissario?" Rossi started the car. "No mistake. Shlomo texted me in code. Roma Rinata's inducting him at midnight in the mithraeum under the Circus Maximus."

"Why didn't he contact me?"

Enzo shrugged. "Maybe because you don't like texts."

"If Shlomo says so," Leone said, "it's likely false information."

"What have you got to lose?"

"Just my reputation. Shlomo made a fool of me at Santo Stefano Rotondo."

"You're right, Commissario. We shouldn't take the chance he's right this time. And then we'd have the misfortune of sweeping the whole terrorist gang into our dragnet and—"

"You made your point." Leone exhaled through his lips. "Get the SWAT team out there tonight."

CHAPTER FIFTY-SIX

Blindfolded and on his knees, Shlomo felt his head forced into water. The ringing in his ears grew louder. Water seeped into his mouth and nostrils. A vice squeezed his chest. When the muscle spasms became excruciating, the hands pressing his head under relented. His face bobbed up, gulping for air.

He would flimflam them. After all, he was the king of cons.

The new inspector promised that Commissario Leone would ride to the rescue and arrest them. The commissario would put him in a witness protection program with a new identity and financial support. He could start a new life far from Rome.

Shlomo cried out with feigned joy.

"You are now baptized a son of Mithras."

It was the voice of the Pater Patrum.

Hands removed his blindfold and lifted him up.

Through a curtain of incense smoking up from braziers appeared the Pater Patrum clasping a ruby-encrusted crosier, his identity hidden under the bone-white mask of Mithras.

To the Pater Patrum's right sat a figure in a saffron robe shot through with orange stripes. Gold powder caking his face, he wore fire-red eyewear. This had to be the Heliodromus, the courier of the sun in Mithraic lore. The Pater Patrum tapped the crosier three times on the floor.

With this signal, Shlomo strutted up and down the cave with arms flapping and throat croaking to the beat of the Lions clapping hands in unison from the benches. He felt like a fool hazed into a secret fraternity of the demented.

The nave ran only about twelve meters long, and the ceiling no more than four and a half meters high. Shlomo thought that the mithraeum of the Circus Maximus should be more impressive. The Pater Patrum and Heliodromus beckoned him forward into the mithraeum sanctuary studded with pumice and seashells.

Wasn't the mithraeum of the Circus Maximus supposed to have been covered with white marble? When will the commissario come? The sheriff always arrived on time in the American Westerns he loved. He fell on his knees before the Pater Patrum and Heliodromus.

"Nama . . . Nama . . . Sebesio," chanted the Pater Patrum, its meaning tongue-tied by time.

In accordance with updated ritual, two Ravens pecked at his bare back with the beaks on their masks.

"Father of all the Fathers," Shlomo said. "This isn't the mithraeum under the Circus Maximus, is it?"

"I changed my mind." The Pater Patrum rested his hand on Shlomo's head. "You deserve the special honor of initiation in this mithraeum under the Palazzo Barberini."

"But it's supposed to be closed."

"Nothing is closed to the Pater Patrum."

"I am honored."

Leone was going to raid the wrong mithraeum.

"But I am not worthy of this honor."

Shlomo beat his chest with his fist for submissive effect. *Calm yourself. You're the master of getting out of tight spots. You'll figure it out.*

"You are more worthy of this," the Heliodromus said, "than you know."

"We should postpone my initiation." Shlomo raised his bowed head. "The attack on the Vatican obelisk has Rome crawling with police."

The Pater Patrum pushed his crosier into Shlomo's chest, pushing him back.

"Do you question me?"

The pecking on his back began to hurt.

"Forgive my careless speech." In a yoga child's pose, Shlomo prostrated himself at the feet of the Pater Patrum. He had to regain favor. "I am only concerned for your precious life. Without you we are lost sheep."

"We do not forgive." The Pater Patrum tapped Shlomo's head with the crosier. "Back on your knees." Shlomo kissed the red slippers of the Pater Patrum before raising himself to his knees.

The Heliodromus intoned, "O neophyte, in the time of ancient Persia, ravens feasted on the dead strung up on funeral towers, and thus thou art dead to thy former life and reborn into the eternal life of Lord Mithras." He took the Raven mask from a silver tray offered by a Lion and placed it over Shlomo's face. "Repeat after me. The will of Lord Mithras is the will of the Pater Patrum, and the will of the Pater Patrum is mine."

Why didn't the Ravens stop hurting his back?

He repeated the words of this bastardized ritual of Mithraic baptism composed of fact and fantasy. The Pater Patrum wandered from the ritual script by blaming Christians for destroying the Mithraic holy books. But as a mystery religion, they wouldn't have kept books, would they? Dismayed at his expectation of rationality from a group of fanatics, he faced another truth: the sheriff wasn't coming. Not to worry. He didn't need the sheriff.

He was still the Houdini of scams. He would find a way out.

"Do you swear by your sacred honor," the Pater Patrum asked, "to obey and never betray Roma Rinata?"

"I do."

"Lord Mithras," the Pater Patrum said, "has swept away Celestine the Sixth, the pretender to my title as pope of Rome. Our time of return is upon us."

Cymbals clashed and drums throbbed.

Hoarse from his vehemence, like an angry drunk, the Pater Patrum rambled on about the coming grandeur of Roma Rinata. It would topple the government and seize power. It would cancel the Lateran Treaty Mussolini signed with the Vatican, expel the imposter pope from Rome, and liberate the mithraeum said to exist somewhere under St.

Peter's Basilica. On the glorious day of national salvation, the leaders of Roma Rinata would reveal their identities to an adoring populace.

"Do you wonder, Shlomo Adorno, why we have specially honored you today?"

Surprised by the Pater Patrum's deviation from his diatribe, Shlomo answered, beating his chest with his fist. "Because the Pater Patrum can raise even the most ignorant to wisdom."

Snickering broke out behind his back.

Had he sucked up too much?

"You undervalue yourself," the Pater Patrum said, patting Shlomo's head. "You are dear to us."

He was dear to them. He didn't need the sheriff. He was still at the top of his game.

"To reconsecrate the Barberini Mithraeum," the Heliodromus said, "we need a fitting sacrifice."

Pain sliced into his back. The Ravens went too far. He whirled around. They weren't beaks. Blood flowed down his back. They held knives coated with blood.

"And you are the sacrifice," the Pater Patrum said. "Shlomo . . . the traitor."

"How did you—"

"Find out?" The Pater Patrum cackled. "When the police raided the Santo Stefano Rotondo church, we knew it was you. We slipped you false information about a planned attack on the church. You failed the test."

Shlomo had a final thought before his death. He needed the sheriff after all.

CHAPTER FIFTY-SEVEN

Cardinal Gustavo Furbone calculated that the odds of pulling off his plan increased to near certainty if the Vatican secretary of state failed to appear. At the head of the conference table in the Apostolic Palace, he prepared to convene what American prelates incomprehensibly called the "kitchen cabinet." To his right fidgeted the English cardinal just arrived from London, and to his left drowsed the Spanish cardinal. Last, and certainly least of eight cardinals, the pope's private secretary took his place at the end of the table.

A Nigerian outsider like Celestine VI, the pope's secretary had the audacity to question the right of the prefect of the secret archives to attend the meeting. Since canon law didn't formally recognize the kitchen cabinet anyway, the cardinals voted to let Carlos Stroheim attend. Furbone spread his thick fingers over his rounded belly in satisfaction at his preliminary victory in the Hall of Constantine. The meeting promised future victories on his way to Saint Peter's throne just like the fresco of the *Vision of the Cross* before his eyes foretold Constantine's ascension to emperor.

To Furbone's dismay, the secretary of state bustled into the hall with an iPhone plastered to his ear. Furbone looked at Carlos Stroheim next to him. The prefect of the secret archives stopped cleaning the table in front of him with sanitizer tissue and returned the look. *This Frenchman spells trouble,* their eyes said.

"You must end your call," Furbone said. "We have a decision to make."

As soon as he terminated the call, the latecomer lashed out at Furbone.

"By what authority did you suspend reinforcement work under the basilica . . . contrary to the express order of the Holy Father?"

"You forget I am now administrator of St. Peter's Basilica." Furbone waved a stamped paper. "The camerlengo has declared the pope in a coma and, sad to say, effectively dead."

"You mistake coma for death."

Furbone dismissed the retort with a flick of his wrist. "A meaningless distinction."

The secretary of state puffed himself up as having the equivalent powers of a prime minister. No one else in the Vatican acknowledged his conceit. He also had a reputation as a hothead and somewhat of a bully. Few of the Vatican staff wanted to work for him, though they respected his abilities. Furbone surmised these character flaws could play into his hands.

"Under canon law," Furbone said, "the camerlengo is now in charge of the Church's property, subject only to the College of Cardinals."

"You well know," the Frenchman replied, "Celestine the Sixth, like his recent predecessors, intended to merge the office of camerlengo into my office."

"Intended?" Furbone repeated the word with derision. "The road to hell is paved with good intentions." He clucked his tongue. "Like so many things the pope intended, he failed to carry out his intent."

"It slipped his mind." The Frenchman looked at the cardinals as if asking support.

"No doubt," Furbone replied, "the residual effect of polio, like so many of his, shall we say . . . lapses." Several cardinals nodded in agreement. "Anyway, the reason for his inaction is irrelevant."

The Spanish cardinal, now awake, nodded his head in assent after seeing the nodding heads around him. The English cardinal looked befuddled. He was too inexperienced for his views to count for much.

"Your carping is uncalled for." The secretary of state chopped the air in a Gallic gesture. "More pressing matters preoccupied His Holiness."

"Please stop waving your hand in my face." Furbone rubbed his cheeks, fixing the pope's private secretary with an icy stare. "What is it?"

"Shortly before this meeting," the secretary said, half rising from his chair, "I received word from the Gemelli Polyclinic. The Holy Father has intermittent moments of consciousness."

"He is still in a coma and cannot perform his duties." Furbone stood up. He leaned over like an alpha primate with his fingers splayed out on the table. "And the camerlengo and I have decided—"

The private secretary's cell phone interrupted the meeting with its Nigerian Christian ringtone remixed with disco sound and drumbeat. Before Furbone could reprimand him, the secretary slunk into the corridor to answer the call.

"As I was saying . . . before the jungle music interrupted me . . . the camerlengo agrees with me. All engineering and architectural work under St. Peter's has ceased and will not be resumed."

"You have no right." The Frenchman folded his arms. "I will not accept this."

"Let's be sensible," Furbone said, pleased to see the Frenchman's face take on an apoplectic glow. "We cannot have the Basilica of St. Peter put on rock-and-roll shock absorbers." He hoped to contrast the Frenchman's growing excitability with his own jocular composure.

"Isn't the analogy a trifle extravagant?"

Who is this English upstart to challenge him? "What is your point?"

"My point is simple. Base isolation, as it's properly called, is a standard architectural procedure. An exorbitant material . . ." The English cardinal paused as the secretary of state whispered to him the correct Italian word. "I mean an . . . absorbent . . . material is inserted at the foundation. The material then buffers the shocks of earthquake tremors. The Japanese have retrofitted buildings with this procedure and—"

"I disagree," said Furbone. "Even if the project does not damage the holy places under St. Peter's . . ." *Why is that pest of a private secretary signaling for my attention at the back of the hall?* ". . . the cost will be enormous. Remember how the cost of building St. Peter's helped spark the Reformation."

"Whatever we do," Stroheim said in a passionate tone, "we must not destroy the past." His demeanor switched to a gold-toothed smile. "That would be a cardinal sin . . . as they say in English."

Who does this South American aborigine think he is, grabbing attention with his juvenile wordplay? "Let's attend to business, if you please."

"Of course, my good cardinal." The prefect's smile flashed gold-toothed impudence.

Ignoring the waving hand of the private secretary near the door, Furbone concentrated on winning over the Englishman. "You must agree this base isolation you speak of has never been used on so large and unique a basilica as St. Peter's."

"I do," the Englishman said. "But any collapse could be catastrophic."

"We must avoid novelty," Furbone said as the pest called the pope's private secretary approached him from the side. The secretary shifted his weight from foot to foot like a schoolboy needing permission to pee. He could ignore the pest no longer.

"For the love of God, what do you want?"

"I'm so sorry." The secretary held up his cell phone. "The architect just called from Bologna. His assistant finished surveying the damage under the basilica caused by the earth tremors."

"You presumed to interrupt me again . . . for that?"

"He discovered something extraordinary."

CHAPTER FIFTY-EIGHT

Opening a top shirt button in the morning humidity, Marco Leone waited in the middle of a gathering mob. With the acquiescence of the minister of the interior, Questore Malatesta had ordered the Polizia di Stato to backstop the Polizia Penitenziaria during the transfer of Otto Fischer from low-level security to the protective custody of Regina Coeli prison. The national police were to keep a low profile so as not to offend the sensibilities of the penitentiary police, jealous of their limelight moment in the public eye. Any minute now, the Polizia Penitenziaria would transport the monster of the Ardeatine Caves down the narrow and crooked street to his new home.

Dressed as a vagrant in sunglasses with cheek stubble, Leone reprised his rookie years as a master of disguise gone undercover to battle crime with other comrades of deceit. Did he still have the magic touch of those glory years? He scoured the crowd for troublemakers with his cap held out for alms.

Reeking of lavender, an old woman in a laced shawl squinted at him through thick glasses.

Did she see through his disguise?

"A euro for your troubles." She deposited a euro in his cap. "God has heard you."

Not a sparrow falls without God knowing about it. So the priest had said at Abramo Basso's funeral Mass. Did God hear Abramo in the Ardeatine Caves? Or Benjamin, before the Nazi blew his uncle's brains out with a handgun? And now Shlomo Adorno found mutilated like the skinned lambs butchers hoisted over their shoulders. The image of Shlomo's bloodied corpse wrapped in a winding sheet and dumped in front of the Questura di Roma from a stolen car still haunted him.

Miriam, I'm responsible for your son's death.

You didn't kill him, Marco, the killers did.

But I insisted he do undercover work.

And I'm the one who cajoled him and charmed you to find a position in the Polizia di Stato.

It's my fault, Miriam, all my fault . . .

You give yourself too much importance, dear Marco.

I will never find peace until I arrest who murdered him . . .

Will you find peace even then?

"You almost fooled me," a voice whispered. Leone turned to confront a street musician with an untamed beard and hair gelled into punk-rock spirals. It took a few moments to recognize Rossi in disguise.

"You upstage me." Leone ran his fingers over the psychedelic-colored surface of Rossi's vintage Billy Boy guitar. "Any leads on the bomb call?"

"The perpetrator phoned from a fifties American-style retro bar, just like I thought." Rossi straightened the red bandana across his forehead. "The owner recognized the caller from the mug shots, a petty criminal named Rocco. We found his apartment."

"Shlomo's source. He knows about Roma Rinata," Leone said. The case was ready to break open. "Did you bring him in for questioning?"

"No."

"No? What's the matter with you?"

"Nothing's the matter with me." Rossi's face muscles twitched. "Something's the matter with him. We found him dead in his apartment . . . a suicide, partially decomposed. Swallowed acid drain cleaner."

Leone's throat tightened.

"The suspect's mother died in the explosion. Rocco left a suicide note." Rossi swallowed hard. "He admitted planting the C-4 sticks, killing his mother. He didn't know she'd attend the religious service. He wanted to suffer before he died."

"How much involved with Roma Rinata?"

"Note didn't say." Rossi strummed a few bars of a protest song on his guitar. "His aunt and coworkers know nothing about his private life. Just a sullen Sicilian."

"Good work, Inspector Rossi."

"Did you actually say . . . 'good work'?"

"I must be getting soft." Leone studied a sidewalk crack. "Now, go back across the street."

On the other side of the street, Rossi played the protest song like a pro, too much of a pro. His musical magic whipped up the crowd into a fighting mood. The shouting for vengeance against the monster dwindled as an indigo police van rumbled down the street toward Leone. The van halted. The words "Polizia Penitenziaria" spread across the side in white letters.

Two penitentiary guards in sky-blue berets and indigo uniforms jumped out.

While newspaper photographers snapped pictures, the guards argued in loud voices with a carabiniere who insisted on helping them unload Otto Fischer and perp-walking him in handcuffs to the prison entrance. Leone overheard the guards insist they had jurisdiction over the prisoner transport, while the carabiniere countered that since his law enforcement agency had arrested Fischer, he should have a role in the transport. The dispute widened to include a uniformed officer of the Polizia di Stato, who claimed the right to place the crowd-control barriers. Grateful only three of the six separate law-enforcement departments were getting in one another's way, Leone went back to soliciting alms, hoping to snuff out the first signs of riot.

The two penitentiary guards trundled Fischer out of the van. A weathered stick of a man, Fischer leaned on his walker while the guards yelled *avanti, avanti*. A bottle hurtled into the street and shattered not far from the prisoner. Hands behind the barriers grabbed for the Nazi. A few protestors broke through the barriers. A uniformed contingent of the Polizia di Stato beat them back with riot shields and batons.

Like a cat intent on a mouse, Leone looked over shoulders to fix on Fischer lurching on his walker toward the prison entrance. The old man behind the crinkly face should have flashed traces of a devil. Instead, he just looked like a stereotypical senior citizen in a television ad. Leone caressed the Beretta 92FS pistol concealed in his wrinkled and stained trousers.

A riot would erupt any minute.

In the confusion and escalating tensions, no one would blame him if a shot from his Beretta was thought to have gone astray and killed the monster of the Ardeatine Caves.

To get a better view, he shoved his way to the first row behind the barriers, people yelling at him and kicking him, just another pushy street bum who didn't know his place.

Someone forced Leone sideways against the bandaged hand of a man leaning up against the barrier. Under the wrapped hand, Leone felt pressing into his ribs a lump hard as steel. Who would bandage a prosthetic hand?

The man tried hiding the hand under a cardigan sweater tied around his neck by its arms. Who would wear a sweater on such a humid day?

Though he kept tugging at his sweater, the man couldn't quite cover his hand. Why would he even try to shield a hand already protected by a bandage?

"Watch where you're going," the man said. The bandage came loose.

The glint of sun on metal flashed into the commissario's eyes locked in a trance with those of the man, both knowing but not saying what the hand held.

He would not bear the responsibility if the man shot the monster. They didn't censure the police guards when Jack Ruby shot Lee Harvey Oswald in broad daylight.

The Nazi relic limping along on his walker like a windup toy made a fine target. Leone pretended not to see the man next to him remove the bandage and jerk the pistol free of the sweater.

The man took aim.

Not to stop the man would betray an oath of office and his self-image as an upholder of law.

To allow the killing of the has-been Nazi would kill a part of himself. He would be just another dog in a mondo cane world where dogs ate dogs.

Leone grabbed the arm with the pistol. The gun discharged, causing the mob to stampede through the barrier. The police beat back the crowd with shields and batons. He twisted the arm behind the man until the pistol clunked on the ground. Rossi rushed to help Leone wrestle the would-be killer into submission.

An egg smashed against Otto Fischer's back followed by a volley of tomatoes splattering Leone and Rossi. The penitentiary guards held up the prisoner, about to fall from his walker.

Personnel from Regina Coeli rushed out a wheelchair. The uniformed Polizia di Stato formed the ancient Roman military formation called the tortoise. They aligned their shields to make a compact marching unit protected with a shield wall on the sides and overhead. In the protected center, Fischer moved forward in his wheelchair. The formation lockstepped toward the prison door as eggs, rocks, tomatoes, and bottles ricocheted off the shields.

The Polizia di Stato dragged the foiled assassin to a police car. Dangling the bandage from his hand, he shook a clenched fist at Leone. "If there were a God, that Nazi beast would have also butchered someone in your family."

CHAPTER FIFTY-NINE

"Time's almost up," the prison guard said. He tilted his chair back against the visiting-room wall and crossed his legs on a desk.

The old man folded his hands. "Can you please help me?" He pressed his forehead against the grillwork.

"Help you?" Will Fisher stared at his father's scraggly white whiskers. He looked withered almost beyond recognition. Did he want money? A lawyer?

"The prison warden helped you." *More than you deserved.* "Without isolated detention, the other prisoners would have torn you apart."

"I need you."

"No you don't. You abandoned us."

"Forgive me."

"Ask your Nazi victims to forgive."

"I beg your forgiveness."

"Hurry it up, you two." The guard plucked an iPhone from his pocket.

"Why didn't you tell me the truth?" Fisher spread his palms across the grillwork. "You were with the SS third battalion in Rome, not at a desk job in Bavaria. You murdered Benjamin Leone in the Ardeatine Caves. It's all over the newspapers and TV."

"Pipe down, you two." The guard followed up his command by plugging himself into the earbuds of his iPhone.

"I was young and drunk. I shot him under orders. They said he was a terrorist." Otto Fischer bowed his head. "Every day I remember. So late we learn."

"Why did you tell the reporters you were my father?"

The old man returned to destroy a son's lifelong struggle to forget. "But I am."

"You lied to me."

"You tell always the truth, my son?"

"I'm not on trial for war crimes."

"Ein neues Leben." His father started to cry. "A new life, I said in my heart. Starting fresh in America."

The son couldn't remember the stone face ever shedding a tear.

"A new life? I remember you as a drunk when you weren't trying to relive your life through me. You deserted us. You left a stack of debts. That was your new life, not mine. Mine is as far away from you as I could get."

Aware of his shrillness, Will Fisher looked at the guard, tuned out on his iPhone.

"I am so, so sorry, my son. Don't be like me."

Don't be like me, not like me, his father would say, hugging him after a drunken fit of rage, leaving him confused and ashamed of a father coming unglued.

"Why do you visit me in Regina Coeli?"

"I'm only here because of my colleague, Dr. Nicole Garvey. Before her father died, he claimed her real great-grandfather was Benjamin Leone. Is it true?"

"It is true." Otto rubbed his red-rimmed eyes, his voice now hoarse. "I saw the birth paper. La Sirena was *die Mutter*—"

"Stop." His father's linguistic contortions and German lapse under stress embarrassed him enough in Milwaukee. "No German."

"La Sirena was the mother and Benjamin Leone the *Va* . . . the father. I showed the police the birth paper. The birth paper said the baby had a . . . how do you say in English? I forget now . . . *Schmetterling*—"

"Butterfly mark?" He'd seen it on Nicole's arm in the Castello of Julius II.

"Ja . . . Yes, I mean. I'm sorry."

"Who betrayed Leone?"

"Jesse Soames, an American spy. Not La Sirena." The father steadied his hand on the walker next to the stool he sat on. "I have Parkin-sohn's disease."

"It's called Parkinson's . . . if you're still speaking English."

"Du *musst* . . . You must forgive."

You must do this—you must do that. He had enough musts from this man.

"Remember, my son, when I took you home?"

His father had bailed him out of jail, a drunk teenager. He cleaned the vomit off his son and put him to bed without blame.

"You only did it because I was a drunk like you." He didn't care if this was true or not. He just wanted to hurt the man who had hurt him. The desire to hurt stung him.

"Not so, not so." Otto Fischer's hand trembled. "My son, what can I do things better to make?"

"Tell me and the commissario about Lucio Piso and associates."

"Piso helped me. How can I turn on him?"

"Do you want more deaths? Help us find the terrorists."

The guard ripped off the earbuds and raced toward them.

"Don't get excited," Will Fisher said to the guard as he put on his jacket. "I'm leaving now."

"You misunderstand," the guard said. "Wonderful news. The Holy Father has come out of his coma!"

"I will tell you about Piso . . . if you visit again."

"I will visit. I will also leave and never come back if you don't tell all."

"Will you forgive me then?"

"I don't know."

CHAPTER SIXTY

In the semicircle of stairs descending into the bowels of St. Peter's Basilica, the glow of nearly a hundred vigil lights flickered across the faces of Cardinal Gustavo Furbone and Carlos Stroheim.

"I'm not postponing the inspection." The cardinal walked farther down the steps. "We're going under without him."

"We should wait." The prefect of the secret archives hesitated to follow. "The pope commanded his participation in the inspection."

"That's why we're leaving." *How dare this outsider from the African bush order a maverick like Fisher to oversee him? After all, Cardinal Gustavo Furbone was the scion of aristocrats, the new administrator of St. Peter's Basilica, and God willing, the next pope.*

They said Celestine VI's deliverance from the coma was God's miracle.

The cardinal thought it the devil's work.

Since his recovery, the pope was not himself. The doctors had warned of mood swings. From a hospital bed he struggled for control of the Vatican bureaucracy as the pace of recovery quickened. He issued commands instead of his former suggestions. He demanded information about things previously of no interest to him. He ordered around subordinates to whom he had once abdicated total discretion.

Wary of the low archways in the Vatican Grottoes under St. Peter's, cardinal and prefect walked single file down into the gloom of what seemed the entrance to the mythological underworld. Whining about germs, the Colombian hypochondriac wiped away the condensation on his wire-rimmed glasses with a sanitizer tissue.

Celestine VI now treated his cardinal like a flunky functionary instead of a more knowledgeable partner. By what right did this darkie pope overrule his decision to stop work on retrofitting the basilica foundation? The pope's disrespect pained him like fishhooks working their way ever deeper into his intestines. He would spin the pope's transformation as a mental dysfunction caused by the trauma on a mind already enfeebled by polio. One way or another, Celestine VI had to go.

They came to the Street of the Dead, an ancient Roman lane about ninety meters long and two stories under the main altar. The necropolis glistened in beaded humidity thick as sweat. Mausoleums with the names of the departed lined both sides of the lane. Walls pocked with niches for funeral urns enclosed courtyard pavements on which lay tombstones. Bare lightbulbs held the enveloping darkness at bay and played tricks with the cardinal's eyes. Ghostly shapes seemed to flit about in the shadows where light and dark battled for dominance.

As they intruded farther into this underworld, they encountered even more mausoleums with cracked plaster and dislodged bricks. Between the mausoleums, boundary walls had tumbled into rubble. Fissures ripped across the ground like the clawing of a monster raging to burst into the upper world.

"Careful." Stroheim steadied the cardinal. "Quakes have made this place dangerous."

The cardinal bristled. "The basilica above is safe."

"The Vatican architect thinks otherwise." The prefect pointed left, then right. "Emperor Constantine used pillars to support his fourth-century basilica. They're under the outer edge of the current one." He kicked mud from his shoe. "This makes the present foundation more rigid at the perimeter. The rigidity makes it more likely to crack under the stress of an earthquake."

"Even so, St. Peter's is safe." Furbone pointed to the main altar above them. "This location is not rigid. It lacks pillars from Constantine's time."

"Trust your eyes." The prefect kicked away debris from a collapsed pedestal. "See the devastation even here."

About to respond, the cardinal froze. Into the murky atmosphere, a shape flitted out of a mausoleum onto the Street of the Dead. The cardinal resumed breathing. It was only the architect's Japanese assistant. When the churchmen caught up to the assistant, he led them to a paved courtyard below the main altar. A linear pile of brick and plaster fragments from a collapsed wall lay next to a red brick wall still standing.

"What happened," the cardinal said, "to this wall where they found Saint Peter's bones?"

"My Italian is limited." The assistant fumbled for the words. "New earth shakes. So sorry."

"Thank God." The cardinal crossed himself. "St. Peter's bones are secure in the Apostolic Palace."

"The alleged bones." The prefect clasped his hands together. "Many deny they're his."

"Those who matter don't." The cardinal dabbed at his forehead with a lace handkerchief. "And that's what counts . . . not the opinion of naysayers."

"Not done." The Japanese assistant gestured forward. "Come see surprise."

Near the end of the Street of the Dead, recent tremors had cracked open a mound of earth. The assistant had had workmen excavate the opening and buttress the limestone walls of the underground burial chamber. "Take look."

Covered by a marble lid, a sarcophagus rested on a platform in the center of the chamber. The cardinal trained a flashlight on the sarcophagus. He strained to make out the Latin inscription incised into the lid. Panic seized him. His eyes must have failed.

It could not be.

With the help of his companions, the cardinal dropped down into the chamber. He landed unsteadily on his feet, almost falling over. He faced the bas-relief around the sarcophagus chiseled into clusters of grapes and garlands of flowers. He shined his flashlight on the lid. At the top, an artisan had sculpted a horseman lancing a foe on foot. His eyes skipped along the grooved Latin letters accentuated with red paint.

HERE LIES MARCUS LOLLIANUS
CALLINICUS, DEVOTED FATHER OF
FATHERS AMONG THE CONGREGATIONS
OF MITHRAS, AGE 45, FIRST CENTURION
OF THE XXII PRIMIGENIA, A MEMBER OF
THE BOARD OF THE MINT, SON OF TITUS,
AND FRIEND OF PAUL OF TARSUS, THE
CHRIST MESSENGER, CLOSEST TO ME
EVEN IN DEATH.

It shall not be.

Clambering out of the crypt, the cardinal feared it was too late. "Do you understand the meaning of this Latin?" he asked the Japanese assistant.

"Not understand." The assistant smiled.

"Good. You must leave us," the cardinal said, his scarlet cassock spattered with mud. "At once, immediately." He clapped his hands when the assistant hesitated.

After the assistant fled, the cardinal bullied the prefect to accompany him back into the crypt. Their feet sinking into the mud, they slid away the sarcophagus lid, which squealed with the grinding of stone on stone, just enough for the cardinal to glimpse inside.

Shining through the murk, his flashlight illuminated a skeleton clothed in fragments of purple cloth shot through with gold thread. A faded red miter headdress lay above cranial bones. At the top of a disintegrated spinal column, a gold medallion hung down between the shoulder blades. The medallion depicted Mithras stabbing the bull for mankind's benefit. The cardinal removed medallion and miter.

They skidded and screeched the lid back into place.

"Not a word of this above." The cardinal wrapped the medallion and miter in his cloak. "Do you understand?"

"I understand more than you think."

"This is a scandal," the cardinal said, heaping mud with bare hands over the Latin inscription. "Why don't you help me?"

"I don't want to ruin my gloves."

"Take them off."

"Too many germs in the mud."

"You need a psychiatrist." Dripping mud, the cardinal reburied the inscription.

Before they reentered the upper world, the cardinal cornered the prefect. "You will have the slab smashed. The simple and trusted workmen the Japanese assistant used will cart away the fragments as an archaeological find needing reassembly. You will have them taken to a workshop I know for reassembly . . . where I predict they will disappear because of presumed theft."

"The medallion and the miter?"

"Melt down the medallion. Burn the miter."

"Don't make me do this. I revere the past." The prefect's breath grew labored. "The past is immutable . . . like a prehistoric insect in amber . . . like God."

"If you so adore the past, don't do what I command." Furbone raised a clenched fist. "You will become past prefect of the secret archives."

CHAPTER SIXTY-ONE

Nicole Garvey leaned against the railing of the Fontana dei Quattro Fiumi next to Fisher after her jog around the Piazza Navona. The piazza glistened in the straw-yellow sunlight of early morning. Street vendors hawking their wares to the tourist horde did not yet mar the stillness. Some graffiti punk had soured her jogger's high by spray-painting "Return Me to Egypt" on the obelisk rising up in the center of her favorite fountain in Rome. "Why did you want to meet?"

"I don't have much time," Will said. "I have to meet Carlos Stroheim."

"Don't let me delay you." She stretched out a cramped leg. "I'm busy too."

"I'm sorry you found out about him from the media."

"It's not about your father." She sat down on the bench. "It's about you." She took a swig of water from her bottle. "My ex-husband hid his affair. I don't want to blind myself again."

"By the way, I think it's great you're meeting Leone tomorrow." He sat down and slipped his hand over hers. "Finding an unexpected Italian relative and all."

"Your concern for my lineage is touching." She removed her hand from his. "But don't change the subject."

"I swear." He crossed his heart. "I didn't know about his role in the Ardeatine massacre until I read about it. You're not the only one deceived."

"Cut the crap, Will." She bolted up, ready to leave. "When the story first broke, the media didn't mention he was your father. But you knew he was. It's not what he did. It's what you didn't tell me."

"Why would I?" He stiffened his torso. "I was always ashamed of him. I wanted to forget, get away as far as possible, start a new life, but my past caught up."

"The past isn't your problem. It's the present." She sat down. "I can't help wondering what else you're hiding."

"What about your affair with Wesley Bemis?"

"My affair with Wesley Bemis?" She put her hand on her hip and laughed. "What are you talking about?"

Will's lips pursed. He looked away. "Wes told me in a letter from Switzerland."

When she saw Bemis after the museum arson, he'd been a mass of red and purple bumps the doctors called keloid scars. They burst across his face like angry cancers. Surgery made things worse. Oozing paranoia and spouting religious gibberish, he had berated her for rejecting him. He took a leave of absence from the Villa of the Papyri and headed for Switzerland. She'd thought he was out of his mind and out of her life. Only one was true.

"Will. It's not true. You know he's troubled. You saw him go ballistic when you took over operations at the villa while he recovered."

"I didn't say I believed him."

"That man." She caught her breath. "That man plagiarized my doctoral thesis. He sexually harassed me at Harvard and at the Villa of the Papyri."

"Who's hiding things now?"

"I had my reasons for not telling you."

"I had mine too." He took his eyes off the fountain and looked at her. "If you want me to tell everything, it has to be a two-way street."

"I wasn't"—she cleared her throat, looking at the pigeons pecking on the ground—"going to let him scare me off, like some helpless bimbo. I had to stand up to him."

"What's that got to do with not telling—"

"We didn't have a personal relationship then."

"We do now."

"Then don't hide things in our relationship." Did this man know himself well enough for a long-term relationship? His only serious romance ended in a crack-up, almost stampeding him into the Jesuit priesthood. Although handsome and older, he had the air of a starry-eyed seminarian on the streets of Rome in a dress cassock and circular-brimmed hat. She wanted a solid relationship as well as her profession.

"Now that we're into full disclosure," she said, "the University of Chicago has offered me a visiting professorship."

"Will you accept?"

"Why shouldn't I?"

**

"The Holy Father asked me to show you this today," Carlos Stroheim said, standing behind Will Fisher. "I must leave you to your work."

As he surveyed the Callinicus sarcophagus in the pit, Fisher barely heard Stroheim, his attention riveted on this amazing find before him.

Callinicus once lived.

The inscription confirmed Mithraism as a highly organized cult composed of different congregations and presided over by a pope of sorts. The man buried down there must have written the Callinicus letter because he claimed a friendship with Paul of Tarsus, the intended recipient of the letter. Although the Unity Report was forged, the circumstantial evidence of this newly discovered tomb made the authenticity of the Callinicus letter a slam-dunk.

Wait a minute.

He didn't want to get ahead of himself this time. The Unity Report had stampeded him into jumping to false conclusions. Getting burned again would not look good on his résumé.

Celestine VI had requested his personal physician, a former specialist in paleopathology, to examine the bones. The examination might shed more light on the man in the sarcophagus.

Why hadn't Callinicus been cremated? In his time, Christians buried their dead, but pagans usually cremated them. Something didn't seem right. And then there was the mind-blowing inscription that—

"Before I go." Stroheim tapped Fisher on the shoulder. "How did you know? My warning about Cardinal Furbone's vandalism was for the pope's ears alone."

It was time to set Stroheim straight. "The pope told me your warning about Cardinal Furbone."

"Why?"

"He's announcing later today I'm the new supervisor of Vatican excavations." Fisher smiled. "The work at the Villa of the Papyri impressed him."

"What's going on with him?" The prefect of the secret archives wiped his hands with a sanitizer tissue. "He dithered over filling the post for almost a year. Suddenly, he's taking actions as though there's no tomorrow."

"I wish I knew." Outraged at the cardinal's near destruction of cultural heritage in the name of Christian faith, Celestine VI expected his supervisor of excavations to report the facts and hide nothing. *God doesn't need a ventriloquist,* the Holy Father had thundered. This was no longer a man to be trifled with. Maybe the Holy Spirit moved in him, as the pious claimed. "He's grateful you reported the cardinal's machinations."

"I had no choice." Stroheim's facial muscles twitched. "I had to stop the ecclesiastical vandalism before leaving for Argentina next week."

"Argentina?"

"Vatican business. Highly confidential."

Fisher listened to Stroheim covering up his involvement in Roma Rinata. He appreciated his father's coming clean about Stroheim and Piso with him and the commissario during a visit to the Regina Coeli prison. Without that information, they would not have known the extent of the conspiracy. He stopped nosing further into the details of the trip. That would put Stroheim on alert and compromise the commissario's investigation.

"I have something for you." Stroheim called over an assistant who handed to Fisher the miter and medallion found in the burial chamber. "Furbone told me to destroy these."

"Why didn't you?"

"To destroy the memory of man is a sacrilege . . . cultural Alzheimer's."

"Where is Cardinal Furbone? The Holy Father wants the Vatican inspector general to arrest him."

"All I know is he left with his chauffeur." Flashing a gold-toothed smile, he held up his hands and shrugged. "Maybe he went to do penance for his sins."

The prefect knew more than he was saying.

"Let me know when the cardinal returns."

"Of course . . . if he does." Stroheim removed a sheet of papal stationery from a folder. "Here's the preliminary report about the skeleton, by the pope's physician."

The skeleton belonged to a robust male about a meter and a half tall with a fracture in the left leg.

It fits.

Callinicus had written about a fractured left leg due to a chariot mishap.

Fisher strained to keep his glee in check.

"I must leave," Stroheim said. "I have packing to do." He had scarcely left when he returned. "Oh, I almost forgot. Before his departure, Furbone told me he worked out a deal to undo your university dismissal."

"That's wonderful."

"Wait. There's more. You must publicly recant your religious syncretism theology. You will be notified when and where. Do you agree?"

Fisher gave a quick nod. "Just do me the favor of keeping it secret."

"Of course." The prefect smirked. "Isn't that how the Vatican works?"

*　　　＊＊＊*

Leone and Garvey nudged their way through the line of regulars and bellied up to the stainless steel bar of the Sant'Eustachio Il Caffè.

Before Garvey had arrived, the barista, who was into genealogy, enlightened him about the terminology. This relative from America was technically a first cousin, twice removed. Looking at her in her fire-engine-red jogging shorts and scruffy running shoes, she seemed not far enough removed for his taste. He now had second thoughts about this getting-to-know-you meeting.

Leone poured a packet of sugar into his espresso. What irked him most was not the male patrons ogling her in the skimpy getup, but his relationship to the object of their ogling. He emptied another packet and stirred. Her entrance half-undressed and unkempt made a bad impression reflecting on the family reputation. The barista kept staring at her until Leone gave the youthful Don Juan the evil eye.

He gulped his espresso in one go before saying what had to be said.

"Dr. Garvey, you're not making a good impression in that outfit."

"I wanted to meet my newfound kin," she said, elbowing a patron pressing too close. "Not to make an impression on strangers."

"You know the saying? When in Rome—"

"Do as the Romans do." She pointed to his three-legged dog. "Doesn't your pooch make a bad impression in this elegant café?"

She was hard-headed, all right.

"Doctor, that's my dog, Mondocane." He tugged at the leash. "Well-mannered dogs are acceptable in bars . . . not jogging shorts and running shoes."

"Just call me Nicole." She stooped to pet Mondocane. "And why don't we skip the stuffy *lei* and refer to each other with the informal *tu*?"

"But we hardly know each other."

"You will." She laughed. "Anyway, we're blood. *Tu* is for family and relatives, isn't it?" Garvey finished her freshly squeezed juice from blood oranges.

"What was Benjamin like?" she asked in a soft voice.

He fumbled in his pocket and brought out the faded black-and-white photo of his uncle in the white shirt with the unbuttoned collar. He wouldn't have shared the photo unless she'd asked. He relaxed into telling everything he knew. The words came out halting and cautious but then gathered speed and abandon. It wasn't just her red hair but the silent empathy, like his mother's. At the end of his monologue, he surprised himself by asking, "Would you like me to show you his grave in the Ardeatine Caves?"

"It would be an honor." She hesitated. "Did Otto Fischer talk to you?"

"To me and his son." Making sure no one could overhear, he moved closer. "But I'm not free to discuss police business." He waited until the barista set down an espresso for her. "Did Professor Fisher tell you what his father said?"

"Not much. Just his suspicions."

"Please keep the information confidential." He planned to further interrogate Stroheim about the meeting with Renaldi and Fischer at Piso's country estate. He needed an airtight case against the super-intendent. If he was wrong . . . Piso would have his head. "We're at a delicate point in our investigation."

"Will's seeing Stroheim today. I'm worried about him."

"Are you involved with Professor Fisher?"

"When did my personal life become police business?"

She made a face upon taking her first sip of espresso.

"It's not. It's family looking after family." He didn't want to rile her up even more by declaring a single-shot espresso wasn't to be sipped. "Next time you try an espresso you might want a little sugar."

She shot him a puzzled look as though he were the foreigner. "I can take care of myself."

"Then why the worried look?"

"It's Will I'm worried about."

"You," he said, slipping into the familiar *tu* form, "have nothing to worry about." With her approval, he emptied a packet of sugar into her espresso. "Stroheim is under surveillance."

"Why don't you arrest him?"

"The kitten will lead us to the cat."

"Stroheim's going to Argentina next week. Will doesn't know why." She took another sip of the espresso and then put it aside. "But I'm sure he told you this new information first."

Like hell he did.

"I'm afraid he overlooked that nicety."

"He does have a way of overlooking things."

No time remained to put a tail on the prefect. He needed to reel in Stroheim before he got away to Argentina.

"I must return to the office." He clinked coins into the tip tray and roused Mondocane from a nap with a gentle hand. "Time to go, my friend."

"Aren't you forgetting something?" She turned her left cheek toward him. "We may be distant, but we're still cousins."

He grazed her cheeks with his before leaving.

"If you need anything, let me know . . . Nicole."

CHAPTER SIXTY-TWO

Will Fisher couldn't wait until his full team assembled. A word in the Callinicus epitaph wouldn't let him. Dead languages were keys to locked doors. And the meaning of one Latin word might be the key to this door.

Jack Daniels, his friend, called out for release from the hip flask. Jack promised to banish the loneliness sapping his resolve in the god-forsaken landscape.

Not now.

Before he changed his mind, he gurgled out the whiskey into the mud like a pagan drink offering to the gods of sobriety. His ascent up the academic ladder would come crashing down if they found the great scholar drunk in the mud and pissing in his pants.

He lowered himself into the pit with a scholar's fierce need to know. The sarcophagus lid remained propped up against a burial chamber wall after the pope's personal physician had removed the skeleton. He remembered the phrase on the lid . . . *etiam in morte mihi proximus.* The Latin words translated as *closest to me even in death* did not mean what the pope's physician thought.

Closest didn't refer to the personal relationship between Callinicus and Saint Paul, whatever it may have been. If that was the intent, the author of the epitaph, presumably cultured and literate, would likely have used the more exact *familiaris*, or even *propinquis*. The author chose *proximus* because it was the appropriate Latin word to highlight a relation between objects based on physical distance.

But what sense did that make? None he knew of. He and the pope's physician had toured the nearby mausoleums. They gave every indication of housing only pagans and certainly no Christian as prominent as Paul of Tarsus. He had to be right this time. People might otherwise question his competency as the supervisor of Vatican excavations.

He climbed into the emptied sarcophagus. The fear of entombment rattled him. He fantasized a giant hand would clap the slab back onto the coffin. He sucked on the flask, now empty of Jack Daniels, whom he had rudely cast onto the ground outside. A few drops fell onto his parched tongue. He craved his friend. He flung the empty flask out of the pit in despair.

Fisher put his unavoidable sobriety to use. He knelt down, probing across the bottom with his free hand while following its methodical movement with the flashlight in his other. At the head of the sarcophagus, his hand touched a vase filled with Roman coins. Not far from it rested a dish filled with what looked like desiccated beans. He picked up the dish to admire its design. To his astonishment, the dish had covered a saucer-sized hole.

The Romans had used pour holes for mourners to nourish the spirit of the dead inside a sarcophagus with wine and other liquids. The lid resting upright outside the sarcophagus had pour holes. But the Romans did not drill pour holes inside the bottom of a sarcophagus. It made no sense . . . unless it wasn't a pour hole. He sprawled lower to peek through the hole.

He saw something.

CHAPTER SIXTY-THREE

In the bathroom of his Maremma farmhouse, Lucio Piso shaved with a straight razor he had once used to cut up an informer. The mirror reflected the next ruler of the country.

In the past week, the European Union had imposed draconian conditions on Italy for a financial bailout. Street mobs clamored for an end to austerity and a restoration of national honor. Mussolini memorabilia leached out of the dark places. The country would fall into his lap like a ripe fig.

He finished shaving and ordered the cardinal's gag removed.

"How dare you?" The cardinal massaged his jaws. "After all I did for you."

The guards shoved the manacled Furbone onto the toilet seat.

"You mean"—Piso admired his face in the mirror—"what you did *to* me."

"I don't understand."

The cardinal lunged up, trying to break free.

"God commands you to stop this sacrilege. Let me go."

The guards twisted his arms. He whimpered, falling back onto the toilet seat.

"Remember this scent?" Piso slapped the cardinal's face and neck with cologne, heavy with the fragrance of cedar and musk plus a hint of lemon.

"I remember," Piso said. The cardinal, then a priest in war-ravaged Rome, had used it while abusing his charges.

"How did you . . ." The cardinal's mouth opened, and his eyes widened. His expression morphed into apparent puzzlement. "I don't recall using that cologne."

"You're a liar."

"You were one of the orphans . . . weren't you?"

Piso nodded. "Did you know, my clever cardinal, you unwittingly paid me to recover the Festus parchment when Renaldi had already stolen it on my behalf?"

"Renaldi was supposed to work for me."

"He did . . . after he betrayed me."

"You promised not to hold it against him."

"I lied."

"If you had him killed, I can forgive you right here . . . if you let me go."

"You're confused. I brought you here for *your* penance."

"It's about ransom money, isn't it? I can get all you want. Just let me go."

"The money?" Piso exploded into spasms of laughter. "Here I thought you a clever man. And you prove a fool. Shame, shame."

"You insult a prince of the Church."

On the edge of a claw-foot bathtub, Piso sat down opposite the cardinal. "What do you think your penance should be for attempting to destroy the Callinicus tomb?"

"That Colombian savage, Stroheim, told you, didn't he?" The cardinal wagged his finger. "Remove these manacles at once, or I'll have you publicly excommunicated."

At Piso's order, the guards removed them.

Looking surprised, the cardinal rubbed his wrists.

This sack of fat enjoys controlling others with his witch-doctor pronouncement of sin, guilt, and damnation.

"Anything but that." Piso feigned terror. "What must I do to avoid excommunication?"

"First . . . kiss my ring." The cardinal dangled a hand adorned with a gold ring inset with a cobalt-blue sapphire. "As a sign of remorse."

See my mushroom, little one. Kiss it.

The words from the past burned through Piso's brain. He shivered, remembering how this man had violated him in the chapel sacristy before Mass.

In a show of mock reverence, Piso cleaned his lips with a towel.

He drew the ringed finger to his lips.

He sank his teeth into the finger.

He ground down into the bone. Blood filled his mouth.

The cardinal shrieked. He pounded Piso's head with his fist until the guards tore Furbone away. Held fast, he howled.

In the sink Piso spat out flesh, bone, and blood.

The guards let Furbone slump to the floor. He sat there rocking and wailing over and over, "Jesus, Mary, and Joseph," cradling his finger stump in his other hand.

He looked at Piso. "Why?"

Piso grabbed the cardinal by his chubby cheeks and stared down into his eyes. "Don't you remember me—Lucio, the child?"

"My God." The cardinal buried his face in his hands. "That was so long ago."

"And there were so many. Just flesh to be degraded and discarded." He kicked Furbone. "For me it was only yesterday."

"Forgive me."

He held out his hands, dripping blood from his finger stump.

"Forgiveness is against my religion." Piso slapped the cardinal. "But penance for the unforgiven exists."

"What penance do you want? I'll do it, anything."

"It is not what I want you to do. It is what I want to do to you."

CHAPTER SIXTY-FOUR

FROM <mattias.boller@fedpol.admin.ch>
TO <Marco.Leone@poliziadistato.it>
SUBJECT: Carlos Stroheim

Dear Marco,

Carlos Stroheim merits your suspicions. Nazi father fled to Colombia through Vatican Ratline and married Amerindian woman. Their son, Carlos, educated in Argentina with scholarship from Piso Global Enterprises, Inc. Informers reported Carlos became secret leader in the neofascist Aryan Force in Colombia while respected archivist. Background check done when the Force tried opening Swiss bank account.

Warm regards,

Mattias

PS: That Mormon guy, Wesley Bemis, now disfigured, back here causing trouble and crazier than ever. Claims he's converting Hitler, Mussolini, Stalin, Mao, Saddam Hussein, Nero, Seneca, and someone called Callinicus. Had to arrest him for peeping into windows. An emotional wreck.

"See this?" Marco Leone held the email printout. "Swiss police just filled me in on your role in the Aryan Force."

"So?" Stroheim put his gloved hands behind his head. "Political activity in Colombia years ago is not a crime here."

"What do you know about Roma Rinata?"

"Never heard of it."

"What's your relationship with Lucio Piso?"

"Beyond a scholarship his company gave me, I have none."

"Otto Fischer confessed to his son and me about Roma Rinata. He heard you and Riccardo Renaldi discussing Roma Rinata on a farm in the Maremma. We've untangled the farm ownership. It belongs to Piso." Leone leaned forward in his chair toward the prefect. "What do you say now?"

"I doubt he'll repeat those lies in court."

Stroheim's denials complicated things. Otto Fischer had died of presumed natural causes in his cell shortly before Stroheim's arrival. No trial would now take place and no autopsy be done before an unpublicized and hasty burial. Certain members of the Italian political class had to be overjoyed. The death ensured the dirty secrets of World War II stayed buried. He had to move to Plan B.

"We'll see about that," Leone said.

Making sure Stroheim could overhear, Leone asked his complicit secretary by intercom to place a purported telephone call to Otto Fischer at Regina Coeli prison. Shortly afterward, Leone's telephone rang with a purported call from Otto Fischer. On speakerphone, Inspector Rossi impressed Leone with a vocal impersonation of an elderly male speaking Italian with a German accent.

"I thank you again, Signor Fischer, for your willingness to testify in court. Goodbye." The commissario replaced the receiver. He folded his hands on the desk as though praying for Stroheim to break down and confess. "Are you ready to talk now?"

"Only when Otto Fischer returns from the dead."

"How could you possibly know, unless . . ." Stroheim knew Otto Fischer's killer.

"Unless what? Otto Fischer's poor health is public knowledge." His gold-toothed smirk of cocky defiance infuriated Leone.

"Professor Fisher and I will testify to what Otto Fischer said."

The prefect's smirk shape-shifted into a pensive look. "I'll take the chance." He rubbed a gloved hand over his chin. "The hearsay statement of a dead Nazi told to a biased police officer and an alienated son isn't enough to convict me."

The blinking and buzzing of the intercom interrupted the commissario's racing mind. His secretary. "Someone's here to see you."

"Does this someone have a name?"

"Won't say. He wants to see you immediately."

"Have someone cool his heels." Picking up his train of thought, Leone slid Inspector Rossi's investigative report across the desk. "Read it."

The prefect removed his gloves. Two hands emerged swollen red. He picked up the report, read it, and dropped it on the desk like a dirty rag. He swabbed his hands and chair arms with sanitizer tissue.

"The report is true . . . insofar as it goes. The dagger used in Basso's murder went missing a week before. And it's also true I had temporary control over the traveling exhibit of Mideast antiquities containing the dagger while the cardinal was away."

"Then another thing is true." Leone tapped two fingertips together. "You had the opportunity to procure the murder weapon."

"You think that's enough?" He rubbed his hands in his lap. "In fact, now that I think of it, I remember misplacing the keys to the exhibit." He glared at Leone. "Funny how it just came to me now."

"Where is Cardinal Furbone? He's your boss."

"I don't know." Stroheim seemed pleased with himself. "Ask his chauffeur. He was the last person to see the cardinal."

The intercom blinked and buzzed again. "Sorry, Commissario Leone. Mister Someone insists on seeing you . . . now."

"Tell him I decide who sees me when . . . and don't interrupt again."

Those raw, cracked hands moved on the other side of his desk, one over the other, like crowded crabs jockeying for supremacy.

And then it came to him.

He rummaged through his files and pulled out the Basso autopsy report. He riffled through it and found the gem. He looked up. "The fingerprints on the murder dagger were worn away, just like I'll bet yours are."

"Prove it."

"The passport office couldn't fingerprint you. Yours were too worn away."

"That's still not enough." Stroheim put on his gloves and stood up. "So long. I have to get ready for Argentina."

"Why are you going there?"

"Confidential Vatican business."

"By God, I'll get you one way or another." Leone slapped his hand on the desk. "I'll tie up your trip in knots until you cooperate."

"Oh no you won't." The prefect sat down. He flashed a business card from his wallet. "Call this lawyer."

Blowing breath through rounded lips, Leone read the name of the same intelligence agent used by police when they contacted the AISE . . . Agenzia Informazioni e Sicurezza Esterna. Right there and then he placed a call to the lawyer. The lawyer confirmed over the telephone that the Agency for External Information and Security, the country's foreign intelligence agency, needed Stroheim in Argentina as soon as possible for reasons of national security. "Keep his cover story confidential and your nose out of this, Marco" ended the conversation.

A baldhead in aviator sunglasses barged through the office door despite the secretary's plea to stop. The baldhead looked at the prefect. "You're coming with me."

"Who the hell are you?" Leone jumped up. "I'm in charge."

The stranger flashed identification.

Agenzia Informazioni e Sicurezza Interna—AISI for short, the country's domestic intelligence agency.

"There's some mistake." Leone scratched his head. "Our AISE go-between just told me the AISE wants this guy on the next plane for Argentina."

It had to be a miscommunication between separate intelligence branches created as a result of the 2007 reform. That reform split the Italian Secret Service after the arrest of a general in army intelligence in the attempted Borghese Coup.

"He's lying through his teeth." The bald AISI officer took off his aviator glasses and twirled them. "This guy and some key AISE higher-up are part of Roma Rinata. They're on the verge of a coup d'état. Their terrorism in Rome is the opening act."

"Not again." The commissario sank back into his chair. He glanced out the window into the past. Was history to be repeated?

Before getting cold feet, neofascists had almost pulled off the 1970 Borghese Coup led by World War II Fascist Junio Borghese, the Black Prince. The attempted overthrow of the Italian government—orchestrated by CIA operatives—shriveled up under the spotlight of lawsuits and parliamentary investigations.

"Stroheim," the AISI agent said, "is going to Argentina to win support for the coup through contacts developed by Piso Global Enterprises. Lucio Piso is the new puppet master, and this man is one of the puppets."

"As I suspected." Leone still had a missing piece. "How does Cardinal Furbone fit into Roma Rinata?"

"He doesn't. Piso abducted the cardinal for reasons not clear to us. We've tracked Furbone to Piso's villa in the Maremma. We're about to move on the villa."

"How do you know all this?"

The baldhead motioned Leone outside the office and closed the door so Stroheim couldn't hear. "The cardinal's chauffeur is our guy working undercover in Roma Rinata."

"Appreciate the heads-up." Leone shook hands with the agent. "I'll take over now."

"This is our parade, friend." The AISI agent reentered the office and handcuffed Stroheim. "We'll question him in our own special way. Basso's homicide is part of the domestic conspiracy. We have jurisdiction, and you don't."

CHAPTER SIXTY-FIVE

The driver braked in front of the locked-up Piso Aquarium outside the town of Grosseto. Lucio Piso piled out of the pickup with his henchmen. A custodian exited the aquarium to inform him all was ready. With the dedication of the building only days away, Piso ordered his underlings to clean up the premises once he finished his mission.

Above the entrance, black lettering on a brushed-gold plaque proclaimed that the Piso Benevolent Association for the Protection of Orphans built the aquarium as a gift to the people of the Maremma region. His right-hand man confirmed opening day was reserved for orphans bused in from all over Italy at Piso's expense. Each orphan was to be admitted and treated to a warm meal, gelato sweets, and a clown act without cost.

He wiped away moisture from his eyes with the pretense that wind-blown dust had stung them.

At the snap of his fingers, workers unloaded a trunk from the pickup onto a dolly. They trundled the load into the aquarium foyer. At his command, the workers stopped at the statue of Mithras he had bargained away from the clerical pedophile. The restoration exceeded his expectations. His artisans had retouched the golden locks of hair and replaced a lost opal eye. The god seemed to see the offering he had brought.

Mithras had returned to Italy.

"What happened," said a henchman, "to the cross on the forehead?"

"I had the desecration repaired."

"Isn't he some kind of saint? Like Saint Michael?"

"Enough." Piso resented the understandable confusion. "We have work to do."

Saltwater tanks swarming with sharks and octopuses glowed around the walls of the low-lit interior. Workers set the trunk before the centerpiece of the aquarium, a cylindrical tank holding seventy-five thousand liters of salt water.

As he marveled at his babies inside the tank, Piso wondered by what happy karma he had made this tank the main attraction before he knew its special purpose.

The tank sparkled with the pinks and blues and yellows of fish playing hide-and-seek around a coral with fissures and crevices. Lying in wait, his darlings darted speckled heads in and out of dark openings camouflaged by undulating stalks of sea grass.

The henchmen jerked Cardinal Furbone from the trunk. A bandage swathed the stump of his ring finger. They cut away the rope from his arms. While they held him fast, the aquarium guards creaked a grooved and mossy millstone end over end to the tank. Ever protective of its chosen one, the Fates had ordained that when he purchased the Maremma farmstead, he would find the abandoned stone once used to grind grain. The mill of the gods grinds slowly, but he would make it grind exceedingly fine.

Piso ripped off the tape from the cardinal's mouth.

Furbone rubbed his swollen lips. "What are you going to do to me?"

"The real question is what did you do to me."

"I helped you." Furbone held out his clasped hands in supplication. "You were an unloved orphan."

Outraged at the sanctimoniousness of what he was hearing, Piso put his hands on his cheeks and rocked his head from side to side. Behind closed eyes, childhood images flashed. His head throbbed. "Don't you remember," he said, whining with a child's voice, "our talk in your office?" The cardinal looked puzzled. "About what should be done to priests who molest children."

"You mean what Jesus said?"

"Bravo." The child's voice became a predator's roar. "You absolutely agreed with Matthew eighteen, verse six." Piso read from the New

Testament. "But if anyone causes one of these little ones who believe in me to sin, it would be better for him to have a large millstone hung around his neck and be drowned in the depths of the sea."

"You can't mean—" Furbone pulled on his ears, wincing in pain.

"Yes I do." Piso rubbed his hands. "I read the Bible literally."

"I didn't really harm you. I helped you, loved you, according to the classical Greek ideal of an adult male mentoring a young male."

His normal voice returned. "You odious piece of dung." He bounced the New Testament off the cardinal's head. "You whited sepulcher."

Piso's henchmen pushed the cardinal up the mobile stairs leading to a platform surrounding the cylindrical tank. Joining them, Piso sliced the cardinal's face with his straight razor. Strings of blood crisscrossed the cardinal's cheeks.

The guards fastened the millstone to Furbone's neck.

"Have mercy."

"Hurry." Piso turned his thumb downward. "Drown him."

The cardinal cowered. "God have mercy on me."

The front doors swung open. Piso's top lieutenant ran inside. "The cops are almost here. Time to scram."

As he sank to the aquarium bottom, Furbone held his breath, failing to climb an invisible ladder of bubbles back to the platform. A swirl of dark forms swarmed up to welcome him. He collided with the coral. Tangled gray and tan blurs spotted in black writhed over his body.

The giant snaggletoothed moray eels tore away at his flesh. They gorged on him. He screamed out a silent volcano of bubbles. His lungs shouted for oxygen. He sputtered and choked as water flooded his lungs. Ripping him apart morsel by morsel, the eels squirmed and slithered over him. He flailed with hands and legs as they slid across his face.

The opal eyes of Mithras beheld him dying and men running into the aquarium with submachine guns.

CHAPTER SIXTY-SIX

Will Fisher strode through the corridor of the Charlemagne Wing in St. Peter's on his way to the press conference. Never had this top floor been reserved for a photographic exhibition as spectacular as his. Journalists aimed cameras at him. Guests parted like the Dead Sea as he deigned to acknowledge with nods and hand waves familiar faces lined up beside his triumphal procession.

He called the shots now. Not bad for the son of a Milwaukee butcher and Nazi war criminal. His fame offset the family shame. The adulation of the attendees jolted him into euphoria without the services of his friend, Jack Daniels.

Along the walls, blue banners spelled out the exhibition's theme in gold lettering: DISCOVERY OF THE DOUBLE SARCOPHAGI. Between the banners hung black-and-white photographs preserving for posterity the chronological record of the great discovery. Near the press conference location, Fisher basked in the sight of a crowd gaping at an enlarged photograph running from floor to ceiling.

The photo recorded the discovery of a second burial under the false bottom of the Callinicus sarcophagus. His team and he, the rather handsome one, stood beside the sarcophagus with the false bottom opened. The team had just removed a skull resting on a deteriorated red satin pillow next to a headless skeleton clothed in tatters. The skeleton was missing parts. Forensic testing confirmed the skull and other skeletal remains were portions of the same body. Christian tradition supported beheading as the cause of Saint Paul's death. A plaque on the wall next to the photograph translated the Latin text inscribed inside the false bottom.

> THANKS TO MATRONA LUCILLA, MOTHER OF CALLINICUS INTERRED ABOVE AND THE PURCHASER OF THIS SARCOPHAGUS, PAUL OF TARSUS LIES HEREIN, APOSTLE OF CHRIST AND ROMAN CITIZEN, DIED A MARTYR AT 57 YEARS, A FRIEND TO CAL-LINICUS, THE FATHER OF FATHERS PRE-SIDING OVER THE MITHRAIC CONGREGA-TIONS IN ROME.

"Congratulations." The voice sounded familiar. Fisher finished signing an autograph and turned around. An usher restrained the rector of the Pontifical Gregorian University and others from crowding the professor.

"Let him pass." Fisher liked being in charge.

"Glad to have our superstar back at the university . . . once you make the statement at the press conference." The rector shifted his feet. "You will, won't you?"

"You'll have to attend and find out." The rector had been the first to turn on him when the Vatican witch hunt began. Let the coward dangle in the wind. This company man needed him. But he was superprof now. He didn't need the rector. Fisher turned his back and strolled to the press conference at the end of the corridor.

In the press conference room, Nicole sat in the back row of folding chairs. Her presence at what would be his bravura performance surprised him. He waved off a photographer who angled on bended knee for a shot. He should have called back as her voice mail requested. He started toward her to make amends only to be redirected by the Vatican press secretary to a table covered with a white cloth bearing an image of the papal seal. The secretary sat down next to Fisher.

"Remember," he whispered. "You must recant here."

"Must I?" They were dealing with superprof now.

The papal secretary glowered at Fisher before he explained the ground rules of the press conference to the media reporters. Fisher waved to Nicole. She didn't wave back. He'd see her after his performance and make things right. Upset over his father's death, excitement over the discovery . . . two good excuses.

In his opening statement, he retold the story of his discovery with a dramatic flair worthy of his best classroom performances, climaxing with the Latin word *proximus* on the upper tomb of Callinicus and its linguistic implication of Saint Paul's physical proximity.

Acting on a hunch—or perhaps divine inspiration, as the press secretary interjected—he had his team insert an optical probe into the opening at the base of the Callinicus tomb. The probe revealed the remains of a dead body.

The team removed bricks from the base and found a slab used as a false bottom to seal off the upper tomb. The inscription inside the lower tomb confirmed Christian tradition. A Roman noblewoman named Matrona Lucilla had Saint Paul buried in a family tomb. The bones dated back to the time of Saint Paul. Other testing corroborated the approximate age of the man as mentioned in the inscription.

"Why," a reporter asked, "would they bury Paul underneath Callinicus?"

"One moment before we recognize questions." The press secretary whispered in Fisher's ear. "Will you recant?"

"Now's not the time." Fisher stood up to avoid the press secretary.

"Back to answering your question." He had figured it out. "We all know Nero blamed the Christians for the fire in Rome. He hunted them down for execution. The surviving Christians and their pagan friends, like Callinicus and his mother, recovered Saint Paul's corpse. They buried it in the lower part of a double-decker sarcophagus.

"When Callinicus died, they laid him to rest in the upper part. The Callinicus letter we found earlier in the Villa of the Papyri shows how friendly the two were . . . 'You will remain close to me in death as in life.' Notice the clever wordplay by Callinicus. What started out in the letter as a close relationship in life ended literally in physical closeness at death."

Nicole took pen and paper from her purse. She was going to take notes of what he said. He must be wowing the journalists. Even she hung on his words.

"Professor Fisher," a florid-faced priest said. "As a fellow American scholar, you surely know Pope Benedict XVI declared Saint Paul's bones rest in a sarcophagus under the altar of Saint Paul Outside-the-Walls in Rome. Are you disputing a pope?"

"Not at all." He planned on his nemesis from the ultraconservative Legionaries of Christ showing up. "Investigators only found bone fragments of a corpse in the first or second century AD. The pope never said they were Saint Paul's bones, only that they seemed to confirm belief."

Nicole stopped writing and folded the paper.

"Come now," the priest said. "The marble plaque over the sarcophagus at Saint Paul Outside-the-Walls reads: 'To Paul, Apostle and Martyr.' It's obvious, like asking who's buried in Grant's Tomb."

Fisher smoldered as the audience broke out in laughter.

How dare this representative of a religious group whose founder had been implicated in sexual scandal rain on his parade?

"Look at the photograph." His voice rising, Fisher pointed down the corridor. "The Matrona Lucilla inscription also declares the remains I found to be those of Paul."

"One set of bones must be a fake," a journalist yelled out.

"Not necessarily." He had thought long and hard about this seeming contradiction. "Tradition says Matrona Lucilla buried Saint Paul in a family tomb. As Christians became socially accepted, the faithful could have reburied Saint Paul's bone fragments under the current Saint Paul Outside-the-Walls. Early Christians dismembered bodies of saints and martyrs as holy and miraculous relics for distribution and . . ."

Why is Nicole handing the paper to an usher?

"Correct me if I'm wrong," the priest said, "but aren't you the person who got taken in by the Unity Report?"

"I'm also the person who admitted publicly I was wrong." He couldn't leave it there. "I don't know about you, but I believe in keeping an open mind."

"Gentlemen, please," the press secretary said. "No personal remarks."

"To complete my thoughts . . . before the interruption . . . Saint Paul's remains were removed at least once. That's why we didn't find a complete skeleton. Early Christians divided up the bones of saints and martyrs for their miraculous powers and to increase the geographic area of veneration." He paused to take a sip of water. "Therefore, it's perfectly possible the bones we found and the fragments under Saint Paul Outside-the-Walls are all from Saint Paul."

"One more question." The press secretary looked at his watch.

"Why," asked a reporter, "don't you compare the fragments in Saint Paul Outside-the-Walls with those you found?"

"Why not?" Fisher smiled. "I agree."

The usher approached the table with Nicole's note.

For me or the press secretary?

"Impossible." The priest from the Legionaries of Christ was on his feet. "A comparison would disturb the only true relic in Saint Paul Outside-the-Walls."

"Not at all impossible." The priest's know-it-all attitude diverted his attention from Nicole. "I have authority from the pope to make a comparison. It's my choice."

"No more questions," the press secretary said. "Any concluding statement to make, Professor Fisher?" He stared icicles at the professor. "This is your last chance."

"I take this opportunity," Fisher said in a flat voice, "to publicly retract the theological views on religious syncretism expressed in my latest book, *One God with Many Names.* My views were ill considered in light of Roman Catholic doctrine and upsetting to many. I apologize for any scandal."

Nicole hurried out of the room. The usher handed Fisher her note.

Contact me when your performance is over. We need to talk. Nicole

CHAPTER SIXTY-SEVEN

Bouncing around in a truck at 3:00 a.m., Marco Leone felt like an interrogation room suspect spied on through a two-way mirror. Across from him sat the "leatherheads" of the police counterterrorist unit known as NOCS, the Italian acronym for Central Security Operations Unit. In dark-olive combat fatigues, the NOCS commander and his men armed with assault rifles scrutinized Leone through the eye slits of their black balaclavas.

They wouldn't be on this dangerous mission if the AISI hadn't botched the capture of Lucio Piso. A tracking device on the cardinal's limousine allowed the domestic intelligence agency to trace the kidnapped Furbone to Piso's Maremma farmhouse. But the AISI agents didn't foresee Piso going to the aquarium in an untracked pickup before they raided the farmhouse. By the time the agents made it to the aquarium, Piso had escaped in a getaway car. Their only achievement was to chop off the head of a flopping moray eel, its jagged teeth clamped to the cardinal's corpse.

"Why did you invite me along?"

The NOCS commander normally would not have given Leone the time of day.

"You deserve it." The commander ran his hand over his holstered Glock 17. "Your guys uncovered Piso's safe house near Ciampino Airport."

That part was true.

His Leone Squad had linked the neofascist owner of the safe house, a cashiered lieutenant colonel, to Roma Rinata. The renegade had helped organize Operation Gladio, set up by the CIA after World War II to wage guerilla war if Italy went communist. The authorities implicated but never convicted him for far-right bombings during the Years of Lead in the 1970s. Inspector Rossi warned Leone the lieutenant colonel had chartered a flight to Switzerland from Ciampino Airport with Piso traveling incognito.

But something wasn't right.

When did NOCS start sharing credit for operations with rivals? And why did the commander invite along a mere civilian cop he had scorned in the past?

"Besides, you trained with NOCS," the commander said, as though he had divined Leone's misgivings. "I always wondered why you resigned."

"What are your assault plans?"

Diverted by the question, as Leone intended, the commander elaborated his attack plan. Leone in tow, he would spearhead a team ringing the villa's main entrance while another team surrounded the rear. On signal, the team leader at the rear would set off a display of confiscated fireworks to distract those inside while the commander's team stormed the front.

The truck whiplashed to a stop behind a thicket of trees surrounding the villa. The commander ordered radio silence. They all slipped out of the truck and slunk toward the front entrance with the stealth of predators. At the edge of underbrush, the commander signaled everyone to take cover. He peered through night-vision binoculars. "What the fuck?"

Leone poked his head up. "What's wrong?"

"Look."

Through night binoculars, Leone detected four black-hooded figures, each holding a Mauser 86SR rifle. The Special Intervention Group of the carabinieri. Who had let this rival counterpart of the NOCS strike force in on the operation? And why did they stand guard under the portico instead of making arrests?

God help us. Leone smelled a disaster of friendly fire in the making.

He had to take the chance they'd recognize him and not shoot.

"Where the hell are you going?" the commander asked. "You'll ruin everything."

In the distance, a thumping sound alerted Leone to a helicopter moving toward the villa. *Must be a carabinieri asset. NOCS isn't using helicopters.*

"Don't shoot." He raised his hands. "I'm Commissario Marco Leone."

"Halt," a voice yelled out. "Or we shoot."

"There's been a mistake." He halted. "A NOCS team is behind me."

The leader of the Carabinieri Special Intervention Group approached with a rifle pointed at Leone. "Get out. You're spoiling our operation."

A shot rang out behind Leone. The head of a wood nymph statue next to him shattered in shards across the lawn. He hit the ground.

"Stop shooting." The officer crouched down. "We're carabinieri."

The NOCS commander emerged from the underbrush with Glock 17 in hand, his brood of commandos straggling behind like ducklings. From the blame game played by the NOCS and carabinieri over responsibility for the near death of the commissario, Leone gathered enough information to fear the worst.

Pursuing their own classified investigation, the carabinieri had raided the villa, not aware the NOCS strike force would arrive. Getting wind of this unforeseen intervention, an AISE agent from the conspiracy-riddled foreign intelligence service insisted on accompanying the carabinieri so he could negotiate a peaceful surrender.

Suspicious of the AISE agent's intentions, Leone shouted, "Let's attack!" to overcome the helicopter noise nearing the villa. "Before they escape."

"What did you say?" the NOCS commander asked, looking up at the helicopter.

"Let's raid the place. We're losing time."

"We can't." The carabinieri leader shouted over the noise. "The AISE representative is inside trying to negotiate a surrender. We are guarding the place in the meantime."

"Is that your copter up there?" Leone asked.

"No." The carabinieri officer looked at the helicopter angling over the roof of the villa for a landing. "I thought it was yours."

The light inside the villa flicked off at the same time a light went on in the commissario's head.

"You've been duped." Leone pointed to the villa "The AISE representative must be in cahoots with Piso. Let's go before they hustle Piso and the lieutenant colonel away."

The air reverberated with a chain of explosions in the villa's rear. The NOCS team had set off the cache of fireworks. The explosion faded away, replaced by the swoosh of Roman candles exploding colored balls in the sky. Green and red pearls of fire. Yellow spinning sparks. And a grand finale of pink peonies across the sky.

"Who screwed up?" Leone pointed to the villa. "If they didn't know we were here, they do now."

"I'll look into it." The NOCS commander shrugged. "We've lost the element of surprise. I'm calling off the assault."

"You're what?" Leone looked at the villa. "They'll get away."

"We'll keep it under surveillance." He ordered his men back to the truck.

"You can't walk away."

"No? Just watch me."

As the NOCS unit departed, Leone rushed the front door with the carabinieri strike force. They battered it down. Two suspects rushed up the stairway. He fired his Beretta. Hit in the leg, one suspect tumbled down the stairs. The other surrendered to the carabinieri and confessed. Leone raced to the roof.

He arrived just in time to see the helicopter buzz away into the night.

CHAPTER SIXTY-EIGHT

The domestic intelligence agency known as AISI drove the handcuffed NOCS commander away in a black Alfa Romeo past Leone. To the commissario's satisfaction, a no-man's land ringed by police sealed off the Baths of Caracalla from the armed insurrectionists inside.

"Are you certain?" Leone asked.

"We broke Carlos Stroheim. He told us everything we suspected about the conspiracy and then some. The NOCS commander was in on the plot." The bald-headed AISI agent twirled his aviator sunglasses. "He was about to defect to the cabal hunkered down under the baths."

"Hold on." Leone closed his eyes and rubbed his nose with index finger and thumb. "He raided the villa with me to capture Piso."

"He was supposed to have you killed . . . accidentally . . . at the villa."

Of course.

How could he have overlooked it? He remembered gunshot shattering the wood nymph statue only a half meter from him. He felt numb. "A raid just to murder me?"

"A feigned raid." The AISI agent squinted through puffy eyes. "Just a diversionary ruse, like Piso's supposed escape to Argentina via Switzerland. Piso was never at the villa. Just the former lieutenant colonel, the co-conspirator and owner of the safe house where Piso stayed. The NOCS commander planned to let the colonel escape in the helicopter so he could join Piso in the baths."

The AISI agent pointed with sunglasses to the Baths of Caracalla. "Piso has set up his command post over there in the mithraeum under the baths." The mountainous structure loomed ominous before them as the morning sun burned off the camouflage of haze.

"Why would Piso box himself inside the ancient baths?" Leone scoured the red-brick ruins of the Baths of Caracalla. "What's he up to?"

The AISI agent came alongside Leone, staring at the Baths of Caracalla, and put his sunglasses back on. "At sunrise, on Easter Sunday, sleeper cells across the country unleash the coup d'état. Piso marches triumphantly from the pagan baths in what he calls the resurrection of Rome. And before you can say Mussolini, Italy's back to the future."

The audacity of the plan staggered Leone.

The Rome Symphony Orchestra was scheduled to play Handel's Easter oratorio, *La Resurrezione*, for Rome's upper crust on Easter Sunday. The performance would take place inside the Baths of Caracalla on one of the world's largest outdoor stages, reopened for this special performance.

The prime minister had lost his head over a golden-haired soprano beauty, forty years his junior, rehearsing the role of Mary Magdalene. With the government facing collapse on the eve of a no-confidence vote, the political playboy scrapped his flurry of emergency meetings. Known more for dancing moves than political ones, the flitterbug of frivolity beelined to a symphony rehearsal earlier in the day without a security detail. An unexpected prize, he fell into the arms of the conspirators who had already taken the orchestra hostage before AISI learned of Piso's whereabouts.

"One more thing." The scar on the cheek of the AISI agent quivered in a smile. "You're taking temporary command of the operation."

"You can't be serious."

"Only until higher-ups name a replacement for the NOCS commander."

"Right. That'll only take a year or so." Leone rubbed his neck. "Questore Malatesta would never allow it."

"I hate to break it to you, Commissario." The agent's voice went somber. "Questore Malatesta has been relieved of his duties. He had knowledge of the conspiracy and his godson's role in it. Yet he failed to report it or act against it."

"He went down for his godson." Questore Malatesta was not an evil man. Just the wrong man for the job. "I still need the Polizia di Stato to approve this."

"The chief of police approved it." The AISI agent put his hand on the commissario's shoulder. "We need you. You trained with NOCS. You're on the front line already. You have the leadership skills that—"

"What about the carabinieri?"

"Their chief of staff remained loyal, but the commander general is over there with Piso. Not a hostage, mind you, but one of the conspirators. We don't know how far this cancer has eaten into the military branches." The AISI agent grimaced. "That's what we get for militarizing the carabinieri."

"They should demilitarize them, like they did the Polizia di Stato." Leone looked at the Baths of Caracalla. "You're in intelligence. You must know why I resigned from NOCS."

"How's this?" The AISI agent rubbed his hand over his bald head like a good luck charm. "You took martial arts training with another cadet. He concealed a pulmonary condition. He died after you put him in a choke hold. You weren't responsible. End of story."

"It didn't feel that way."

"That was then. This is now."

"His brother's a big shot in NOCS."

"His brother has gotten over it. So should you."

"I'll take command . . . but on one condition."

"What is it?"

"Give me a cigarette. I need one."

"You told me you don't smoke anymore."

"To be exact, I said I no longer buy them."

CHAPTER SIXTY-NINE

"I'm against a direct assault." Leone returned to scrutinizing an architectural survey of the Baths of Caracalla in the command trailer. Finished in AD 217 by the Emperor Caracalla, the baths, covering the space of three soccer fields, had accommodated more than fifteen hundred bathers at a time. They were now a UNESCO World Heritage site.

"The risk of damage is too great." He looked up and opened the top buttons of his shirt to cool off. "We could cut off outside communications and wait him out."

"That won't work." Inspector Rossi fanned himself with a newspaper. "All Piso has to do is play out the clock. Rebels operating independently across the country, most still unknown to us, automatically start the coup on Easter Sunday. Time is on his side."

"That's what Stroheim told the AISI. It doesn't mean it's true."

"Want to take the chance?"

"You know what Piso's messenger told us." Leone drew his forefinger across his throat. "If we attack, they'll slaughter all the hostages."

"The Alpine detachment could scale those walls at night." Rossi removed binoculars from his neck. "They'll surprise the guards and free the captive orchestra."

"Even if we seize the outdoor stage and free the orchestra without a massacre," the commissario said, "Piso and his inner circle are holed up in the fortified bunker of the underground mithraeum. They'll kill the prime minister and the negotiator held inside the mithraeum."

"Kill the prime minister?" A wicked grin spread across Rossi's face. "Italy should be so lucky."

"Get serious."

"I am. If we crush the conspiracy in its shell, it'll never hatch after the media blitz. Piso's ringleaders won't try a coup d'état with their leader dead or in chains."

"Let's at least wait for the negotiator." Would the sociopath inside let him go? "At least for now. We'll know what Piso wants."

"You can't negotiate with the devil. He's just stalling."

"Have you forgotten? The Red Brigades murdered Prime Minister Aldo Moro when the government refused to negotiate."

"A little before my time." Rossi scratched his head. "But not yielding was the right thing to do. I heard it broke the back of the Red Brigades."

Leone felt clammy and tired. "Easy to say when it's not your life." The humidity mired further thoughts. "We'll decide when the negotiator returns."

"If he returns," Rossi added. "Piso doesn't have all his screws in place."

CHAPTER SEVENTY

Across the esplanade abuzz with cicada songs, a figure zigzagged in the shadows toward the security perimeter set up by the Polizia di Stato around the Baths of Caracalla. After passing a watchword challenge, sentinels escorted the figure to Leone. He welcomed back the negotiator with a hug. "What did he say?"

"He warned us not to storm the baths. Else everyone dies."

Leone waited for an armored personnel carrier to rumble past.

"What about our offer?"

"Went nowhere." The negotiator wiped sweat off his brow. "The recommendation of leniency in return for surrender enraged him. He thinks he holds all the cards."

"How many men inside?" Leone fanned away twilight mosquitoes with his hat. "And the armament?"

"Machine-gun emplacements outside the mithraeum entrance. The roundabout way they took me blindfolded through the grounds suggests land mines." The negotiator twisted open a bottle of mineral water. "Kept me near the entrance, so I couldn't determine the fire-power inside." He chugalugged the bottle and wiped his mouth with the back of his hand.

Leone stooped to pet a panting Neapolitan mastiff accompanying the police canine unit on their way to patrol duty. He returned to the task at hand. "What about releasing the hostages . . . including the prime minister?"

"Piso wants till Monday after Easter to consider it," the negotiator said. "If we attack, everything's off."

"The bastard's trying to hoodwink us." Leone clenched and unclenched his fists. "He thinks we don't know the coup start time . . . sunrise, Easter Sunday."

"I let him believe we don't know," the negotiator said, tossing the water bottle aside. "We might be able to play this to our advantage."

"Damn." Leone sighed. "He's forcing us to take action before then."

"Looks that way." The negotiator hesitated. "But he dangled one possibility . . . totally unacceptable. We give him a substitute hostage in place of the prime minister."

"Simultaneous exchange?"

"Yes."

"When?"

"Tomorrow morning . . . Good Friday."

"What hostage does he want?"

"You . . . and no one else."

CHAPTER SEVENTY-ONE

Enzo Rossi's simmering silence made Leone feel more on edge. The inspector drummed his fingers on the dashboard of the parked squad car. Then Rossi erupted. "You can't play hostage. Hostage exchanges are against departmental policy."

"You heard the negotiator." Leone rolled down the front passenger window a little farther in search of a breeze. No one around to eavesdrop. "The prime minister screamed for me to be exchanged for him."

"Holy mother of God." Rossi threw up his hands and turned to Leone. "The prime minister is saving his ass under duress. His orders have no validity."

"We need the prime minister."

"No we don't. Prime ministers come and go. The country survives."

"Don't let your emotions run away with you." Leone opened the passenger door for more air. "Without a government in place . . . miserable as it is . . . Piso has a better chance of filling the political vacuum."

"Come on." Rossi opened his door on the driver's side. "If ever I saw a candidate for the Stockholm syndrome, it's the prime minister."

"Where are you going with this Stockholm syndrome business?"

"You saw the prime minister's profile . . . a dependent personality with no core values. If he gets out, he'll likely agree to whatever Piso wants, maybe even joining Roma Rinata and having us arrested."

"Spare me the psychobabble. We're cops, not psychiatrists."

"Who's supposed to take over when you're inside?" Rossi waved to laborers working under the yellow glow of mobile sodium floodlights to cordon off the Baths of Caracalla with a final load of barricades and sandbags.

"You can . . . until I come back," the commissario said, remembering something in the architectural plans of the baths. A current of excitement pierced his lethargy.

"What if you don't . . ."

"Come back?" He rubbed his chin. "Commissarios are replaceable."

"The new ones don't have the military training you had."

"Brains are needed for this, dear Inspector Rossi. Not just guns."

Asking what the commissario was up to, Rossi followed Leone to the command trailer. Leone crouched over the architectural survey for the Baths of Caracalla.

Three point two kilometers of tunnels ran along three different levels underground. Each tunnel measured six meters high and six across, wide enough for two ox carts to pass through with the tons of wood needed daily to fire up the fifty bath furnaces. And those were only the known tunnels. From the depths of his mind, a childhood memory about the tunnels floated to the surface of awareness. Leone grinned.

That could be my subterranean surprise.

"I know that look." Rossi tapped Leone on the shoulder. "What's up?"

"I have a plan, Inspector Rossi." The commissario rubbed his hands together. "But I need to get inside to scope out their defenses."

"One problem." Rossi crossed his arms. "How can you give us the scoop if you're a hostage inside?" He then tapped his head with his finger. "You're always telling me to use this."

Rossi tapping his head. Tapping. Body language. That was the answer.

The negotiator poked his face inside the trailer door. "What do I tell Piso?"

"One minute before you turn me over to Piso." Everything depended on coordination. "I must let Inspector Rossi know what I'm up to."

CHAPTER SEVENTY-TWO

Under the Baths of Caracalla, reed pipes warbled the revival of the sacred taurobolium rite as a passing storm cracked thunderbolts on Good Friday morning. Clad in buckskin trousers and star-studded cape, Lucio Piso grew giddy behind the alabaster mask of Mithras in the swelter of a pit dug into the mithraeum.

Above the pit, costumed Ravens, Bridegrooms, and Lions crowded the two stone benches running the length of the chamber to witness their leader's beatification. Even those Soldiers guarding the entrance would witness his elevation. Just as he anticipated, the rising incantation of *Nama . . . Nama . . . Sebesio* and the sweet smell of incense trapped by limited ventilation intoxicated his besieged acolytes into a communal state of desperate destiny. Like berserkers, they would fight to the death.

Crouched like a fetus within the dark pit topped with perforated planks, Piso shivered in anticipation of his blood baptism. The clomping of the white bull calf dragged in chains reverberated on the planks. As in classic days, the Ravens crowned the drugged beast with a garland of jasmine and magnolia blossoms and adorned its flanks with gilded cloth and tiny bells. He fought back against the near loss of consciousness in the fetid constriction of the pit.

The Pater appointed to replace Carlos Stroheim the traitor intoned a prayer overhead before slitting the bullock's throat. The hypnotic thumping of the drum accompanied bovine bellowing. Blood seeped through the perforations of the planks and plopped droplets one by one on the alabaster mask of Mithras. The Pater Patrum closed his eyes as the crimson blood of the baby bull fell faster, like a summer shower, in tune with the music, spattering his mask and stippling red his star-specked cape. He could not, must not, black out at this critical time.

They, the upstarts of a Judean cult, thought they could obliterate Mithras by mocking his adherents.

But we are not deceived in the caves.

The inscription on the mithraeum wall above—UNCONQUERED MITHRAS—had survived as did the images of Sol, the sun god, and Luna, the moon goddess. Even the fresco of Mithras in his stocking cap and solar disk had weathered the ages. They deceived themselves in thinking they had smothered the old ways. What they covered over was rising again and would soon poke its head above the earth at sunrise on Easter Sunday to spread its seed.

The clash of cymbals joined the rising drumbeat. Blood streamed into the pit with the whiff of musky incense. Hunched over in the mithraeum's womb, he licked the metallic-tasting blood from his lips. The musical frenzy stirred up thoughts of revenge while he hovered in a dream state on the edge of consciousness. Once he emerged victorious from the cave of Mithras, he would re-create the bronze bull of ancient torture and bake Stroheim inside until he moaned like the dying baby bull.

The music ended. Two Ravens raised him up from the pit, his tunic dripping blood. The bullock knelt on its forelegs as though in prayer. He straddled the animal and stabbed it in the neck with his dagger.

The creature collapsed dead in its own urine.

Fanning out his cape like the wings of an avenging angel, the Pater Patrum proclaimed the dawning of a new age and the destruction of the old. At his feet, the prime minister rattled a cage whose dimensions forced him to crouch on hands and knees. He begged for release at whatever price the Pater Patrum demanded.

The Pater Patrum drank from the chalice of the bull's blood and passed it among the inner circle of Roma Rinata gathered round him. Chimes resonated through the mithraeum. With a blood oath they swore loyalty and hailed him with outstretched arms as the Father of Fathers, the anointed representative of Mithras on earth.

He held up his hands. "You are mistaken."

Events showed the Mithras revival more than propaganda, more than his becoming the vicar of Mithras. Had not Virgil, the Roman poet, referred to the coming of a savior to restore the golden age? Lucio the puppet could not ascend to the truth, but the spiritually enlightened Pater Patrum could.

"I am Mithras reborn."

The Heliodromus broke the stunned silence with the cry "Mithras is reborn."

The congregation chanted the cry over and over, beginning in faltering tones and ending in a full-throated mantra. With eyes closed and mind numbed by the adulation, he felt the Heliodromus perfume his hair and wipe away the gore from his face with a warm sponge.

"Commissario Marco Leone has arrived," cried a guard at the entrance.

CHAPTER SEVENTY-THREE

With a butt kick, the Roma Rinata sentry propelled the prime minister toward the police negotiator waiting to receive him in the Good Friday hostage exchange. The playboy politician fell in the mud. He struggled to get up. Marco Leone cringed at the spectacle of the prime minister trying to adjust his toupee.

They had broken the prime minister.

They would not break him.

On his way under guard to meet Lucio Piso, Leone calculated the number of defenders and their weapons. The armed men he passed had military training. A generator, air conditioner, and medical supplies showed foresight.

Blood slicked the paving stones surrounding the pit in the main aisle like crimson gelatin. He placed his hand over his nose to block the stench. Not even improvised air vents could dispel the odor.

Had Piso squirreled away reserves in the auxiliary chambers and web of tunnels running under the largest mithraeum in the Roman Empire?

Everything depended on Piso not discovering the subterranean surprise.

"My dear Commissario, welcome. I told you at the Hotel Elysian we would meet again." Piso rose from his camp stool at the front of the main aisle. "I would like you to meet my cadre."

A Lion seated to Piso's right lifted his mask. The minister of justice. Another Lion seated to Piso's left raised his mask. The minister of foreign affairs. A Lion standing behind them lifted his. The minister of economy and finance. The commissario steadied himself, aghast at the extent of the conspiracy.

"Where's the minister of defense?" Without him the conspiracy lacked a key player.

"In the United States on a fact-finding tour." Seeming to enjoy the commissario's consternation, Piso's eyes brightened. "The minister will remain neutral. But many subordinates, except the navy people, are either sympathetic or neutral." He snickered. "I doubt a navy cruiser will stop our march on Rome."

"And the Americans?" Leone left the question hanging.

He didn't need to spell it out. Every European knew their world turned on what the Americans wanted. They were the superpower inheritors of Rome. Without them, Piso had no chance.

"As long as Roma Rinata keeps the radical left from power and does not threaten American military presence in Italy, they will wring their hands in public but do nothing."

"How can you be so sure?"

"The defense minister would not stay neutral if he thought the Americans would intervene." Piso flashed his winning card. "Moreover, let us just say we have friends in the CIA and NSA."

The former lieutenant colonel who had escaped the Ciampino villa rushed in with the latest news. In retaliation for a governmental decision to disband their unit, ex-members of the Mechanized Brigade of Sardinian Grenadiers near Rome promised to help seize major media and governmental offices and block any military units racing into Rome to crush the takeover.

"Lest you underestimate us, I must tell you." Piso put on his stiletto smile. "A few hours ago our assassination team terminated the interior minister in her sleep."

They had killed a brilliant jurist turned politician well on her way to the premiership. She had kept law enforcement free of political ideology and curtailed police surveillance of political groups. For her scrupulousness, she and society paid a high price.

The ascent of Roma Rinata from the underground blindsided them all.

"I invite you to join us in fashioning the new Italy."

New? It was a con game as old as the Caesars. A mania for personal power sugarcoated with the rhetoric of patriotism.

"I'm prepared to make you public security chief." Piso seemed puzzled by Leone's reticence. "You realize you'll control all law enforcement, do you not?"

"Not on your life."

"Let me warn you." Piso snarled. "Your life hangs in the balance."

An attendant reminded Piso it was time to get ready.

"Confine our hostage." Piso motioned for the guards to seize Leone. "Let us hope he comes to his senses before it is too late."

Pursuant to the hostage agreement, every hour on the hour, a military officer called a Soldier of Mithras had armed guards in combat fatigues escort him to the mithraeum entrance. They paraded the hostage outside the bunker like a slave before auction to show off the good state of his health. Unknown to them, Leone had prearranged a secret code of body language with Rossi. His intricate set of hand and leg movements during the hostage walks tipped off the Polizia di Stato about the underground defenses.

When the hostage walk took place at 10:00 p.m. on Holy Saturday, he would flash the go-ahead signal for the preemptive attack on the Baths of Caracalla unless he could convince Piso to surrender before then. He would rush toward the advancing attackers if that increased the odds of his rescue. The chief of police reluctantly approved the plan on the condition that if the conspirators failed to parade him unharmed at the agreed times, the coordinated attack would automatically begin a half hour later.

Everything had to go exactly to plan.

Otherwise he would join Abramo Basso in the land of the dead.

CHAPTER SEVENTY-FOUR

On Holy Saturday morning, his guards frog-marched Leone, groggy in handcuffs, to the main chamber. He rubbed his eyes in disbelief. The leader of the coup sat on a backless ivory stool with curved legs—the curule chair of an ancient Roman dignitary. A makeup artist had just finished applying a facial foundation on Piso in preparation for his television address to the nation after the takeover.

Next to the leader of Roma Rinata stood a camp table with a silver coffee set. Guards shoved Leone into a kneeling position on the mosaic floor at Piso's feet. Piso poured an espresso shot and held it to Leone's nose. The dark-roast aroma of caramel and smoky chocolate penetrated the cotton residue of insomnia.

"Will you join me in an espresso?" Piso pressed a demitasse to Leone's mouth. "Sip from my hands since yours are occupied."

Leone shook his head and pursed his lips.

Piso would not humiliate him as he had humiliated the prime minister.

"As you will." Piso withdrew the demitasse and took a sip.

The makeup artist applied a finishing touch of rouge to the age spots on her client's face. She removed the apron protecting Piso's bespoke Italian blue suit of wool fibers plucked from vicuna and musk oxen. His tie bore the tauroctony emblem of Mithras slaying the bull.

"You can have a great future." Piso put down the demitasse. "Will you join us?"

"You can't hold out forever." Leone could not let slip that he knew the coup began Easter Sunday sunrise. Surprise was his best ally. "They plan to starve you out. You're trapped like Hitler in the Berlin bunker."

"So that's your plan." Piso slapped his thigh and roared with laughter. "Here's my little secret. I wanted that spineless prime minister let go. He agreed to back our new government. So, the proper analogy is Hindenburg handing over power to Hitler."

"The prime minister has outdone himself with disgrace." Leone struggled with his handcuffs. "No one will obey him."

"Even if he proves useless as well as spineless, I still have you." Piso stopped to whisper an order out of Leone's hearing and continued. "Your men might well have let that scumbag of a prime minister die at my hands." He pointed his finger at his hostage. "But they will never let die one of their own, their dear Commissario Leone."

"You are mistaken." He had to try another historical analogy. "In the Moro crisis, the government refused to negotiate. They let the Red Brigades riddle Prime Minister Moro with bullets and stuff his corpse into a car trunk. 'The state must not bend,' they said." Leone tried getting up. "Do you think they give a crap about the life of a pawn like me?" The guards shoved him back onto the floor.

"The distinction is elementary." Piso stood up with demitasse in hand. "The Americans wanted no communists in government. Unfortunately for him, Moro was open to it. But they will tolerate me . . . me, the only guardian against the radical left boogeyman."

He ordered the commissario lifted up.

"You're living in the past." The handcuffs bit into his wrists. "Haven't you heard? The Soviet Union has collapsed. The Communist Party has shattered. The Americans have no fear of Italy going communist."

What more could he say to this madman? Only Piso knew the distorted logic of the fantasy world he lived in.

"What do you want Lucio to do?" Piso said in a child's voice the commissario found chilling. A far-off look clouded over Piso's face.

The AISI agent had clued him in on what Carlos Stroheim reported. With increasing frequency in times of stress, Piso slipped into a child's voice and referred to himself in the third person. In his investigations, Leone had found the mental instability of an intelligent man like

Piso the most dangerous because it combined unpredictability with cunning.

"I want you to surrender." He had to get through while Piso's psychological defenses were down. "Somewhere inside, you know you can't win. Even if your coup succeeds, Europe will quarantine your government. The Resistance will return and topple you."

"Never." The Pater Patrum's voice had returned. A switch had flipped. He jutted his jaw in a Mussolini pose. "Better to live one day as a lion than a hundred years as a sheep."

It was hopeless. Piso had retreated into the narcotic of clichés.

"This is your last chance," Piso said. "Will you join us?"

"Not now, not ever."

"Take him and break him," Piso said to the guards. "What's he hiding?"

CHAPTER SEVENTY-FIVE

Dangling on a rope tied to the handcuffs behind his back and fastened to the mithraeum ceiling, Leone spat out blood from a blow to his cheek. Pain seared his arms pretzeled behind his back. His shoulders slumped forward, collapsing his chest into his diaphragm, choking off breath on the way to strangulation. A line of sweat across his forehead leached into his eyes. An invisible pair of hands throttled him.

How did he, a Jew, wind up hog-tied in what they called a Palestinian crucifixion on Holy Saturday at the hands of a pagan lunatic? He would die in this theater of the absurd. Mondo cane—a dog's world after all.

Agony tempted him to squeal what they wanted to know. He now understood how Colonel Soames felt before betraying Uncle Benjamin. To fortify his resolve, he fantasized his lips sewn shut. He refused to backstab his comrades the way the colonel had backstabbed his uncle. Without the specter of his uncle's betrayal, would he have held out so long?

Teetering on the rim of surrender, he felt the rope snap slack. He collapsed in a heap on the floor.

"We'll continue after his beauty walk," one of the two guards said over the buzzing in Leone's head. "We have to keep him in one piece . . . for now." A kick in the ribs rolled him over onto his back. He endured another kick in the groin with the knowledge the attack would begin when he gave the signal outside the bunker, at 10:00 p.m. this

Holy Saturday. They dragged him to his feet and wiped off the blood so his comrades could see him alive and uninjured.

When they took him out for the hostage walk, he'd give the signal and attempt a dash across the esplanade toward his comrades coming to the rescue under cover of darkness and a barrage of police bullets. He had only a long-shot chance at salvation.

One of Piso's officers regaled as a Soldier of Mithras barged into the chamber. "What are you doing? We're already late for the hostage walk. Get going."

"How late?" Leone asked, trying to suppress his anxiety.

"None of your business," the Soldier said. About to leave, he turned and asked, "Why do you want to know anyway?"

"I'm supposed to take medication for Addison's disease."

"Not now." The Soldier of Mithras spat on the ground. "Go and bring him back unharmed . . . but put him in leg irons this time."

"Why? Your guards watch my every move." He rattled his handcuffs. "I've also got these."

"I've watched you," the Soldier said. "You're up to something."

He'd never make it to the police line.

The thwacking of helicopter blades and then the popping pulsations of gunfire filtered through the mithraeum. A sentry stumbled inside, yelling that attack helicopters had opened fire on the outdoor stage.

It had to be 10:30 p.m. The attack was underway. They'd kill him for deception. A guard dropped the leg irons and hustled Leone away. The other guard rushed the entrance with an Uzi submachine gun. Grenades exploded outside over the whining patter of a gunfight. The tripod-mounted M240G machine guns out front fired rat-a-tat bursts.

The police had to be advancing on the mithraeum as planned while the helicopters stormed the orchestra stage in the other prong of the attack. Assault teams should soon rappel down from helicopters to rescue the orchestra hostages.

A thin trail of tear gas released outside snaked through the entrance. Tears burned in Leone's eyes. The gas pricked his throat like needles. He convulsed in hacking coughs. Defenders ran inside, one hobbling on a leg streaming blood.

The renegade lieutenant colonel waved his pistol and threatened to shoot wavering defenders unless they returned to their posts. "Everyone to the front," he ordered, as Piso's fighters sealed off the entrance. To mitigate a gas attack, a Lion passed out goggles and masks to selected fighters. He did not have enough for everyone. The lieutenant colonel pistol-whipped a fighter grabbing someone else's.

Just maybe. Leone pinned his hopes on the subterranean surprise.

"Keep Leone at the front," Piso ordered, forcing his way through his fighters. "If they try to break in, tell them the commissario gets a bullet in the brain. We just need to hold out until sunrise when the coup begins."

The guard held a pistol barrel against the back of Leone's skull. He steadied his trembling. If he had to die, he didn't want to give them the satisfaction of smelling fear. His mouth felt hot and dry like sand in the sun.

Reaching the barricaded entrance, Piso turned to his warriors. He donned the pointed Phrygian cap and alabaster mask of Mithras. "I am Lord Mithras." He pounded his jewel-encrusted crosier on the ground. "We shall fight to the last man."

Lucio Piso had jumped the rails of sanity for good.

The outside shelling stopped and so had the circulation of air. The attackers must have cut off the ventilation. The uncertainty of silence weighed as heavily on Leone as did the rising humidity. The mithraeum stank of sweat and blood. He exhaled tension as his guard removed the pistol from his head and raced to shore up the crumbling defenses.

While Piso's demolition expert used the lull to booby-trap the entranceway with explosives, Leone heard scratching like the sound of rats within walls. The scratching changed into a pounding. At Piso's command, two of his personal bodyguards with bandoliers across their chests ran back into the mithraeum to check out the disturbance.

The rear wall of the mithraeum erupted into an explosion of stone and brick. In a bug-eyed gas mask, a NOCS commando jumped out spraying submachine gun fire. One commando after another popped out of the opening with weapons firing into the defenders surprised from behind. Shooting broke out from every direction. Men groaned and fell.

The gamble on the subterranean surprise paid off.

The Romans had built a service tunnel from the upstairs baths to the mithraeum below, but no one knew it was passable until he dared to take a chance.

A grenade exploded, throwing him to the ground.

Breaking through the booby-trapped entrance of the mithraeum, the attackers raced over rubble and bodies to meet up with fellow NOCS commandos coming forward from the rear. Shrieks of the wounded resounded off the walls.

A tear gas canister whooshed through the demolished entrance before exploding into a white cloud. The shooting sputtered into silence as the sound of coughing men amplified. Handcuffed behind his back, Leone used a wall to steady his way up to a standing position. Through the spreading miasma of tear gas, he made out Piso running back and forth near the blood pit as NOCS attackers pressed the defenders from front and rear like predators surrounding prey.

Fighting off burning eyes and chest pain, Leone stumbled his way toward Piso just as the billionaire slid on the blood-slippery pavement headlong into the pit full of blood from the sacrificed bull calf. He wanted to pull Piso out by his legs. Leone's hands wouldn't move from behind his back. The handcuffs.

Bubbles popped through the putrid red ooze of the pit and collapsed.

The bubbling slowed and stopped.

Medics among the living and the dead fished Piso out of the pit.

They covered the body with a sheet and moved on.

CHAPTER SEVENTY-SIX

Early on Easter Sunday, an unshaven Inspector Rossi burst into Commissario Leone's office. "The pope's in the waiting room."

Had he misheard? His head ached. He should have taken the medic's recommendation of an overnight hospital stay. Leone had Rossi repeat his pronouncement.

"The . . . pope . . . is . . . in . . . the . . . waiting . . . room."

"What's he busted for? Selling indulgences without a license?" Leone just wanted to go home with Mondocane and fall into bed. "Quit pulling my leg."

"It's true. Come see."

Sure enough, Celestine VI sat on a bench normally reserved for pimps and thieves awaiting interrogation. The pope doffed the green baseball cap of the Nigerian national team. He smoothed his salt-and-pepper hair. Standing beside his boss, the personal secretary looked dashing in the helmet and leather chaps of a motorcyclist.

If word got out about the pope's surprise visit, the Curia was sure to fuss and fume. Through back channels, they had promised Leone to prevent the pope from creating security nightmares for the Polizia di Stato by his impromptu excursions in a motorcycle sidecar. And yet here he was, back to his old tricks. What did he want at police headquarters? In a few hours, he had Easter Sunday services to attend to.

The Leone Squad sprung back to life in the presence of the Holy Father after the exhausting firefight at the Baths of Caracalla. One minute, they were filling out postincident reports and being debriefed while trying to stay awake. The next, they scrambled to attention, jarred by the unexpected presence of the Vicar of Christ.

"What can I do for you?" Leone added, "Your Holiness."

A wary Mondocane hobbled around the pope and sniffed at his clothes. Leone commanded the dog to heel. Mondocane ignored the command.

"The question, Commissario Leone, is not what you can do for me." Celestine VI stood up with the assistance of his personal secretary and straightened his white cassock. "It's what I can do for you."

"I don't understand."

"I want to personally invite you to attend Easter services in St. Peter's Square today. You will receive the Benemerenti medal in public recognition of your service to the Church and society."

"But I'm not a believer."

"The medal is for doers, not believers."

"On one condition." Leone indicated his fellow officers. "That I accept it, not for me, but on behalf of the Polizia di Stato of Rome. They did the fighting . . . and the dying."

"Agreed."

"Please give us a blessing, Your Holiness." Though the cry came from behind, Leone recognized the voice of Inspector Rossi. How could this be? His right-hand man was the in-your-face anticleric from Turin. He knew more colorful blasphemous curses than anyone in the department. An officer knelt on the floor to the inspector's right. Another to his left. One by one they all fell to their knees except Leone. The pope blessed him anyway.

Mondocane barked at the pope as he raised his hand in blessing. He stooped to let the three-legged canine sniff his fingers and papal ring.

"If you, too, want a blessing," the pope said, "you must stop barking . . . and lie down."

Mondocane obeyed and wobbled down onto his stomach to Leone's astonishment. He had never been able to command such obedience. Patting the dog's head, the pope blessed Mondocane before an officer full of apologies for the dog's behavior shooed Mondocane away.

After blessing the police, Celestine congratulated each for their heroism. Following the lead of the first officer in line, each knelt and kissed the pope's ring. When Celestine VI approached Leone standing off to the side, he offered his ring.

"I won't kiss your ring." Leone looked at the ground. "Nothing personal."

"Thanks for not doing so," the pope whispered, winking and lowering his arm. "Just between us, all the grabbing and kissing aggravates my arthritic fingers."

His identity blurred under motorcycle goggles, a green baseball cap, and a black leather jacket over his cassock, the pope told his secretary the time had come to return to the heavenly prison. As they sped away, Leone tipped his hat in farewell.

CHAPTER SEVENTY-SEVEN

In blue uniforms, the Swiss guard marching band struck up a brassy musical fanfare heralding Celestine VI's Easter Sunday urbi et orbi address to the city and the world.

The afternoon sun broke through a previously overcast sky and illuminated rows of yellow tulips and purple azaleas decorating St. Peter's Square under a crystal-blue sky dappled white with powder-puff clouds. GOD HAS DELIVERED US FROM EVIL read a banner held aloft by three nuns while church bells gonged across Rome in thanksgiving for the failure of the coup d'état.

Overcome by the applause of a crowd he estimated at two hundred thousand, Leone hastened back to the section reserved for honorees after receiving the Benemerenti medal. Trying to avoid stepping on toes, he made his way through the seated row of honorees wearing identical Benemerenti medals glistening in the sun. He returned to the seat beside Professor Fisher, wearing a medal for his exploration of the Villa of the Papyri and the Callinicus sarcophagus.

He might as well tell the professor now. "My newfound American cousin is displeased. You haven't returned her calls."

"Mea culpa." He tapped his chest with a fist in a gesture of theatrical contrition. "I've been very busy. His Holiness appointed me to a committee studying the theological implications of our recent discoveries."

"I'm too busy at work . . . That's what I told my now-alienated daughter."

The crowd rustled and murmured. Celestine VI would appear at any moment above them in the Loggia of the Blessings framed by three other balconies on each side of the Loggia.

"I promise." The professor's face turned serious. "I'll call today."

"My advice is—"

Shouts and clapping erupted in St. Peter's Square. Fisher pointed to the Loggia of the Blessings. Flanked on each side by an assistant in a white surplice, the pontiff entered the central balcony in the cream-colored vestments of skullcap and cassock. A flight of doves released into the air circled the papal chair in the loggia before flapping away. Celestine VI raised his right hand over the swirling tide of humanity in the piazza.

"No more tiara, no more chasuble, no more red shoes like an ancient Roman patrician." Fisher laughed. "Prada's losing business with this pope."

Professional instincts on alert, the commissario scanned the facade of St. Peter's and the surrounding roofs for the glint of a sniper's rifle. It would take time to mop up all of Piso's supporters. Did a desperado survive, ravenous for revenge? If only the Secret Service had looked up at the Texas School Book Depository Building in Dallas, his hero might not have died. The assassination of a pope on Leone's watch was an if-only nightmare he'd never live down.

Everything looked as it should. Only police sharpshooters stood on the rooftops where he wanted them. The Vatican had its security on full alert. Besides the Swiss guards and the gendarmes, the Vatican Inspectorate of Public Security surveilled the crowd from blue-and-white mini Lamborghinis looking like souped-up golf carts.

About to begin his address, Celestine VI stumbled, grabbing at the microphone near the papal chair. The microphone squawked and screeched. Gasps and screams broke out around Leone. Leone jumped up.

Did somebody shoot the pope?

Two assistants guided the pope onto his chair and readjusted the microphone. Speaking into it, Celestine VI apologized for the alarm his clumsiness had caused. He quipped that infallibility did not extend to his feet. Silence greeted the pope's remark until isolated titters in the crowd avalanched into laughter booming throughout St. Peter's

Square. A pair of prelates seated in front of Leone turned around to
view the spectacle in lemon-lipped disapproval.

"Humor and laughter." Fisher nudged the commissario with his
elbow. "Something new in Saint Peter's Square."

"Dear brothers and sisters," the pope began, setting aside the prepared text. "The Church needs to be forgiven as well as to forgive.
Whatever was twisted in those who sought to overthrow our faith
and country . . . the misguided among us helped twist. The misguided
sought to bury truth, but truth cannot stay buried. It will rise, just as
our Lord, Jesus Christ, arose from the tomb where his enemies thought
him buried and forgotten."

The microphone shrieked. The pope tapped it with his fingers. The
noise subsided.

"Those who suppress truth in God's name blaspheme by presum-
ing to protect a God who needs no protection. They protect only their
own fears of doubt and uncertainty."

The pope's voice cracked. He paused.

"We are but caterpillars, creeping along, heads down, searching
our way, day by day, on the complex tapestry of life, unaware of the
whole, but wandering . . . straying . . . until we . . ."

Celestine VI stammered.

A stroke? Leone looked around for medical assistance.

"Become butterflies," the pope blurted out.

Celestine VI recovered his train of thought with an ever stronger
voice. Humankind, he said, had to cling to the tapestry of life in faith,
in love, and in the hope that someday they would, like butterflies, fly
above the tapestry and see more of the grand design in what was once
a tangle of threads.

The microphone emitted a series of squeals syncopating the pope's
thought into intelligible and unintelligible disconnected phrases, something about the invisible Church of Saint Augustine . . . not corrupt-
ible institutions with wolves within while sheep remain without . . . a
community of God embracing all seeking truth with goodwill . . . The
microphone stopped squealing.

"I intend to follow the examples of Benedict the Sixteenth and my
namesake, Celestine the Fifth." The pope's voice came through loud
and clear. "I have decided to retire from the papal office. I long to

rejuvenate the remainder of my life in the service of the poor and the afflicted in my native Nigeria."

The pope waved down the no-no chants of the multitude into a muttering of discontent, trailing off to acquiescence.

"My brother bishops are asked to submit resignations at seventy-five years of age. Why then should I . . . the Bishop of Rome . . . be exempt?"

He blessed the crush of people in the square and concluded with the words of Paul of Tarsus at the end of his mission. "I am poured out like a drink offering, and the time has come for my departure."

Leaving the national greetings in over sixty languages to a cardinal rumored to have the inside papal track, Celestine turned to leave.

A cascade of cheers from the common people below followed him into the Papal Palace.

CHAPTER SEVENTY-EIGHT

Was he just late again or had he stood her up? Nicole Garvey shaded her eyes with her hand. She squinted down the Spanish steps for his arrival.

The Barcaccia Fountain in the Piazza di Spagna below fueled Garvey's agitation. Chipped, scratched, and graffiti-riddled by waves of soccer hooligans from beyond the Alps, the hull-shaped sculpture lived up to its representation of a sinking . . . relationship . . . He should have phoned . . . It was sinking . . . Government funds for repair dried up . . . like their relationship . . . Rome never falls, it just crumbles . . . like their . . . Fifteen more minutes and—

He waved his way up the Spanish steps framed with potted bougainvilleas and crowded with lunchtime loungers. Composing herself, she held up a brown paper bag in a half-hearted salutation.

He stumbled against a cadaverous young man with a purple Mohawk haircut sitting on a step. The hooligan sprang up and kicked at Fisher. She hurried her way down to hear Fisher plead, *"Scusi. Scusi."*

"Speak English. I'm not some bloody foreigner." The hooligan waved a smashed panino in Fisher's face. "You stomped my lunch. Now pay up."

Fisher dropped coins into the outstretched hand.

"Go start a soccer riot somewhere," Garvey said. "You shouldn't be eating on the steps anyway."

He wiggled his gimme-gimme fingers until Fisher donated more coins.

The shakedown rankled her. She held her peace. He wasn't going to change. "Let's go." She nodded up the stairs to an open space by a staircase wall. "We have to talk."

He followed her up the greater part of the 135 steps. She braced her back against the wall. "Why did you avoid me?"

"I didn't." He ran his forefinger along the inside of his collar. "Just busy."

"You sold out."

"What do you mean?"

"I was in the Charlemagne Wing." She set the paper bag down. "I heard you recant. All your brave talk about taking a stand went out the window."

"Aren't you overreacting?"

"Don't patronize me just because I'm . . ." She bit her lower lip and looked up at the twin belfries of Trinity Church on top of the hill. "Just tell me why you did it."

"They gave me back my professorship at the Greg. Now that I'm famous, if I may say so, I can't just leave Rome and burn my bridges. I've got follow-up work here. I've got to—"

"A man's gotta do what a man's gotta do."

"The Greg is my home. It's part of me."

Thirty pieces of silver. They paid him thirty pieces of silver.

"What's in the bag?"

She picked it up. "Are these yours?"

She pulled out three empty Jack Daniels miniatures.

"Why would they be?"

"I found them after you left my place . . . in my toilet tank."

"I haven't done airplanes in a while." He took her arm. "What about us?"

"Us?" She moved away. "We can always be friends."

"How?" He pointed to the home of John Keats at the foot of the steps. "Keats wrote his sweetheart that love was his religion and for love he could die. That's more than friendship."

"Don't go maudlin on me. Keats was a hormone-riddled twenty-year-old about to die of tuberculosis."

She regretted her tone. This man so mature in other respects had the romantic vulnerabilities of a pimply teenager.

"Is this what I get for trying to be honest?"

"Trying isn't enough, Will." He wasn't making it easier for her. She hugged herself. "It just doesn't feel right."

"How can you say that? After everything . . . all the magic moments."

"Please, Will. We're not on stage." Aware of people staring, she sat down on the steps. He sat beside her. "It won't work," she said.

"What am I supposed to do, then?"

"How about writing your own life script and not rehearsing someone else's?"

"When can I see you again?"

"That'll be hard to do." She stood up and smoothed her slacks. "I'm accepting the visitorship at the University of Chicago."

"What about me?" He looked up at her with puppy eyes.

"It all comes down to that, doesn't it?" She waved goodbye. "Good luck."

And then she was gone.

CHAPTER SEVENTY-NINE

Suitcase at his side, Leone downed his afternoon espresso inside Da Pappagallo.

SEISMIC TREMORS VANISH

The front-page banner headline barricaded the face of the patron jammed next to him at the bar. Leone leaned in to skim the article under the subheading "Vatican Shores Up St. Peter's Foundation."

A bulbous-nosed man lowered the newspaper and shot the violator of his space a sour stare. Leone looked away, pretending to assess the qualities of a puff pastry in the showcase. The man harrumphed and returned to reading. Leone checked the time. They would have to leave for the airport soon.

"Much better inside than outside, no?" asked the owner of Da Pappagallo.

"I'd say so."

"What? You agree?" The owner stooped across the bar and touched Leone's forehead. "Hmmm . . . you must be sick."

"Must be your coffee." He looked toward the door.

"Relax. They're always late."

A moon-faced patron with a Roma fan scarf swirled around his neck grabbed the remote from the counter. "Time for the championship game between Roma and Lazio." Other patrons shouted a chorus of approval.

The fan clicked on the TV above the gold, gleaming La Marzocco espresso machine flanked by bottles of liquor on the shelves. The maroon-and-orange jerseys of Roma, the city team, and the white and blue of Lazio, the regional team, poured onto the field amid the pandemonium of the packed stadium. Not even the Mithras conspiracy could derail a cultural ritual more enduring than any governmental upheaval.

His claws clattering on the tile floor, Mondocane scrambled through the doors of Da Pappagallo on a leash held by Inspector Rossi. He barked a greeting to Leone. The inspector released Mondocane. Mondocane cavorted and begged for food and attention as though he were showing off his prosthetic leg donated by the Leone Squad as a going-away present. The pointer made whole wagged his tail and waddled over to Leone. He sat on his haunches with four-legged ease.

"Thanks, Enzo, for walking him before we go."

"No problem, boss." Rossi looked worried. "Still not here?"

"Still not here." Leone opened the travel carrier as Mondocane circled the trap. He tricked him inside with a dog biscuit and snapped the lid shut. "I got you."

The patrons gathered round the TV and hooted approval. Roma won the coin toss. Leone cheered along. For him, Roma represented the nitty-gritty proletarian heart of the city against the right-wing team favored by Mussolini. Even with gentrification ripping through the old Jewish ghetto like typhus, knee-jerk loyalty for city fans like him remained a traditional badge of leftist sentiment.

Rossi handed the leash to the commissario. "With Malatesta gone, the boys in the know say you're favored to take over as questore."

"Are you trying to cheer me up or depress me?" Leone hugged the inspector. "Thanks for everything."

"Time to get back to the questura." He shook the commissario's hand. "Good luck . . . my friend."

Soon after Rossi's departure, Nicole Garvey entered, dragging her roller luggage with a carry-on bag perched at the top.

Happy to see her, Leone brushed her cheeks with his.

"Anyone meeting you at the Chicago airport?" she asked.

"Officer J-im Mur-phy, I think." He pulled Murphy's letter from the inside pocket of his jacket to confirm the name. He hoped to remember the spelling. "Chicago Police Department. Office of International Relations. He's meeting me with a limousine and driver."

The letter warned of an anonymous threat against his life if he came to Chicago. He was used to threats. No need to worry her. "And what about you?" he asked.

"I'm just a visiting professor in archaeology. Not some big shot who put down a coup d'état." She nudged him with her elbow. "I have to make my own way to the campus."

"Will I see my American cousin in Chicago?"

"Naturally." She linked her arm with his. "You and I are family."

"Time to go." Leone picked up Mondocane in his carrier cage. "Mondocane and I are about to discover America."

ACKNOWLEDGMENTS

I am grateful to the team at Girl Friday Productions for their top-notch assistance in the production of *The Mithras Conspiracy*. Without their help, the technical aspects of launching a novel into the marketplace of ideas and imagination would have daunted this writer. I am indebted to Sara Addicott for seamlessly coordinating the production of this novel from one end of the country in Seattle, Washington, to my home in Sarasota, Florida, despite a three-hour time lag.

My hat goes off to Scott Calamar and Wanda Zimba, whose copyediting and proofreading skills made *The Mithras Conspiracy* a better read than when they received it. Thanks is also owed Paul Barrett, Rachel Marek, and Georgie Hockett, for their design and marketing skills. I also extend my appreciation to any unknown soldiers at Girl Friday Productions who may have helped in the fight to get *The Mithras Conspiracy* published and to the late Jim Agnew, dogged researcher, who shared his love of fiction and never let me forget that writers are supposed to write no matter what.

I would be remiss not to acknowledge two persons in Rome, Italy, who aided my research. The first is Sara Magister, Italian art historian and archaeologist, who guided my wife and me on a tour of Mithraic sites mentioned in this novel and helped us understand their historical significance. The second is Giuseppe Righini of the Polizia di Stato who, without a prior appointment, graciously answered a foreigner's impromptu questions about the operations of this police force.

And last, but certainly not least, abiding tribute is owed Donna, my dear wife, who suffered through the first draft and told me what I needed to hear and not what I hoped to hear. Without her fresh perspective, *The Mithras Conspiracy* would be less than it is.

ABOUT THE AUTHOR

M. J. Polelle is a Harvard Law School graduate, an emeritus professor of the John Marshall Law School in Chicago, and an award-winning legal writer. He honed his fiction writing at the summer writers' workshop of the University of Iowa and the Writers' Loft in Chicago. Polelle's passion for Italy has led him to travel there numerous times, for pleasure as well as to direct a summer law program in Parma. He speaks Italian and was a columnist for *Fra Noi*, an Italian-American newspaper in Chicago. This is his first novel. He lives in Sarasota, Florida.

Made in the USA
Columbia, SC
22 March 2022

58027002R00198